Cast of Characters

Richard Ringwood. An Oxford-educated Scotland Yard inspector who frequently resorts to unorthodox methods in solving his cases.

Clare Ringwood. His new bride, also Oxford-educated, who is a great help to Richard in his work.

Sir Alban Worrall. A self-proclaimed archaeologist who has funded and supervised several digs in Crete. He dies before the book opens.

Janet Coltman. A serious-minded, dedicated young archaeologist who idolized Sir Alban and who survives a stabbing shortly after his death.

Ian Shrubsole. Another earnest young archaeologist, an expert on pottery, who is both colleague and rival to Janet.

Jack Macdonald. The Assistant Keeper at the British Museum.

Iorweth ap Ifor. A Welsh nationalist, also an archaeologist, whose expertise is architecture and religion. He feels a kindred spirit with the Cretans.

Zoe ap Ifor. Iorweth's sensuous, voluptuous Cretan wife, whose very presence brings to mind the Mother Goddess.

Costa Mikhailopoulos. The volatile proprietor of the Minos, a Cretan restaurant in London patronized by all the archaeologists.

Georgios Aiakides. A slender, handsome young waiter at the Minos, who is Zoe ap Ifor's lover.

Stavro Mikhailopoulos. Costa's brother.

Sergeant Frewin. A sensible, sympathetic middle-aged policewoman.

Mr. Semonides. Clare's talkative Greek hairdresser.

Mr. Coltman. Janet's uncle, her only relative.

Mrs. Shrubsole. Ian's good-natured, voluble mother.

The Bloodhound. Richard's superior at Scotland Yard.

Books by Katharine Farrer

The Inspector Ringwood Trilogy

The Missing Link (1952)
The Cretan Counterfeit (1954)
Gownsman's Gallows (1957)

At Odds with Morning (1960)

Being & Having by Gabriel Marcel (1949)
(Translator)

THE CRETAN COUNTERFEIT

By KATHARINE FARRER

The Rue Morgue Press
Lyons / Boulder

Author's Note

I know that all the characters in this book are imaginary, but hope that some of the archaeology is real, since various learned friends have allowed me to bother them incessantly

K.F.

The Cretan Counterfeit
Copyright © 1952
New material
Copyright © 2004 The Rue Morgue Press
ISBN: 0-915230-73-9

FIRST AMERICAN EDITION

Reprinted with the permission of
The Trustees of K.D. Farrer Estate

The Rue Morgue Press
P.O. Box 4119
Boulder, CO 80306
800-699-6214
www.ruemorguepress.com

Printed by
Johnson Printing

PRINTED IN THE UNITED STATES OF AMERICA

About the author

KATHARINE FARRER (1911-1972) and her husband Austin belonged to a small, very select group of Oxford Anglican Christian intellectuals who were collectively known as the Inklings and were among those privileged to read J.R.R. Tolkien's *Lord of the Rings* trilogy long before it went to the typesetters. It was such a closely knit group that Austin and Katharine took care of fellow Inkling C.S. Lewis, creator of the Narnia Chronicles and a leading Christian apologist, during his final days. Another Inkling, metaphysical novelist Charles Williams, was the butt of a sly joke in Katharine's first detective novel, *The Missing Link.* While the Inklings obviously were concerned with weighty issues, primarily the destruction of the mid-twentieth century reliance on scientific materialism, they had their lighter side. None would have chastised Katharine for turning away from her work on Christian existentialism to write detective stories, since another prominent Inkling was Dorothy L. Sayers, the creator of Lord Peter Wimsey, though admittedly she had deserted the genre herself in the late 1930s to devote herself to writing on Christian theology. While husband Austin might not have been as famous as other members of the Inklings, the Archbishop of Canterbury referred to him as "possibly the greatest Anglican mind of the twentieth century." In 2004, the centenary year of his birth, conferences were held on both sides of the Atlantic to honor and study his teachings and writings. If you take the C.S. Lewis walking tour of Oxford, one of the stops is Katharine and Austin's gravesite.

It was only natural that Katharine would involve herself in both scholarship and religion. Her own father, F.H.J. Newton, was a noted minister while on her mother's side she was related to the Des Anges family who were involved in the Port Royal movement in France during the reign of Louis XIV. The movement was started by Cornelius Jansen, who taught that people were saved by God's grace, not by their own will power, a theological position that fits in quite well with Austin's own teachings and ministry while a Fellow and Chaplain of Trinity College from 1935-1960. He finished his career as warden of Keble College, dying one day after his final sermon in 1968.

There was never any question that Katharine would go on to university, although this was a time when few women earned college degrees. On her mother's side, she was related to Miss Frances Mary Buss, a pioneer in higher education for women in England in the nineteenth century. Miss Buss, as she was known, opened the North London Collegiate School for Girls in 1850 and later worked with Emily Davies in opening exams for women at Cambridge in 1865. Katharine herself was educated at St. Helen's School in Northwood and went up to St. Anne's, Oxford, at the age of 18, where she read Classical Mods and Greats.

While at Oxford, she published her first short stories under a pseudonym. She married in 1937 and put her own writing aside to care for her daughter until she was able to attend school. In 1949, she translated Gabriel Marcel's major 1935 work, *Etre et Avoir*, into English as *Being & Having: An Existentialist Diary.* Her first detective novel, *The Missing Link* (1952), was set in Oxford. It was followed by two more novels featuring her Inspector Richard Ringwood and his wife Clare, both Oxford graduates: *The Cretan Counterfeit* (1954) and *Gownsman's Gallows* (1957). Her last published book was a mainstream novel, *At Odds with Morning* (1960), a satire involving a self-appointed saint.

Although Katharine and Austin were serious theologians, her books are free of any overt religious propaganda, although one can see a bit of Austin's philosophy in action when Clare visits a grief-stricken couple with tremendously good news, only to be dismissed quickly and with little thanks. Richard explains that this is a copper's lot. Austin Farrer might have elaborated further by saying that you don't do good deeds to earn a reward, you do good deeds because that is what good people—and good policemen—do.

For further information on Katharine Farrer see Tom and Enid Schantz' introduction to the Rue Morgue Press edition of *The Missing Link*.

Chapter 1

"How heavenly it is not to have you bolting your breakfast and dashing off to the Yard! Almost worth a sprained ankle. More coffee, darling?"

Her husband shook himself up and down. "I'm making a noise like a hot-water bottle already. Still, perhaps half a cup. I say, listen to this. Someone's died in *The Times* called Pompilia Dudgeon. No flowers, no letters, by request."

"Huffy to the last. See if there's an obituary."

"No, not for her. But here's one that looks promising. Shall I read it and you guess what sort of chap he was? *Sir Alban Worrall, the archaeologist, whose death is announced on another page, was born at Buxton in 1898. Educated at Marlborough and at New College, Oxford ...*"

"Then why was he born at Buxton?"

"Father a cotton nabob, I should think ... *He interested himself in the practical aspects of archaeology from an early age, and before his thirtieth year had taken part in the excavations at Skaiai and Mataiorycha; besides rendering them considerable financial assistance*. Did you get that?"

"Mm."

"No you didn't, darling, or you wouldn't say mm. He got a poor sort of degree, for they don't mention it, but he managed to buy his way into the archaeology racket by financing digs."

"Go on."

"*The results, however, proved unrewarding, and it was not until 1928 that he was able, by the exercise of special influence, to arrange for excavations under the monastery of Hosios Markos in Crete, a coveted site to which he gained access by the wealth of his local contacts*. Pretty, isn't it?"

"*The wealth of his* ... Oh, I see. He bribed the monks. Go on."

"*Not unexpectedly, he made some important friends – no, finds – and with great skill and munificence negotiated the transfer of many good examples of seals and faiences to the British Museum; others were with equal astuteness left in the Museum at Herakleion, upon which he also lavished a large subscription for repairs after it had been damaged by earthquake. While not adding perhaps appreciably to our knowledge of the period, these finds were picturesque and attracted wide notice in the popular press. Their discoverer financed (and himself took part in) a film expatiating upon the excavation.*"

"I don't know which is nastier, the writer or the corpse. More coffee?"

"No, six cups is enough. *Worrall received his knighthood just after the war, and shortly afterwards became curator of the museum at Herakleion, an office never before offered to a foreigner and which he has held ever since, though the width of his interests has often obliged him to exercise it through deputies. He has since led no less than four expeditions to Minoan sites (chiefly at his own expense) of which the last, interrupted by a sudden illness which necessitated his return to England, promised to be interesting. Sir Alban claimed that he was on the point of proving, by archaeological evidence, that Corfu was the Phaeacia described in the Odyssey, and while it would be rash to base a theory on such slender evidence, a seal found just before the expedition broke up may well begin to substantiate the claim.*"

"That sounds important."

"Very, if true. *It is chiefly, however, as patron and publicist that he will be remembered. Even the pioneer work of Sir Arthur Evans did not arouse such public enthusiasm, presented as it was by his more austere and unobtrusive scholarship. Sir Alban brought Minoan art to the common man in a form he could understand, not disdaining to enlist the aid of film, radio, and television, and even influencing contemporary fashion. His leonine head and impressive utterance were to be noticed alike at foreign embassies and in London society. Archaeologists will agree that his death is a material loss to British* … why, what's the matter, Clare?"

"This academic malice rather gives me the creeps."

"Cheer up. It's bogosity they hate, not people. I should say that the man who wrote this really knew his stuff, and didn't have time to disguise his feelings. It looks like a rush job. Generally, of course, they have obituaries ready years in advance, and the old men all have fun writing about each other and showing it round. I wonder what he died of."

"*Suddenly, in London*," said Clare, looking at the back of the paper, "*aged fifty-five*. Oh, well! What shall we do with this morning?"

Like farmers and doctors nowadays, detective-inspectors are primarily civil servants playing the game of Hunt the Slipper with batches of official papers: and next day Richard Ringwood decided to go to the Yard and catch up arrears. Otherwise, he said, they would have no weekend. He left after an early breakfast, and limped home late to dine on the huge sofa by the drawing-room fire.

"You're tired," said Clare. "Bad day?"

"Boring and sordid. Mean and dirty. That's what people are." His mouth and his level black eyebrows drooped. "Is it really any good trying to cope with the crime wave? It's just human nature."

"Nuts, darling. Oh, by the way, I saved you this. It's very un-mean and rather interesting – a sequel to that catty obituary you read me yesterday." She curled herself up beside him and spread out *The Times*.

"*Miss Janet Coltman writes: May a colleague of some years' standing add a tribute to your notice of Sir Alban Worrall? While many scholars were aware – and some possibly envious – of his gift for vivid public exposition, only the few privileged to work with him closely could truly appreciate his inspiring leadership and his tireless attention to detail. Generous in encouraging the other members of his expeditions to publish their own accounts of finds, he nevertheless always made time to read their work and add his illuminating criticisms and suggestions. And even in his own province, he would ask the advice of scholars of far lower standing than himself; than which they could have had no greater honor or encouragement, save one – occasionally bestowed – the privilege of coauthorship with Sir Alban himself. On fieldwork, he held the whole team together, and was himself ubiquitous – now on the site, now consolidating those local friendships which so added to the success of his work (he had an unaffected love of the Greeks), and now closeted with his books and seals, often far into the night. A last glimpse of him at Corfu seems, in the light of subsequent events, symbolical. Returning from a late stroll shortly before midnight, I saw his unmistakable figure standing in moonlight beside the newly opened trench, in earnest conversation with a young Greek workman. It was a key to his whole life, and perhaps to his death; for such unsparing activity may well have sown the seeds of that fatal illness which led to his untimely end. He is said to have left no close relatives behind him: but his friends will not forget*."

"Well, that's handsome, don't you think?" Clare's view of her husband's face – one of those upward shots taken from just below chin-level which are so rare on the films and so common in married life – though it revealed little but nostrils and eyebrows, reassured her. He was clinging to his pessimism now with a clear enjoyment.

"Handsome, you say? Well, but notice that she's *Miss* Janet Coltman and 'of some years standing.' Don't you think perhaps *he* was the handsome one?"

"What, Worrall? Richard, your mind is like a sink. Or no, the trouble is, you're too innocent. If she *had* been in love with him, she'd never have made such a show of it."

"Couldn't her feelings have been too much for her?"

"Oh no, not once he's *dead*. He'll never see the letter. Women don't let their feelings get too much for them unless there's an end in view."

"All right, realist. I'll remember that next time you weep on my bosom. But listen, this article's bursting with feelings, isn't it? So according to you, it must have an end in view. Well, what?"

"Simple debt of gratitude, I think. Maybe a touch of loyal defense, too. It's so British one can hardly tell."

"I know. How do you account for the curiously *Tom Brown* flavor?"

"Well, it could be Girl Guides, but I expect it's just the old school. Girls' boarding schools are the last stronghold but one of the Arnold tradition. Why, do you know, they actually used to make us *confess* if we'd been talking after lights-out, and if we had, we lost a mark for our house. And *everybody* confessed. Even me."

"Poor little mugs. Moral blackmail, that's what it is. You ought to be a screaming mass of jangling ganglions. Instead of which, you're purring and you don't feel as if you had any bones at all. Come on. You start your bath while I lock up."

He had undressed and was sitting on the edge of the bed winding the alarm-clock when the telephone rang. He ran downstairs to answer it, and Clare was snug in bed by the time her husband returned.

"I say, do you know what?"

"Mm?"

"A most extraordinary coincidence. That was the Bloodhound ringing up from the Yard. A woman's been found stabbed in the back. Still alive, but only just. Happened this afternoon, in Soho. She's in the Middlesex Hospital now."

"Oh dear, poor thing. And have you got to take it on? Your ankle …"

"Yes, but listen. This woman is a Miss Janet Coltman. And she was carrying a briefcase with archaeological notes in it."

"Good heavens! What, you mean she's *The Times* one? The loyal colleague?"

"Almost certainly. And quite certainly attempted murder." He towered beside her, dressing as he talked. "They want me to go along to the Middlesex now, in case she comes round. The Bloodhound was kind enough to say that I was the only man he could trust with academic cases."

"Of course. They won't forget that Oxford case in a hurry."

"Unfortunately he went on to say that I'd already had three days off with my ankle and anyway no one else was free."

"Beast! How is the ankle, actually?"

"It'll do. I'll get a taxi. Well, it would have been nice to go to bed, but still …"

"Still, this'll be better than black market and bogus companies?"

"Lord, yes. I'll try to ring up soon, darling. But go to sleep if I don't."

When he had gone, Clare went down to the drawing room to get the obituary from yesterday's *Times* and the letter from the current number. But she was too late. They were already cut out and stowed in Richard's wallet.

Chapter 2

RICHARD RINGWOOD had seen the surgeon's report, and the ordinary policeman who was waiting for him had told all he knew and gone away. Now he sat in a chair at the foot of the bed in the small private ward, while the nurse on special duty sat on the other side near the head. A green-shaded lamp threw a little circle of light, just illuminating the bed-table and charts, and leaving the rest of the room in darkness. The hospital noises rang hollowly in the corridor outside. He tried to summarize what he knew so far.

The weapon – a kitchen knife, originally quite ordinary, with a burn on the handle that suggested it had been used in cooking. Originally quite ordinary. But the blade had been filed to a fine point at the end, and the edge sharpened like a razor. Also, where handle and blade joined, it was neatly and cunningly wound with many turns of fine copper wire, twisted and plaited as elaborately as a naval Turk's head so that it stood up like a collar more than half an inch high, a hilt for the stabbing hand to push against and drive home hard. The handle, made of some yellowish synthetic substance, was an ideal recorder of finger-prints. It showed those of the policeman who had found the victim, the surgeon's (in rubber gloves), and the nurse's who had received it from the surgeon's hands after he had pulled it out. (They had only just been in time to stop her from sterilizing it.) Under all these prints were a few others, fragmentary and all but obliterated.

A knife is really a less murderous weapon than a pistol; yet this knife inspired Ringwood with a peculiar horror, and he began to ask himself why. Partly, he supposed, it was because it had clearly once been an innocent kitchen knife, and someone had perverted it – had filed and hilted and sharpened it to kill. Sheepdog turned wolf. But that was not all. The someone who had worked on it was resourceful, inventive, even a bit of an artist. That copper wire had been sensitively applied, and the altered shape of the blade had a kind of functional beauty. The knife didn't look mass-produced any more. It had become an arte-fact, almost the kind of thing one finds among primitive peoples, or that archae-ologists dig up in the middens of ruined cities. He drew a deep breath. That was it. The thought-stream method looked like proving fertile.

He glanced again at the bed. No sound or movement but the tiny bright drop that fell rhythmically through the tube of the saline-machine into an opened vein in the patient's arm. The nurse raised her head, caught his eye, and looked away shyly. Her youth had grown accustomed to death but not to detectives.

The victim had been found face down in a passage between two buildings, off a quiet street in Soho. There had been a little blood on the pavement of the street and a pool of it in the passage, which suggested that she had been stabbed in the street, perhaps from ambush, and then thrust into the passage at once. A briefcase had been found beside her. No handbag, but she may not have carried one; there was a purse containing just under two pounds in one pocket of her mackintosh and a fountain pen in the other. The briefcase with its papers was still being tested for fingerprints. The knife had passed between the ribs at the back, but only touched the heart. She was dextro-cardiac, according to the surgeon; that is, the large valve of the heart was on the right, not the left. This abnormality had been lucky. In most cases the knife would have gone right home. As it was, the damage had been bad enough; there had been great loss of blood and serious shock. Two transfusions had already been given.

A French pastry cook had found her lying there, but not for at least half an hour; she had bled so much and turned so cold. That was at five o'clock, and by half past she was in hospital.

She was officially described as a fairly well-nourished woman in hard physical condition, probably in her middle thirties. Under her Burberry she wore a brown tweed skirt and a navy-blue Aertex blouse; on her feet, brown brogues over gray woolen ankle-socks. No gloves, hat, or bag could be found. Her stout and ample underclothes, clean but in need of mending, were all marked with name-tapes, *Janet Coltman*. An incomplete typescript found in the briefcase also had *Janet Coltman* on the title-page. Inquiries were made, and late in the evening – just before the telephone call, in fact – it was discovered who she was.

It was significant – and, Richard Ringwood thought, pathetic – that her identity had not been established through anyone's having missed her and made inquiries. It was through the British Museum authorities that the police had obtained the names of other scholars who knew her, and even they had not been able to do more than give her permanent address. She had a cottage of her own at Cholsford, a village near Reading, where she lived alone whenever she was in England. Telephoning to her home village, they had learned rather more. Miss Coltman had gone to London three days ago to work in the British Museum, leaving instructions to the postmistress to forward her letters to a students' hostel near Gordon Square. Richard had at once rung up the Cholsford policeman to make sure that the locked cottage should be sealed as well, and left for him to inspect himself. He discovered at the same time that Miss Coltman had no near relatives, but there was a paternal uncle, a retired army chaplain, who lived near Haslemere.

The uncle, he thought, is practically in the bag; the hospital will see about him. They're good at producing relatives for patients on the danger list. But the friends and colleagues – he must find them in the morning and question them thoroughly. He would like to go down to Cholsford too. On the other hand, he could not afford to neglect the possibility that Miss Coltman might come round and speak some crucial words. If she did, he must hear them himself, for they might be her last, and much of their value would depend on skillful prompting and intelligent interpretation. He decided to wait until midday, and the decision plunged him into gloom. Waiting was his nightmare; it drained away his confidence drop by drop. On an impulse he rose, whispered to the nurse to call him if there was any change, and went into the sister's room next door to telephone to his wife.

"… so that's how it is, you see. I do the wrong thing either way. If I wait here, the clues get stale, and if I don't, she makes a deathbed accusation and some fool gets it down all wrong."

"There! I'm sure you're right. Anyhow, you can't have long to wait, can you, if she's all that bad. Poor thing! What's she like?"

"Frightfully remote at the moment. It's hard to tell. Straight sandy hair, done in an uncompromising sort of bob. Face? Well, it's quite still, you see, not a drop of color, and her eyes have been shut so far, so it's hard to say. Very weather-beaten and freckled, light eyebrows and a blobby sort of nose."

"Clever-looking?"

"So much of that is eyes. But a good forehead, yes. Rather a nice face, I thought. Though of course that look of patient resignation may just be illness."

"Did you see her clothes?"

"Lord, yes! They'd shock you to the core, but I found them rather touching, actually; so unworldly. But of course I would. I get angry every time I look at that beastly knife. She'd put on a mourning-band for Worrall, by the way. At least, it was brand new, so I suppose it was for him. She doesn't seem to have any close family or friends."

"Poor thing! I say, is there anything I can do?"

"Yes. Look, I must get back to the ward. Will you ring up your father in the morning and see if he knows anything about (*a*) Sir Alban Worrall, (*b*) Miss Janet Coltman, (*c*) anyone else who worked with them? He did a bit of archaeology for his County History, didn't he? And he's so sociable, he might have picked something up. He's good at remembering about people. And will you ring up *my* father …"

"Oh … yes."

"Sorry, darling. He's generally all right after breakfast. Ask him if he ever came across an army padre called Coltman. That's the uncle. Father's my only army contact, and he doesn't like parsons, so he might remember him. What's the joke?"

"Just the nice balance of your style. Shall I ring you back?"

"Better not. I'll ring up tomorrow, but don't stay in or anything, will you? Sleep, darling."

* * *

Back to the stillroom, the rhythmical drip of the saline-machine, the hollow noises outside, the treadmill of his thoughts. Why had she been in Soho, and why had she been attacked? For robbery? But her purse and her watch were on her, and she did not look the kind of woman to wear expensive jewelry. Could her briefcase have contained a valuable antique? She specialized in the Minoan Age, the civilization that flourished in Crete long before the Greeks were a name in the world. He had learned a little about it when he was at Oxford, and it had fascinated him: the great labyrinthine palaces they had discovered in Crete, their frescoes with groups of crinolined, big-breasted women, snaky-locked, postured like dancers; the slender youths vaulting unarmed between the fierce bulls' horns; the animals so spontaneous in movement and feeling, the humans so hieratic and remote. The many inscriptions written in letters no one could yet interpret. And above all, the jewels, the rings and seals engraved with tiny, perfect pictures, some as flawless as if they had been carved yesterday; nearly all depicting the rites of their religion – virtually unknown except through their art. At the center, clearly, stood the Mother Goddess, voluptuous and sovereign. A stripling god or king attended on her ways like a shadow. Was he son, mate, or victim, or all in turn, during the sacred dance of his ambiguous reign? His choreography was set for nine years, but hers went on forever. Presented with such beauty of form, and so far distant in time, even that cruel cult had a strange fascination; deep down, we all had it in us. If we went among modern savages the blood and stench and howling would revolt us; here, it was disguised in formal beauty, and we could still exclaim "What pipes and timbrels! What wild ecstasy!"

Richard recalled himself to his inquiry. Miss Coltman might have been carrying a valuable antique; probably Minoan, certainly small – a ring, a seal, or a plaque – easily removed and concealed. Such a thing might be of fabulous value if the thief chose his market wisely. But the robbery presupposed personal knowledge – of Miss Coltman, of what she was carrying, and of where she was going, too, unless the suggestion of an ambush was misleading them. This was no casual smash-and-grab raid. There must be a personal factor. But what was it? He stared at the quiet, drained face on the pillow. Was her life as impersonal as it seemed?

As he looked, his mind offered the words "unravished bride of quietness." Then he mocked himself. A bit long in the tooth for a bride, surely! And look at that hair and those freckles. And yet the face did hold a look of dedication, even of content. He thought of the few nuns he had known – brides of Christ. Most of them looked just as unbridal as Miss Coltman; plain, shiny, businesslike, not lilies in fenced gardens, not roses of fire.

Miss Coltman lived by herself and no one worried about her. She had not, perhaps, inspired strong personal devotions. Yet her letter to *The Times* seemed to show that she was herself capable of feeling devotion, for it had been as openly pro-Worrall as the obituary on the preceding day had been covertly anti-

Worrall. (He must find out who wrote that obituary.) But was the devotion personal? Was she defending Worrall the man or Worrall the archaeologist? Perhaps the second, since attacks upon the value of his work might reflect upon her own. Still, there was the new mourning-band on the Burberry sleeve. What had his death meant to her?

The light was changing. It was the hour before dawn, the hour when neurotics wake and the dying find their last sleep. Janet Coltman's head stirred on the pillow, her lips moved, and he approached and leaned over her. A glint of white eyeball showed between the closed lids. She spoke in a tone of great distress, and the words were so strange that he wondered if he had heard them rightly. Later, he found that he had.

"But look! It's like the other amygdaloid ones. It isn't a question of loyalty. They all belong to the same glyptic cycle, don't you see? Oh dear, what shall I do? Daddy …"

Her voice faded.

"Could she be roused, do you think?" he whispered to the nurse.

"It's no good, she's unconscious. You can see she is, and it's not surprising, considering her temperature and pulse. It's like someone talking in their sleep. You couldn't get her to answer you back, and she's better left quiet."

"How's she doing, actually?"

"No change. But that's a good sign, really. We didn't expect her to last the night. There's the tea coming round. Would you like a cup?"

He drew the chair closer to the bed, his notebook ready, but she was quiet again. At five, she cried sharply, "Oh, Daddy!" and a little later, "But there *was* a baetylic shrine!" She began to cough blood and breathe with dreadful hardness, though the nurse said she was still unconscious. The sister was called in to help, and asked him to leave the room. She suggested that he should rest on her couch next door, promising to wake him if the patient seemed likely to speak again. He assented, and though the couch was narrow and a foot too short for him, he slept at once.

* * *

At half past seven he started up at a touch on his shoulder. A small middle-aged woman was standing beside him. Still half-dreaming of the brides of quietness who had been in his thoughts during the night watch, he saw her as a personification of the dedicated woman – formidable in virtue of her devotion to her calling, at once practical and remote; a woman in whose presence you could hear a pin drop. But surely none of her nurses would be so rash as to let a pin drop with such an eye upon them.

"Good morning, Inspector Ringwood. I'm the day sister."

"Oh, good morning, Sister. Has Miss Coltman come round yet?"

"No, she hasn't been fully conscious so far. But there is a slight improvement in the general condition."

"Really? You mean, she may recover?"

The day sister allowed herself to smile briefly.

"As far as we're concerned, all our patients may recover. That's what we're here for. Miss Coltman may pass into a normal sleep presently, if she can be left perfectly quiet. So …" she frowned at a clash of crockery in the corridor "… I'm afraid we can't let you go back into the ward just at present."

"But, look here …"

"Just a moment, Inspector Ringwood. Matron asked me to tell you that a relation of Miss Coltman's has just arrived – her uncle. He's very anxious to see you. Would you like to have him in here?"

He had never been easily managed, even as a child; and this maneuver was altogether too simple. His dark sidelong smile mocked her as he replied: "That's very kind of you, thought I must be dreadfully in the way. But I'd like to be a little clearer about Miss Coltman first. You realize that she's the only person who can throw any light on this attempted murder, don't you? Could she make a statement yet? If she can, it's my duty to be there and hear it, you know."

She folded her hands lightly over the silver waist-buckle that was her badge of office.

"It's very unlikely that she could speak to you. She's been given a sedative and we hope she'll get to sleep presently. She ought to sleep till about midday."

"And then?"

"Then we must see. We hope for an improvement."

"But if not? Don't you see, this may be our last chance of getting at the truth?"

"I'm sorry. This is my patient's last chance too, and it's my duty to see that she has absolute quiet. She has already been given the injection."

A laden trolley clattered by outside, but he did not even raise an eyebrow. He knew better than to quarrel with facts.

"Just as you say, Sister. Then could I see Mr. Coltman now, and perhaps I might have a word with you later."

"Certainly, Inspector. I'll have some breakfast sent in for you."

They parted with mutual respect.

* * *

Mr. Coltman could only be described as an army clerical codger. At first sight Richard Ringwood found his mustache annoying, for mustaches on the clergy denote Lowness and Richard was inclined to be High; but he had a weakness for codgers and Edwardianism, and the old man was touching in his indignation and concern for his niece. They had made friends by the time Richard finished answering questions, and when the breakfast came in Mr. Coltman was explaining how he had caught a train from Hampshire at four o'clock in the morning.

"But we get used to that in the army, you know. Don't think anything of an early start. Only too glad to find her a bit better. She's my last living relation, you see." He wiped his eyes. "She's a topping little girl, too, straight as a die. And brainy."

"I'm sure she is. Have you seen her lately?"

"Oh, yes. Only last week. She came down to see how her old uncle was getting on, although she'd only been back in England a fortnight. She's been an … an absolute brick to me since my dear wife died."

"I suppose she was just back from Corfu."

"That's it. Very disappointing. They stopped the dig when that feller … you know, in *The Times* …"

"Worrall?"

"That's it. They stopped when he got taken ill. Don't see why they couldn't have gone on without him. Still, there it is. Janet said he was against it. Yes, they all came back together on his yacht. Last week, let's see, Tuesday last week, Janet came down to Fleet for the day to see me."

"Did she seem at all upset or uneasy? Any feeling of strains or quarrels?"

"Well, that's uncommon clever of you I must say. How did you guess? I was just thinking of that in the train; always think better in trains; it jogs up the liver. Yes, she didn't seem the thing at all. Jumpy. Quite unlike her usual self."

"She's placid usually?"

"Wouldn't find a steadier little girl anywhere. And another thing. She looked older. Of course, she's … she's over, er, over thirty. But still, she's wholesome-looking. But last week the poor girl really looked quite wretched. Shocking. Due for a spell behind the lines, if you ask me."

"And did she give you any idea of what it was that she was worrying about?"

"No, not in so many words. But when I asked her how soon they were going to start again in Corfu – you see, everyone was taking it for granted that the feller … what's his name?"

"Worrall?"

"That's it, that he'd be better soon. Well, when I asked her, she put me off – hedged. Then she sort of pulled herself together and said 'Soon, I hope.' And d'you know, I had a feeling that she wasn't telling me the truth. And that's very queer, you know, because Janet's as straight as a die. I can only suppose things'd gone wrong somehow and Janet'd promised not to say anything."

"Did you question her at all?"

"Well, I sort of said 'anything wrong, my dear?' But she said not. I don't think she'd had a very happy mess, though."

"Happy mess? Oh, you mean the archaeologists had been getting on each other's nerves?"

"Mind you, Janet didn't say so. Too loyal. And of course, she was devoted to – to …"

"Worrall?" Richard almost shouted, for the third time.

"In a perfectly *healthy* way, of course. Don't misunderstand me. He might have been her father. (You should have seen Janet with her own father; regular little pal she was. She lost her mother early, you see.) As a matter of fact – mind you, this is in confidence – *I* think the feller exploited her rather. She had a great deal too much on her shoulders."

"Too much bottle-washing and too little credit? Could that have been the cause of the trouble?"

"Oh, no, no, Janet was perfectly happy to take the second place. She's such a little brick, that wouldn't occur to her. No, if anyone felt like that, it would have been one of the others."

"Who *were* the others?"

"There's a young man called Shrubsole," he replied without hesitation. "He's the pottery expert. Janet says he's good at his stuff – got a First at Oxford and all that. But not … not *educated*, you know. A bit of a rough diamond."

"Who else is there?"

"There's a Welshman called ap Ifor. He does architecture and religion. Funny combination, isn't it? But he's a funny fellow, by all accounts. Grew a beard, you know, and married a native – a girl in Crete. Between you and me, I got the impression that he was a bit *cracky*. Taffies often are, I find."

Richard was amazed at how much the old man seemed to know about this party of archaeologists. It was only the name of the leader that he forgot consistently. Encouraged, he put his next question more bluntly.

"You see what I'm getting at, sir. Someone tried to murder your niece."

"The scoundrels!" he exclaimed, as if the idea were quite new to him.

"And the attacker had to have certain qualifications, as I told you. He had to know the construction of primitive weapons – I showed you that knife, didn't I? – and he had to know your niece's movements in advance, because she was ambushed. And he hadn't an ordinary robbery motive, because her money and watch weren't taken. So what I ask is – could it be one of her colleagues who wanted her out of the way?"

"Holy Moses!" Mr. Coltman's rheumy eyes widened. "They wouldn't do that, surely! They're educated people. British, too. No, depend upon it, it was one of those Wops. Soho's stiff with them, they tell me. We had just the same trouble when I was serving in Egypt. Italy, too. A soldier'd go down one of those little native streets – not enough lampposts – no self-control. Ten to one he'd get a knife in the back. It's the religion, you see. Moslems and R.C.s, they don't know any better. You're not an R.C. I hope? Glad to hear it. No, my dear boy, you're barking up the wrong tree, I'm sure."

"No doubt you're right, sir. But the fact remains that unless we can find someone with a personal knowledge of your niece's movements and a personal motive for attacking her, we're very unlikely to make an arrest. Meanwhile, a dangerous criminal is at large. Well, I've got the names of her colleagues. Can you suggest anyone else who might have a grudge against her? What circles did she move in?"

Mr. Coltman, looking suddenly old and bewildered, apologized and asked him to repeat the question.

"Oh yes. Yes, I see. Well, she's kept up with some of her old college friends. They're mostly schoolmistresses. Then of course there are the people at Cholsford, where she has a cottage. But she took up this archaeological work when she was quite a girl, and she's been at it hard ever since – mostly abroad with, er, Worrall. I don't think she's had much time for anything else."

"No … no engagement, or anything like that?"

"Oh no! Dear me, no! I don't mean she's a bluestocking or anything like that; she's a dear girl. But she's so wrapped up in her work. And she doesn't make the best of herself. My dear wife always said that."

"I see. So we can roughly limit her acquaintance to fellow archaeologists, old Oxford friends, and the village of Cholsford. Well, I'll go and take a look at the place in Soho where she was found, and then I'd better talk to her colleagues. Will you be staying here for a bit?"

The sister interrupted them. Her patient was asleep, a little better, and likely to sleep till midday. Richard rose to go. As he left the room, he heard the sister telling the old man, with unexpected gentleness, that he had better rest now and leave her to find him a room in a hotel for the night.

Chapter 3

THE alley in Soho where Janet Coltman had been attacked was near the corner of Peter Street and Berwick Street, and there Richard dismissed his taxi. He had never been in Soho as early in the morning as this, and was struck by its unfamiliar quietness and domesticity. In Berwick Street, market stalls were being decked for the day; large perfect fruits glowed in rich pyramids of color, but he noticed that the small bruised ones were being packed into the bottoms of bags weighed out ready for customers. A palsied old man crept about with a sack collecting waste paper, at which he jabbed inaccurately with a spike until a lucky shot impaled it. Latin-looking women stood about in carpet-slippers bargaining for vegetables. They looked slatternly as yet; but their black hair, now twisted uncombed into careless knots, and their greasy sallow faces, still unwashed, would later in the day become triumphs of elegance and art. Later, Richard knew, the lights and the shouting exotic crowd would transform Berwick Street. There would be loitering Negroes, curiously natty in their draped

American jackets and brilliant shirts, laughing like bassoons or softly lurking in silence, but always in couples and never at ease unless they were touching each other, feeling the reassurance of black flesh against warm black flesh. The prostitutes would stand, as they always did, every ten yards down the left-hand side of the road, as though, like the fruit-barrows, they were bound by rule to keep to fixed pitches for the sale of their overripe wares. The unidentifiable Mediterranean types would be talking at the corners in their vaguely conspiratorial and dramatic way. On the whole, they were the most respectable members of the crowd. Then there would be visitors who always turned out to be crooks or Bohemian celebrities – in either case, they had the same long hair, horn-rimmed glasses, and look of defiant but furtive vanity. A few Americans, too, would have come in search of nightlife, young, passive, and slightly drunk. He remembered an indignant, baby-faced A.A.F. policeman who had gone there one night last year, with thirty pounds in his pocket. Next morning he had come to himself on the pavement of a side street, with empty pockets and an itching skin. He went into a public lavatory, stripped off his clothes, and found himself tattooed all over, and with designs that he could never show his Momma. There was no remedy and no redress.

Richard turned off Berwick Street into Peter Street, a less lively place, where the shops sold meat, brawn, and deadly-looking sausages. Turning again to the right past a little corner shop which made its unlikely living by the sale of secondhand "comics," he came into Hopkins Street and saw at once how strategically it had been chosen as the scene of the attack. It was a small, empty street. On one side there was a school and some tenements; on the other, past the shop, a narrow, vaulted passage ran into it at right angles between tall, blank buildings. But the rest of that side of the street had perished and left only an empty bombed site somewhat below road level. Richard walked down the passage far enough to see the stalls and hear the chatter of Berwick Street at its far end. There would have been more noise in the afternoon.

Yes, the attacker had found himself a secret place to hide, with two entrances; a quiet street for the deed, where it was unlikely to be seen, but with a clamorous market nearby to cover any sound of struggle. Janet's blood was still blackening in the cracks between the paving stones of the passage, but Richard found no clues there, although he searched minutely – nothing but dirt and old paper bags and orange-peel, the anonymous litter of any London alley. He still had no idea why Miss Coltman should have been walking in this part of London, so apparently foreign to her background and interests. From where to where had she been going, to come along this narrow, out-of-the-way thoroughfare? And how on earth had her attacker known that she would choose to walk along the side of the street where the passage was? If she had been walking on the other side, all the advantages of his ambush would have been lost. Or was this one of her walking routines, which he had known well? It looked like it. Suppose she was on the same pavement as the passage. Which way would she be walking? If south, the way led into other back streets of Soho. If north, it was in the general direction of the British Museum, which lay to the northeast an easy walk away.

The police had found no one who had heard or seen the crime. The people in the tenements, most of whom were British and elderly, had noticed nothing amiss, and the school had been closed. Henri Puissesseau, the Frenchman who had found her, lived a few streets away, and had merely, he said, been taking a shortcut back from the market. His local reputation was good. He was a *pâtissier* of some renown, and law-abiding if you did not ask how it was that all his cakes were made with real butter and eggs. In all else, *honnêteté* was his policy. For him, the only way to kill a cat (or a customer) was to choke it with cream. He attended lectures on existentialism at St. Anne's House.

No, there was nothing more to be done in Soho at present. At least Richard could now visualize the scene, but he was no nearer to finding suspects. The British Museum was his next objective, but it was too early yet to hope that the archaeologists would be at work there. He filled in time by drinking excellent black coffee in an Italian workmen's restaurant, where the waiter told him a completely new version of the crime. There were many dead, many wounded, all women of abnormal passions. You could tell by their clothes; they were wearing men's mackintoshes. You pay me, sir, I give you a nice story, no? No. Richard finished his sketch-map and notes and sent for a taxi.

A little before half past nine he was limping up the steps of the Museum, leaning on his stick. He would have taken them three at once but for his sprained ankle, and no one would have had time to notice his length of limb and dignity of bearing. But today even the wooden-faced porter admired his approach and gave a respectful answer to his greeting. The respect diminished when Richard asked for Mr. Shrubsole.

"Mr. Shrubsole, let me see, Shrubsole. Have I got a key for him? I'll have a look. It's a bit early yet, you know."

He poked about in his cubbyhole and found that Shrubsole was in, for his key was not on its hook. He summoned a second man in uniform, whose equally impassive face seemed carved in knottier wood by an inferior artist.

"Mr. Shrubsole, Greco-Roman," he said with a jerk of the chin, and returned to his stool and his *Daily Mirror*.

The second man led off without a word. *Bang, bang*, his feet struck the empty floors; *dot down, dot down*, Richard's, limping after him, syncopated the rhythm. They went down a stone staircase and into a lift, which bore them slowly and interminably upwards. At last it stopped, and the man led him out on to a roof under the open sky. They crossed it and plunged down an iron staircase, spiral, steep, and slippery.

"Sorry I'm so slow," said Richard. "Sprained my ankle."

The man became suddenly human, apologized, and asked how he'd done it. Richard (who had in fact, by a flying tackle, stopped a malefactor from riding off on a motor-bicycle under the noses of the patrol) replied that it was a road-accident, and they exchanged amiable platitudes about traffic as they plodded on – this time down empty passages, occasionally stumbling over buckets which stood in the middle of the fairway, generally in a poor light and just round a corner. They came to a row of doors.

"That's the Keeper," whispered the attendant, pointing to a door with a frosted glass panel, and he creaked past it on tiptoe. The Keeper, evidently, kept state as well as antiquities.

They now paused at the threshold of a large room, divided into open-ended cubicles by a series of projecting bookcases filled with dusty textbooks, with a table and chair in each cubicle.

"If you'd just sign the book, please," said the man with all his former woodenness.

It was a portentous volume with four columns. The last, headed *Object of visit*, gave him most trouble. Legal retribution? Moral scavenging? *Personal*, he wrote, combining truth with discretion.

"Mr. Shrubsole! Mr. Shrubsole!" called the man in his loud harsh voice.

There was shuffling and whispering in some of the unseen cubicles, and a voice farther down the room replied to the call.

"That'll be him," said the guide, pointing to an embrasure. Richard turned into it and almost ran his face into an upended mop, sticky with floor polish, which was leaning against the bookcase. He sneezed, recovered, and looked up to see a young man just rising from a table littered with papers and sherds of pottery. He had a lean sallow face, dark hair oiled straight back from the forehead, and very black eyes. Most eyes that pass for black have a touch of some other color to give them expression and softness. But this man's eyes were an opaque and glittering black like coals or pieces of jet. They expressed nothing but wary challenging intelligence. One wondered if they could soften with amusement or sleepiness. Incidentally, Shrubsole looked as if he slept badly.

"Mr. Shrubsole?" began Richard. "I'm afraid I must ask you to spare me a little of your time. I'm a police officer from Scotland Yard."

A dead silence had fallen over the whole room. Shrubsole pushed back his chair with a clatter.

"Not here!" he said in an excited sibilant whisper. "Can't you hear them listening? Come outside. Half a mo', I'll just take my papers." He led the way out into the passage. As they passed the frosted glass door, he whispered, "That's the Keeper," and tiptoed past it on squeaky shoes. Once round the corner he spoke with more assurance. Richard noticed that he used the BBC-Oxford dialect of English, with undertones of Cockney. He was evidently in a high state of nervous tension.

"I don't suppose you want everyone to hear what you've come about. This is a heck of a place for gossip. I'd better take you to one of the galleries. Not ours, that'll be too crowded. Maybe we'll try the Ethnographical. It's darned inconvenient not having a proper room to myself."

He led the way down a stone staircase. Richard, not wishing to put any serious questions until he could watch Shrubsole's face, offered small talk to the spotty back of his neck, and complimented him on his early arrival at work.

"I mostly clock in before the others," he replied. "Matter of fact, my family have breakfast at half past seven, because my father" – he glared challengingly back over his shoulder – "my father has to be at work at eight. He's an ironmonger's assistant in Lewisham."

So what, thought Richard, wondering why he felt so ashamed that his own father was not also an ironmonger's assistant. He grinned and said:

"*My* father always insists on an early breakfast too. I find it's a great relief to have got married. You can at least fix your own mealtimes."

Shrubsole made no reply to this, but led on into the Ethnographical Gallery, and paused in the middle of the room by a case full of brownish untidy objects like very old mops, not immediately identifiable.

"Now," said Shrubsole, nervous but jaunty, "fire away. No eavesdroppers here. What the heck! You can't be too careful in this place. It's an absolute hotbed of gossip. As a matter of fact, I've been half-expecting something like this, and personally I don't mind answering any questions. Is it about Sir Alban or ap Ifor?"

Richard hid his surprise. "Sir Alban's dead, isn't he? And I hope to have a chat with Mr. ap Ifor later. No, I've come to ask you about Miss Janet Coltman."

"Janet!" cried Shrubsole, surprised but wary. "I don't believe it! Why? Has she been talking to you?"

"Not much. She got stabbed in the back yesterday afternoon and she's in hospital."

Shrubsole's sallow face turned still sharper and paler, and his black eyes glittered feverishly in their bony sockets. For a moment he seemed unable to speak. Then he ejaculated:

"My godfathers!" The foolish expletive was charged with an extraordinary intensity of feeling. "She's not dead?"

"No." Richard watched for signs of relief or disappointment, but the jetty eyes betrayed nothing but nervous alertness.

"Is – is she going to die?" he asked in a quieter voice, looking aside at the showcase, which Richard now perceived to contain tiny dried human heads. That accounted for the curious smell.

"She's on the danger list," he replied, "but they said there was a hope of pulling her through."

"What hospital's she in?" Richard did not answer. "I say, what hospital's she in?"

"Perhaps I'd better get my questions over first, hadn't I? Now you say you were expecting this news, Mr. Shrubsole?"

"Me? What the heck! Of course I wasn't!"

"You just said now that you were expecting to be questioned by the police. What did you mean by that?"

"Nothing. I – oh, what the heck, it isn't important now. It hasn't got anything to do with this about Janet."

"You prefer not to answer my first question," said Richard, taking out his notebook. "All right, we'll leave it like that for the moment. Can you tell me anything about Miss Coltman's movements yesterday?"

"No. I haven't seen her since the day Sir Alban died. That's three days ago." He seemed easier.

"Can you give me any idea why she should have been in Hopkins Street, Soho? It's just off Berwick Street."

He was silent for a moment, thinking. "Why, surely that's a bit of Sir Alban's patent shortcut back here from the Minos! That's a Cretan restaurant in Rupert Street, and it gives special prices to archaeologists. Sir Alban went there quite a bit, specially when he had guests."

"Did Miss Coltman go there often?"

"No, she mostly gets a snack here. Still, that's the only place I'd expect her to go in Soho – that district's not really her line – and of course she would have come back here his way. Still, as I say, I haven't seen her since he died. I'd have thought she'd have been too upset to go there just now."

"They were great friends, I gather?"

Shrubsole laughed bitterly. "Friends! You didn't know him, did you? If you mean he exploited the whole-time services of a much better archaeologist than himself, and got all the credit, and she was dumb enough not to see it – O.K., they were friends."

"You don't think she was in – in love with him?"

"My godfathers! No! No, she can't have been! She may be dumb, but she's not that kind of dumb. And she's too matter-of-fact, and – oh, what the heck's it got to do with you, anyhow?"

Richard repeated the little speech he had already made to Mr. Coltman about the special nature of the crime and the need to question all who had been intimately associated with the victim. Some little boys came in and made a dash for the human heads with cries of "Coo!" and "Look, man!" Richard and Shrubsole moved to the other end of the room and continued their talk beside the model of a Polynesian war canoe.

"You wrote that obituary, didn't you?" asked Richard suddenly and at a venture.

"What the …! Well, yes I did, actually, if you want to know."

"Been writing it for some time, hadn't you?"

"No, I … Darn it, I might as well admit it. I showed it to a bloke once, and I suppose he's been gossiping. You won't understand, but –"

"Oh yes. Lots of people have that kind of safety-valve. With me, it's writing rude replies to annoying letters – I don't send them, but it lets off steam. I suppose when he died suddenly and *The Times* hadn't a bit ready, you sort of bunged it in on an impulse? It's been quite useful to *me*. Look, I'm trying to get a picture of the various members of this dig, and I want your views. Let's start with Sir Alban. I gather you didn't think much of his work."

"Work! I never saw him do any! Oh, sometimes he'd pick up a sherd that one of us had found and washed, and hold it the wrong way up while somebody took his photo … Janet wrote most of his descriptions, and I bet she gave him the stuff for his lectures too – the good bits, that is. You can take it from me, he was the darnedest rotten archaeologist that ever bought his way into the racket. And I suppose" – he turned his look of fanatical challenge on full blast – "you'll say that's disloyal of me. Because he paid me four hundred a year to do his work for him, and he had oodles of the stuff and he's dead anyway. O.K., O.K.! Next question, please!"

"You say Miss Coltman was good. If so, why didn't she see through him? Or did she?"

He knitted his brows. "I don't know. I don't know. Maybe she did, a bit, over that Corfu business."

"Ah!" said Richard, guessing again, "that's what you thought I'd come about, I suppose. You'd better tell me, you know. If it really hasn't got anything to do with the attack on Miss Coltman, it needn't go any further."

"I don't know. In a way, I'd like to get that at least off my chest. But – oh, what the heck! You wouldn't understand what it was about."

"I've dabbled a bit in Minoan archaeology. Rather amateurish, I'm afraid, and it was only at Oxford a long time ago. Still …"

"I'm not really in a position to judge, either," said Shrubsole with unexpected modesty, "because this isn't my line, I do pots, and Janet does gems and seals. But look – I've got it with me. I daren't let it out of my sight."

After a quick glance around him, he took a matchbox out of his pocket and opened it. Inside, knocking about in an irreverent way, was a great seal ring of pale gold exquisitely engraved.

"What d'you make of that?" He watched with all the street urchin's cynical eagerness for the toff to make a fool of himself. Richard could not help rising to the challenge. He studied the ring for a moment in silence and replied:

"Middle Minoan III, I should say, though I wouldn't know if it's genuine or a good fake. Isn't it the type they describe as a Religious Scene? Sacred Tree, one male worshipper possibly the Sacred King – Great Goddess or her priestess with three attendants. Found in Crete?"

Shrubsole's shrill crow of laughter was pure Cockney. He was clearly delighted.

"What the heck! So you really *do* know a bit! Aren't our British policemen wonderful? Actually, it's Late Minoan I, and it's not exactly a fake, I don't think. Notice anything queer about it?"

"Not specially. Of course, all this stuff is queer to me – that's half the fascination. The men's waists are too small, and the women's breasts are too big, and they have hair like live snakes, and they all look as if they were doing some fantastic ballet and their life depended on doing it right – and yet no one seems to have quite discovered what they *were* doing ..."

"*I* wouldn't have any suggestions. I'm a plain field archaeologist." And proud of it, his manner added.

"Where *was* this ring found?"

"Ah! Sir Alban Worrall found it on Mouse Island, Corfu. There's a very old shrine there, you know, and we were looking under it for classical and pre-classical remains. He picked this out of the trench with his own hand. We were all there. He saw to that. We'd been on the site all the afternoon sweating away, when he strolled up, as fresh as a daisy. 'I'll just look along the trench once more,' he said, 'in case we've missed anything in this stratum.' *We!* And he went along with a brush, and he *found* this ring straight away. We'd all been pretty careful, and I'd been over that particular section myself. '*Eyes and no eyes*,' he said." He snorted.

"Was the ring clean or encrusted with earth?"

"Good question. It *was* encrusted with earth – and the right kind of earth too, by the look of it – just the same as that wall of the trench. '*I'll clean it myself*,' he says, very complacent. '*Everyone clean his own finds. That's always been my rule*.' Still, I came with him. And I swear this is the same ring."

"But you think he put it there for himself to find? That he salted the trench?"

"Mind you, I'm not dead sure. There was some dark-on-light Late Minoan I pottery sherds found in the same stratum – not much of it, and none of it first-class, but still – some kind of corroboration for the ring."

"Alternatively, he *could* have put in the fragments too?"

"Could have. He was there during the lunch break. The main thing is, everyone says they've never found that particular type of ring outside Crete. And there's one very queer thing about it. Look, here's Sir Alban Worrall's description of it. He wrote it himself, for once." He passed over a typed sheet from the sheaf of papers he had carried off with him. It read as follows:

> Gold amygdaloid seal ring found by Sir Alban Worrall on Mouse Island, Corfu, May 1953. (His own description.)
>
> On the left of my impression a half-kneeling nude male figure grasps in his right hand the branch of a tree (perhaps a wild olive) and turns

his head and the upper half of his body towards a draped female figure in the center. His left arm, bent at the elbow, is extended towards her in an attitude of supplication. In the center stands a splendidly formed woman, dressed in the typical Minoan crinoline and close-fitting jacket, leaving the breasts bare. She is facing us, but her head is turned towards the male figure, and her right arm, bent at the elbow, is extended in an attitude of gracious welcome. Behind her and to the right of my impression stand three similarly garbed female figures of smaller size, with floating locks, and arms raised above shoulder-level in energetic motion. Over their heads is a large spherical object. On the ground under the feet of the male figure is a line of spherical dots, the conventional Minoan symbol to denote running water. No other objects have been found in this stratum as yet to assist in dating, but the ring belongs to the type of Late Minoan I.

It has great interest and importance as being, perhaps, our earliest representation of the story of Nausicaa as told in Book VI of the Odyssey. The central figure is the princess herself in the act of welcoming the shipwrecked hero. The smaller female figures are her maidens at their ball game, and the ball may be seen over their heads in the air (not in the bushes as in Homer, doubtless for convenience of representation). Odysseus himself is depicted in the act of picking the leafy bough (line 128) to cover his nakedness. The river flows at his feet. The "salty crusts of brine" on his body (mentioned in Od. VI. 225–6) may perhaps be seen lightly indicated on loins and legs.

This find confirms my theory that Corfu is the Homeric Scherie, last and latest outpost of the great Minoan culture.

"Find that sort of stuff convincing?" asked Shrubsole with a sneer.

Richard hesitated. "I know so little about it. If he *were* right I suppose everybody would agree that it was a very thrilling discovery. He'd get enormous prestige for it."

"You can bet your sweet life he would. Especially with people who know next to nothing about archaeology – what *he'd* call the Wider Public. *Wide!* My godfathers! *Now*, look at Janet Coltman's description. She did one too, but Sir Alban persuaded her to pipe down and not publish it."

Richard wondered how, in that case, Shrubsole had managed to get a copy out of her, but for the moment he reserved the question.

Janet Coltman's description.
(Positions described from impression)

On the left, a male figure clad in the loincloth and leg bindings of a

Minoan athlete half-kneels and grasps in his right hand the trunk of a tree in full leaf, which he shakes to invoke the Mother Goddess (cf. Persson, *Religion of Greece in Prehistoric Times*). He simultaneously extends his left arm, bent at the elbow, towards the center in an attitude of supplication, turning his head in the same direction. In the center the Goddess, clearly represented in her fertility aspect, has appeared, dressed in the usual flounced skirt and frontless jacket. She extends her right arm, bent at the elbow, in an attitude of greeting. Slightly behind her and to the right are three female figures similarly dressed. Their smaller size, uplifted arms, and swaying bodies indicate them as votaries engaged in an ecstatic dance. The sun, large, round, and immediately overhead, indicates that the season is summer, as does the full foliage of the tree and the two lily-like plants in the right foreground. The nine spherical dots in the left foreground are the conventional Minoan symbol to indicate a rocky terrain. The portion of the seal immediately below the tree has suffered wear or defacement and does not give a clear impression; but comparison with similar designs in the same glyptic cycle would lead us to expect that this space was originally filled by the representation of a small baetylic shrine.

This ring closely resembles two found last year in Crete by Sir Alban Worrall. The type has already been well described by Persson (v. supra) as representing a religious scene. The baetylic shrine, however, does not appear owing to wear or defacement. The sun is represented as a plain sphere not inscribed with rays, which is unusual in L.M.I., to which period this object should probably be assigned on stylistic grounds. But for a parallel, cf. Tsountas, *Révue Archéologique* 1900, pl. VII, 3.

"This is much more what I'd have expected, certainly," said Richard, handing it back. "The stuff about baetylic shrines foxes me a bit. What *are* they, anyhow?"

"Baetylic shrines? Bethels, if that means anything to you. Sacred stones into which the deity descends. In Crete, they're generally long-shaped stones planted in the ground, and they have an ordinary stone on each side like a doorpost and a flat slab across the top to make a sort of table, probably for offerings. They seem to have been built out-of-doors."

"Oh, yes, I know the things. Didn't know what they were. They're fairly small compared with the figures, aren't they? About waist-high?"

"Yes. Though it's often a mistake to take scale too literally in Minoan art. But you see Janet's point?"

"I think so. There ought to be a baetylic shrine under that tree, where it looks blank? May I look at the ring again? … M'm. There *isn't* a hollow there as if the surface had been rubbed away."

"No, but it could have been rubbed down with emery and then filled up with gold. That is, if the right kind of gold could be got. It's not so pure as the modern kind."

"Are there any tests that you could make to see?"

"You could file off a specimen and have it analyzed. That's Janet's business. She won't have anything to do with the idea. Says it'd spoil the seal, and anyhow Sir Alban was against it."

"But if there was never a shrine at all, then there *is* a sort of case for the Odysseus-Nausicaa interpretation? Or anyhow, it's an interesting idea and bound to get a lot of publicity. They always said, didn't they, that Nausicaa's island was a picture of a Minoan city – really a pre-Greek setup?"

"Yes, and there's a quite unreliable tradition that Corcyra, Corfu, that is, was the actual place referred to by Homer."

"Did you tell Sir Alban your suspicions?"

"What the heck! Accuse him of planting a forged object? And lose my job? Not till I could prove it up to the hilt and all the rest of the expedition backed me up."

"Miss Coltman didn't, though you say she was worried. What about ap Ifor?"

"What the heck! Him share suspicions! He'd just lap it up and say it all went to show Homer was a Welshman after all. He's either blind balmy or in the racket up to the neck. I'm not sure yet which."

"Homer a Welshman? What *do* you mean?"

"Iorweth ap Ifor" – he pronounced it *Ee-orroo-eth ahp Eefor*, mimicking the pure-voweled Welsh with contemptuous fidelity – "or Beavor, is a Welsh nationalist – also our architect and photographer. Also a darned good publicity man for those who like it. Well, he thinks the Minoan civilization moved to Wales, bag and baggage, when what he calls 'the Greek invaders' got power in the Aegean, about 1400 B.C.. In fact, Nausicaa's probably at the top of his family tree. He's all for romance, is friend Iorweth. Even that wife of his is a reincarnation of the Great Goddess, according to him. *I* wouldn't know. *I*'m just a poor pot-mender trying to get field experience."

"What made you choose this particular job?"

"Choose! It's the only one there was, and I was darned lucky to get it. I'm working class, get that, and if I do any excavation at all beyond digging drains for the L.C.C., I have to do it on a subsistence wage under whoever'll have me. And when my father's past work, I'll have to snap out of the whole thing and be a schoolmaster, or the family won't eat. You can't keep going on archaeology."

"I'm sorry. I'd forgotten how few paid jobs there are. Were Miss Coltman and ap Ifor in the same position?"

"She was, more or less, though I imagine she had relations who'd have helped at a pinch. Ap Ifor's in clover. His father owned a coal mine. The real version of the family surname's Beavor."

"And what happens to your jobs now Sir Alban's dead?"

"Wouldn't we like to know?" said Shrubsole, with a wolfish smile that stretched the skin over his sharp jaws. "We were supposed to be employed by the Museum at Heracleion, but it's no secret that Worrall provided the cash. He paid the workmen too – we had a small gang of Cretans who'd been specially trained and were very good at the job. He even took them to Corfu on his yacht. Well, either he's left us money to carry on, or he hasn't. I suppose we'll be told after the funeral. We'll go, just for that." The staccato words were charged with venom and aggressiveness. But Richard knew that attack is a common form of defense, and he counterattacked.

"Had any quarrels with Miss Coltman lately?"

"Who, me? No, of course not! Why?"

"It's odd you haven't spoken to each other since the death of Sir Alban. You've both been working here, I understand. Surely you must have had things to discuss, in such an unexpected situation?"

The black eyes darted nervously to and fro. "Must have missed each other. Anyhow, she's got lots of fancy friends if she wants to weep on their shoulders. Me, I've got my pots. And I'm busy on them till I'm kicked out. Get that. And I'm not making any more statements today. What hospital did you say she was in?"

"I'll keep in touch with you. Can I have your home address? You won't of course leave it without letting us know."

"So you're tailing me, are you?" said Shrubsole shrilly. "So you think I murdered her, do you? You're afraid if you told me the hospital, I might get in and finish her off? O.K., O.K.! You'll let me know if she dies, won't you? Save me a bit of trouble, see?"

"Don't be silly, I haven't even taken a signed statement off you yet. She's at the Middlesex, and you can ring up and inquire. Of course she isn't allowed any visitors. Now, can you take me to Mr. ap Ifor?"

A subdued Shrubsole led Richard about and discovered that ap Ifor had not yet put in an appearance. His home address was found after some trouble, and Richard set out there at once.

Chapter 4

IORWETH AP IFOR and his Cretan wife lived near Baker Street in a furnished flat, one of a hundred and fifty like it, in a block called Missenden Mansions. Richard Ringwood disliked such dwellings on aesthetic grounds, but his professional hatred of them was even greater. They were warrens with too many bolt-holes, and so vast that no one took any notice of his neighbors. The lift that carried him to the third floor was automatic and soundless; the branching corridors he wandered down were softly carpeted; only the chromium-plated number 108 distinguished the ap Ifors' glossy green door from a hundred and forty-nine others.

When he rang, the door was not answered at once, though he could hear a whispering and scuffling behind it. He was just going to ring again when it opened. It framed a startling vision. For the woman who stood there, high-nosed, dominant, and inscrutable, was a living replica of the Great Goddess whose picture he had been looking at with Shrubsole half an hour ago – flounced skirt, snaky hair, voluptuous limbs and all. Or no, not quite all. It was true that her cobalt-blue robe with its dark red flounces looked very Minoan, especially over those heroic hips and thighs, but it was really only an elaborate dressing gown. True, a serpentine girdle was thrice wound round her hourglass waist, but it was of yellow cord, not hieratic gold. And her great swelling breasts were not actually exposed, though they looked as if they might come bursting up over the top of the low bodice any moment. He hoped not. It would be the last link with the ordinary world snapping. She looked more like a fertility fetish than a human being as it was. And to crown her resemblance to the Goddess of the ring, she was even now extending her left arm, bent at the elbow, in an attitude of …? What will it be this time? Archaeologists, it seemed, were allowed to interpret that gesture in almost any way they chose, but detectives had to make up their minds.

Then Richard saw the youth, who had been out of sight behind the door. He was a dark graceful creature with an unnaturally slender waist, and he looked frightened. Just like the male figure on the ring. Contemplating it in the museum, Richard had been reminded of the mating habits of spiders. The female spider, like the Goddess, was big and eager, the male much smaller and very nimble. He had to be, for unless he made a lightning escape, the female would eat him the second after the act. *Vénus toute entière à sa proie attaché* … This time, however, Venus, in the rather overwhelming avatar of Mrs. ap Ifor, was evidently telling her prey to get to hell out of here. Richard stopped him.

"Don't go, please. Are you Mr. ap Ifor? I'd like a word with you. I'm a police officer from Scotland Yard."

The youth said nothing and looked more frightened than ever. But the woman, unmoved, intervened in broken English where a Greek accent struggled (as so often) with that of Broadway.

"No, no. He is jost a salesman, that's all. He comm in while I tell him to bring me" – she paused – "food. You want my hosband, he is right here, taking a bath, yes? Comm right in."

I'll let the boy go, thought Richard. It's probably black market, but I can't waste time on that at present. Anyhow he obviously isn't any kind of archaeologist.

The woman rapped on a door and called through it in a language that Richard could identify as modern Greek, but not understand. Her remarks were brief. Then she took him into a sitting room, pointed to a sofa, and seated herself sinuously upon an upright armchair, feet together and one long olive hand along each arm – an effective attitude that seemed to turn the chair into a throne. Apparently she did not consider it necessary to speak. Presently Iorweth ap Ifor came in.

He was splendidly clad in a robe of green silk. Turkish slippers turned up at the ends adorned his feet, and a small black beard his chin. But he was no match for his wife in physical magnificence. He was stocky and short-legged. Spectacles perched across a long Cymric nose pointed like the nib of a pen, and pink from the bath. When he spoke – as he began to do at once – there was little accent, but his tenor voice, light as running water or a jackdaw's cry, was as Welsh as a whole Eisteddfodd.

Richard was trying to assess the ap Ifors' reactions to a police visit. The woman's worried him. She had seemed displeased rather than surprised. Had she been expecting something? Was this impassivity natural? Or was her silence defensive? It was clear, he thought, that her husband had expected no policeman's visit, and he seemed charmed with the honor. He looked the kind of man who would flourish in the fierce light that beats upon a soapbox – witness the mobile mouth, the assent-collecting eye – so perhaps it was the hope of notoriety that pleased him.

"There's really no need for me to waste Mrs. ap Ifor's time, I think, at present. I've come to ask you some questions about the Corfu expedition."

Ap Ifor glanced at his wife with a look of questioning respect. In reply, she merely bent her brows at him (they were black and met over the bridge of her nose) and said:

"I stay."

Her husband supported her volubly.

"Yes, indeed, Inspector, I think that would be best. I can't imagine what we've done to deserve the honor of a visit from such a very distinguished officer" – he glanced at Richard's card again – "but it must be something important. And if so, I'm sure Zoe will be able to help. Women's intuition, you know. That's what it's vulgarly called. I'd prefer to say" – he smiled deprecatingly – "that women have access to a deeper kind of knowledge than we have. Indeed, the older civilizations were sure of it, and I'm not prepared to say they were wrong. It's the Life Principle, you see – they're so much closer to it. Women are surely part of the great Rhythm of Nature. And that's the reason why ancient Crete – yes, and ancient Wales, too; they're not so different as people think – were in a sense matriarchal. And of course it's a known fact that there were priestesses long before there were priests. They're closer to the Life Forces, you see. Zoe specially. Zoe has so much Life, I feel."

He gazed fondly at her immobile curves. She seemed to gather sap as you looked, like some juicy plant expanding without visible movement. Yes, she had Life all right – but the inhumanly fleshy life of a tropical greenhouse. It was uncanny, and did not assist clear thinking. Richard took a grip on his fancies and said:

"Yes, yes, I'm sure you're right," and ap Ifor looked gratified. "Do let her stay if she cares to. I *have* come on a serious matter, as you say. I take it you don't know that your colleague, Miss Janet Coltman, was stabbed in Soho yesterday afternoon?"

"My God indeed no!" he exclaimed on a single shocked breath. "This is a terrible thing you are telling me, Inspector. Is she – is she – ?"

"Alive this morning, but only just. There's no doubt someone tried to kill her." He repeated his introductory speech for the third time that day. As he spoke, he watched the woman. Her face was still the same opaque-eyed, high-nosed archaic riddle, but he could sense that she had relaxed. Her body looked softer, and she rubbed one bare shoulder against her cheek as though the contact pleased her. When he stopped speaking, she rose to her feet in a single smooth movement.

"Too bad," she said. "That's okay, Oorweth. I go."

Richard intervened. "One moment, Mrs. ap Ifor. Just for the record, would you mind telling me where you were yesterday afternoon?"

"That is easy. Ollways, from two to four, I take off my clothes" – What *is* that gesture, thought Richard? *Ayesha Unveils*, that's it! – "I lie down on that sofa, where you sit now. I sleep. Yes."

"And can anyone corroborate this?"

She bent her brows again on her husband, who hastened to reply:

"Oh, yes! I rang her up from the museum between half past three and four. I – I'm afraid she was still asleep. The operator had to ring several times before he got an answer. I – I expect he'll remember."

I bet he will, thought Richard.

"That's right, buddy. He wake me. Was I mad! I go."

She left the room like a panther, and suddenly there was more air to breathe and more room to move. That almost dehiscent bodily exuberance was a strain – as much of a strain as talking to a pure intellectual. Zoe was at the other end of the scale – a pure physical, as it were – and equally hard to apprehend as a person, the more so for being cast in the mold of the most ancient goddess in the world. He briskly began his questions.

Ap Ifor ("Call me Iorweth. In Wales we do not have surnames, except where the English have imposed them.") confirmed Shrubsole's estimate of Miss

Coltman's character and interests. He had seen her yesterday morning at the museum, and had asked her to look at some seals that had come into his possession; but she had said that she was just going out to lunch and would examine them in the afternoon. He had looked for her in her cubicle at three but she was not there. Yes, she generally kept appointments. No, she did not often go out to lunch. She looked strained, but no doubt Sir Alban's death had been a blow, and perhaps too she had been anxious about the future. In Iorweth's opinion, there was little real doubt that Sir Alban would have left money to carry on the work, as he had often said he would; but Janet and Ian Shrubsole were both hoping for the leadership and each feared that the other would get it. Only this could explain the quarrels they had been having lately.

Quarrels? Yes, whenever he had found them together, since their return to England, they had been arguing bitterly in low voices. In fact, since Sir Alban's death, they had not even been on speaking terms. And look how they had attacked each other in *The Times*!

Richard objected that if they had begun to quarrel *before* Sir Alban's death, the leadership of the party could hardly have been the point at issue. No one had expected the man to die. Or had they?

"I did," said Iorweth solemnly, but rather tentatively. "Not on the so-called scientific level, I grant you. But he'd had his lesson, in Pontikonisi, and he'd disregarded it, in spite of the warning I tried to give him."

"What on earth do you mean? What did he die of, anyway?"

"Gastric ulcer, Inspector. He had a sharp attack at Corfu, and as you know, he had a much worse one in England, which was fatal. The ulcer perforated."

"But what did you mean when you said he'd had his warning?"

Iorweth smiled again and caressed the upturned point of his little beard.

"You'll probably say it's just my fancy, Inspector, if I tell you. (Though I could quote other experiences, and in our own time too, that bear it out.) Pontikonisi – Mouse Island, that is – is an odd place, you see. It's been holy ground for thousands and thousands of years, ever since anyone can remember, and there are – well, shall we call them influences? Vibrations? Anyway, something not quite – in the common run. Now nobody could be a keener archaeologist than I am. (For I've got better reasons than most people for thinking the Past is important.) But keen as I am, I'd never go to a place where the – the influences were hostile, without taking certain precautions. Oh, I don't say I'd go so far as to kill a lamb for a blood offering. After all, blood's only one of the forms of Life, and it doesn't do to antagonize people."

"So what *did* you do?" asked Richard, fascinated. The unearthly lightness of the jackdaw voice made the words sound almost convincing.

"Well, mind you, it was just a precaution, Inspector – I *did* just pour a small libation of honey in the part of the pit nearest to where I thought the shrine would have been. I didn't mention it to anyone, except just a hint to Sir Alban, when we arrived. That was a bit unfortunate in a way because Ian Shrubsole stepped in it next morning in canvas shoes, and he was very rude about it – very rude indeed. He rejects the Life Forces, you know. He exalts Intellect above Nature, and of course his nerves suffer as a result, poor man. The tragic modern dichotomy. I knew it would be no good talking to *him*. But I did try to warn Sir Alban again, after that poor boy was killed. I *knew*, you see. We ancient peoples, some of us, do still at times feel ourselves in touch with that deeper kind of knowledge. Zoe felt the same. But even the first victim didn't convince Sir Alban."

"Victim? The boy, you mean? What boy? How was he killed?"

"Ach, it was a terrible tragedy. He was the only son of our Cretan foreman, a boy of sixteen, and shaping very well, too. He fell down a high cliff one night, poor lad, and was picked up with his neck broken and so on. His father found him on the rocks in the morning."

"How did it happen?"

"The others all said he was climbing for gulls' eggs and had a fall. But there was more to it than that. He'd been working closest to the center that day, you see. And he wouldn't have fallen like that if he'd been in a normal state. He was very sure-footed. Ach, no! Poor boy, it's only too clear his mind was affected – he'd come dangerously near the influences of the place, and they'd affected him like a shock. Have you ever read the *Bacchae?* That's the sort of thing I mean. Why, he'd even left his knife lying about in the trench – and no Cretan peasant in his senses will ever part with his knife. They even take them to bed. No, it wasn't a natural death – not as modern men understand Nature. I saw it as a warning."

"What happened after that?"

"Well, the foreman found the body, as I said, early next morning, and Sir Alban was told at breakfast. Two hours afterwards, about ten o'clock, *he* was struck down. He was taken very bad – ach, he was groaning in agony – and he kept saying over and over again that he must get back to England quickly. He didn't trust foreign doctors. So Miss Coltman settled the legal details – luckily they were content with a signed statement about the boy's death – and paid off the workmen and gave them their fares back to Crete, and we got off somehow by the end of the day. But of course I knew it was already too late."

"You mean, he didn't get to his doctor in time?"

"Indeed, yes, he saw his doctor. He *seemed* better, after we got back. There was some talk of his going into hospital for observation later, and he was going about very much as usual. But he was never the same man, really. It was just a fortnight after that, he had his second attack, in the Minos – and, notice, *that* was in a way Greek soil – and he died very quickly. I can't help blaming myself, in a way, for not speaking out more boldly. I might have saved him."

Richard was puzzled. The sequence of calamities did seem rather too close to be natural. He must look into them. But did this excited little man believe that they could have been averted by his heathenish mumbo-jumbo? Surely not. He had the reputation of being a good archaeological architect, and the photographs on the walls here showed him a brilliant photographer. Could a man of such ability really be so credulous? Or was he acting? If so, was he deliberately laying a false trail to cover some human and punishable malignity? Or had he, as he claimed, the Celtic power of second sight? Had he scented trouble to come, and was this talk of vibrations and influence a kind of romantic rationalization? In any case, the events in Corfu clearly must be taken into account.

"Where were you and your colleagues when the boy died?"

"Well, let me see. Zoe and I were asleep in bed in the hotel at Corfu. I think Sir Alban and Ian Shrubsole were too. They slept there. Janet Coltman was sleeping on Pontikonisi, in a tent. She liked to keep an eye on the site, and anyhow she enjoyed sleeping out. The workmen slept on the island, too."

"And where were you and your wife when Sir Alban died?"

"On Monday? I was going over to Highgate, to lecture to a school. Zoe – let's see, he died after lunch, didn't he? She'd have been asleep on that sofa as usual. Zoe has to sleep a great deal," he added importantly. "It's an astral necessity. It seems to me that perhaps her Life-Forces demand a wider range than our limited space and time can give them. But in sleep there is liberation."

"Oh. You don't happen to know who Sir Alban's doctor was, do you?"

"Indeed I do. Chevet, that was the name. Doctor Chevet, of Queen Anne Street. Sir Alban talked about him a lot on the way home."

"You all came home with him, I gather?"

"Certainly we did. He had his yacht there, with the permanent Greek crew, so it was much the quickest and most economical arrangement."

"Was there any need for the whole expedition to be broken up like that?"

He shrugged. "Sir Alban particularly asked for me to see him home. I think he felt I was a kind of protection to him. Otherwise of course I'd have stayed. Janet naturally went with him to look after the day-to-day details, as she always does. Did, I should say. Ach! I hope from my heart that she may be spared to do so again, yes indeed I do! But as I was saying, that only left Ian Shrubsole."

"And one's not enough, I suppose. You need a team. Or do you mean he wasn't up to it?"

"Indeed, I wouldn't venture to pass a judgment on a colleague. But excellent as his work is, he's just a narrow academic. A pot-mender, as he says. Ian isn't really what I call Minoan-minded, poor man. He has no imagination, no historical sense, no vision, no – no soul! The Saxons are too young a people …"

Oh dear! thought Richard. He's raising the hwyll again. How tiring these fanatics are. They have no sense of personality. They can only distinguish between the people who agree with them and the people who don't. Still, can he really think that a Vibration made that knife and stuck it into Janet's back? I can't believe it. I'll play him along, though. He's let slip a lot by the way, and I feel that Zoe of his has been up to something. I'd better try to get a look over the house before I go. He rose.

"Well, thank you, er, Iorweth. Very helpful and interesting. I'd like to come back for another talk some time. You won't go away without letting us know, will you? We might want you as a witness. I say, this is a very nice flat, if you don't mind my saying so. How many rooms have you got? Actually, I was wondering if you'd be leaving it, if you go back to Corfu. May I really look over it? That's very kind of you."

Iorweth conducted him eloquently round every room but the bathroom, where the Great Goddess seemed to be secluded for ritual ablution. (Judging by the silence, she was making up some astrally necessary sleep in her bath. It was fairly easy to imagine her out of Time, but Space was another thing. Surely her function was to fill it?) Richard noted that an iron fire escape led from the bedroom window to the car park below; and having thus achieved the object of his tour, took his leave. But he went no farther than the next passage, and after a few minutes stealthily returned. Zoe was talking hard. Her impassivity, then, was feigned; she had been playing possum. Now, at any rate, there was no mistaking the tone of her voice, though the words escaped him. She was both angry and alarmed.

Chapter 5

The interview with the ap Ifors had yielded very little evidence of the kind that makes sense in a law court. The story of quarrels between Janet Coltman and Shrubsole might perhaps figure in the official notebook. The rest seemed fantastic, but there were some features worth noting. First, Zoe had expected trouble. But when the trouble turned out to be merely the attempted murder of Janet, and she had been told that Janet was still alive, this enigmatic and alarming woman had not thought it worth while to stay and hear the matter out.

Next, the attack on Janet had been preceded by two other deaths within the same small group of people. The boy's death had been violent; Sir Alban's unexpected, for he had seemed better after his return home. There would be no harm in looking into these two deaths more closely. And if so, the sooner the better, for Sir Alban's funeral was to be tomorrow. Richard looked up Dr. Chevet in the telephone directory and took a taxi to his house in Queen Anne Street.

After a sharp engagement with a receptionist and a secretary, both of them determined and highly polished young women, skilled to defend the shrine of Aesculapius from the profane, he managed to burst through the luxurious waiting room to the inner sanctuary, the consulting room, glistening with glass and chromium plate, where the great man himself sat at his walnut desk. He looked too clean-limbed and trustworthy to be real; fine head, thick hair a little grizzled at the temples, short clipped mustache, long legs, impeccable tailoring, even a pipe. Slightly sunburned, too – he must play golf at weekends. He was annoyed at Richard's irruption, especially as he was caught without a patient in his chair or a paper in front of him. But Richard applied the tactics he always knew he should use on his own father. (Colonel Ringwood was a retired Guards officer, and belonged naturally to the type to which Dr. Chevet so strenuously aspired.) Richard was modest, monosyllabic, and manly; upright, forthright, downright; too public-school to talk back to his senior, but too honorable to abandon his duty. Arnold's Best Boy. He took an ironic pleasure in the performance, and, being a Salopian, rather overacted it. But it worked. Dr. Chevet was presently eating out of his hand, and told him the full story. The facts had been as follows.

* * *

The wires began buzzing even before Worrall touched the shores of his native land. There was a telegram asking Dr. Chevet to meet the yacht on arrival, signed Coltman. Then there was another, canceling the first arrangement and proposing that an ambulance should convey the patient to Queen Anne Street on arrival. Finally, one from Sir Alban himself, saying, "Better stop walking stop please arrange appointment your house tomorrow." Dr. Chevet considered putting him off for a few days – a doctor who let his patients order him about only lost caste in the end – but on reflection, he yielded. Worrall was so very well known. And he had sound views on the National Health Insurance. So many patients took advantage, these days. The secretary telegraphed that Dr. Chevet could spare him half an hour at ten-thirty.

Worrall settled himself massively in the chair, and began to talk, smoothing the bristly hair over the roll of flesh on the back of his neck.

"Well, I can tell you, I'm damn glad to have got to you in time. I don't know what's the matter with me – that's your business, eh? Trust the expert, that's always been my rule – but, my word, when I had that attack on Corfu, it was ..."

"Lot of pain?" Chevet's blend of sympathy and professional alertness was nicely judged.

"Well, I'm not a man to exaggerate, I hope," said Worrall with a game, tight-lipped smile. "But it was – just about as much as I could take. A sort of sharp, burning pain *here*." He indicated the ample but still fairly flat region under the lower buttons of his gray herringbone waistcoat.

"Any vomiting? Yes? And tell me, did you feel better when you'd vomited? Yes ... yes, I see. Did you try taking anything for it? Bicarbonate? Magnesia?

That do any good? Yes, relieved by alkalis and vomiting, quite. What about meals? How did you feel after food?" He gave his patient another keen glance. It was all part of the service. They appreciated it.

"That was the queer thing, Chevet. I should have *thought* there was something badly wrong with my digestive system, but – I enjoyed my meals. Had a good appetite, and felt all the better for my food."

"But an hour afterwards?"

"Exactly. You're a wonderful chap, I must say I'm glad I came straight back to you. An hour after the meal was over, I was in agony. How on earth did you guess?"

"We doctors don't do much guessing, Worrall. It's too risky. Now tell me, did the pain come on at all at nights?"

"It was worst at night." A gruff, valiant understatement.

"H'm. You're playing it down a bit, aren't you? Now, come and lie over here and let's have a look at you."

The knightly stomach, white, extensive, and still not really flabby, was exposed and prodded inch by inch, up and down, round and round. To each inquiry whether it hurt, Worrall replied "No." When the exploring fingers came closer to the pit of the stomach, he modified it to "No, not really." But then the doctor touched one particular spot more lightly than the rest – a spot about the size of a shilling – and the patient gave a short yelp of pain. "Sorry!" he added. "It's there, isn't it?" said Chevet, touching it again.

"Fff! Yes, that's the place. Don't do that again without warning me!"

"That's all right. All over now. Sit down again when you're ready. Well, Worrall, it looks to me as if you'd got a slight gastric ulcer. We can't be sure, of course, until we've had a barium meal and an X-ray. We won't jump to any conclusions. But as I say, that's what it looks like at present. A lot of brain-workers get these internal ulcers at some time or other, you know – writers, Cabinet ministers, public figures of all kinds. Anyone with a lot of responsibility. Half my patients, in fact. I won't say it's psychosomatic exactly. That's putting it too dogmatically, and I don't like dogmatism. But put it like this. We *can* say that there is a very considerable psychogenic factor. I'd like to talk over your case with my friend Sir Willoughby Jebb. He's made some rather interesting discoveries in gastric surgery lately. You know him?"

"Yes. Actually he was knighted at the same time as me. But …"

"Was he now? Yes, yes I remember that Honors List. You were the only two I felt really happy about that year."

"Listen, Chevet. Jebb may be a friend of yours, but I'm not going to have him carving me up. Nor anyone else either. I won't have an operation." Worrall spoke with great vehemence. "I've never let anyone get a knife into me yet, and I'm not going to start now. Good God! I've even put it in my will. Yes, I've just made a will. Buried whole and unmutilated. Surgeons! I – I can't stand the idea,

I tell you. If you knew as much about sacrificial methods as I do …"

"There now! Don't let's be alarmist. We needn't jump to any conclusions, need we? I only meant I'd have a word with Willoughby about *treatment*. I'm pretty sure we can get you right with dieting and so on. We're taking it in good time, after all. Now, get these prescriptions made up. I'll tell my secretary to give you a copy of my diet sheet. It should help you, I think … Yes, by all means stay at your club, and go on as usual. But take things quietly."

"Any idea how long this will take? I want to get back to my work, you know. And it isn't my idea of archaeology to sit back in London. No, I've never been an armchair archaeologist. Plenty of fieldwork. That's always been my rule."

"We-ell, I can't give you a snap judgment about that, of course. No conscientious doctor would. But don't worry. Well now, that's all for the present, I think. I'll have to do the checkup on heart and blood-pressure next time you come. Actually, I've got rather a queue of patients waiting to see me. My secretary will let you know when we've fixed up for your barium meal. I take it you'd prefer a private nursing home. Good, good. I'll try to arrange it soon, then."

A firm handshake, and a smile implied "You're a brave man. I can see you're suffering and I'm proud to think I can cure you." Then the room was empty, and Chevet composed his features into a somewhat softer mold, preparatory to steering yet another aging charmer through the migraines of her late forties.

* * *

A week later, the matron of the Burton House Nursing Home rang him up in considerable indignation.

"It's your patient, Sir Alban Worrall, Dr. Chevet. We've got him here for his barium meal and X-ray. But he won't take it. He just spits it out. We can't do anything with him."

"Dear, dear, Miss Armstrong!" (He made a point of remembering the names of important nurses. It helped.) "Well, we can't have that, can we? I'm afraid I can't come along myself. I'm just going out to a case in the country. Perhaps I could have a word with him now. Can he come to the telephone?"

"Certainly, doctor. At once. But I must warn you, he seems very determined."

"No harm in trying, anyhow. I'm afraid you'll have to send him the usual bill, whether he takes the meal or not. Did you make that clear?"

"Very clear, doctor. It made no difference. He says he can't face it now, we must put it off. Quite childish, because I can *see* … Oh! Here *is* Sir Alban, doctor."

"Hallo, Chevet," said a weak but stoical voice. "My dear chap, I'm afraid I've put these good people to a lot of trouble for nothing. I just can't seem to swallow this morning. Feeling so sick and wretched. Very sorry. Of course I'll, er, see that they don't lose anything by it except their time. You take my meaning. The laborer is worthy of his hire, that's always been my rule. But I can't face any more just now. That's final, I'm afraid."

Dr. Chevet did some quick thinking. Then he said:

"Well, we must see if we can fix something up later. It's a pity, but … tell me, how have you been lately? Diet helped you? Good, good. I thought that would relieve it. It's probably a question of nervous strain – getting over the journey and so on. It doesn't do to neglect the psychogenic factor. It might be wise to give you a fortnight or three weeks to settle down a bit, and then try again. Will you tell the matron I'd like another word with her? … Miss Armstrong? What is the general condition like? Is he still in the room? I'll ask the questions, you say yes or no. Respiration and pulse normal? Yes. Color good? Yes. Sleep? Yes. Bowels? Yes. Temperature? Yes. Sounds like nerves, doesn't it? You'd be surprised, these big men often are. Well, I don't think there's any risk in putting it off for a bit. It doesn't seem acute. Though as a matter of professional ethics, I think we'll have to ask him to pay twice. Otherwise we'll have everybody doing it. Yes, he is rather a special case, you know. Very distinguished figure, lives under a considerable strain. We have to make allowances. Yes, you tell him, will you? I know you'll be tactful. Good, good. I'll be coming along tomorrow, yes."

* * *

It was only three days later that his secretary came running out to the car as soon as it drew up in Queen Anne Street. She looked worried and quite human for once.

"It's Sir Alban Worrall. He's had a very bad attack. They've rung up several times. About an hour ago. I couldn't get you, I *did* try … It sounded like a perforation to me. He's in the Minos Restaurant, Brewer Street. It was the proprietor ringing up. I'd have suggested their calling another doctor, but I thought you'd be back earlier. I do hope that was right? He sounded very bad, yes."

Ten minutes later, Dr. Chevet was standing in the back-room of the Minos, reserved for private parties except on unusually busy days. On the walls, in crude imitation of frescoes at Cnossus, the Goddess and her priestesses postured, snaky but pneumatic, bare-breasted Medusas, with slender boyish partners; some wrestling naked with bulls; some catching blood in buckets as it streamed from struggling bulls trussed on sacrificial tables; some sprinkling it with long-handled brushes over the assembled worshippers. Even in these bad copies there was that typical Minoan feeling of primitive passion expressed in the style of a Diaghilev ballet – violence enacted in plasticity.

But there was nothing tranquil, nothing stylized about the real figure that thrashed about on the floor, writhing and groaning. They had unfastened his clothes and put down blankets and cushions for him, but he had churned them into a lumpy mass and rolled right off them on to the bare boards. His yellow distorted face was streaming with sweat. Occasionally, through his inarticulate noises of animal pain, a word broke through; sometimes a call on divine powers, sometimes on gross physical functions. The proprietor and a young waiter stood by in silence.

"Help me to hold him still." It was almost more than they could manage, though the proprietor was a man of bull-like strength. The doctor made a swift examination. Worrall howled on a dreadful shrill note at the least touch on his stomach. Chevet was glad he had brought his morphine syringe. He stood up and asked for the telephone. Luckily Sir Willoughby Jebb was available. Yes, he could operate today. Yes, the patient could be sent to Burton House at once.

Dr. Chevet put through a second call for an ambulance, and returned to the back room. The patient was quieter. The injection was beginning to take effect. He turned to the proprietor:

"He'd been lunching here, had he?"

"Yes, sir. Very good lunch, very clean, very fresh. I eat him myself. He comm often, two days, three days every week, yes."

"What did he have?"

The waiter was consulted. Sir Alban had had a special Cretan kind of bouillabaisse with Dublin Bay prawns and octopuses in it. He followed this with stuffed veal fillet fried in batter, with aubergines and fried potato straws. Then he had a sweet of Turkish origin, made with almonds, rosewater, and many spices, called khadaif, and finished up with a hard salt goat cheese. He had drunk resinated wine with the meal, and ended with Turkish coffee and a glass of neat *ouzo*, a Greek liqueur rather like absinthe, consisting of almost pure alcohol with a burning flavor like furniture-polish.

The doctor whistled. Well, he'd asked for it. If he'd been doing this kind of thing three times a week, he'd certainly got it coming to him. This messed-up foreign food, too. You never knew what they put into it. The proprietor was regarding him steadfastly from behind his magnificent black curly whiskers.

"He was seek, yes? He not tell me."

"He was a sick man, all right. He oughtn't to have eaten anything richer than milk or boiled fish."

"Ah! I not know. Today, he have no milk. But the fish, the *octopodi*, octopod, you say, I boil him myself, yes. Very young, very fresh. He not hurt a child, a sucker child. You won't make no trouble for me, doctor?"

"Good Lord, no! He knew perfectly well what he was allowed, and he ordered all this himself. No fault of yours."

"Ah, thank you! That is very O.K. You comm here one day, I make you special price, yes? Thirty percent reduction. Boy, you'll love it. He's the best Greek cuisine in London."

Here the ambulance arrived. Worrall was now lying quite still.

"He dead, yes? Too bad, doctor."

"No, no, of course he isn't. Just drugged, that's all."

"Ah, O.K.! I don't want no trouble here."

"Look, somebody ought to go with him in the ambulance. I'm afraid I can't. D'you think one of your customers ..."

"No, no, I don't want no trouble. I go."

He removed his apron, revealing an enormous red cummerbund, shouted some last instructions to the waiter, and helped to carry the patient out.

* * *

"Hallo, Chevet? Willoughby Jebb here, speaking from the Burton. About that perforated gastric ulcer of yours, Worrall. I'm afraid he was dead when he got here."

"Well, I'm not surprised. He was in a pretty bad way when I saw him. And I must say, he'd been asking for it, after the lunch he'd eaten. Octopus and fried stuff and neat spirits and God knows what. In a Greek restaurant too."

"Like me to do the P.M.? I could get it in now, if so; I've got half an hour to spare."

"Well, I don't know. It's a rather complicated position. I've just been in touch with his secretary or whatever she calls herself – woman called Coltman. She put me on to his lawyer. Apparently there's a clause in his will forbidding it. At least, it says that if his body's buried whole and unmutilated, he leaves his money in trust to go on with his archaeological work. If not, it goes to the Anti-Vivisection Society."

Jebb groaned.

"You remember, I told you his peculiar views about surgery, don't you, Willoughby? I'd have insisted on an operation, of course, in spite of it, if we'd been in time. But as it is ... I think we'll be rather unpopular if we let a deserving cause lose the money, just over a P.M., when it's such a clear case, don't you?"

"H'm! That's all very well, but I can't put peritonitis just like that, without having a look. It doesn't usually finish them off for a couple of days, you know."

"Obviously, no. But there'd have been a considerable element of shock in this case, I should say. Very nervous subject, you know."

"H'm! What about his heart?"

"Not too good, I should think, with all those cigars. Wish I could afford the damn things. He was always smoking them in my consulting room – never offered me one."

"I suppose," said Jebb, in a voice as sharp as one of his own scalpels, "you checked up on heart and blood pressure when you examined him?"

"Yes, yes, naturally." He had done so last time Worrall was in England. "It wasn't too good. He was fifty-five, you know. Older than he looked."

"Right. Well, I'll put peritonitis caused by perforated ulcer, and consequent heart failure due to shock. You agree? Good. See you at Moor Park on Saturday."

Chapter 6

THE doctor did not, of course, tell the story quite as it is here set down. Richard Ringwood filled in the gaps for himself, partly now, by sizing up Chevet more shrewdly than he allowed him to suspect, and partly later, by questioning the other people involved. This morning, he simply pressed for an immediate post mortem, and won his point without difficulty. The doctor preferred to offend no one, but faced with a choice between the police and the archaeologists, he yielded to the former. Richard undertook to handle Sir Willoughby Jebb himself, which he did later, picking up some useful knowledge in the process. Jebb was a doctor one could respect.

The body was awaiting burial in one of those monstrous undertakers' refrigerators. He shuddered at the thought. Even after ten years' police work, he did not like the thought of corpse factories. Churches were different. A body, coffined and candle-lit before an altar, lost its power to horrify. But refrigerators, funeral parlors, and crematoria were a masking of the fact of mortality; and as every child knows, a mask makes a bogy.

A police surgeon was instructed to do the post mortem at once, so that the funeral could take place next day as announced. As for the will, it seemed that the archaeologists might still get the money if Worrall's death turned out not to have been a natural one. Otherwise – well, justice had higher claims than archaeology. Suppose there were a connection where he suspected it, an inquiry into Worrall's death might be the means of calling Janet Coltman's would-be murderer to his account.

And now it was midday. He returned to the hospital to find out whether she was in a state to be questioned yet. The news was good. She was better, and he might see her alone for five minutes if he promised to be careful not to exhaust her.

She looked extraordinarily different with her eyes open. Asleep, with that carroty cropped hair, those freckled, ordinary features, she might have been any of the excellent conscientious women who are so unconscionably far from womanhood and who so seldom manage to excel – second-rate headmistresses, second-class scholars, first-class social workers – dedicated, earnest, and uncouth. Her eyes added a different quality. He found their alert and capacious intelligence disconcerting. Yet clever people did not usually disconcert him, unless they were being unfriendly or arrogant, which this woman was not. No, that was just it. She wasn't "being" anything. Women – especially plain women in their thirties – generally betrayed some consciousness of Richard the man. They were shy, or confiding, or even prickly. But this woman's mind just looked out of her eyes like a hawk looking out of an open cage, ready to fly on command. It made him uneasy.

"The sister's told you why I'm here, Miss Coltman. Someone attacked you with a knife in Soho. Luckily it missed your heart and you're going to be all right soon. Now will you tell me all you can remember about it? Did you see your assailant?"

Her voice, weak though it was at present, suggested the loud abrupt tones of a schoolboy's voice before it breaks.

"No, I didn't see anyone. I was walking rather fast and not looking at things much. Suddenly someone took hold of me from behind – my mouth. Yes, that's it, a hand over my mouth. And then I felt a pain here, in my chest. And the hand over my mouth still, but forcing my head backwards against their shoulder – I could feel it was a shoulder. I had an idea that I was being held round the waist, too, but I can't be sure about that. At least, I've no memory of actually falling. In fact, I'm afraid that's all I *do* remember."

"It's a lot. Did your, er, assailant – I'm sorry to use this jargon – make any sound? Speak, or grunt, or anything? Could you tell if it was a man or a woman?"

"No. There was no sound, I'm sure of that. I may have tried to say something, but of course there was this hand over my mouth. Oh!" Her mind took wing, with evident pleasure. "The person was stronger than me, but not much taller. Because I was already slipping down when my head came into contact with the shoulder behind me, and I'm just about average height. And the hand was a large one. It came right across my face. So surely my assailant was a not very tall man. Don't you think that's right?"

For a woman who enjoyed reasoning, and did it so well, she was curiously anxious to have her findings confirmed and approved, like a schoolgirl showing up her essay. Incongruous and a bit alarming. But he smiled and complimented her.

"You didn't manage to scream or anything, you say?"

"No, my mouth was covered straight away. And anyhow, I – well, I wouldn't *scream*, you know."

"Like the Spartan boy and the fox?" He said it in Greek, in a parody of Aristotle's most elliptical manner – a funny but recondite joke. The boy in question, also brought up not to scream, had stood in silence while the fox, which he was hiding under his tunic, gnawed away his inwards. Surely both his fate and Janet's indicated a mistaken educational policy.

She saw the joke instantly and chuckled. But then she coughed, and tears of pain came into her eyes as her wound jarred under the strain. She sipped the water he held for her and lay back exhausted.

"I'm terribly sorry. I ought to have remembered that it hurts to laugh. Can I call the nurse, or something?"

"No, I'm all right. I say, are you Classics too? How topping!" For a moment she beamed just like her old uncle. Then, still laboring for breath, she extracted a detailed account of Richard's classical career. His little gambit, advanced as a friendly claim to share her interests, was unexpectedly turning into a presentation of credentials, and Janet's close questions embarrassed him no less than her ready admiration. He cut her short.

"Look, I'm sure you oughtn't to talk too long, and we ought to be thinking about this attack on you. It wasn't robbery. It looked more like a deliberate attempt to kill you. Now you've told me that you didn't see or hear your assailant. But can't you, all the same, form some idea of who he might have been?"

"No, I'm afraid not." She was puzzled but still objective. "I don't think I know anyone who would. Want to kill me, I mean. I'm not important enough to have enemies."

He noted the implication but did not press it at that time.

"Any idea who this knife belonged to?"

He laid it on the sheet. She turned it over with a weak, uncertain hand and looked at it interestedly.

"No, none. What a lovely bit of work, though. Why, it's an ordinary kitchen knife that's been adapted. How ingenious." A pleased pause, then, still interestedly, "Is this what I was stabbed with?"

"Yes," he said, between anger and amusement. "Tell me, what were you doing in Soho?"

"Just getting my briefcase from the Minos restaurant. I'd left it behind, last time I was there."

"When was that? On Monday?"

"Yes." For the first time, she avoided his eye.

"The day Sir Alban Worrall died?"

"Yes." She was panting and spoke in a distressed whisper.

"Were you lunching with him?"

"Yes." He had to bend close to her to catch the words. "That is … I was going to. But I … I left early."

She choked and coughed again. This time the paroxysm was longer and far more agonizing. She brought up a little blood. He offered her water, but she could not drink it, and some spilled on the bedclothes. He was conscience-stricken and alarmed.

"I'm terribly sorry. Look, don't worry, please! I'm not going to bother you any more. Nurse! Nurse! Could you come? I'm terribly sorry. She was all right till she started coughing. I do hope it isn't my fault. I won't come again till she's better."

He picked up the knife and stood uncertainly for a moment. As he stole out, he heard her whisper hoarsely on a hard-drawn breath:

"I'm – all right. Honestly!"

Perhaps there was something to be said for the Spartan Boy after all. But he did not care for himself in the role of Fox.

* * *

Lunch at home on a working day was not a luxury Richard often allowed himself, but a night out and a very uncomfortable ankle justified it today. He telephoned to his wife that he would be back in half an hour. She rose to the occasion. Soon he was lying on the sofa with his ankle bathed and bandaged. On a low table in front of him was ham in thin curling slices, olives, gherkins, salad, shells of butter, and crusty French bread, besides a jug of home-brewed cider. Strawberries and cream were on the mantelpiece in reserve. Clare sat on the windowseat. Her beauty is no less than Zoe's, he thought, and yet of an entirely opposite kind – airy and translucent. But why especially today? He looked again and chuckled; it was too absurdly like an advertising strip cartoon. Married life Before and After the use of Our Product.

"You've done your hair a new way, haven't you?"

"Yes. I went to Semonides this morning – you know, my Cypriot chap in Gerrard Street. I half hoped to see you, being so near Soho. Is it nice like this?"

It flowed up from her temples in two wings of dark gold, and exploded into feathery crescents on the crown of her head.

"It's charming. He's made you look like an Oread."

She purred and waved away the extravagant compliment. "Yes. Semonides *is* good, though I don't know if I can stand all that sales-talk and temperament much longer. And he does *sing* so. Very tuppence-colored and time-wasting."

"Greeks tend to be. I've got to see some today too – at the Minos. By the way, did our respective fathers have anything to say about the Coltman family? I do hope mine wasn't tiresome?"

"Actually, he couldn't remember anything about them. He said to look in the army list. Don't look so cross, darling; he was really trying to be helpful. And isn't it heaven, he's dug out a ring he had, stashed away somewhere, an emerald, and he's going to send it for my birthday."

Richard whistled. Colonel Ringwood had never unbent to anyone as he was doing to his new daughter-in-law.

"After that I rang up Daddy. My dear, he *knew* them! He and Major Coltman got together about tactics, apparently, for the Civil War part of Daddy's County History. Janet's father seems to have been a complete innocent – a sort of mixture of Don Quixote and the *Boys' Own Paper*. That's why he only got to Major. He always believed hard-luck stories. But a good tactician, Daddy said, and he and Janet thought the world of each other. They did everything together. Janet even helped with the tactics, which is how Daddy met her."

"When did he?"

"A few months before her father died. So he went to see her afterwards."

"Good heavens! He must have known her quite well really."

"No, he didn't. But he wanted to see what she was like without her father. It was partly pity, I think, and partly curiosity. You know how eccentricity fascinates him."

Richard could picture Mr. Liddicote sitting with his pointed chin propped on his ivory walking stick, dispensing his elvish inquisitive kindness. Not heartless; just separate. "Lord, what fools these mortals be!" But Clare was continuing.

"She was shattered at first, apparently, and keeping such a stiff upper lip that she was practically dumb. But then she got this job with Worrall, and Daddy thinks she gradually accepted him as a kind of substitute father. A very bad one, because he was bogus *and* selfish. Daddy described him as a cross between a sunfish and a shark."

"A bit of walrus, too, by the photos. He doesn't think she was in love with him?"

"No, he says not. His theory was that she's an emotional axolotl."

"What's an axolotl?"

"It's a kind of huge Mexican tadpole. It ought to develop into a sort of salamander, and if you take it to a different climate I believe it does. But in Mexico it stays at the tadpole stage all its life. It's a grown-up tadpole, I mean, it breeds all right and so on. But something in the climate stops it from ever completing its development."

"What a feast of zoology! But how does this apply to Janet?"

"Daddy thinks she's got stuck at the emotional age of fourteen, when girls simply adore their fathers and don't notice other men much. Her intellectual development's O.K. Mentally, she's grown up; a salamander, as it were. But emotionally, a tadpole. If she can find an older man to hero-worship, and do things for, and be approved of by, she asks no more."

"That's possible. She doesn't look or behave like a person who's been emotionally starved, or got dried-up, or queer. She's not spinsterish exactly. Worrall as the father-substitute might be the answer."

"But you say something had gone wrong with the Worrall thing?"

"Yes. First, this business about the ring. And then this lunch in the Minos that she was so upset about. Tension with Shrubsole, too. All sorts of cross-currents."

"Perhaps she'll grow up a bit now."

"It's her immediate future I'm concerned about. What to do with her when she comes out of hospital."

"Comes *out?* But she was practically dying last night. Surely that won't be for ages."

"I saw the Sister just now, and she says that if the improvement keeps up, she'll be better in about three days – not *better*, I mean, but past the serious stage when she needs hospital nursing. And then they'll have to chuck her out, as they need the bed. I don't like the idea of her in that country cottage of hers."

"But, listen, why don't we have her here? I mean, Daddy *does* know her, and it would be so fascinating to see if she really *is* an axolotl. Besides, I could take care of her. We might even turn her into a salamander."

"Bless you, Clare. You *are* an angel."

"Not at all. I'm like Daddy. I want to see what makes her tick."

"Well, I'd better go and have another try at seeing what nearly stopped the works. Look, shall we go out to dinner tonight?"

"Where? The Minos?"

"Clever. Yes. We'll do some observing on our own and I'll leave the official interview till later. Now, I'll just ring up the museum and make sure my archaeologists are there and keeping out of mischief. If they are, I might try to get into Iorweth's flat and find out what his wife's up to."

"But won't she be there? I thought she always had a siesta."

"That's the story. If she does, well and good. I won't wake her. Yes, I know it's risky, but at least *he*'ll be out of the way. And I shan't be surprised if *she* is too. I feel she's carrying on some funny business behind his back – smuggling or blackmail or something."

"Well, mind you don't get into her clutches. She sounds frightfully bitchy to me. How will you get in? Will you dress up?"

"By the fire escape. Yes, perhaps I will dress up, in case I'm recognized. A workman? No, they probably have their own."

"Be a government snooper. Seeing if the fire escapes are safe, or something."

"I *am* a government snooper, when you come to think of it. Hell!"

"Never mind. It'll be an adventure if you dress up. Go on! And mind you come and show me before you go."

* * *

A different man came in ten minutes later, walking with a stoop and a shamble that concealed his height. He wore flannel trousers, a carrot-colored sports coat, and a thin maroon pullover, and he carried a green felt hat trimmed with a frayed cord. His hair was sleek, his eyes hidden behind sunglasses, and his skin disfigured by a convincing (though artificial) crop of spots. A row of fountain pens was clipped into one pocket and a fancy handkerchief hung out of the other. He carried a shabby American cloth briefcase.

"You look *revolting*," said Clare proudly. "I do hope that stuff on your hair will wash out. But dirty your nails a bit, darling, and take off your seal ring. You wouldn't consider a small mustache?"

"Actually, old dear" (you could tell by this man's voice that he had been in the RAF) "I don't go much on spiv types, and the wife isn't too keen eether. Frankly, the people at Sutton wouldn't be impressed. Well, cheers. I must be toddling. Be good, and if you can't be good, be careful."

On his way out, he passed Mrs. Bean, and lingered to hear if she would make one of her comic entrances. It tickled her sometimes to pretend that she was a large staff of servants instead of a single charwoman, and she was always inventing a fresh character. He was not disappointed. In a deep and portentous voice she announced:

"It's all right, madam. Just the butler come to remove the cold collation." Then, in her own comfortable Cockney, "Mr. Ringwood looks ever s' smart today, don' 'e? Going somewhere special?"

* * *

It was amusing to walk across the car park of Missenden Mansions, while the mechanic, after one contemptuous glance, returned to the wheel he was changing. It was amusing to clamber up the fire escape, stopping to tap it and shake it and jot things down in a notebook. It was amusing to see how the woman who indignantly asked his business popped back into her flat reassured by his reply, "Just testing" – a phrase which practically never failed to soothe. You didn't need to say *what* you were testing. To test was a good activity in itself. He supposed that this was symptomatic of the Age of Anxiety.

Now he was at the third floor, dizzily high, and no one was looking up at him, though there were several people in the car park. He recognized the ap Ifors' drawing room by the Minoan pot on the sill. The fire escape passed below its window-level, but by stretching he could catch a glimpse of the interior. Zoe was not asleep on the sofa, or, indeed, in the room at all, as far as he could see. He went on cautiously upwards to the open bedroom window. This room, too, was empty. He looked down again. The car park seemed full of people, and if someone saw him lingering and peering, there might be trouble. He had better make his entry now and risk it, not wait and listen. He climbed in. It was something of an obstacle race, but managed without noise, and he had just let himself down from the chest of drawers to the floor when he heard footsteps coming across the hall. There was no time to climb back. He slipped behind the curtain of a hanging wardrobe which, he was pleased to find, contained Iorweth's clothes and so would probably not be invaded at the moment. He peeped through the crack in the curtain to see who was coming.

It was Zoe, and she was dressed for the private rooms of a Cairo *boîte de nuit* rather than for a solitary afternoon in a London flat. Her black lace negligee, in the unforgotten phrase of his goatish old Art master, *conshealed, and yet revealed, the most exquishite female figure*; her golden-brown flesh glowed through it as smooth as an egg. She was heavily made up, and she was humming to herself in a throbbing contralto as she put some last touches to an already elaborate toilet. She smoothed the lace with a slow enjoying gesture over her waist and hips. Richard could see her face reflected in the glass. She looked flamboyantly vulgar and (for the first time) entirely human. No enigma about that expression. Who was she waiting for? "Not for me," Richard told himself rather too emphatically. "Oh God! I wish I hadn't come."

The doorbell rang. With a soft *a-ah* of anticipation, a catlike sound from deep in her throat, she went out, leaving the door open so that the hall was in full view and Richard could not leave by the window unobserved. Yet he no longer wished to stay. He was prepared secretly to search a private house for incriminating objects, but it disgusted him to play peeping Tom to an illicit amour. He was just about to come out of the wardrobe, whatever the consequences, when the tone of the voices in the hall made him pause and look again. They were standing by the half-open front door, arguing in Greek, Zoe and – yes! The dark young man who had been there when he arrived this morning. Richard did not need to understand the words to guess their purport. She was hanging round his neck coaxing him in, and he was holding her away and protesting. He looked half-frightened and half-fascinated, while she pressed against him, stroking his neck and shoulders, slipping a hand inside his shirt, and kissing him as often as he gave her opportunity. Still he shrank away, talking faster and with a sharper note of alarm and refusal. Gradually her blandishment turned to fury. She was kissing to hurt and to provoke; when that failed, she bit him hard in the cheek, and when he cried out, she stood away from him and hit him twice with her hand where she had bitten him already. Her palm had his blood on it. Then she came storming into the bedroom, opened a drawer, and from under a pile of clothes snatched out a tissue-paper parcel. She flung it at him violently, while he stood there staring with his hand to his cheek. "Here it is!" Her tone said more clearly than any words. "Now go!" The parcel hit him on the temple, fell to the floor, and burst as it fell. The contents clattered on the tiles like a handful of pebbles. He knelt down and began to pick them up, while she stood over him still hissing out her unknown insults. Every word sounded more stinging than the last, and his silence seemed to spur her on. At last, as he crouched there unresponsive, she kicked him. He whipped to his feet with a fierce exclamation, hit her in the face, ripped the lace from shoulder to waist, and took her as if to throw her down. But she did not resist. She simply melted against him with another of those catlike sighs of desire, and this time he did not shrink back. He seized her with a blind angry desperation and clung to her. Presently, without letting her go, he felt for the door behind her – it was the sitting room – and opened it. Still entwined, they disappeared from sight, and Richard heard the key turn in the lock.

He was glad to escape. He took off his shoes and crept across to the front door. The unshod sole of his foot was pricked by something small and hard. He looked. It was a sherd of ancient pottery. Near it lay a great gold ring, shaped like the one Shrubsole had showed him. And not far off lay the little broken parcel. He picked up everything he could find, crammed it into his pockets, and got safely out to the lift. All the way down, he was still tingling with shame, excitement, and the beginnings of an idea.

Chapter 7

DRIVING home in a taxi, Richard reflected that, although he had gathered some useful knowledge, his superiors would not have approved of his methods. Romantic, undisciplined, incorrect, they would say; Ringwood at his damned cloak-and-dagger stuff again. This time he agreed with them. Anyway, he thought, I won't make them pay for the taxi. He told the driver to wait.

Having removed his disguise, he looked into the drawing room, but Clare was out. Mrs. Bean was watering the window boxes.

"'S all right, sir, on'y the gardener, 'osin' the 'erbaceous."

He returned to his taxi, drove to the museum, and asked for Shrubsole. After a repetition of this morning's admission ceremonies, he found him in the same cubicle as before, poring over what seemed the same bits of broken pottery, and once more Shrubsole jumped up and hissed at him:

"Sh! Sh! Ap Ifor's just along there. Come outside!"

He hurried Richard past the Keeper's room in silence, but in the first empty stretch of passage gripped his arm so hard that he could feel the separate pressure of each bony finger.

"How is she?" It was extraordinary that a face could express such intensity of feeling without giving any clue to its nature. "I rang up the hospital twice, but they were cagey as usual."

"She's a bit better. They say she'll recover, barring accidents. I talked to her today."

Shrubsole withdrew his hand, but not before Richard had felt it quiver. The defiant black eyes, however, still sought and held his own, not to communicate, but to repel communion.

"Well? I don't suppose you came snooping back just to tell me that, did you? What are you after this time?"

"Come up on the roof and I'll tell you. We can't talk here."

Richard led the way up a spiral staircase and they came out under the open sky and sat on the parapet. Around and below them were bomb-scarred walls and roofs and sooty chimneypots. The heat of the afternoon sun beat upwards in waves from the asphalt at their feet. Pigeons cooed somewhere out of sight.

"First of all," said Richard. "Oh, perhaps I ought to have cautioned you first."

"Anything I say will be taken down and used in evidence against me?"

"Not necessarily *against* you. Just used in evidence. Cigarette?"

"I can still afford my own when I want them, thanks."

"As you please. First – it's just routine, of course – where were you yesterday afternoon?"

An uneven purplish flush crept over Shrubsole's sallow face.

"You had to ask that, didn't you? I was with a Miss Montagu. Fourteen Edward Street, off the Charing Cross Road. Having an elocution lesson, if you want to know. Go on, laugh!"

Richard's earlier adventures today had made him sensitive to charges of prying, and now his naturally hot temper got the better of him.

"Damn and blast you!" he exclaimed, flinging his burning cigarette in a wide arc over the chimneypots, "come off it, for God's sake! No one's laughing at you. You're not funny. You're just a bore. You're so busy looking for imaginary insults that you make rational talk impossible. You *could* talk perfectly good sense. If you'd stop being so jumpy, you could really help me. Dammit, I'm not doing this for fun. And I don't suppose *you* really think people ought to be allowed to get away with attempted murder, do you? Or … do you?"

He broke off short, alarmed, as always, by the violence of his own anger, but still more by its effect on Shrubsole, who had turned white and gasped as though at a voice from the grave. His hands fidgeting in his trouser pockets, he said in a dry, harsh whisper:

"Jumpy! Jumpy! That's what … oh, what the heck!" He pulled his hands out of his pockets, and some of their contents spilled – a very dirty handkerchief, a matchbox, a pencil, a file, and a little coil of copper wire. The small accident recalled him to a sense of his surroundings. He picked the things up, looking foolish, and said, "Sorry. Go on. I'm rational, don't worry."

"I gather you and Janet Coltman had been on bad terms lately."

"Yes." Though quiet, he was still discomposed.

"About the ring?"

"Yes. That and – other things."

"This sort of thing, for instance?" He opened the box into which he had put the contents of Zoe's parcel. Ian Shrubsole looked at them, and the last vestige of color left his face.

"Where did you get these? Were they with Janet's things? Does she know you've got them?"

"No. I'm waiting till she's a bit better. Why? What do *you* know about this business?"

His face set. "Nothing. I've never seen these things before."

"Sure? Well, at least you can tell me what they are."

"I can give you a rough idea about the pottery. It looks genuine enough. This is a bit of E.M. III – the top of a spout. This one's later – M.M. II, I'd say. You can see it's made on a fast wheel but the technique is still uncertain. Oh, here's a bit of the dark-on-light. You see what it is, that reddish-brown mark? It's the end of a tentacle. No, you've got it the wrong way up. See? It'll be from just below the shoulder of one of the big two-handled pots with the octopus decoration – say, roughly, L.M. II. Curious mixture of periods, isn't it?" He spoke, for the first time, unemotionally and with assurance. Richard was impressed.

"Good Lord! Do you mean you can really tell what the complete pot was like, just from a little bit like that?"

"Of course. But no one's any the wiser, if the locale and stratification haven't been noted. And they haven't, have they?"

"Why are you so sure?"

Shrubsole was silent, and Richard waited. But he merely said, after a moment, that of course he didn't know. Richard continued:

"Can you tell me about the value of these things? And what about the rings and the seal? You haven't said anything about them yet."

"I told you, they're not in my line. I don't know if they're valuable. The pottery isn't, not by itself. It might be, indirectly, if it were being used to fix the other things – used honestly, I mean. All the conditions of the find noted by a properly qualified person. If so, I suppose the seals would be worth between two and three thousand pounds each."

"You mean, if the ring and the seal could be proved to have been found in the same bit of soil as pottery of the same period, that'd show they were genuine." He nodded. "Well, who *can* tell me about the rings and the seal? Janet Coltman?"

"Oh, no! No! Not now! I mean … she – you said just now she wasn't well enough. You – you insist on knowing about these things?"

"Certainly I do. They're an important part of my case. And I'm asking *you*, not merely as a citizen but as the only qualified scholar available, to recommend me to the right expert."

"Oh heck! Well, if you put it like that … well there's a South African," he said unwillingly, "he's an Assistant Keeper here – his name's Jack Macdonald. He knows about Minoan glyptics. And he's got nothing to do with our lot. That ought to please you. But …"

"But what?"

"Nothing." Shrubsole's defensive look had returned. "Any more questions?"

Richard asked him about the course of events in Corfu, and his answers were rational and straightforward. He confirmed the bare facts of the boy's death and Worrall's sudden illness. He said that he had himself been in the hotel on the mainland on the night of the boy's death, and assumed that the ap Ifors and Worrall were too. When Richard asked him about Worrall's being on Mouse Island during the evening, he said that he had only learned of it from Janet's letter to *The Times* after his death, but it did not surprise him; Worrall had spent several evenings in the little hut he had for an office, there on the site, working. What did surprise him, he added bitterly, was that Worrall was working at all, instead of standing over somebody else while they did the work for him. Apart from that, he found nothing unusual in the state of things that evening. He was sure Worrall had slept at the hotel, for he was breakfasting there when the boy's death was announced. On being asked whether he thought the boy had died a natural death, he smiled contemptuously and said, "Oh! I see Iorweth's been prophesying at you, has he? The fairies got him, didn't they?" Clearly he did not take the question seriously.

"What about the fact that his knife was found in the trench, not with his body on the rocks? Iorweth said he'd never have parted from it in the normal way. Is that true?"

Shrubsole thought a moment before answering. "Mm. Cretans *do* hang on to their knives as a rule, yes. But I suppose they're liable to lose things like everyone else. I don't think he was murdered, if that's what you mean. Murder's pretty common among Cretans, I know, but it's according to rules, so to speak. Some of the peasants keep up the family blood feud, but it's pretty well known who's gunning for who. And I'm quite sure there was nothing like that in our gang. I know them well, and they've been together for years. Unless Zoe ..."

"Yes? Tell me about Zoe. What was she before she married?"

"She was just a common ..." He hesitated, embarrassed.

"Come!" said Richard. "There are at least fifty synonyms. A hundred and ninety-one in French, they tell me. No need to get stuck for a word."

Shrubsole smiled sourly. "I haven't got a public-school vocabulary. Well, Iorweth picked her up in some low cabaret in Candia. It's given us a lot of trouble with the workmen, actually. All the Greeks are touchy, and the Cretans are the touchiest of the lot." He clearly admired them for it.

"I see. They couldn't bear to have a fellow Cretan set over them, as it were. Being one of the bosses."

"A bit of that, maybe. Though they're too independent to think of us as bosses. That's what Sir Alban never understood. No, mostly I think they just loathed her for being such a bad Cretan. They're very proud, you know – very anxious for foreigners to think well of them. And Zoe's reputation was ... well, they wouldn't have let their own womenfolk speak to her. And they'd kill them if they went on like she did. They're touchy about the honor of their women. So they didn't much like it when a song started going round Candia about Zoe and her manifold uses to the expedition ... A pretty crude song."

"Have she and Iorweth been married long? Has she got any family?"

"They married last winter. She came of a decent peasant family, up in the mountains. Her mother was a fine woman, one of the leading partisans in the war, and a great wit. People used to come miles, just to hear her stories. That made it worse, somehow, when Zoe – got like that."

"Children of outstanding parents often do. I suppose it's the only way they can assert themselves. How *did* she behave at Corfu?"

"Fairly correctly to us. I suppose she had *some* caution. But the workmen – well, she just couldn't let them alone. The four older ones told her where she got off, all right. I heard them. But the boy – I don't know. I wonder."

Remembering the young man in the flat, Richard wondered too. A sensual woman, she would in this small community be naturally attracted to her own race. If she had at first succeeded with the boy, and later been repulsed, could she have exacted such a revenge? She looked quite capable of it. Or alternatively, had she been stealing antiques, and had the boy found her out? True, her husband had said she was asleep in the hotel. But his silence might be one of complicity. Or she might have frightened him into saying it, even if he was partly in the dark. He was not a strong character. Was this, perhaps, the factual basis of all his romantic nonsense about the Goddess's revenge? And anyhow, what had it to do with the murderous assault on Janet Coltman, and (possibly) Worrall? There were so many seeds of murder here – intrigue, superstition, money, or prestige to be gained by traffic in Minoan objects, professional and personal antipathies – but each pointed to a different victim, and none seemed to point surely to Janet Coltman. Richard shelved further consideration for the time being, and began asking Shrubsole about Worrall's illness.

He confessed that in Corfu he had not taken it seriously. The man was making such a fuss. Nobody could possibly be as ill as he claimed to be. In fact, he had not looked a very sick man. As for the breaking-up of the expedition, Shrubsole had been furious about it. Why stop eight people from working because one man was ill? In his opinion, Worrall was simply unwilling to let the others have credit for any discoveries that might be made; especially after the doubtful reception which two of them had accorded to his own *finding* of the ring the previous day. Shrubsole still felt resentment at being taken from his dig, though he owned he was wrong in making light of the illness.

"Still, what the heck! If you'd seen him playing for sympathy, you'd have thought the same. *I* could see him looking at Janet out of the corner of his eye, to see how she was taking it."

"And how was she?"

"Oh, she seemed worried all right. Couldn't do enough. And Iorweth sat there egging him on. You know how he loves a spot of drama. But I saw the little snacks going into his cabin, on the way home. My godfathers! There was nothing wrong with his appetite. And he kept Janet hard enough at work, writing *his* lectures as he called them. But I don't know much about illness. I suppose this came in bouts. I see now he must have been really bad after all; for once, it wasn't a fuss about nothing."

"By the way, where were you when he died?"

"Me? I was right there, on the spot," said Shrubsole with that false jauntiness of his. "Lunching in the Minos."

"*What?* With Sir Alban?"

"Not likely. I was with a friend – Jack Macdonald as a matter of fact – and you can bet we sat as far away as we could get."

"Then you were with him when he was taken with his second, and fatal attack?"

"I was in the room. But I wasn't taking much notice, actually. There seemed to be people to cope with it, and they took him out somewhere, I believe. Frankly, I thought it was just another of his acts."

Richard was shocked. Could Shrubsole really have failed to notice that Worrall was in his death agony?

"Miss Coltman said she was lunching with him and left early. Is that so?"

"She said so, didn't she?" He spoke with all his former aggressiveness.

"Yes, I'm just asking you to confirm it."

"O.K. I confirm it. She was lunching with him and left early."

"Did she seem at all distressed when she left? What made her go?"

"I tell you, I wasn't attending. I'd had to do quite enough listening to Sir Alban Worrall in working hours, without putting in overtime eavesdropping in restaurants. *I'm* not a detective."

This time Richard kept his temper. "Well, I am," he replied, measuring his words. "And I'm here to find out who tried to kill your colleague. I must say, I hoped you'd be more cooperative. But of course – you'd quarreled with her too, hadn't you? So you didn't notice her distress at the lunch, or Worrall's death agony, and you don't think it your business if her life's in danger now. I wonder if anyone is capable of such pure detachment? Weren't you perhaps rather attracted by the prospect of getting rid of them both?"

Shrubsole plunged his shaking hands into his pockets. His eyes were like coals in his white face. He shouted:

"*Both!* How dare you say *both?*" His breath failed, or so it seemed, for he was unable for a moment to speak. Then he said, flatly and reasonably:

"O.K. I don't mind admitting it. I was glad when he died. He was bogus, and I think he was dishonest too. But … my colleague …"

"Yes?"

"She was a darned good archaeologist once," he said wearily. "And she's a darned fool. And I didn't try to kill her, and I haven't a clue who did. Can I go and get on with my pots now? I'd like to finish them before …"

"Before what?"

"Oh, before I lose my job. Before you decide to arrest me. Before tea. What does it matter? I never shall finish them, anyhow."

At Richard's nod he rose and walked towards the staircase. Richard thought he had never seen a man look so exhausted.

Chapter 8

THE spring weather, so hot at midday, had turned to a cool gusty evening when Richard came down his own street in St. John's Wood to take Clare to dinner at the Minos. On his left were graceful little Regency houses set back behind high garden walls; on his right, raw red blocks of flats and a neon-lighted concrete garage; behind him jungle cries from the Zoo came distantly through the hum of traffic. The London sky, a tatter of smoke and gold, seemed to gather up the splendor and the squalor of the capital in one, and restate it as harmony. Other cities, he thought, might take their character from buildings or people, but London was most truly itself in its sky.

He burst into the hall, blew his nose on a trumpet note to announce his arrival, and came upstairs to find Clare at her dressing-table frowning at a string of pearls in one hand and a filigree gold chain in the other. She dropped both to welcome him, and they plunged at once into eager conversation. Richard gave a satirical but uneasy account of the scene in Iorweth's flat, and passed quickly to a fuller description of Ian Shrubsole's curious behavior at his second interview.

"I can't make him out, you know. He's so rude and so jumpy, one feels he must be hiding something. He's as prickly as a hedgehog, and I should say that nervously he's about at the end of his tether. And yet, he's been honest in a way. He's admitted to a lot of damaging things, like writing the obituary, and quarreling with Janet Coltman, and hating Worrall. Of course, it could be double-bluff – I don't know. Anyhow, he's done one good thing – put me on to a decent Minoan archaeologist who hasn't got anything to do with Worrall's setup. I went to see him and took him this parcel that Zoe had, and he's going to report to me about it tomorrow. He seems very sane and nice. Oh, and I rang up ap Ifor, really to sort of feel his pulse, but the pretext was to ask if he had any snaps of the people on the expedition, workmen and all. He has, as it happens, and he's posting them off to me tonight. He didn't seem a bit rattled, by the way, so he must be in the dark about that business this afternoon."

"Well, I suppose he would be in the dark about his wife's lover. He might have reasons of his own for not mentioning the loss of the parcel."

"Bad, if so. After all, I did steal it. Oh Clare, I'll never make a proper policeman! If I keep the rules, I don't get anywhere. There's this hitch about the post mortem too. It seems they've got to thaw Worrall's body out, so they can't do it till the morning. And that means putting off the funeral; there'll be some undesirable publicity. Our name'll be mud if it's all for nothing."

"Oh dear! And they'll be cross enough about the P.M. anyhow, won't they, since it means the money's lost to archaeology by the terms of the will. Was it a lot of money?"

"A hundred and twenty thousand. Worrall had provided for a permanent trust for work in Minoan archaeology. The head of the show was to get twelve hundred a year, the first assistant eight hundred, the second one five hundred, and there was a tidy bit over for expenses and workmen and so on. There wouldn't be heavy death duties, you see, because it was a kind of charity trust. Yes, it's a lot of money. I can't help wondering if Worrall knew that someone wanted him out of the way, someone who would benefit by his will, and put in that odd bit about his body being whole and unmutilated to guard against some sort of funny business. He seems to have talked a lot about that particular clause. And as you know, he made the will only when he got back from the Corfu expedition."

"Yes, I see. Did he actually nominate the new head of the show?"

"No. The present members were each to have a vote on the election committee, but in fact they were outnumbered by the other electors. Still, I suppose Janet's got a good chance. Or (if they don't like to choose a woman) even Shrubsole. So the plot does thicken a bit."

"But surely, if you hold a P.M. on Worrall's body, the money won't go to archaeology at all, will it?"

"We got Counsel's opinion on that. The position seems to be that *if* it is found that Worrall didn't die a natural death, it may be possible to get an exception, in such an obviously deserving case. It may not be so easy to justify if the death was a natural one after all. It's very tricky. The Bloodhound hates it, and I'm not too happy myself. After all, I'm only going on a hunch – hardly more than that."

"Your hunches have a way of being right. Perhaps you'll get something more solid at the Minos tonight."

"Get something indigestible, more likely, and we'll be carried off screaming in a plain van. Oh well, off we go. I must say, darling, you look absolutely lovely. All set to encounter darkness as a bride."

"Not much of an effort," said Clare, picking up her gloves. "After all, I *am* one."

There were not many people dining in the Minos and of those half looked mousey and the other half raffish; the Ringwoods were a pleasant contrast, and the proprietor came over to welcome them in person. He had a great smile under his luxuriant whiskers – welcoming without the least trace of obsequiousness. He took them to a table by the wall, situated, as it happened, at the exact point of the frieze where the blood streamed downwards from the neck of a sacrificed bull. Richard shrugged his shoulders and looked round for somewhere to hang his hat. The proprietor took it and hung it on a strange double peg that seemed to grow out of the wall picture.

"What is it? Oh! I see, horns of sacrifice!" said Richard. "Very Minoan. You've got it all in, haven't you?"

The big man was shaking like an earthquake and his black eyes almost disappeared in a net of laughing wrinkles.

"I tell you good joke, no? What I say. The horns – you know what that mean, horns? For husband?"

Yes, they said hastily. They had heard of the cuckold's horns.

"Good! The horns, and sacrifice too, that is for the fool. The horns, with profit, is for an Italian. But for man of honor, no horns, no sacrifice. Fonny, no?" he roared putting his arm round Richard's shoulder and laughing enough for all three of them.

"Marvelous!" Richard was racking his brains for a suitable rejoinder. Unnecessarily, as it turned out, for it was impossible to get a word in edgeways. His joke fully savored, the proprietor whipped out a menu card and began to expatiate on food. Unlike his brothers in the trade, he did not recommend the most expensive items. Patriotism, not avarice seemed to inspire his choice. Cretan rice pilaf, Cretan wine, were puffed beyond the game birds and vintage French growths that were listed with them. Clare was eager to experiment, but Richard persuaded her against the exotic and they chose a good simple meal on French lines.

"You not like Greek cuisine, best in the world?" The proprietor twirled his mustache like a musketeer, and frowned.

"I like it with Greek sunshine, and Greeks to talk to," said Richard. "It doesn't taste the same in London. But why don't you join us over some real Greek *ouzo* afterwards, Mr. ...?"

"Mikhailopoulos. Sta – Costa Mikhailopoulos. Thank you, sir. Lots of fun, very good *ouzo*."

He left them with a gesture at once zestful and ceremonious.

The soup was brought by a young waiter, a dark graceful creature with an extremely slender waist. Clare, her eye for good looks unimpaired by matrimony, was watching him as he approached, and naturally it was at her that he looked first. Then he saw Richard, and suddenly his long eyes widened and he turned pale. Half the soup slopped out of the plates on to the floor. With a whispered apology, he fled. Richard hardly seemed to notice, and sat there impassive with his eyes on the table. Clare wondered why; as a rule his face was alive and changing every moment. Surely, too, he was talking in a very forced way? The waiter came back with a cloth and mopped up the soup. Then he brought fresh platefuls, but still Richard did not look at him and still continued his dull monologue. The waiter was less nervous now. When at last he had slipped away, Clare said:

"He's exactly like the men on the Minoan frescoes, isn't he? What is it, darling? Mustn't I talk about him?"

Richard looked up and for the first time she realized that he was excited and trying not to show it.

"Talk, yes, if you can talk in riddles. He's the young male partner of the Great Goddess in person." He dropped his voice. "I saw him once this morning and again this afternoon. He only saw me once, but he's recognized me. I hope he'll think I haven't recognized him. For God's sake don't look so interested, darling. Talk about the frescoes."

Clare transferred her gaze to the wall and said aloud, "He has the look of a victim, hasn't he? There's something pathetic about him. The woman was obviously the one who did any sacrificing that had to be done."

"The man must have done some of it – decoyed the bull and got him helpless and roped down. The woman stayed in the temple, you see, we've got evidence for that."

"In the case of the cow, we have." Both repressed a smile at this unkind description of Miss Coltman. "But are we sure the Goddess wasn't present at the immolation of the bull?"

"We can't be sure. She was unattended. But of course the bull may have died a natural death."

"Yes, and anyhow, why pick on the bull? A Welsh goat or something of that sort would be more reasonable as a victim. The horns would fit better."

"You have to consider," said Richard as the waiter offered him bread, "that there are two possible motives for sacrifice. They sacrificed either to turn away something they were afraid of, or else to get something they wanted. For the first, the bull would be the obvious victim – a powerful, dangerous animal, remember. Isn't that good sense, even if it's bad anthropology?"

"I *see!* They played with the bull first, didn't they, and perhaps they got to a point where he wouldn't play any longer. The bull *did* take part in games first, didn't he?"

"Yes, rather secret and nasty ones, I think. In fact, the games may have involved a human sacrifice – the slaying of a Cretan boy. But we can't be sure till all the fragments have been pieced together. Some of the most interesting ones may turn out to belong to quite a different picture. … No, you may never eat octopus unless you know the man who caught it."

"If the cow wasn't immolated effectively," said Clare, "and the bull was a bad bull anyway – oh good! He's gone. I couldn't have kept it up much longer. I mean, if Janet gets well and Worrall was a crook, I won't feel so bad about things, will you?"

"Yes, I shall. I don't like not knowing, and I don't like chaps knifing people in my London. Still, I see what you mean. Drink up and don't look so sicklied o'er with the p.c. of t."

She obeyed. But Richard paused, his glass half raised, straining his ears. There was some kind of violent altercation going on behind the scenes, and he thought the woman's voice was familiar.

Presently the voices ceased, and the waiter came back, looking flushed but less frightened. The proprietor was in the room again too, busy at other tables. Richard wondered what had been going on. Did Mikhailopoulos know he was a policeman? He was watching them covertly, and when he saw their last course being served, he hurried offstage. Well, two can play possum, thought Richard, and sat on, hiding his anxiety. The proprietor's reappearance dispelled it. Clearly he had been looking forward to their party and had been smartening himself up. His apron was gone. A wide crimson cummerbund set off his sturdy waist, and his blue-black curls and whiskers glistened with highly scented oil. He had even waxed the ends of his mustache. The impression was spectacular but overpowering at close quarters. A bottle of *ouzo* was brought, and tumblerfuls of cold water, which puzzled Clare, until she discovered what *ouzo* does to the inside of your mouth.

"To your health!" said Richard in Greek; it was one of the few phrases of modern Greek he knew. He had to wave away the flood of Greek in which he was answered, with apologies for his ignorance.

"Too bad. You go to Greece many time, sir? You go to Crete?" His voice lingered lovingly on the name of his native island, in his mouth a musical dissyllable.

"I've been at Athens and Corinth and Sparta. Never Crete, I'm afraid."

"And you, madame?"

"I've never been to Greece at all, but I hear a lot about it from my hairdresser. He comes from Cyprus."

"Cyprus!" The Cretan spat fiercely but neatly on the floor. "Sir, madame, I tell you about the Greeks. First" – he raised his hand high to mark a level – "we. The Cretans. We are the best. We have all honor. Next" – he lowered his hand (a short square hand with grizzled curly hair on the back) – "the Epirotes – of Athens, of Saloniki, mainland. Since Venizelos, they not too bad. They cheat, but they stop the enemy till we come. Then the Corfiotes – no good. Lazy, cowards, sleep with their goats. Then the bad peoples of all the sea, who kill father, who sell sister in street, who …" he glanced at Clare and cut the list short. "Yes. But after them, much after" – he swept his hand down till it pointed at the spittle on the floor – "there, the Cypriotes! If a Cypriote evven weenk to my wife, my daughter, I kill him. All bastards."

His eyes and teeth flashed. It was a warning conveyed by one man of honor to another, and Richard thanked him gravely.

"Have you got your family here in England? Have you been here long?" In Greece, he remembered, personal questions are considered a courtesy.

Mikhailopoulos paused. "Yes, very long time. My wife and daughters in Crete."

"But I suppose you brought one or two sons along with you?"

A longer pause still. "No," he replied at last in a voice that discouraged question. They saw that big tears had rolled down his furrowed cheeks and were glittering in round drops on his bushy whiskers. For a moment they were all three united in a wordless human sympathy. Then the Cretan shook off his tears as a bull shakes off flies, and smiling a little to show there was no malice in his reserve, asked proudly and politely:

"And you, sir? You are archéologue, no?"

Richard confessed to amateur status, but soon had him talking of archaeologists, especially the Minoan ones. He seemed to know most of their names and (which was unlikely, though good business) claimed them all as customers; but Richard, try as he might, could not get him to discuss their personalities. Strange, for Greeks are usually so interested in character – but perhaps it could be explained by business discretion. About their archaeological achievements he was surprisingly animated and well-informed. Mr. Macdonald had found a statue of gold and ivory, Sir Alban Worrall a set of frescoes, Mr. Shrubsole a new type of rhyton. He had it all pat, though he was more inclined to praise his native land for containing these objects than the British for unearthing them. After about a quarter of an hour of pleasant conversation not much to Richard's purpose, the waiter brought the bill. Mikhailopoulos intercepted it and crossed off an item.

"The *ouzo* is on me, sir, madame. The dinner, yes, that is business. But you drink with me in my house, you are my guest. Sure?"

Richard was suddenly shamed by this proud, primitive hospitality. How could he accept it from a man on whom he was spying? It was contrary to that Homeric code of honor which to some extent he himself shared with the Cretans. Now, when confidence had been established but not (thanks to the failure of his efforts) abused, now was the last chance to declare himself honorably. He wished he had done so before. This man could help if he were not antagonized.

"Send the waiter away," he said. "Look, I'm sorry, Mr. Mikhailopoulos. I can't accept your hospitality today. I'd like to another time. But today I – I haven't come as a guest. I've come officially, from Scotland Yard – here's my warrant – to make some inquiries."

The Cretan did not look at the warrant card; he stared at Richard in bewilderment.

"Scotland Yard? What is that?"

"Police."

The man's face hardened and closed. (So, thought Clare, Odysseus must have looked, silent and wary and implacable as he sat with the traitors in his own house.) He made a sudden movement and Richard was on guard. But all Mikhailopoulos did was to take up his own glass and empty the little liquor it contained on to the floor. Richard understood the symbolical force of the gesture and winced.

"I'm sorry. I ought to have told you sooner. I – I wanted to get to know the place first and leave the official interview till later." The excuse was feeble even to himself, but perhaps his direct, troubled eyes pleaded for him better; for a touch of pity came into the tragic Odysseus-mask of Mikhailopoulos, and he said slowly:

"I understand. Good man sometimes have to do bad thing. You want, sir?"

"I want to ask you about Miss Coltman."

Mikhailopoulos stood up, turning his broad back. "We go into other room. I don't want no trouble in here."

They went into that same inner room where Worrall had suffered his death-throes, and sat bleakly round a bare table. Clare got out her notebook, and Richard began his questions.

"You know Miss Janet Coltman."

"Yes. She come here sometimes."

"Did she come yesterday afternoon? Yes? What time?"

"After lunch, maybe two, maybe later. The lunch was nearly finish."

"What did she come for?"

"She ask me for address of my brother in Crete. He sometimes work for archéologue, she think maybe he help her next year."

Richard thought: First discrepancy. Janet's story was that she called back for a forgotten briefcase.

"Did you give her the address?" No address had been found among her papers.

"Yes."

"Did she write it down?"

"No. She say she remember." He jerked up his chin in the Greek gesture of negation – the logical opposite, when you come to think of it, of a nod.

"Was anyone else with her?" Another nod in reverse. "Anyone leave here the same time she did?"

"I don't know. Maybe. The lunch just finished, many pipple go out."

"Was anyone there she knew?"

"I think – no."

"Was that the last time you saw her?"

Mikhailopoulos hesitated. Richard waited.

"O.K. I tell you. Just after she go, I remember she left a bag here – big bag of leather, with papers …"

"Her briefcase, yes. And then what?"

"I run out after her to give back the bag."

"And did you catch her?"

"Yes, I catch her."

He had overtaken her in the very next street and restored her property. She was walking by herself.

"And then what did you do, when you'd given her the case? Come straight back?"

"I? I was looking in shops a little. I buy cigarettes, coffee. No hurry, lunch is finish. I come back in perhaps ten minutes."

Richard made a note of the shops he had visited. They were in Brewer Street.

"And now, I want you to tell me about Monday – the day Sir Alban Worrall was taken ill on your premises. Was Miss Coltman with him?"

"She have sherry with him, and he order lunch for her. But she go away, not stay for lunch."

"Did they have a quarrel – you know, angry words?"

"Ah! I understand. Yes, they were angry, both, and Miss Coltman go."

"What was it about? Did you hear what they were saying?"

"A little. I serve them myself. I think, first, it is quarrel of archéologue, like often – that is fake, you wrong. Not too bad. But then, he call her bad things, not for archéologue – for woman."

"Ugly, interfering bitch?" suggested Richard at a venture.

"Ah, you know." It seemed to give him a sombre satisfaction. "Yes. Then Miss Coltman begin to …"

"To weep?"

"Yes, and she go out damn quick. She forget her bag."

"Did she speak to anyone on her way out? Mr. Shrubsole was there, wasn't he? Oh, and Mr. Macdonald too? Lunching together? Yes. But she didn't speak to them. Well, what happened after she'd gone? They all went straight on with lunch. Where was Sir Alban Worrall sitting?"

"Where you sit just now." He smiled a little grimly. Clare's pencil slipped on the paper.

"And where were Macdonald and Shrubsole? A good way off? Well, you can show me in a moment. Now, when Sir Alban was taken ill, did he call to them? What? What do you mean, perhaps?"

"There was much noise, and perhaps I not hear. All the pipple were looking at rabbits. Ah! You not know?"

He launched into the story, comic if it had occurred in another setting. Rabbits, it seemed, were kept in the backyard of the Minos ("for ze creamed chicken," explained Mikhailopoulos incautiously) and somehow they had got loose and into the restaurant. Yes, they often got out, but had never actually got into the front before. The proprietor, the waiters, and many of the lunchers had been shooing and grabbing at them. It was really a very unlucky time for a sick man to call for help (though the doctor had said that nothing could have been done for him in any case.) By the time Worrall was observed, he was practically beyond speech, and the staff had got him into the back-room. Shrubsole might not have noticed. Later, Macdonald had asked if anything was wrong, and either he or Shrubsole had given the name of Worrall's doctor. Questioned about Shrubsole's attitude, Mikhailopoulos was unhelpful. He had not noticed, he had been too busy with Worrall. By the time the crisis was over, Shrubsole and his friend had gone.

Richard went on to question the Greek about Sir Alban's illness, and his answers, steady and careful, filled up the gaps in Dr. Chevet's account that morning. Worrall had eaten, as he always did, fast and copiously. He drank with equal dispatch. Mikhailopoulos seemed especially affronted by one particular trick of which Worrall was proud – to drink *ouzo* in a single draft.

"It is good *ouzo*, no? But gllp! He drink it quick, like always, and then he say 'Bad *ouzo*, Costa, very rough.' I say 'You not taste it good, sir. Just wait. You feel the quality in a moment.' Ah! The doctor is very angry when he hear what Sir Alban have for lunch, but he say 'Not your fault. He ask for it.' That's O.K., yes? I give what he order."

"Of course. I'm sure a Cretan wouldn't poison a guest." The Cretan looked up fiercely. "Even by accident, I mean."

He laughed. "Ah! No! My cuisine's very healthy. But, sir, I tell you about guest in Crete. He don't pay. I give him. If he order dinner and pay, that is business, he is customer, not guest. One day you drink with me here in my house, I pay, you are my guest, lots of fun. But Sir Alban, no. He will not drink with poor *restaurateur*. He pay, with thirty percent reduction like I always make for archéologue."

How touchy he was on the point of honor. Primitive laws of hospitality must take a lot of working out if you're a restaurant proprietor. Worrall, no doubt, had treated him as a "native" and insulted his dignity; hence this insistence that Worrall was merely a customer.

"You didn't like him?"

"Listen, sir. He is good customer, come often, I give him best attention. When he's ill, I get him doctor. I take him to hospital myself when doctor ask me. Good, no?"

Richard recognized the evasion, but felt his question had been unfair. It was too much to expect an open avowal of dislike for a man whose death was at least the proximate result of one's own cookery. Indeed, in the circumstances, the answer was scrupulously truthful.

"Yes, I'm sure you did all you could for him. Thank you for answering me so carefully. That'll be all for now. Before I go, I must see the waiter. And I'll have a look at your back premises too – kitchen and so on. He can show me."

"My God, sir! Go in kitchen in dinner hour? What happen? Everyone rush around, food spoiled, womens give notice, customers angry like hell because there's no best attention! You want to ruin me? Why not come in morning, all clean, no rush, no customers?"

To Clare's surprise, Richard yielded. Yes, he would come in the morning if Mikhailopoulos preferred. But he would speak to the waiter now. Mikhailopoulos shrugged.

"He's a very stupid boy, don't speak English good. In morning, I interpret for you. Now, if you take him, I must do his work."

This being Richard's desire, he once more insisted. The man left the room sullenly, Richard close behind him. He summoned the boy with a jerk of the head and spoke briefly to him in Greek. Richard could not follow the rapid words. But he could see contempt and domination on one side, and alarm and – was it? – hatred on the other. Of course, in Aegean lands employees *are* treated like dogs, and there is no R.S.P.C.A. There are several sides to the Homeric code of behavior.

* * *

The waiter came in, and Richard told him to sit down. He sat, but his weight was on his feet, his body poised for flight, his eyes wide open like a deer's. *Fauve*, thought Richard, there's no decent word in English. But what beauty! Antique and pastoral, youthful, but with a strict perfection of shape and motion quite unlike the puppyish charm of Frankish youth. *Fair youth beneath the trees, thou canst not leave Thy song* ... Damn him, must he stare at my wife like that?

"I'm from Scotland Yard," he began. The boy looked suitably alarmed.

His English was on about the same level as Richard's Greek; that is, he had learned the phrases one needs in a restaurant. His French was better though vilely accented. His name, to Clare's surprise, was spelled Georgios. (It sounded like Yor-yo. That was the nominative; you addressed him in the vocative as Yor-yi.) The surname sounded equally Oriental and came out as the comparatively familiar Aiakides. He also was a Cretan. He had been six months at the Minos and a year before that in Paris, he said, learning the restaurant business. When he was rich, he would go back to Crete and start his own hotel. (Pathetic, typical ambition!) No, he was no relation of Mikhailopoulos, and though Mikhailopoulos lived alone on the top floor over the Minos, Georgios slept out in a room of his own a few streets away.

Richard now began to question him about the two afternoons, Monday when Sir Alban had died and Thursday when Miss Coltman had been stabbed. His answers agreed with those of his employer, and were given sensibly and with increasing confidence. On Monday, he had served Shrubsole and Macdonald, while the boss, as he called him, had served Sir Alban, who had arrived first and was sitting near the front of the room. Shrubsole, following Macdonald into the restaurant, had knocked into Worrall's table in passing, and upset a dish of olives, but gone straight on without a word of apology to the far end of the room. The waiter had picked up the olives. It was all over in a moment, while Janet and Worrall were drinking their sherry. (An accident, or a diversion? Time to drop something into Worrall's glass? Wait! We don't know yet whether he was poisoned or not. Stick to facts.)

The rabbits. How many rabbits? He asked, and how had they got loose? Five rabbits, a doe and her young. The back door into the yard from the kitchen must have been left open, though it was shut when he and the boss took the rabbits back. Who was in the kitchen? Two Englishwomen, a washer-up and a kitchen maid; Mikhailopoulos attended to the fine points of the cooking himself. Well, wasn't it rather odd that the rabbits hadn't been noticed? The waiter laughed like a child. Really, he was extraordinarily attractive.

"All too busy, monsieur. Not see evven" – a vivid pantomime of horns and leer.

"The devil?" Richard understood and laughed too. He had been in these Soho kitchens before, and seen the hurrying and swearing, the spitting on the floor, the smear of gravy removed from the edge of the dish with a licked finger or a used handkerchief; the half-enjoyed sense of crisis, no room for the extra hand they needed. If the devil himself came in, they wouldn't have time to see him. Why, the waiter hadn't even noticed that Miss Coltman quarreled with Sir Alban, nor had he seen her leave; and the boss had to call him before he realized anything was wrong with Worrall.

As for Shrubsole and Macdonald, whom he was serving, they had enjoyed their lunch and Shrubsole had paid. He had also done most of the talking. He was "very happy." How did Georgios know he was happy? He drank a lot, he gave a good tip, he went out arm-in-arm with his friend, laughing loudly. Drunk? No. He could walk and he had not broken anything. But there again, thought Richard, we must remember the difference of race. High spirits in a Greek may have the same effect as distilled ones in an Englishman. Get Macdonald's version.

Georgios confirmed that Miss Coltman had come in after lunch on Thursday and stayed a short time talking to the boss, who had afterwards run out with her briefcase. He had returned very soon with some coffee he had bought while he was out, and when he came back, the waiter left. Lunch was over and he got an afternoon break. He had, he said, gone for a walk. Richard could guess its direction – Missenden Mansions.

"Now listen!" he said. "You know someone tried to kill Miss Coltman?"

The youth nodded, serious but unsurprised.

"How do you know? Who told you? It wasn't in the papers." Zoe must have told him.

"The boss tell me. He …" a hand to the ear.

"Heard it? Yes, where?"

"In the … where you buy fruits, in street … *enfin, au marché*."

"In the market?" It was possible. There might be that sort of grapevine in Soho. He remembered the talking women in Berwick Street early this morning. But Mikhailopoulos had not mentioned his knowledge of the attempted murder to Richard. Too cautious, no doubt: the prudent Odysseus.

"Well, what do they say about it in the market? Why do they think she was attacked?"

He looked interested. "Some say – *pour l'argent. Mais elle n'avait pas le sou, ça se voyait*. Some say, *crîme passionel*. I don't think. She was like *religieuse, et d'ailleurs très laide*."

"And what do *you* think?" This boy was not stupid. He enjoyed being asked to think.

"*Affaire de famille*, per'aps? Or *politique?* Or per'aps Sir Alban not like, pay a man to kill her? He's very rich, and you say they *se disputaient au déjeuner*, no?"

Fantastic suggestions, of course; but he made them with an air of helpful intelligence, as he might help a client plan a dinner – and with equal personal detachment. It was curious that, like Zoe, he seemed to stop worrying as soon as he discovered that the crime under investigation was merely attempted murder. The mere word frightens most people. He was either very sure of his innocence on that count or very anxious about his guilt on another. Was it the affair with Zoe, or something to do with the parcel of Minoan antiquities? I'll crack the pair of them tomorrow, Richard thought, when Macdonald tells me about the stuff and when I've heard the result of that post mortem. Meanwhile, we'll give him something to think about.

"I'll be coming back to make a search in the morning. Just give me your address before I go."

Mikhailopoulos came in to say good-bye and present the bill, which was neither steep nor moderate. The waiter lingered for his tip. Handing it over, Richard said casually to Mikhailopoulos:

"By the way, did Mrs. ap Ifor pay you a visit this evening? I thought I heard her voice out at the back."

Georgios took the tip without looking at it. He was very pale.

"You hear everything, sir." The proprietor spread his hands in a gesture of rueful capitulation. "Always more trouble! All right, I tell you the truth. Yes, she come. She say, I'm passing, speak to Georgio for table tomorrow. Ah, bah! Why go to kitchen side to get table? That's too stupid. She come for him. Ah! Georgi, I see you look at her like dog at bitch, many time when she come with Mr. ap Ifor, dirty little son of Corfiote goat for mother, you want to make me trouble for wife of good customer? You think I not give you wages, I wait for you to get pay of woman?" Overcome by his indignation, Mikhailopoulos seized his own mustache, looped it out of the way behind his ears, waved a clenched fist in front of his hooked nose, and gave himself free vent in his own tongue.

The boy wilted, Richard gasped, the torrent did not falter.

And then suddenly there was the boy slipping out, Mikhailopoulos unlooping his mustache and smiling.

"Pff! I been waiting one hour to say that. Good. You see, I look after honor of my house. She won't come again, only with husband. All finish now. You won't make me no trouble?"

"No, I won't talk about this. But why on earth should *you* mind if your waiter's carrying on with Mrs. ap Ifor? What's it matter to you?"

"Outside" – his shrug disclaimed knowledge or responsibility – "he carry on with devil if he want. But not in my house, not when he work. Bad honor, bad business, yes?"

Chapter 9

"WELL, I *must* say," said Clare, as they walked away, "lots of the things you've done this evening seem to me quite bats. But, being you, I'm sure they were all right really."

"That's the ideal wife. Absolute skepticism combined with perfect trust. Well, what?"

"Why didn't you ask Mik-whatever-it-was about his past life? How long he's known this bunch of archaeologists, and where he's lived and so on. You did the waiter. Surely it's important."

"It is. I asked Macdonald about it this afternoon, and got my facts verified by the Home Office. He's been running that joint for twenty years, darling. He's a political exile – got involved in one of those violent Cretan factions in his youth and made the place too hot to hold him. There were only two ways open to him; go abroad, or join the outlaws in the mountains – they're a sort of perpetual Robin Hood feature of the island. Well, he'd done some digging for Evans's lot, and some of them wangled him permission to come over here. He had to leave his family behind, poor chap. Still, no doubt they're better off like that than roughing it on the heights of Mount Ida."

"I wonder. There are worse ways of living. Funny, I'd have expected him to make the heroic choice. It's more like him."

"Yes, there is a Homeric quality about him. But don't forget, Odysseus knew which side his bread was buttered, too. I expect he's made more money for his sons this way. Anyhow, there you have his past. The exciting part's a long way back. Worrall's gang have been coming to the Minos for a long time, though Macdonald did mention that the thirty percent reduction for archaeologists is a new stunt. He was amused to see that Worrall fell for it in a big way. He began to do all his entertaining there instead of at his third-best club. Funny how mean rich men are in little ways."

"Inherited technique, probably. Well, I see now why you let off Mik – oh, call him Costa, I can pronounce that – from telling his life-\ story. But why didn't you grill young George? He might have broken down and told you a lot if you'd taxed him with Zoe. Or if you want him in a state of false security, why did you let on you'd heard Zoe's voice in the kitchen?"

"Oh, I did that to get Costa's reaction. I'm saving up the grilling of Georgios till I know about that parcel of antiques. Are he and Zoe faking them, or stealing, or just smuggling? Obviously they're up to no good, but I'll frighten them much more if I wait till I can accuse them of something you go to jug for, and not only adultery."

"I see. By the way, what *did* you think of Costa's reaction?"

"Absolutely in character, wouldn't you say? Combining a high sense of personal honor with a keen eye to business. After all, it can't do him any good to have his waiters getting off with the wives of regular customers."

"No. He does fascinate me. I have the impression that if he wanted to lie, he'd do it more convincingly than anyone I know; and yet somehow I felt he was telling you the truth, didn't you? Even to his own disadvantage. Look how he wouldn't pretend he liked Worrall."

"Ye-es. Just for the sake of argument (though mind you, I feel the same as you) he might have said to himself, 'If I say I'm Worrall's friend, it will follow that I'm Miss Coltman's enemy, because she and Worrall had a flaming quarrel. So Worrall might have hired me to kill her. And I had an opportunity, too, when I ran after her with the briefcase.' Three days after Worrall's death, true, which makes it less likely. Still …"

"Yes, and don't forget that he was only about ten minutes, and he knows you can check up on the shops he visited. Surely the waiter's a better proposition. Quicker on his feet, and he didn't have to hurry back. Also, if he's faking antiques, he's got a better motive for killing Janet, supposing she'd found him out. Also, I can't believe, one, that Costa's a hired assassin, or, two, that a hired assassin carries on with his job when his employer's been dead three days."

"I do agree there. Somehow Costa Mikhailopoulos doesn't smell to me like a hired assassin, even allowing for the hair oil."

"It would drown almost anything, wouldn't it? Whereas I suppose you'd suspect young George at sight … Just because he's so beautiful, poor lamb."

"Because he's so weak. He's much more the criminal type. Well, have I committed any other batty actions, or is that the lot?"

"Really, my dear Holmes, I am amazed by your imprudence in actually *warning* the miscreants of your intention to search their premises. Whatever incriminating clues the back parts of the Minos may contain, you may be sure that all traces will be carefully removed by the time of your expected visit."

"You have, my dear Watson, albeit unconsciously," said Richard with a vulturine grimace, "hit upon the very purpose of my warning. They will remove the incriminating clues, if any, tonight. But not – ha-*ha!* – unobserved. I shall be there, lurking in my ulster."

Clare began to protest, and Richard went on hastily.

"It's perfectly safe. I've got a description of the premises out of the ex-A.R.P. chap, and there'll be a bobby within call if anything unexpected turns up. I've already told ap Ifor that I'm going to search the place tomorrow, and I shall ring up Shrubsole and tell him the same. Ah! Here's a callbox. Let's do it now, and give *him* a chance to demonstrate his guilty conscience."

Three minutes later he put down the receiver.

"Well, that was unexpected."

"Why? What did he say?"

"My godfathers!" Richard was a good mimic. "What sort of a detective do you think you are? Don't you realize they'll have got every single clue out of the way by the morning? Why the heck couldn't you do it tonight? ... And so on. Odd, you know, that man never swears, and yet he gives off a constant aura of bad language."

* * *

The house looked ramshackle from the back, but Richard found it well fortified. A narrow alley running into a back street brought him to the yard of the Minos, which was enclosed by a high smooth wall and secured by a locked gate with barbed wire along the top. Most people would have given up the approach as hopeless, but Richard was an Oxford man, and grateful tonight for the wide scope of a university education. Climbing into college after hours had trained him for this sort of thing. He crawled over the top of a public-house lavatory, picked his way along a wall encrusted with broken glass, rolled gingerly over a corrugated iron roof (being careful to roll against the grain and so avoid making a noise like stage thunder), crossed a garden, and found himself high on the wall of the backyard. Even then he would have been puzzled for a way down and a hiding place, if it had not been for the big fig tree that grew against the wall, its leaves just unfolded and its trunk still swathed in sacking and straw against last spring's frosts. Mikhailopoulos must have cherished it well for a long time to bring it to such a size in this climate. Perhaps it reminded him of his beloved Crete. At any rate, he often sat under it, for there under its shade stood a dilapidated basket-chair which had taken on his very shape and nature. Flanked though it was by stinking dustbins and rabbit hutches, it seemed still to wait affectionately for its master, and now and then it emitted eerie creaks and whispers as though to give warning of the intruder who crouched in shadow among the topmost leaves above. Low clouds whirled across the sky, reflecting the glare of the London lights downwards as an incomplete darkness; the faint oval of the moon dodged in and out of the clouds like the white face of an idiot lost in a wood.

All the windows but one were in darkness. Light shone behind the skimpy kitchen curtains and there was a bright line of it under the kitchen door which led into the yard. Someone was doing a bit of carpentry, it seemed; Richard heard the tap-tap of a hammer, the faint tinny jangle of wire, the clatter of wood on wood. It was half an hour after midnight. He began lowering himself to the ground for a closer view, but just as he stretched one leg out of the tree, the kitchen door opened, and he scrambled back behind the leaves. Mikhailopoulos came out into the yard, a cigarette at the corner of his mouth and a rabbit hutch in his arms. He was humming a barbaric tune of five notes in a minor key, jigging a little to the strongly marked rhythm. On the last note of the phrase, he set down his homemade hutch with a bang like a final chord. The rabbits inside squeaked indignantly and Mikhailopoulos spoke a soothing word or two in Greek. Then he opened the hutch and took a very young rabbit out, sitting it on his hand and talking to it. Richard wished he could follow, for it was clear that Mikhailopoulos wasn't really talking to the rabbit at all – he was talking to himself, and with some emotion. His voice was both angry and sad. If life in Soho really inspired the man with such passionate regret, surely he would have done better to stay as an outlaw in his native mountains. The words *honor* and *father* seemed to come in a good deal. Perhaps he was secretly ashamed of having run away and cut his home ties, and perhaps that was why he indulged in monologues to rabbits instead of in confidences to his fellow Greeks in exile. Poor chap! Still, people who think themselves alone *do* show signs of unexpected melancholy. Few men walk an empty road with untroubled faces; hardly a traveler on the Underground but seems to have his private torment; human beings, in fact, tend to look unhappy in solitude, but they are seldom as unhappy as they look, and Richard, after ten years of watching, was wary of taking such private exhibitions at their face-value.

The rabbit, meanwhile, sat still and stared at its owner with that look of timid obstinacy only found in rabbits and minor functionaries. But then it stopped attending. It had become aware of Richard in the fig tree. Mikhailopoulos broke off suddenly, with something between a laugh and a sigh. He said a phrase Richard recognized – "So you don't speak Greek, eh?" He put the rabbit back with the others and turned heavily towards the house. A few drops of rain began to fall and he frowned up at the sky.

When the kitchen door banged, Richard climbed down and stole across the yard to the window, which was shut and not quite covered by its curtains. It was easy to see in. The room was littered with tools and bits of wire, and there was one large piece of wood propped against the table-leg, measuring about a foot square. Mikhailopoulos put away the tools in a packing case, threw the chips into the boiler stove, and then began to chop up the piece of wood with a hatchet. He chopped hard, in short, ringing blows, and the tough, newly cleft wood glistened pale under the light and clattered sharply as it fell on the stone floor. When the work was finished and the firewood thrown with a final rattle beside the stove, the quiet seemed oppressive. Mikhailopoulos turned to the bottle and glass that stood ready on the table and poured himself a drink. Beside the bottle lay a primitive but rather lovely little instrument like a guitar, and now he picked it up, fingered the strings for a moment, and began to play the same five-toned air that he had hummed in the yard. He played well. Under his hand the strings seemed to speak. "*By the rivers of Babylon*," thought Richard. That theme is timeless and nationless, and he's got it all there, I find myself recalling the words from first to last. But … all? Suddenly Mikhailopoulos stopped in the middle of a phrase as if he could not bear to go on, and wrapped the instrument up in its cloth again. "*And we hanged our harps upon the willows in the midst thereof.*" Yes, the whole psalm, it was all there. But the less poetic, inevitable aftermath followed. Mikhailopoulos returned to the bottle. He drank three times more, quickly and without pleasure, and then rose and left the room by the inner door, switching off the light as he passed. Richard heard his dragging feet plod up the stairs and presently a light went on in the first-floor window.

Richard did some more mountaineering, his rubber shoes slippery on the brick, and climbed to a place where he could see into the bedroom, which was small but comfortably furnished. There was a huge wardrobe and chest of drawers, a trouser-press, and even a fixed washbasin with a looking glass above it. Odd. One would have expected the owner of such a room to look – yes, and smell – rather more civilized than this old warhorse. But of course it was a matter of prestige nowadays, this *confort moderne*. It did not, in the Near East, necessarily mean that you washed. It might not even mean that the taps worked. So long as you had shown your rivals that you could afford to have taps, honor was satisfied.

Mikhailopoulos's behavior bore out Richard's theory in the most delightful way. He did not wash. He did not put his trousers in the trouser-press. True, he contemplated his own whiskers in the glass over the basin for a long time, parting and twirling them this way and that with comical vanity. But that was all he did do there; after that he just undressed. Jacket, waistcoat, collar and tie came off. Then he unwound the red cummerbund from his waist – there seemed to be yards of it – and picked something from among its folds, which he placed under the pillow. Socks, shoes, and trousers in turn were thrown on the floor but the shirt he kept on. Perhaps he slept in it. Anyhow he had stopped undressing and was standing by the bed motionless. He seemed to be looking at a picture. He raised his hand and Richard suddenly realized what he was doing. He was crossing himself with the ample gesture of the Greek Orthodox Church. He was saying his prayers. Richard disliked spying on him in these circumstances, but it was his duty. Besides, it was fascinatingly incongruous to see this hairy, thickset Odysseus joining his hands and moving his lips with the simplicity of a child in a night nursery. "*Bow, stubborn knees: and heart, with strings of steel. Be soft as sinews of the newborn babe!*" But of course even Odysseus had never made the mistake of thinking himself as good as the gods.

The prayers were as short as they had been unexpected. Mikhailopoulos crossed himself again, scratched in his armpit, and turned off the light. Richard hoped he had got into bed, but there was no means of making sure. At least, there was no point in staying up here on the wall. Richard clambered down again into the yard. It was raining in earnest now, and he must get under cover, or he would leave wet traces of himself everywhere when he got indoors. He pressed into the shallow recess of the kitchen doorway and dried his rubber soles on his handkerchief, standing first on one foot and then on the other. It was very quiet. Was Mikhailopoulos asleep? If so, he slept soundlessly. But perhaps this was in character. An Odysseus does not snore, or suffer from catarrh or indigestion, though he may go to bed rather drunk. No: if he *had* snored, he would almost certainly have been shamming. Richard gave him twenty minutes extra for safety and then prepared to go in.

He felt in his pockets. *Had* he lost his little oilcan? No, here it was, and the torch with it. He oiled the keyhole and hasp. But to his surprise, the door was not locked, at least not with the key. It might of course be bolted. He turned the handle softly and the door opened. Either Mikhailopoulos had been so depressed that he had forgotten to lock it, or he trusted to the barrier of the yard gate. Richard tried the bolt. It was loose and easy with frequent use.

He went into the dark room, and groped at the sink till he found a dishcloth to wedge in the door, to prevent it from banging and yet keep it unlatched. Then he tiptoed round the room, learning his way about. There was a tall dresser with shelves of china above and drawers and a cupboard below. There was an Aga cooker, a boiler stove, and the sink with plate racks at the side of it. The only other furniture was a table and two chairs. You could cut the air with a knife, it was so thick with stale cooking, garbage, and Greek tobacco. He would have to be careful of his feet, there were so many packing cases on the floor, stacked in corners. A pile of onions nearly cost him a fall, rolling hard and slippery underfoot. The bump he made sounded very loud, and he froze and listened, but it was still quiet upstairs. Yet he could have sworn he had heard something, just after his own bump and not in the room. Yes, there it was again. Outside, in the yard. Could the rabbits have made that heavy metallic clank? Surely not! He looked out. There was somebody with a torch in the alley on the other side of the wall. Well, he can't climb in *that* side, thought Richard. The wall's too smooth and high. You couldn't get a purchase, unless you had a Roman scaling ladder or something of the sort.

The torch was extinguished, leaving the yard very dark, since no ray of light fell on it now from the house and the sky was obscured by rain. Yet he thought the top of the wall looked different. Yes, its line was broken by a figure. Another clank, a soft slither and a bump, and the figure had dropped into the yard and was coming across towards him. He must hide, but where in that bare room? There were no large pieces of furniture to give cover. It would have to be the cavity under the sink, small and reeking of unemptied garbage. He coiled himself in, a tight fit. It felt as horrible as it smelt, like the inside of an ungutted fish.

Richard wondered what the new invader would think when he found the door wedged on a cloth and not even latched. But the person outside did not even try the door. His steps came straight to the window – a sash-window directly above the sink, shut and fastened with a catch. Again there was a glimmer of faint torchlight, and then the grate of a blade against metal. Richard could not see but he knew what the sound meant. The catch was being pushed back from outside with a thin knife-blade inserted in the crack between the two halves of the window. Very amateurish. No professional burglar would have risked such a noise at night, though a tramp might safely have used the method to break into an empty house. Suddenly the spring shot back as he knew it would. Surely that ringing snap would wake Mikhailopoulos. Here was a clumsy housebreaker indeed.

Clumsy he might be, but he had the self-control to wait for five minutes in absolute silence. Richard timed him, and it seemed an age. Then, very slowly and cautiously, the window was opened. It stuck several times and had to be coaxed loose with the knife-blade, and the sash-ropes squeaked against the pulley-wheels. A burglar would have taken fright and decamped at half the noise, but the person in the yard persisted, with pauses of absolute silence between the attempts. At last there was a different sound – the rumble of the whole window as weight was pressed on it, and then the soft pat of rubber-soled shoes on the wet sink. The torch shone from immediately above Richard's hiding-place on to the floor, lighting up a pair of dangling legs in flannel trousers and two feet in dirt-encrusted canvas shoes. Then it went out again. The feet scraped down over the rough brickwork supporting the sink, missing Richard by inches, and touched the floor. The man stood upright and used his torch again, which must have cloth or paper tied over the glass, so small a light did it shed. Richard thought the man was slight in build but it was hard to be sure even of that. He groped his way round the kitchen as Richard had done until he came to the dresser. Then he stopped and got to work.

One by one, with infinite precaution and long pauses after the least sound, he opened the drawers and shone his dim light into them. He must be looking for some particular thing, for he shut three drawers up without touching their contents. The fourth took longer. It rattled as he opened it, and when he put his hand in, something reflected the torchlight enough to show Richard that the hand was gloved. The face, peering in, was invisible. Presently something flashed and rattled as the man lifted it, and then he shut the drawer again softly and began to move towards the window. Richard was ready for him. He would slip out by the door as the man was climbing out of the window (he could do it very quickly and softly because of the cloth in the door) and tackle him in the yard. He knew a way to overpower a man without a sound and without injury. So he would find out who he was and what he had taken. All his senses were deliciously sharp with the hunter's joy of final action. So a hawk might feel perhaps as it stoops to kill.

But suddenly a sound in the house made him pause – downstairs not upstairs, and towards the front – the sound of a Yale key stealthily fitted into a lock. Richard, swiftly reviewing the plan of the building, remembered that the restaurant had a glass door with an ordinary key, and shutters too. It was not the restaurant door, it was the one next to it, which led down a passage to the stairs and kitchen. That had a Yale lock. He was torn between desire to catch the man here in the room now, and curiosity about the new arrival.

His dilemma was unexpectedly resolved. The man in the kitchen, instead of taking alarm and making his escape quickly – surely the natural thing to do – turned back. Richard heard his feet softly padding over to the far side of the room, where the inner door led to the passage. There he stopped. The silence hung like a guillotine. It lasted even when the inner door opened.

At first Richard could only guess that it was open because of the chill air rushing across the room. Then a car passed along the street in the front and a faint light came down the passage, just defining the oblong door-hole. So he's left the passage door open, thought Richard. Otherwise how could the light get in? But where was the fellow? There was neither sight nor sound of him; a spirit could not move more noiseless and invisible. It was almost uncanny.

As though in mocking confirmation of the thought, a melodious twang suddenly filled the room – a sound so disembodied, so unearthly, that it gave him a thrill of primitive panic horror. *Iorweth said – Welshmen know these things – he said Something got loose from that shrine on Pontikonisi. Perhaps It's in the room now*. There was a single hollow rap. *One!* Richard did not know why he was counting. His spine crept.

Then he suddenly understood and nearly laughed. As suddenly, the room came to life. Somebody gave a startled gasp; there were a few sharp whispers in Greek – two voices. And then they were fighting. There was no mistaking that hard-drawn breath and desperate shifting of feet; though they fought in silence, they fought in earnest, and Richard rose up to intervene. But just as he got to his feet there was a twangling crash. The guitar had fallen off the table. And as he came on, he and somebody else were enveloped in voluminous folds of stuff. One of the combatants had thrown the tablecloth over his opponent and Richard with him. Gripping his companion, Richard got his head clear just in time to see the other, a dim shadowy mass, climbing out of the window. At the same time he heard heavy steps on the stairs. The man he was holding wriggled like an eel and got loose. Richard let him go and dashed through the door into the yard. The other man was astride the wall already. Richard grasped at his foot but only caught the toe; it rasped against his fingernails and pulled away, and the man was down on the other side. Some heavy iron object dropped with him. Then he was running for dear life down the alley towards the back street. Richard tried the gate but the key had been taken out. The wall was hopeless – how had the man climbed it? He turned back to the house.

No one seemed to be there. A light now shone in the passage and partly illuminated the kitchen. The tablecloth and guitar were on the floor, and a chair was overturned. Mikhailopoulos was shouting in the road. Richard hastily covered his own traces. He picked up the cloth he had wedged in the door and threw it back into the sink. He shut the door exactly as he had found it. Then he had to hurry and climb up into the tree, for Mikhailopoulos came back, running. The street door slammed behind him and the kitchen light snapped on as he entered. Richard could hear and partly see him as he moved about muttering to himself. He must be trying to see what's gone, thought Richard. Oh Lord, he's coming out.

He looked extraordinary and rather splendid striding out in the light from the room behind – a light that fortunately did not fall on the fig tree. He was wearing nothing but a shirt. His square brown feet were bare, the muscles stood out on his legs, which were so heroic-looking that the shirttails weren't even funny, and he held in his hand a bright long knife. He stood at gaze, breathing deeply, but not out of breath, and looking about him. Then he strode over and tried the yard gate. Finding it secure, he pulled the rabbit hutches into the light from the window and counted over the rabbits. Richard heard and recognized the Greek numerals. Once he had made sure all was safe, he looked content and seemed likely to settle down again. But then he noticed the open kitchen window. He turned in his tracks and came straight for the fig tree with his knife. Richard kicked – he hated doing it – at the man's diaphragm. Most men would have collapsed. Mikhailopoulos reeled a moment, shook his big head, and began climbing. But Richard was over the top and away by a route he knew. He increased his start easily. Just before he dropped into the street from the top of the public-house lavatory, he heard Mikhailopoulos coming over the corrugated iron shed in the next-door garden. He was stamping on it and making a noise exactly like stage thunder.

Chapter 10

RICHARD arrived early next day at Scotland Yard. The night's adventures seemed to have cured his sprained ankle, and raised his spirits; even the prospect of an interview with his superior, the Bloodhound, inspired him more with militancy than depression.

But for once even the Bloodhound was complaisant. The post mortem on Worrall had been carried out and proved to have been completely justified. Worrall had swallowed a large dose of hydrochloric acid, probably administered in capsule form, since there was hardly any mark of burning in the mouth. There were burns in the throat, naturally, as some of the acid had been vomited. Worrall's general physical condition – apart from the hardening of arteries and softening of muscles common in self-indulgent men of fifty-five – was healthy; no heart disease, and above all no gastric ulcer.

Richard only paused to ask for the services of certain experts, while his chief was in a complying mood, and then hurried off to catch the surgeon, an old Scotsman whose lectures on forensic medicine he had once attended. His comments were generally illuminating when they came, though he had an annoying habit of recapitulating his own reports first. He spoke with a singsong lilt that gave certain words a quite delusive emphasis; a kind of Doric Gregorian chant.

"So ye see it *looks* like a perfectly straight *case* of hydrochloric acid *poisoning*, when death would *occur* say thirty-six hours after administration."

"Thirty-six!" Richard was surprised. "Why, wouldn't the poison start working at once?"

"Come away!" the surgeon rebuked his former pupil. "Ye know verra *well* that immediate and severe *pain* is the first symptom produced by the caustic *action* of the acid. It starts working *instantly*. What *ensues* upon this? I mind ye had the question in your *paper*, Mr. Ringwood, just eight years *ago*. Ye did moderately *well*."

"General peritonitis," lilted Richard in unconscious parody of the lecturer, "ensues due to the caustic *action* of the acid upon the internal *tissues*." He had never been quite sure what that meant but it was easy to memorize for the exam.

His master looked at him with austere pity.

"I'll describe the process ana*logically*, that being the only form of statement that a man of literary education can *grasp*. Suppose your interior is a delicate system of *containers*. Each contains something useful in *itself* but dangerous to the others. You burn a lot of holes in the containers and what *ensues?* An unholy *mixture* of things that ought to have been kept *apart*, which ferments and poisons the whole *system*. But not at *once*, mind. Ye'll need a day or two to brew up a fatal *dose*."

"But this man died four hours after the pain started, I think. Is there bound to be bad pain straight away? You couldn't delay the pain by giving some other drug at the same time as the acid?"

"Short of a general anes*thetic*, no. The pain is too *severe*. The acid might be given in a thick gelatine *capsule* that took maybe a quarter of an hour to dis*solve*."

"That's not long enough. Well then, he didn't die just from the poison. The peritonitis wouldn't be bad enough after four hours to kill him. So why did he die? Shock? What *is* shock, anyway?"

"That's quite an intelligent *question*. Well, laddie, ye've seen plenty die of shock. What do you think it is?"

"Fear? Pain? Sensitivity? Lack of will to struggle?"

"Ye're putting it just a wee bit *emotively*. But … Mphm, Mr. Ringwood. Have ye noticed how few of the *martyrs* appear to have died of shock?"

Richard shunned this fascinating red herring.

"But Worrall died of it?"

"That is what the data would appear to sug*gest*. The hearrt was in quite a healthy con*dition*. And shock does occur in these *cases* of acid poisoning. The alarm and *pain*, ye see, would be con*siderable*."

* * *

At nine o'clock the party set off in a car. It consisted of Richard, a fingerprint expert with a camera, and a policewoman called Sergeant Frewin, a plain comfortable woman of forty-five, rather like a welfare worker and rather like the best kind of maiden aunt. Richard had always admired her extraordinary talent for finding things – she would be a born champion at Hunt the Thimble – and after half an hour in a strange house she knew intuitively where everything was kept. She had not attained high promotion because the more brutal forms of sexual vice still caused her to be sick at unsuitable moments.

They called first at the waiter's lodgings. He had already gone out to work, but his landlady, a woman if possible even more squalid than her house, showed them his room. Leaning against the doorjamb in her grubby wrapper, she kept up a running commentary while they went quickly and methodically to work. This was a respectable house, this was. Never took nothing but waiters, see? Women? She'd like to see a woman poke her nose inside the door. The colored gentleman in the top back had tried it on once. Asked if he could bring in his sister. Sister, she asked them! If she was really his sister, they could go to a Lyons, couldn't they? Unless … here she became really scabrous and Sergeant Frewin turned a little green. Richard intervened to ask whether the lodgers had keys at night or were let in by the landlady. They had keys, but the landlady kept her eyes open, and if they came in late they got the rough side of her tongue. Richard wondered if it would be worse than the side *he* was getting – the slimy side, perhaps? Also, she turned off the electricity at midnight. Mr. Aiakides was never later than half past eleven, and nor was the Negro, but the Italian sometimes gave trouble. No, the three were not friendly, and just as well too; friendship led to noise and uppishness and the sharing of gas fires.

Georgio's wretched little room contained no papers, no weapons, and no antiquities – nothing but cheap smart clothes, carefully cleaned and pressed. The only fingerprints in the room were those of himself and his landlady; of hers, several were found inside the drawers. If Georgios had any valuables, he was wise not to keep them here. Assuring her once more of the routine nature of their search, urging her in vain to believe that no reflections were being cast upon her house or her lodgers, they left and were glad to go.

At the Minos, the atmosphere was humane but frenzied. All hands had been mobilized to receive the police in style, but not mobilized quite soon enough. The kitchen floor was still wet from a recent scrubbing; the garbage pails had been emptied; the packing cases, full and empty, bundled into the yard with the onions and other boobytraps. One of the women was peeling potatoes at the table, the other busy in the flat upstairs. The waiter was cleaning the restaurant.

Mikhailopoulos was squatting in the kitchen sink, nailing wire-netting over the window, but he jumped down now and then to stir a saucepan on the stove, and he kept up a flow of hearty and abusive admonition over his shoulder to the others.

"Maureen! That's a good potato you drop in with the peelings. You ruin me. Georgi, you ain't polished under the big table. Move him out, lazy —! Shirley! Shirlee! You ring up Louká, now, now, and ask him where in hell is my vegetable. You finish later, sure! Quick! Quick! Quick! Quick! My God! You want to worry me to death?"

A rhetorical question; Mikhailopoulos obviously had enough nervous energy for six, and enjoyed using it. When the police party came in, he jumped down from the sink and whipped the saucepan off the stove.

"Good morning, sir. Hey you, Maureen, pour this in the big bowl, quick, quick, I don't want no lumps. There's a strainer somewhere around. Good morning, madame. Excuse me, I hear the vegetable. I don't want him in my yard."

He dashed off to the yard gate and returned staggering under five boxes of greengrocer's stuff, remarking apologetically that he didn't want no trouble. What could he do for them? His house was a good house, there was nothing bad in it, everyone could see for themselves. He addressed himself to Richard, but eyed Sergeant Frewin with fascinated disapproval.

"We'll start in here," Richard said. "It won't take long! Will you all go out, please?"

Mikhailopoulos shooed his staff out like poultry, but himself remained standing in the doorway. Richard saw no reason to exclude him.

"I won't keep you a minute, Sergeant Frewin. Fowler, will you try both the doors, the window, the dresser and inside that drawer, and the door of the front passage? We won't touch anything till you've finished. Here are the five sets of impressions. You may find the set labeled six, too, but don't worry about them. They're known."

Fowler laughed. The sixth set of fingerprints were marked R.A.R. – Inspector Ringwood's own initials. He set to work.

Richard went out into the yard, taking Miss Frewin with him. She was to look for Minoan antiquities, hydrochloric acid containers and capsules, and copper wire (for the knife that stabbed Janet Coltman had a homemade hilt of copper wire). It was like her to begin work on the dustbins, and continue, though Richard tried to displace her at the job of picking over their unappetizing contents by hand. Feeling a beast, he got to work on the packing cases. One contained elementary carpentering tools, another onions, another miscellaneous ironmongery, another tinned soup. Some were empty. He unwound from the fig tree the straw and sacking that swathed its trunk and searched the tree. Nothing was hidden there. Sergeant Frewin looked up and with an "Excuse me" shook out the sack before Richard replaced it. Nothing fell out except a few balls of rabbit dung. He went over to the hutches. The occupant of the first, an old buck rabbit, bit him when he opened the door. He swore and became aware of Mikhailopoulos watching him.

"Here, hold this, will you?" he said, handing the creature over by the ears. Mikhailopoulos took it casually, tucked it under his arm, and asked if he could help.

"Yes, please. Will you take all these rabbits out of their hutches? I want to look inside."

"But where I put them? Not together, that makes fight or too many baby." Mikhailopoulos's intelligent eyes ranged over the fig tree, the basket chair, the dustbins, and the packing cases. "Ah! I know, sir. You leave it to me."

In no time he had arranged a system. Each hutchful was transferred to a separate packing case and kept there by putting another on top. The last hutch contained a doe and her young and they went into the last empty packing case. There was no other to act as a lid, but Mikhailopoulos resourcefully supplied one by sitting on it. Richard had watched him and made quite sure he had not taken anything but rabbits out of the hutches. But he found nothing inside them. He helped put back the rabbits.

"Which were the ones that got out on Monday?" he asked. "What, the young ones? Why? Did someone leave the door open?"

"No. They break it. Bad door, old wood. But after, I mend him."

It was true, there was a new door, closed by a simple but ingenious wooden latch.

"That's very neat," said Richard. "I say, Sergeant Frewin, come and look at this. Isn't it a clever repair job?"

"The whole thing looks as if it'd last forever," she agreed. "I don't know where you get these lovely packing cases. Most of them are so flimsy nowadays."

"Listen, Madame. I get you some real Cretan wine of Archanes, it come in a box like this, box is free. Special wine, special price for police-girl, yes?"

She refused quite kindly and went back to the dustbin. Richard helped her finish. Then he climbed up on a pile of packing cases to examine the top of the wall. It had fresh scratches on it. Mikhailopoulos steadied the boxes and watched with passionate interest. Richard, sitting astride the wall, pulled out of his pocket a thing like a big meat-hook with a knotted rope fixed to it. He had found it in the back alley when he crept back in the early hours of this morning, and now he was trying it out. It worked. The hook held to the top of the wall and the knots made it easy to slide down the rope. He did so, and turned to meet the indignant eyes of Mikhailopoulos.

"So …!" he shouted, fumbling at his waist, "it was you! It was you. What for you come creeping in? What for you don't trust me? I'm nice, no? I show you all my house, I don't hide nothing, I don't do no politic …"

Richard explained.

"This isn't mine. I found it in the alley outside. I also notice you've been putting wire netting over your kitchen window. Why didn't you tell me you had a burglary last night?" His tone was sharp.

Mikhailopoulos shrugged fatalistically. "What's the good? I don't want to make you trouble. I don't lose nothing. I see he won't get in again. I never have no burglary here before. But I tell you. Sure I tell you. Listen. I was asleep. Then I wake up. There is a noise in the kitchen. Quick, quick, I am on the stairs. I see the burglary rushing out of the kitchen, rushing out of the front door. I rush too. I run after him down the street. But he's damn quick. And I'm not dressed, too. So I come back to see what the burglary take. But my God! He ain't take nothing. Only, he break my *kithara*, which is of my father's father, very beautiful, but I think I can mend him. O.K. I say. Not too bad. But then I see the window is open. I never open him. I rush out, there is another burglary in the tree there. But he goes off damn quick. I nearly catch him, too … But why …?" He frowned in thought. Then his face cleared. "Ah! I understand. Listen, sir! He come in with the rope, yes. But he drop it so he can't go back. *So*, he have to use tree. Sure thing. Too bad he find the tree there. Maybe I better cut him down."

"You say there were *two* burglars – one at the back and one at the front. How did the one at the front get in? It's a Yale lock, isn't it?"

"If he's clever, maybe he work it some way. Or … No! I understand. Listen, sir, the two burglaries, they both come in by the kitchen window. Then they open the door at the front to run away quick if I come. Sure."

"What d'you think they were after? What were they looking for?"

Mikhailopoulos shrugged. "Money, perhaps? Electric machine? Linen? My house very nice, plenty for a poor man to steal. But I stop him too quick. Ahh! I wish I catch that guy in the tree. He's a bad thief, sure, very quick, very quiet … The police pay money, maybe, to catch a clever guy like him."

"Not much money," said Richard, thinking of his salary. "Where's the key of the front door?"

"Somewhere around in the kitchen."

"Well, show it to the man in there when he's finished. But don't touch it. We'll be going upstairs now."

On his way through, Richard inspected the rough brickwork that supported the sink. Yes, there were the traces of mud that had rubbed off the first man's canvas shoes when he slid down last night. A little of the same mud had been left in Richard's fingernails when he had grabbed at the man's feet later, and he had saved it. But this was an easier sample to work with. He scraped some off into an envelope. Then he and Sergeant Frewin went through the dresser drawers and cupboards. The third drawer, which the man last night had searched in, contained assorted kitchen utensils – eggbeaters, spoons, cutlery, and so on. Sergeant Frewin remarked that they seemed to be rather short of knives. The cupboard was well stocked with groceries, many of them exotic, but they found no hydrochloric acid or capsules of any kind. There was more butter and eggs than they had seen for years in the larder, and three live lobsters in the downstairs lavatory, but otherwise nothing of interest. They went upstairs.

Besides the bedroom there was a sitting room. The brown easy chairs were well worn but the room somehow did not feel lived in. There was also a bathroom. On the bathroom shelf there was an amazing array of bath salts, talcum powder, brilliantine, and other masculine cosmetics, mostly made in England, but no drugs apart from a bottle of quinine tablets. In the bedroom they gasped at the extent of Mikhailopoulos's wardrobe. He had thirteen good suits, a drawerful each of ties and socks, and quantities of shirts and pajamas. On the bed, wrapped in a silk scarf, lay the broken guitar. There was nothing hidden under the pillow or mattress. Mikhailopoulos had removed whatever he put there last night. On the basin the soap was wet, so Mikhailopoulos must have had a morning wash. A bottle of hair oil with a Greek label on it gave out, even corked, the strong scent of which his hair and whiskers had smelt last night. Under the bed was a well-worn pair of Macedonian slippers with turned-up toes. Richard left Sergeant Frewin to finish in the bedroom and looked through the papers in the sitting room. Mikhailopoulos was roaring at his subordinates below. The morning was running on.

The papers were simple and orderly, stored in boxes. Receipted bills were in one, outstanding bills in another. A tin box contained personal papers – passport, naturalization, permits, and licences, as well as the stubs of old checkbooks for ten years back, all perfectly in order. There was no money, but Richard already knew that whatever was not locked in the till or paid into the bank was kept in Mikhailopoulos's own pockets. A pile of old Cretan newspapers, well thumbed, was the only reading matter; and a handsome wireless set (if wireless sets can ever be called handsome) stood on the table. Richard began to think that

Mikhailopoulos had been telling the truth when he said that there was nothing bad in his house. And yet … Worrall *had* been overcome by a quick-acting poison while lunching there, and Janet Coltman stabbed while coming away three days later.

"Well?" he said, rejoining Sergeant Frewin, "it all seems most desperately respectable, doesn't it?"

"Yes. I wouldn't have expected him to be so civilized, would you?"

"Every Greek's a dandy so far as he can afford to be. The show's the thing. Have you drawn a blank too?"

"Not quite, Inspector Ringwood. I wonder if *this* can be what you are looking for? It was inside the guitar."

It was a Minoan seal-ring of agate. On it was carved the Great Goddess, flanked by a pair of strange heraldic animals. It was a lovely thing and, if genuine, was worth well over a thousand pounds – or so Macdonald had said of a similar one yesterday.

"I didn't handle the guitar, Inspector," continued the policewoman conscientiously, "except with a hanky. The ring shook out quite easily."

"Sergeant Frewin, you're a wonder. In fact, you've probably saved the case. What on earth made you look there, of all unlikely places?"

"Oh, my sister once lost her engagement ring, and it turned up in her ukulele. Should I take this down to be fingerprinted, Inspector? Or do you want Sergeant Fowler up here?"

"No, I don't think he need bother. Nobody got up on to this floor last night. But I must go and take statements from the boss and the waiter, and then I'm due to see Mr. Macdonald at the museum. I wonder if you'd mind dropping a couple of notes for me at the Yard?"

FROM RICHARD RINGWOOD'S PERSONAL AND PRIVATE NOTEBOOK

Friday, May 8th. Fingerprints at the Minos.

Outer Kitchen Door … Self, Mikhailopoulos, Georgios, Maureen, Shirley.

Kitchen Window … Mik. superimposed on gloved prints.

Inner Kitchen Door … Mik. and staff as above.

Dresser … Ditto, and gloved prints (gloves dirty).

Street Door at end of passage.… Mik. and Georgios. Unidentified print on outside.

Key … Surface won't take prints.

Guitar … Mik. and Georgios. (Mik. says G. might have played it but wasn't allowed. Kept in scarf when not being played. G. admits to taking it out once and looking at it – can't remember when. Fowler says fingerprints would last a long time on that surface.) Ring could have been inserted without handling wooden part – just feel along strings for hole by bridge.

Ring ... Won't take prints.

Scaling-hook ... (Really a large meathook.) No prints.

Analysis of mud from first man's shoes. "Pale type of rab soil (Wales? Cornwall?). Mixed with another substance which so far defies analysis." I must try to make them a synthetic sample and see if they can tell the difference. Ask J.C.

Bouillabaisse. Mussels, octopus, sea-snails, Dublin Bay prawns, halibut. Flavor wonderful, texture rubbery. Worrall bolted his food and would certainly have swallowed a lot of this stuff whole. Was capsule disguised as *fruit de mer?* The bouillabaisse was actually on the table when J.C. and W. were finishing their sherry, and when I.S. passed table and knocked over olives. Could he have slipped in capsule then? Or did waiter act for him? If so, capsule could also have been put inside a raisin in the sweet. Fits better for timing unless the capsule was very thick and took extra long to dissolve.

Reactions to statement Worrall was murdered. Waiter frightened to gibbering-point. Mik. seems put on mettle, full of suggestions, says it "make him trouble" in business, not horrified however. I suppose he's seen a lot of this kind of thing at home when young. Steady as a rock but keeps trying to do my job for me. Haven't tried news on anyone else yet.

Macdonald on the antiques. In Zoe's parcel: pottery genuine but valueless. Rings he thinks are fakes, all but one which might be genuine but if so several better specimens of the type have been found. Very good faking indeed. Won't quite commit himself. Wants to ask J.C.

Ring in the guitar possibly a v.g. fake. If not, worth about £1,000.

He hasn't seen the "Nausicaa Ring" – i.e. the one Worrall found(?) on Pontikonisi. If genuine a really fine example, might fetch any price.

Symptoms of Gastric Ulcer. Violent pain about an hour after meals, also at night. Pain relieved by food, by vomiting, and by taking alkalis such as magnesia. (Ask J.C.) A doctor prodding the patient would find great tenderness in a localized spot about the size of a shilling in the pit of the stomach.

If the ulcer perforates, it causes peritonitis. Patient usually operated on at once. If not, agony may last for days. If patient dies at once, it must be shock or heart.

Worrall fulfils all these conditions. Could old McK. be wrong? Did he have real ulcer before? Caused perhaps by his being half-poisoned (unsuccessful first attempt) on Pontikonisi. If so, everyone but members of expedition are automatically exonerated.

Hydrochloric acid easily obtainable in powder form for getting stains out of linen. Capsule could be homemade with leaf gelatine.

Must Do. See "ironmonger's assistant". Contact Corfu and Crete, also ring up Patrick at British School at Athens. Minos laundry. Bank. Get Janet to come clean about the "Nausicaa Ring". Could perhaps use it as method of grilling Shrubsole? For some reason it gets them both on the raw. But I must wait till Janet's better. Meanwhile, find out more about faking – where, how, by whom. Probably the field is limited, as few people combine the necessary archaeological knowledge with the training required by a skilled engraver.

TABLE OF THOSE SUSPECTED OF
THE MURDER OF WORRALL

Mikhailopoulos

Motive. None that I can see, though he admits having disliked Worrall. Plenty of motives *against* his being the murderer. (*a*) He had no personal relations with Worrall, who only started using the Minos this month. (*b*) If a restaurateur poisons people, it's bound to be bad for business. Mikhailopoulos "don't want no trouble." (*c*) If Worrall's pains, diagnosed as ulcer, were really the results of an unsuccessful attempt to poison him at Corfu, Mikhailopoulos is out – he's been in England for the last twenty years. (*d*) He's a good chap (if uncivilized) and has strong ideas about the sacredness of hospitality, honor, etc. (This last point isn't evidence but I think it's true all the same.)

Opportunity. None at Corfu. Obviously excellent in the Minos. If he did it, could he have been bought or blackmailed by one of the others?

Georgios

Motive. He wouldn't gain by the will. But he may have feared exposure if Worrall had found out that he was selling faked Minoan antiquities, or that he was having an affair with Zoe ap Ifor. In character he is weak type. He wouldn't be in it on his own, I think, but as the tool of somebody else – either Zoe (see above) or possibly Shrubsole.

Opportunity. As for Mikhailopoulos.

Zoe ap Ifor

Motive. Fear of exposure for faking or adultery; for though she is obviously all in favor of adultery, it would nevertheless suit her book to stay married to ap Ifor, who is idiotically trustful, completely under her thumb, and much richer than anyone else that she's likely to nab permanently. As for the faking, she's clearly deeply involved.

Character. A human volcano. (N.B. Strong-minded and intelligent whores v. rare.) Could have planned murder for prudential motives already suggested. But she is equally capable of doing it for revenge (if Worrall had injured her first) or in order to get Georgios more completely into her power (he seems to be making feeble attempts to escape) by holding the murder over him as a threat. I'm sure that nothing would stop Zoe from getting anything she wants badly. She really is a corker in her own line. What, if any, were her relations with Worrall, who seems to have been at least *moyen sensuel?*

Opportunity. Shared hotel at Corfu with Worrall. Wasn't in the Minos but would have used Georgios as a proxy.

Shrubsole

(My favorite, despite colorful foreign competition.)

Motive. He had a hysterical dislike of Worrall, but no hope of any employment in his own line other than that provided by his position under Worrall. Would certainly benefit by the will, as he was sure to be reelected by the committee either as leader at £1,200 per annum, or (if Janet got the first place) as first assistant at £800 – both an improvement on his present income, and he is wretchedly poor. Also greater security of tenure. He must long to do the work he likes in comfort, and without the constant humiliation (and possibly threat, see below) of Worrall over him.

In character, he is a really clever and determined man, with a fanatical hatred of rich men and of bogus archaeologists. Both *bêtes noires* were typified in Worrall. He quarreled with Janet when she supported Worrall. These quarrels interest me, because both Janet and Shrubsole are being cagey about them. I wonder if Janet knows something about him that might point to him as the murderer? It could be something that happened out there – some previous attempt on Worrall's life – or she may have some reason, not certain enough for her to feel it her duty to reveal it to me as yet, for thinking that he poisoned Worrall in the Minos. Or possibly she suspects him of some other kind of dirty business. Did he (for instance) obtain and "plant" the Nausicaa Ring in the trench for Worrall to find, in order to trap Worrall into hailing it as a great discovery and then being discredited when it was shown up as a fake? And if so, does Janet know? And did he get the fake ring from Zoe and Co., or is he really the brain behind the whole faking racket? I'd have said he had too much archaeological conscience, but there might be a certain cynical pleasure in showing how gullible his more successful colleagues were – fooling them to the top of their bent.

He's certainly as nervous as hell now. Wish I understood him better. I dislike him extremely and feel guilty at doing so because I pity him as well. All this stops me from thinking as clearly as I should.

Opportunity. Shared table at Corfu. Could have dropped the capsule into Worrall's bouillabaisse this week while passing his table (he's very neat with his fingers) or alternatively, bribed or blackmailed Georgios or Mikhailopoulos to do the job for him. He'd be more likely, on the face of it, to have a hold over Georgios.

Note. He refused to rally round Worrall in his death agony, in fact he got drunk and very exhilarated. I'd say that this behavior wasn't natural to Shrubsole at any time (he seems a puritanical type) and surely, at that particular moment, it was worse than heartless.

Ap Ifor

Motive. Not discernible. The will means less to him, because he's a rich man. Had he any cause to suspect Worrall of cuckolding him? He has two rather fishy lines of conversation. (*a*) "Ancient magic," etc. (*b*) He claims to have liked Worrall and admired his work. (Still, bad as that is, it's hardly an excuse to hang the fellow.) Lord, he is a bogus man!

Opportunity. At Corfu, good. At Minos, improbable. He wasn't seen, and alleges that at the time he was on his way to lecture at Highgate, and the school says that he arrived punctually and embarrassed them all very much by his views. If he poisoned Worrall, he did so by bribing or blackmailing the waiter or proprietor. Bah! This bores me.

Janet Coltman

Motive. Seems nonexistent in view of her well-known devotion to Worrall. But (*a*) Hell hath no fury like a woman scorned – and he was very rude to her. I know that she gives the impression of a woman who has never been in love or is likely to be – but couldn't this very sexlessness of hers be a sign of sexual abnormality? Couldn't she have sublimated (or distorted) her normal sexual feelings in such a way that they were gratified unconsciously by her purely intellectual relationships with men? I'd better talk to a psychologist about this. Though I never quite trust them. (*b*) Could she have a motive for killing Worrall connected with the Nausicaa Ring? Why did she refuse to do further tests on it when Shrubsole demanded them? Did she really know it was a fake? If so, whom was she shielding? Worrall, or Shrubsole? She quarreled with them both. (*c*) She was the person most likely to benefit by the will. She was the likeliest candidate for the leadership which would give her a great increase both in income and in prestige. And *she helped Worrall to draft it* during the voyage home, according to the solicitor, who admired her competence. Did she persuade Worrall to put in the clause warning off the surgeons? A case could be made out against her on these lines, as that clause protects the poisoner from being found out by the doctors. N.B. She's very, very intelligent.

Opportunity. Good in the Minos – she was sitting at his table. Not so good at

Corfu, because she wasn't staying in the hotel with the others. But we don't *know* that the illness that brought him home wasn't a perfectly natural one.

I find it hard, nevertheless, to suspect Janet seriously, despite all this. After all, quite apart from what I think of her character, she *was* stabbed, and it does look as if the stabbing was inspired by her letter to *The Times* in Worrall's defense.

SUSPECTS IN THE ATTEMPTED MURDER OF JANET COLTMAN

Mikhailopoulos

Motive. None, unless she killed Worrall and he was Homerically avenging his guest. Or someone paid him to kill her. *Friget!* No motive really.

Opportunity. Possible, when he ran after her with her briefcase, but he'd have to run pretty fast and be in good training to manage that and his (checked) shopping in ten minutes. I wouldn't expect a stout Soho restaurateur of middle age to have the requisite turn of speed.

Georgios

Motive. None, unless you say he was doing it for someone else.

Opportunity. Better. He had the whole afternoon off, is, I should say, very quick on his feet, and left the restaurant ten minutes after Janet, which tallies all right with her having reached Hopkins Street, if she was going at a slow pace, or if he really left a little earlier than he said.

Zoe

Motive. Did Janet reveal, purposely or unintentionally, in her letter to *The Times* that she knew something dangerous to Zoe?

Opportunity. She is alibied only by her husband, who says she answered his telephone call at 3:30 that afternoon. She is strong and has long, though not broad, hands.

Iorweth

Motive, if any, something like that suggested for Zoe. Or acted as her tool. She gives him his only alibi, as he does her. Matrimony (even theirs) invalidates witness.

Shrubsole

Motive. To remove Janet. Already his most serious rival for the now vacant post of leadership of the expedition, having already shown herself an intractable (or insufficiently gullible) colleague, she has now provoked him past endurance by writing that letter to *The Times*, which in some secret, allusive way, shows him that she knows of his guilt in killing Worrall, or planting fakes, or both.

Opportunity. Went to elocutionist (checked by telephone) but was ten minutes late. Is the only person in the case who certainly has the skill and the tools to have made that knife. Had copper wire in his pocket, too.

The First "Burglar" Last Night.

I think that the first man who entered when I was watching in the Minos last night was Shrubsole, for the following reasons:

(1) That huge meathook he used to get over the wall with looked as if it had come straight from an ironmonger's. Shrubsole could have got it easily from his father.

(2) The hook-and-rope method of scaling walls is familiar to classical scholars from the ancient accounts of sieges – *I* thought of it too, at once. But it isn't generally known about nowadays. I've never seen it used.

(3) The man's whole behavior showed a determination, intelligence, and self-command that I wouldn't expect to find in the others – e.g. wearing gloves and sand-shoes, making himself wait in silence for so long before entering, reconnoitering the room before starting what he came for, etc.

(4) If, as I think, this first man took a knife out of the dresser drawer, it wasn't Georgios. Georgios could easily have done it in daylight without arousing the least suspicion. Though I can't think what on earth Shrubsole wanted that particular knife for – a complicated plan to attack Janet again later and have the knife identified as M's, so as to put him under suspicion? Also, why on earth did he stay and fight the second man? I'd have expected him to clear out as quickly and quietly as possible.

Unnecessary speculations, I hope. I've got a specimen of the very unusual mud from the First Burglar's shoes. I hope shortly to find a shoe encrusted with the same mud, and then I'll be sure. I think the mud, which puzzles the analysts, consists of dust from Pontikonisi stuck together with honey from Iorweth's "propitiatory libation," which Shrubsole, as we know, stepped into, to his great annoyance.

The Second Burglar

Had a latchkey to the door of the front passage. Moved soundlessly. Planted the ring in the guitar. Whispered in Greek. Ran like a hare. This fits Georgios, or possibly Zoe. Their object would be to draw suspicion on Mikhailopoulos by making me think he sold fakes (if the ring *is* a fake.) Or anyhow to involve him and save themselves. The ring is uncatalogued and if genuine would sell for over £1,000, which makes it unlikely in any case that a man like M. would have been in possession of it honestly. But now it isn't just *odd* for a member of Worrall's entourage to possess such things; it's downright incriminating. True, when Zoe and Georgios came out into the lobby of her flat yesterday afternoon and found the things gone off the floor, they didn't know that it was I who had taken them. It might have been Iorweth, or Shrubsole. But whoever *had* taken them knew their secret. It must have given them a nasty jolt. So they made haste to unload the one remaining seal on to Mikhailopoulos, to whom they owed a bad turn for his treatment of them yesterday when he turned Zoe away and abused Georgios.

Which of them was it? Her voice is contralto and his is tenor – the whispers last night might have been either of them. But Georgios is the likelier. Zoe would have been missed by her husband (or is he in the faking racket too?). The landlady didn't hear Georgios go out or return; but he has his own key, started late, and can move like a shadow; also he had good opportunity to get hold of the key to the passage door, which Mikhailopoulos seems to leave about his kitchen in the most casual way.

If Janet is still being regarded by one of the party as an unexploded bomb full of damaging knowledge or curiosity, they may make another attempt on her life even now. She'll be out of hospital the day after tomorrow, and coming to stay with us. How far am I justified, even with police protection, in using her as bait?

Ah! cruel choice! That it should come to this!
We miss the catch, or jeopardize the Miss.

Addition, in Clare's writing.

Go halves with me. While you contrive the hit
The Miss shall occupy my humbler wit.

Chapter 11

AT the museum, while Jack Macdonald, the Assistant Keeper, was giving his opinion on the various rings and sherds Richard had brought him, the detective was studying his personality. Appearance as well as name betrayed his Scottish origins; he had that look of hardy anxious integrity. Africa, the land of his birth, had softened the dourness and ripened the pale northern coloring. An easy, handsome, likable man. People would trust him. So Richard tried to draw him on to talk about the members of the expedition – Worrall, Shrubsole, Janet Coltman, the ap Ifors. At first he simply gave conventional, noncommittal answers; but when Richard, after a particularly direct question, said:

"Can't you give me an opinion? I thought Shrubsole was a friend of yours?"

He replied, flushing a little, "Yes, he is. But honestly, I don't see why that makes me more liable to discuss him with strangers, do you?" A smile softened the blunt words, but they reduced Richard to momentary silence.

"Not," continued Macdonald, "that Ian could conceivably have anything to do with fakes. But look, the police don't usually take any interest in fakes anyhow. *Caveat emptor*, it's the mug's fault for being had; unless it's a question of genuine stuff being stolen and fakes left in place of it. It isn't that this time, I know. There's been nothing exactly like these rings in any of the published collections. What *are* you after?"

"Well, there again," Richard smiled, "there's a kind of honor even among policemen. We don't broadcast our suspicions. But I can tell you a bit what I'm after. I'm after the murderer of Alban Worrall. Also the would-be murderer of Janet Coltman."

Macdonald's sunny geniality was gone. He looked as Scottish and uncompromising as the Day of Judgment.

"I'd heard that Miss Coltman was knocked down in Soho. But – Worrall murdered? Are you sure of your facts?"

Goodness, thought Richard. If I wasn't I shouldn't care to have that eye on me.

"Of course I am. Here's the report of the post mortem. You were there yourself when the poison began to take effect."

"*I* ...! Yes, I see." He looked ashamed. "I left it to the Minos people to cope with, I'm afraid. Could I have saved him?"

"No, I don't think you could. But listen. First he's killed, then Miss Coltman's stabbed. Surely there's a connection there?"

"Looks like it, certainly."

"And now we find certain people who knew them both passing round these fakes here. There were also some people who thought the Nausicaa Ring affair suspicious. Isn't that likely to tie up too? Or anyhow, oughtn't we to make sure if it does or not?"

"I think – yes."

"Well, that's where you come in. We – the police – can't tell a fake from a genuine Minoan antique. We don't know a sound archaeologist from one who is incompetent or plain dishonest. And as for the personal setup – well, obviously we can't take it that any members of Worrall's lot are disinterested, and anyhow the whole thing is colored for them by their likes and dislikes. We need an objective view, and so far you're the only person I've come across who could give me one."

Macdonald paused. He was thinking seriously. Then he said:

"I'm prepared to give you full information about the archaeological side. The country employs me for that purpose as it employs you for your job. But I'm not just sure about the other. You're asking me, I take it, to repeat any personal confidences I may have heard from these people or about them? I don't altogether like that."

"Of course you don't. Nor do I: it seems like disloyalty. But surely you'd agree that the most important kinds of loyalty override private loyalties to individual persons?"

"H'm! I don't know that I do. When people start thinking like that, you get things like the Spanish Inquisition. And the seventeenth-century witch hunts. And the color wars in my own country today. Betraying your neighbor for the sake of your principles."

"I don't agree. Those things *weren't* based on the most important kind of loyalties. They were based on fear and herd instinct – mostly fear, which always breeds persecution."

"And you? What's *your* non-personal loyalty?"

"Well, truth, I suppose. Truth about the facts so that no one is unjustly accused. And truth *in* society. I mean, human society'd be a sham if it didn't enforce its own laws. We *must* catch our murderers, or we might as well all go off and live separately in caves and chuck rocks at strangers. I sometimes think," added Richard with a deprecating sidelong grin, "that that might be the easiest arrangement."

"You wouldn't, not if you knew any prehistory."

They laughed and suddenly liked each other.

"All right," Macdonald said, making up his mind. "You've convinced me. I'll answer any questions you like to ask. Though anything I can tell you will be pure anticlimax, I'm afraid, after making all this fuss. But you'll understand it was the *principle* I was defending; I'm ready to yield on the application to individual persons."

"No one like the Scots for principles" – Richard passed over the logical *volte-face*. "Well, I'll just take you through my list of characters, shall I?"

Macdonald had known Worrall slightly but never actually worked with him, he said. As an original archaeologist Worrall was not perhaps quite in the first flight, but his money and enterprise had done great service to Minoan studies, and distinguished scholars had served on his digs. For instance, Miss Coltman would never have been able to do so much valuable fieldwork if Worrall had not made it possible – lack of funds would have forced her into teaching or a museum job long ago. She had been with Worrall a long time. The others came and went. He believed some of them had found Worrall a little difficult to work with. Archaeologists were a pretty temperamental lot.

What did they dislike in Worrall? asked Richard. Was he bogus? Exigeant? Unwilling to give his colleagues their due share of the credit? Macdonald looked shocked at such specific denigration of the dead, but did not altogether rebut it. Still, he added stoutly, but for Worrall certain sites could never have been excavated.

"What d'you mean, never?"

"Well, Hosios Markos, for instance, and Zero. There's a monastery built over one and a village over the other. Worrall gave them splendid new buildings to compensate for undermining the old ones. In fact, Zero's practically a model village now, instead of a collection of unsanitary hovels. And people have long memories in Crete, for kindnesses and the reverse. They're still trying to make up their minds whether they love the memory of Arthur Evans for discovering their ancient treasures, or hate him for carrying some off and throwing others into the harbor in a rage because they put on a new export duty. You know, Worrall doesn't understand them as Evans did – and he hasn't (I mean hadn't) a tithe of Evans's qualities of genuine greatness – but they *do* know where they are with him. He's always behaved very correctly. Taken good advice and so on."

"The Cretans like him?"

"As I say, they expect well of him. They're prepared to do deals. You know he rebuilt the museum at Herakleion last time it was knocked down by an earthquake? Well, they made a special exception for him. They invited him on to the staff. A foreigner. That's practically unheard-of."

"H'm. I see. Well, now we come to Janet Coltman."

Unqualified approval. Accurate, industrious, generous with help, modest in disclaiming credit – all the scholarly virtues, in fact.

"Why, only last week I happened to show her rather an unusual seal that reminded me of another I couldn't place. You understand, I thought she might just happen to remember. Well, she insisted on going right through the *Palace of Minos* – a colossal book in umpteen volumes – just to make sure her guess was right. (It was, of course.) She wouldn't hear of me doing it. Interrupted her own work too."

"She a friend of yours?"

"No, not really. I never seem to see her outside the museum. But that's typical, you see. She wasn't going to all that trouble for *me*. It was for Minoan studies. I don't know anything about her private life. Don't expect she's got one really. And yet she seems quite happy. Or at least she did till recently."

"Ah! Shrubsole's told you about their quarrels?"

"No, he hasn't. I've noticed them standing about in corners whispering in a tense sort of way, though. Nobody has any privacy here unless they're V.I.P.s. So that was it! What were they quarrelling about?"

"They won't tell me. Miss Coltman had a quarrel with Sir Alban, too, didn't she? In the Minos?"

"I was there," said Macdonald again formidable. "That wasn't a quarrel, it was an outrage. She didn't say a word. She just sat there getting whiter and whiter while Worrall abused her in the most filthy way I've ever heard. Ian and I were just going to throw him out when she got up and left. Actually, that's why we weren't awfully keen on holding his hand when he was taken ill later."

"Why, what did he say?"

"What didn't he say? At the top of his voice, too. It was bad enough when he was attacking her as a scholar – cocksure, inexperienced, ungrateful, battening on other people's training, arrogant – oh, fantastic accusations. But then he went on to pull her to pieces as a woman – ugly, unnatural, frustrated, do anything to get a man, no man'd look at her. … That's where she went out."

"I wonder you let him get so far."

"I wouldn't have. But I was with Ian, and of course Ian depends completely on this job with Worrall. Did, I should say. Lord knows what he'll do now. I wonder if the old man's left money to carry on the work."

"Surely he'd get another job? I thought he was supposed to be extra good at his stuff."

"He is, very good indeed. But he was at Athens for a time, you know, and I'm afraid they found him a bit of a square peg, even there … There aren't many field jobs, you know. It's not Ian's fault, really. He's had a fairly tough time."

"How?"

"Well, his father's a working man. No harm in that, but he's also a rabid socialist. He brought Ian up as a fellow traveller. Well, when Ian was at Wadham, he naturally thought he ought to do a bit of political propaganda there. Reeducation classes. Perhaps he wasn't very clever at it. Anyhow, he got pretty badly persecuted, poor chap – you know, had his room smashed up, and notices and red paint and things all over his doors and windows. He was de-bagged, too. He minded that more than anything. Funny, some people do. Well, ever since then he's been awfully bitter about what he calls public school types. He doesn't count me because my school was in South Africa; also I don't take the conventional line about the color question. It's a pity about Ian, though. He ought to do well, and he puts people's backs up."

"He makes no secret of having disliked Worrall, certainly. And I gather he didn't hit it off with ap Ifor, either."

"Well, Beavor's got a very different type of mind, you know. In justice, I must say that he's a competent architect and a first-class photographer and draftsman. But he holds rather … unsupported theories. I don't wonder Ian lost patience a bit, cooped up with him."

"How about his wife? She made a bit of trouble, I gather. Having seen her, I don't wonder, really."

"Yes, I remember Ian boiling over a bit about her. She would keep talking to the workmen, apparently. And her husband refused to speak to her about it. I suppose in a way it was natural. I mean, she must have felt more at home with them."

"Did she make any passes at Ian?" Again both men laughed.

"I shouldn't think so. It's a funny thing," he added reflectively, "I've walked around London a lot with Ian, one way and another. And you know how one's always getting accosted by women. Well, it's never once happened to me when I've been with him. I suppose they must have some sort of sixth sense that makes them realize he's frightfully pure-minded, or something."

Richard thought it was unlikely. Poor Shrubsole, the dice had indeed been loaded against him. He reverted from persons to objects.

"Now about these seals I brought you – three gold rings and an amethyst yesterday, and this agate today. You say you're still not certain if they're genuine ones or very good fakes, and you want a bit more time to make up your mind. Well, that's all right, mustn't hurry you, of course. But from what you've said already, I suspect that the owner might have had good reason to hope that he could *sell* them as genuine, whether they really are or not. If so, what price could he have got for them?"

"Depends who he was selling them to."

"Yes, yes! But can't you make a rough guess?"

"Well," replied Macdonald with maddening deliberation, "you'll understand that I've only had experience of the *official* purchase and sale of objects. Private collectors' prices might be different according to the personal factors involved. I daresay that Sir Alban, for instance, if he had bought such things, would have been willing to pay a higher price than the museum, in present circumstances."

"Mm!" Richard forced himself not to be impatient. "Have you heard a price quoted for rings like this?"

"Large seals of the best period, that is, Late Minoan I. Well, they're pretty valuable, if they're good examples, that is, and not defaced in any way. I'd say a good specimen might fetch between two and three thousand."

"What? Two to three thousand *pounds?*"

"That's my guess. I wouldn't like to say how far, or in what direction, the price might fluctuate if it were paid in dollars, though. Some Americans are getting things cheap now because Europe needs dollars so badly. Others, again, are still under the Duveen spell, and think that good works of art must be expensive, or they can't be good."

"I see. But putting your estimate at its lowest, that is, two thousand, the contents of the parcel might fetch – let's see, three gold rings makes six thousand. … Good Lord, and what would the Nausicaa Ring be worth if it's genuine?"

"I haven't seen it. But if it's really genuine and undefaced, and vouched for by the dig, it has an enormous extra value because of the historical interest. It'll have made Worrall's name – given the whole dig colossal prestige. Of course it's legally the property of the Greek government and I don't suppose they'd dream of selling it, though I hope they might let us have it on loan. You can't talk about market values with a thing like that."

"What about if it turned out a fake? What happens to fakes?"

"I'm afraid we've got plenty of those in my department already," said Macdonald dryly. "Yes, they *are* a problem. We'll have to do something about them one day. We don't exhibit them, of course. They get put away, you know, with the electrotypes and things ..."

"You don't sell them?"

"Good gracious, no! It would be dishonest. Besides, they might turn out to be genuine after all."

"Are they kept locked up, like the real things?"

"Well ... theoretically I suppose everything is, but people working in the museum can take them along to their rooms, and I'm sorry to say that they aren't always as careful as they might be about minor objects. Such things do get lost sometimes, even the valuable ones. But they usually turn up again."

"So that if the Nausicaa Ring turned out to be a fake, nobody would worry much if it got lost?"

"I didn't say that. Of course all reasonable and due care would be taken."

Richard was not convinced, and his mind flew to the question whether anyone had intended to "lose" the Nausicaa Ring later on, and if so, for what reason. But he did not want to talk any more about it to Macdonald, so he said:

"Well, counting the Nausicaa Ring out, we've still got the three gold ones and the amethyst from the parcel I brought you yesterday, and this agate I've found today. The gold ones, if genuine, are worth more than six thousand all told. What about the other two?"

"The amethyst is a common type. I doubt if it would fetch much more than five to seven hundred. But the agate is interesting stylistically. I can only recall one other that's like it so far. Personally, I'd be willing to give quite as much for that as for any of the three gold ones."

"Good Lord! It adds up to a tidy sum, doesn't it? Upwards of eight thousand five hundred pounds worth of stuff, just knocking about in your pocket in a matchbox!"

"Only if it's genuine." Macdonald did not seem to be impressed.

"Still, I wish you wouldn't be so, er ... For Heaven's sake, go and lock the damn things up before they drop down a drain or something, there's a good chap! After all, I suppose I'm responsible for them at this stage."

* * *

Richard walked into the Greco-Roman galleries and halted before a caseful of Minoan seals, deep in thought. He had not realized until now how much money could be made out of them; not hundreds, but thousands. Even rich men, like ap Ifor or Worrall, would have found it worth their while; even conscientious scholars, like Janet or Shrubsole, might have been tempted. Yes – but tempted to the point of murder? Perhaps even that. For exposure did not only mean a total loss of reputation. It also meant not being able to sell your remaining stock. And the five seals alone, the ones now in Richard's hands, would have sold for close on ten thousand pounds. Which member of the expedition had an equal interest in money and reputation? Surely Shrubsole, who was poor, unpopular, and had only got his present job on his reputation for being a sound scholar.

Again, who was likeliest to have put the agate seal in the guitar? A thing that might have sold for over a thousand pounds. The owner must have been seriously frightened before he decided to part with it. Which of the people concerned was frightened enough for that?

Zoe and Georgios had only had one fright so far – the loss of their parcel yesterday. But Shrubsole had already been in a nervous state at Corfu. He had exhibited symptoms of horrible, hysterical relief when Worrall was dying. He had shown signs of strain and alarm when he heard that Janet was stabbed but not yet dead. He had appeared even more frightened when he saw the contents of Zoe's parcel in Richard's possession. His midnight invasion of the Minos (Richard was practically sure that his first man was Shrubsole) had been the risky action of a desperate man.

A man driven desperate by a *series* of alarms, not just by one. If Shrubsole *had* been selling faked seals, and had been threatened with exposure (which meant the wreck of his whole career) those threats may have begun at Corfu, where a sure-footed boy had fallen over a cliff and a healthy man had been seized by sudden illness. Those two "accidents" may have been Shrubsole's first attempts to eliminate people who threatened his precarious security. But all this was mere guesswork. From his own observation Richard could construct a clearer pattern of Shrubsole's cumulative alarms since his return to London.

Worrall died and Shrubsole was hysterically relieved. But two days later, Janet's letter to *The Times* somehow gave him reason to fear her too. She was stabbed the same day, but she did not die. But she didn't expose him either. He waited.

Then danger appeared from a new quarter. The police began to show unexpected interest in Worrall's death. And they discovered that fakes were passing, and seemed inclined to link up the faking with their murder inquiries. They would very soon find out that Worrall had not died a natural death. Suppose Shrubsole had one fake left on his hands, having palmed off the others on Zoe at an earlier stage. What was he to do?

Obviously, if he could "plant" the fake on someone else, someone who also came under suspicion for murder, he would not only clear himself, but divert suspicion too. It was worth the risk of climbing into the Minos by night. Yes, Shrubsole must have put the ring into the guitar before he began his mysterious work on the dresser drawers. It was physically quite possible; he had slowly reconnoitered the whole room in the dark.

But in that case, what had the second burglar come for? The second one was a Greek, light on his feet, and dressed as a man. Probably Georgios. Well, once one had made up one's mind to accept the idea of Shrubsole selling fakes, one would also have to assume that there were agents under Shrubsole's orders – you needed a gang for such work. Zoe and Georgios were ideal material; Cretans who might have come by Minoan objects honestly, picking them up as surface finds on their native soil, or being given them by their rural uncles. They were perfectly placed, too. Not only were they Cretans, but they were constantly meeting archaeologists. Shrubsole might well have other agents besides, here or in Greece, but certainly this pair must have been working for him.

Yes, but if Zoe and Georgios were working on Shrubsole's side, why did Georgios make an entry into the Minos independently? And why the fight? That too Richard could explain from his previous criminal experience. If the police begin to take an unhealthy interest, and particularly if it is a question of murder, gangs *do* split up. The underlings turn against the ringleaders, the ringleaders try to jettison the underlings, and there is an orgy of double-crossing and mutual suspicion. Honour among thieves is a myth. If Georgios *was* a member of Shrubsole's faking gang, his presence, and Shrubsole's reaction to it, could be easily explained. Georgios had come to catch Shrubsole out and so save his own skin. Probably the idea was Zoe's. It was the sort of thing she *would* think of – simple, bold, and ruthless. A pity that such a woman should have been forced into being a mere member of a gang, thought Richard (adopting for the moment an entirely technical and unmoral view of crime). She had the temperament for really big stuff.

Had Shrubsole? Richard thought over again what Macdonald had told him of the man's character and early life – unpopular and persecuted at Oxford, ignored by women, rejected as impossible to work with by the archaeologists at Athens. Was his defensiveness, his resentful, jumpy attitude under questioning, just a symptom of his inferiority complex? Or did it mean that he really had more reason than any of the others to fear questions? He was a clever man, everybody said so. Wasn't he *too* clever to be so nervous unless he really had something to be nervous about?

Or, to approach the matter from another angle, what did Shrubsole most want in life? What was his heart's desire? According to himself, security to "get on with his pots" and not to have to worry where the money was coming from. To that one might add a general desire for success. But Richard was not sure if success, to Shrubsole, would include fame or ostentatious wealth – he had despised them too much in Worrall. Unless that bitter contempt of his was really disguised envy? Shrubsole was a complicated character, and if he had really been at the bottom of the whole business – fakes and murders too – his motives would certainly have been many-sided. Such a man would be moved at least as strongly by resentment and fanatical dislike as he would be by the desire for self-advancement.

He had told Richard – not once but many times – that he didn't know anything about Minoan seals. He was "just a pot-mender". Surely this was unconvincing. He had had an all-round archaeological training and must at some time have studied Minoan seals. Did his profession of ignorance cover a knowledge too great to be safely revealed? Did he know enough to have made the fakes himself? Macdonald, when Richard asked him, had only been able to suggest one group of persons who were likely to have acquired both the knowledge and the technical skill to carve pseudo-Minoan gems. Sir Arthur Evans, more than thirty years ago, had employed skilled workmen to make replicas of his finds. Richard had seen the replicas in museums. *If* any of Evans's craftsmen were still alive, and *if* they had become corrupted, said Macdonald. … Two "ifs" already, and even if you got over them, you would still have to establish a link between these craftsmen and the members of Worrall's expedition. It would be more plausible to think that they were being made "on the inside."

Richard stared again at the seals in the case before him. Certainly they were very beautiful, and quite unlike anything else in ancient or modern art. Here was a ring of the same type as the agate from the guitar; but the animal-headed daemons – Calves? Wild asses? – were more elongated and pop-eyed, and the Goddess, hook-nosed and balloon-breasted as usual, appeared to be standing on a piece of Brighton rock. Here was one of those young male figures who appeared by contrast so slight and pathetic; yet if you looked more attentively, his muscles stood out round and hard on thigh and torso. He was no weakling. Here again – but no, this was not he after all. The head was wrong, horrible. It was the monster, the Minotaur, the legendary offspring of the lustful queen Pasiphae and her bull. A reality as horrible underlay the legend. It was the Minos, the king, wearing his hideous priestly vestment, the bull's hide, the bull's huge cruel face whereby he put off his humanity and grace when once a year he held his human sacrifice. But you could still see the lithe waist and the round, young muscles on the thighs of the man-monster. Was Georgios such another?

Pasiphae had threatened her servant Daedalus with destruction if he would not pander to her unnatural desires, she the snaky-haired, the big-breasted, the merciless-mating spider queen. So Daedalus had made her a fake – the first fake in history – a fake cow. She got inside and the bull couldn't tell it wasn't a real one. To Ovid a joke, to Virgil a horror. To me …? Well, whenever I think of Pasiphae after this, I shall always see her with the face and body of Zoe. How do I account for that?

He started. He had been dreaming, and time was short. He must see Shrubsole. But Shrubsole was not in the museum. So much the better. It was time to have a look at him in his own place. Richard took a bus to Lewisham.

* * *

It was a long bus ride. You passed first, with lines from the poets springing in your head, by the Abbey, the Houses of Parliament, and Westminster Bridge; then, climbing imperceptibly, into London-South-of-the-River, a shabbier place but not ignoble. You bowled past the rope-makers where they had made the rope for every execution for a hundred years past, and wondered again about capital punishment. Then the buildings, some carrying scars of war still unhealed, became meaner yet, the shop windows were scrawled in white paint with ill-spelled news of today's offers – jellied eels, surgical belts, cheap permanent waves – a meretricious and saddening quarter. The Elephant had long ago lost his chastity, the Castle was fallen. Never mind; up on the left there, Blackheath still kept something of the space and dignity of eighteenth-century suburbia; and below it the old Royal Hospital dreamed over the reflection of its twin cupolas in Thames, while the Observatory watched the stars as it had watched them first for Charles the Second. But no, you were to miss it this time. The bus turned down to the right, away from these glories, to where the traffic jarred and hooted, and jerry-built shopfronts shrieked to an apathetic crowd their message of bargains unrepeatable and constantly repeated. Richard got down in Lewisham High Street.

Walking through the side streets, he was reminded afresh of the war. Many of the houses were still shattered and tenantless, and the rubble was still piled high here and there, a feature of the landscape; man-made hills under whose shadow the little Elizabeths and Winstons of the prefabs had been born into an uneasy peace.

The Shrubsoles' house was one of a row built at the turn of the century, red-brick picked out with yellowish cement ornament. Not all the row was still standing, but this house was in good repair though the front garden was a wilderness. The paint was fairly fresh, and the window curtains all matched. When Richard pressed the button of the bell, it went off with a noise like several fire engines. A large woman in royal-blue slacks and a pink silk jersey answered the door.

"Sorry I made such a row," began Richard. "The bell …"

"Nothing today, thank you."

He hastily thrust a foot inside the already closing door, but she kicked it back with a force and accuracy that could only come from long practice.

"Hey!" he called through the letterbox, "I'm not trying to sell you anything. I'm looking for Mr. Ian Shrubsole."

"Why the Little Nell couldn't you say so, then?" the woman replied, opening the door again. In spite of the regimented black curls and the orange rouge, she looked human and nice. "Sorry, dear, but I thought you was another of these vacuum fellows, you know what they are. Can't blame them reely, they get paid for a dem, see. But I'm blessed if I'll have them demming all over my front carpet. Ian's out with the boys. But they won't be long. You'll have to come in the kitchen, dear, I've got the iron on. Now which one'd *you* be? Jack?"

"Jack Macdonald? I've just been talking to him. No, my name's Ringwood – Richard Ringwood. I missed your son at the museum so I came on down here. I say, what an amazing iron. It's like a steam engine. Where's all the steam coming from?"

"It's one of these new electric steam models," replied Mrs. Shrubsole with placid pride. "Ian gave it me. Just new out, they are. Of course Dad got it cheap at Merricks, see. They damp and iron all in one. Look, just watch it on these trousers, see?"

"I say, do let me try!"

Richard insisted on pressing Shrubsole's trousers. Like many newly married men, he had become interested in domestic techniques, and the iron really intrigued him. Nothing could have endeared him to Mrs. Shrubsole more.

"Please let me do something else. Can I try this?" He held up a shapeless grayish garment. She roared with laughter.

"Look all right, wouldn't it, if Ian come in and find you ironing his Mum's whats-its! There, don't be shy, dear. Sit down and I'll be done in two twos and then I'll give you a cup. I could do with one myself. Mind Stuart's engine. O.K., you can put the kettle on if you want to. Not the hot tap, it's poisonous."

"It *isn't!*" Richard was vehement. "The deposits are precipitated in the pipes and the water is if anything purer than in the cold tap. Ask any plumber. I don't know where women get these ideas. You're all the same, though. *My* wife won't fill from the hot tap, either."

"Well, my dad, he *was* a plumber," retorted Mrs. Shrubsole. "And he said if you saw what water, so-called pure water, does to the insides of tanks, you'd stick to beer, same as me."

An argument was inevitable at this point, and they both much enjoyed it. By the time the tea was made, they were well away. Mrs. Shrubsole had discovered that Richard had been married for four months and was telling him not to worry (as of course he did) that there was no sign of a baby yet, she'd known people wait ten years and then have six straight off. Be thankful for a bit of p. and q., that was her motto. She'd had a gap of ten years after Ian, and then three more sons in four years. "Dad would keep on, see. 'E was set on 'aving a girl." Since then, she alleged, she had not had a moment's peace.

"You should train them to do things for themselves," said Richard. "That's what we're going to do."

She snorted. "What with Ian training them to speak proper, and their Dad training them to be democratic, they couldn't take a drop more, pore little sods.

Even if I could get a word in edgewise, which needless to say I can't."

"Poor old Mum, creeping round like an overworked mouse," suggested Richard mockingly.

"You're all the same," she cried, hooting with mirth. "Laugh, laugh, laugh. *I* don't mind, bless your little cotton socks, better laugh while you can, we'll all be dead soon. They're lovely boys, my boys are. Give that clock a shake, dear, it must've stopped. They ought to be back by now, unless they've decided to see it through again. Ian's taken them to *Ivanhoe*."

"Oh dear!" said Richard as one remembering his duty. "This is awful. I've been having a nice time under false pretenses. I never told you. I'm a policeman. I'm frightfully sorry. I was enjoying myself so much I forgot to mention it. Would you like me to wait outside or something? I'm supposed to be asking your son some questions about the attack on. Janet Coltman and the murder of Alban Worrall. I'm afraid you took me for one of your son's archaeological friends."

She did for a moment look both affronted and betrayed. But her instant liking for Richard, and even more her curiosity about Worrall's death, predominated. Richard found himself giving her an edited account of the story, which she received with sympathy not unmixed with excitement.

"Hydrochloric acid? That's a new one, innit? What *is* it then, some kind of rat poison?"

"No, it's ordinary spirits of salt. You know, people use it for getting out stains on linen."

"Well, I'm jiggered! I've got a packet of it somewhere here – where is it? No, that's bicarbonate, and that's valve rubbers – here it is. Well, I'll put it straight down the sink, after this. I wouldn't keep it in the house, not with the boys about. My soul, dear, you give me a turn, straight you did."

"Sorry. Let's just make sure this *is* the same stuff. Mm. Yes, this is it all right. Do you often use it? It looks an old packet to me."

"Yeah, Dad got it for me at Christmas when Bert knocked over the port wine. He said it was the best thing out for fetching it off. You just put a titchy little bit in a saucer, see, and let it soak. … Don't it taste, though?"

"Oh yes. But they think it was made up into a capsule. It's quite easy to do, with gelatine. You know, leaf gelatine."

"Can't say I've ever heard of it."

"You know, what you make jellies of."

"Don't be so soft! They come in packets."

Richard found himself explaining that some people made jellies with real fruit-juice and gelatine. Once more they were in danger of a domestic digression. He broke off abruptly.

"I suppose Ian's worrying a bit about his job?"

She instantly looked worried too.

"'E hasn't said so. But I could see he'd got something on his mind. Why? Will he be redundant or somethink?"

Richard had not the heart to tell her that her son was one of the suspects. But he did disclose that there was some doubt whether Worrall's money would be available to carry on the work, and added that in that case Ian and his two colleagues would be out of a job.

"Ap Ifor's got some money of his own, I believe," he said, "but it won't be easy for Miss Coltman, either. Have you met her?"

"No, Ian's never brought her here. Too posh, I expect. 'Course in the old days he couldn't talk enough of her – it was Janet thinks this and Janet says that, as if Ian didn't know twice as much! We got fair sick of it. But I ast him how she was getting on the other day – just to be nice, like – and he fair bit my head off. 'Don't let's talk about her,' he says, 'she's no better than the rest of them. I thought she was a decent scholar once.' I suppose it's the change of life, pore thing."

"Oh, surely not!" said Richard in surprise. "She's only thirty-one."

Mrs. Shrubsole looked astonished. "Go on! Only thirty-one! Well, to hear Ian talk, you'd think she was my age at least. 'Course, Ian don't go much on girls, and that's a fact. Wish 'e did, sometimes. It'd take him out of himself a bit. What's she like, then?"

"Straight bobbed hair, freckles, wears an old mackintosh and ankle socks. Treats you like a brother. Not a glamour girl. Nice, though."

"One of these intellectuals, I s'pose, it doesn't sound as if she had much nature to her. Ian's not like that, though. He talks ever so sarcastic, but he don't mean it, I know, and I only wish he'd get fixed up, I do reely. 'Course, I'm ever so proud of him, doing so well and all, but I do wish he'd bring a few girls home, like. He's always *said* he'd never be ashamed of his family. And he's twenty-nine. Well, I ask you. It don't seem natural, do it?"

Twenty-nine, thought Richard, and remembered the rope-maker's shop. He had thought of Ian as he passed it. Would he see thirty? Compassion made him answer the mother gently and not recall her from her digression.

"Don't you think intellectuals like Ian often marry rather late? They grow up so quickly in their minds that they seem to take a long time catching up in other ways."

"Not Ian, dear. He was shaving every day at sixteen."

Another cause for Ian's nerves and restless ambition! So many of the guilty had never got themselves a girl. This old trout was no fool, even a bit of a saint. It wasn't many proud mothers that grieved if their firstborn stayed with them after due time.

"Still, you'd miss him, wouldn't you, if he set up on his own?"

"My soul, wouldn't I just! And what's more, our Bert'd have to leave school and get a job. Ian's giving me thirty bob a week for him to carry on and work for Higher. Still, we wouldn't want to stand in Ian's way, like. If he'd just be happy, that's all. It's enough to make a cat sick, seeing him fidget. And if Dad starts a bit of an argument, like he used to enjoy, Ian fair jumps down his throat. What I say is, if a boy can't be happy with 'is family, it just shows, don't it?"

She sighed, the pouches under her eyes heavy with worry. But then she cocked her head and listened.

"Talk of angels! Here they come! Listen, duck, don't say nothing to Ian, will you? I must've been half barmy to go on like this, as if you'd care. But one thing led to another, as the girl said when she 'ad triplets. And I can't seem to think of you as a policeman, somehow."

"There!" said Richard patting her hand – she had worked herself into a great state of agitation – "Cheer up. I'm lousy with other people's secrets, I'm a sort of human dustbin. Don't mind me. And anyhow," he added as the door opened, "he didn't find me ironing your whats-its."

There was a clatter of heavy shoes and the two younger boys burst in at the back door with loud cries of "Mum!" and had given her a smacking kiss each before they became aware of the stranger. Then they halted, stamping like startled colts, and the little boy, Stuart, made a dive for his scarlet engine and clasped it to him. The two elder sons came in more quietly, Ian with an arm about his brother's shoulders, looking more at ease than Richard had ever seen him; but only for a moment. As Richard stood up, he drew back, saying "You again!"

"That's a nice way to talk!" said his mother with scolding affection, "and after Richard's been pressing your pants, too! We had a bit of fun, didn't we? Well, don't look like that, you'll turn the milk sour. He's got to do his job, hasn't he?"

"I missed you at the museum," said Richard. "And some new evidence has come in since yesterday that I want your help on. It won't take long. Now first, I need a specimen of topsoil from Pontikonisi. I understand from ap Ifor that you fell over a pot of honey he left lying about there when you had on a pair of canvas shoes, and that you went on wearing those shoes for the rest of the dig. Right? Well, could I borrow them? Being sticky, they'll have held a good bit."

Shrubsole had turned pale, but replied steadily:

"Sorry, I'm afraid they're thrown away now."

"No they're not, duck," said his mother. "I know you put them in the dustbin this morning, but I got them out before they came to empty it. Thought I'd clean them up for Ted, there's plenty of wear in them. Here they are, mud and all. Seems it's your lucky day, ain't it?"

As she bent to get them from under the table, the tight blue trousers made her behind look enormous. Ian laughed so hysterically that Richard was surprised when the family took no notice; only the little boy, Stuart, edged with his engine to the door. A nut dropped off and Richard picked it up and gave it to him.

"What the heck!" Ian said, still laughing without mirth, "can you beat it? She got them out! You ought to have been a rag-picker, that's what you ought to have been!"

Her heavy raddled face flushed a dull purple, and a tear trickled from each toffee-brown eye on to the bistred wrinkled flesh under it, but she said nothing. The boys stood in resentful uncomprehending silence.

"Could we go up to your room, Shrubsole?" said Richard, trying to keep his dislike out of his voice. "I'm sure we're in the way here."

"All right, if you must. S'pose you want to see how the poor live, eh?"

As they left the room, Richard heard the boys begin to chatter of the film as though nothing were amiss. But their mother still stood leaning on the kitchen table, like a boxer who can barely keep his feet after a hard blow.

* * *

Shrubsole's room was shabby enough, but cleaner than the rest of the house and arranged with a kind of austere artistry. A few really beautiful drawings hung on the walls – designs from archaic vase-paintings – and a small mended black-figure drinking cup from Attica stood alone on the chest of drawers. There was a Greek sheepskin on the bed. Otherwise, nothing but a deal table and chair, quantities of books on homemade shelves and piled up on the floor, and a great number of cardboard boxes with labels on them under the bed. His few clothes hung on pegs behind the door.

"You'd better sit down," said Richard, his back to the window so that the light must needs fall on Shrubsole's face. "I warn you, I've got to search this room. Here's my warrant. No need to upset your mother. It's only fair to warn you that since I last saw you the scope of my inquiries has widened. Yesterday I was investigating the attack on Miss Coltman. Today I'm also investigating the poisoning of Sir Alban Worrall, which was established by a post mortem early this morning. Here, hold up! Put your head down! Here, drink some water!"

He took the jug from the table. Shrubsole seemed only half there. He opened his eyes and pushed the jug away weakly.

"No," he whispered. "That's not water. That's hydrochloric acid."

Richard's heart missed a beat. Fate seemed to be playing into his hands with a gruesome jocularity. With an effort he kept his voice level as he asked:

"And the leaf gelatine? Where's that?"

"In the box under the bed," answered Shrubsole mechanically in the same flat faraway voice. Then his faintness passed and he sat up again, his face alert and strained.

"What the heck d'you want that for?"

Richard told him.

* * *

But it was not after all so simple. All archaeologists, it seemed, kept hydrochloric acid for cleaning pottery, and gelatine for making certain types of impressions. Shrubsole pulled out book after book and proved it to him on the spot, besides referring him to the museum authorities. He gathered energy and confidence as he talked. He even cleaned a sherd with acid there and then to show how it was done.

"Very nice," said Richard. "You've convinced me. But I'll have to carry out my search just the same. Will you stay or go downstairs?"

For a moment he looked at the door as if he wanted to make a dash for it. Then he met Richard's eye with his old aggressive stare.

"I'll stay. And any handling of pottery that's done will be done by me. See? This is all Greek government property on loan and it's got to go back safe when I've finished working on it. Also, I'm not going to have you mucking up my arrangement."

"All right," Richard said. "That's fair enough. But I warn you, you'll have to take out every single thing."

"Don't worry," said Shrubsole mockingly. "I often do."

* * *

Boxes and boxes full of sherds; some mere muddied eggshells, others glossy and delicately painted or incised, all tumbled with apparent carelessness into the dilapidated cardboard containers, which Richard vainly tested one by one for false bottoms. One box was of wood, and in it was a complete jar which Shrubsole was unwilling to move; he had only mended it yesterday, he said, after a week's work identifying all the fragments. The design was beautiful – a kind of underwater garden of seaweed and sea-anemones and octopuses, so free and fluid that they seemed to wave as you looked at them, in spite of the many cracks in the surface. They rippled even through the cradle of wire that Shrubsole had made to hold the vessel. It fitted exactly and was beautifully constructed.

"So you use copper wire too?"

"I know what you're thinking." Shrubsole's hands, generally as jerky as the rest of him, were steady and gentle as he laid his find back into safety. "You're thinking of that knife, aren't you? The one Janet was stabbed with. It had a sextuple plait of copper wire where the blade joined the handle. Well, I can tell you that for once I *am* the only archaeologist who uses the stuff. It's a dodge of my own. And as for the knife-blade – well, I'd say, that was done with corundum. I haven't got a corundum stone of my own, but I've easy access to plenty at the museum. And as for my alibi – I was reading Pausanias in a corner of the B.M. library after lunch on Wednesday, and then I went on to Miss Montagu as I told you." He looked at Richard tensely.

"Mm," said Richard. "All right, you can put the boxes back now.

Anything I'd spoil in the table drawer?"

Shrubsole did not reply, so Richard opened it. It was full of penknives, old screwdrivers, tubes of glue, pencils, tweezers, adhesive tape, brushes, scissors, labels, bits of rag, lumps of plasticine, and it was lined with newspaper. Richard took everything out and ran his finger over the newspaper. There was something hard under it at the back of the drawer; he lifted it, and found a kitchen knife, a large one with a yellowish handle. Unlike the other things in the drawer, it was bright and clean.

"What d'you use this for?"

"Scraping," said Shrubsole quickly – surely too quickly? "It makes a good paper knife, too."

"Did you buy it?"

He shook his head. "Pinched it out of the kitchen. Why?"

"Look!" Richard pointed to the maker's name.

"You wouldn't make a bad archaeologist." Shrubsole showed his teeth – you could not call it a smile. "Yes, I saw it too. That's the same make as the one Janet was stabbed with. Well, where's the handcuffs? What more do you want?" In spite of the warm day, he was shivering.

"What are you trying to say?" cried Richard, almost hysterical himself. "Are you confessing you stabbed Janet Coltman?"

"Don't be a fool!" Shrubsole was spitting a little as he spoke, and the drops of spittle stood glittering on the sheepskin beside him. "Of course I'm not. But I can see you've got a case. I hated Worrall, you know that. I could have poisoned him, both at Mouse Island and at the Minos. I had the materials. So had everyone else. But then comes the second attempt. Janet gets stabbed – presumably because she's got to know more about the murder than she should. (Incidentally, I suppose that means she didn't kill him herself.) Well, this time I've got the materials and none of the others have – nobody uses copper wire but me. I'm known to have quarreled with her recently." He began to speak very fast and shrill and to stammer uncontrollably. "My behavior is – is – is abnormally nervous. I don't know anyone im-important enough to make a fuss if you arrest me on this con-con-considerable though by no means con-conclusive corpus of facts. You want to make an arrest. Well, for G-g-god's sake get on with it!"

"Mrs. Shrubsole!" called Richard, opening the door.

"No! No! I don't want to see her. I'd rather go straight off."

But she was panting up the stairs already.

"Listen, Shrubsole. You're not a stupid man. You must know this evidence still isn't enough. I can only presume that you want me to charge you on this because you know a court wouldn't convict on it, and you hope to get off and so out of danger, because you can't be charged twice, can you? Well, I'm not playing. That's all. Oh, hallo, Mrs. Shrubsole! Will you take Ian down and give him some hot tea with lots of sugar in it? He's had a bit of a shock. I'll just finish here and then I'll come down."

Looking worried, but purposeful now that there was a definite task to be done, she took her son's arm. He let himself be hustled and clucked down the stairs.

Richard went through the chest of drawers – remarkable only for a paucity of shirts and a large stock of patent medicines – and the books, which were simply books with nothing hidden in or behind them. He looked through six folders of papers. One held all the certificates Shrubsole had ever won, from the first school examinations to the Oxford Baccalaureate of Letters. There were many testimonials, all sounding the same note of exasperated approval, from tutors and the heads of the various bodies which had employed him. In the other folders there were archaeological photographs and photographs of groups of archaeologists; drawings, rubbings, and quantities of notes, rather unintelligible, such as *Test Pit 2 m. 50 wood ash, clay floor, M.M. kamares, string-cut base*. Most were in his own hand, some in Janet Coltman's. Richard wondered if he'd be any the wiser if they were all in code. Last of all, he pulled the bedclothes down. Yes, this man slept badly. The sheets were crumpled and spotted, and gave out a sour, invalidish smell. Richard began to feel that familiar intimacy, almost sympathy, that strange unwilling bond that links the detective to his chief suspect. He must see how Shrubsole was getting over his hysteria.

He found him slumped over the kitchen table.

"All finished," he said. "Hope I've left everything tidy. Could you lend me an old knife a minute, Mrs. Shrubsole? In there? Don't bother, I'll get it."

Ian made as if to rise, but subsided again with a shrug. Richard had a good look in the knife drawer; there was nothing of the same make as the one which he had found upstairs, and now lay wrapped in his case. He used a knife from the drawer to scrape the mud from one of the canvas shoes into an envelope, and then handed the shoes back.

"Your statement's being typed, Shrubsole," he said, "and we'll bring it along for signature later. You won't change your address without letting us know."

"Change it?" muttered Shrubsole with a ghost of his former petulance. "Why, where else could I go?"

His mother made an inarticulate comforting sound. Richard asked if they were on the telephone.

"No," she replied. "But if you want a message took for Ian, you could ring up Merrick's in the High Street, that's where Dad works, and the young lady'd tell him. Half a sec, I'll take you out the front."

On the step she whispered:

"Don't mind Ian. He's funny sometimes, it's his nerves, see, he can't seem to give himself a break, but he don't mean nothing. You're – you're not *after* him? He won't tell me."

"He won't talk much sense to me either," Richard said, "and of course that doesn't do him any good. Sorry. I'll have to come back, I'm afraid."

He lifted his hat and turned away.

Ian Shrubsole was already in his room, reading the note that Richard had left on his table.

If you decide to give me full information about the passing of false antiquities among the members of your dig, together with full personal details, either of these addresses and telephone numbers will find me. Why don't you, if you really think as you say that you've nothing to lose? R.A.R.

He crumpled it up; but after a moment smoothed it out again and put it in the folder with his testimonials. Then he took a couple of Aspros, swallowing them dry, and lay down on his sheepskin.

Meanwhile Richard was buying a large iron hook and some rope at Merrick's, the ironmongers in Lewisham High Street. A boy served him, but Mr. Shrubsole senior, a small, sardonic, irascible-looking man, had to tell him where they were. Hooks and rope of the kind required were in good supply.

Chapter 12

AFTER a short call at Scotland Yard to enlist the further help of experts, Richard went on to the hospital. Janet Coltman was now in a state to answer questions, and much hung upon her answers. The hospital visiting hours were almost over, and the corridors echoed to the steps of a throng uncertain of their way and in awe of their surroundings. He was dodging through them with sure impatient strides when he heard his name spoken.

"Uncommon lucky thing, uncommon lucky!" Mr. Coltman beamed. "Me niece insists on sending me home tonight, and I did so want a word with you first. The very man! Hope you can spare a minute. Nice bench we can sit on, just round the corner. Wonderfully well they arrange everything in these civilian hospitals. Marvelous recovery she's making, isn't she? Well, my dear boy, I've just been meeting your wife. Charming little girl too, regular little fairy I call her. I'm going to send her my paper on Coptic superstitions. She's been delivering your very kind invitation to have my dear girl to stay when she comes out of hospital, really uncommon kind. Can't thank you enough. Regular Good Samaritans you two dear young people. Of course Janet was going to refuse, didn't want to give trouble, you know. But I persuaded the nurse to let Mrs. Ringwood talk to her, and of course that did the trick. Janet was quite bowled over, pleased as Punch. We both are. Regular little fairy godmother. Uncommon kind."

"Least we can do," said Richard. "I'm very glad that's settled. Otherwise I'd have had to get her police protection, and some people find that a bore. But we'll need to keep an eye on her. We haven't made an arrest yet, you see."

"Holy Moses! D'you mean to say the brute's still at large?" Mr. Coltman looked as fierce as an enraged Sealyham. "Tell you what, my dear boy, I'd better stay on in town after all and help you guard the house. Quite used to sentry duty, y'know. Like the fresh air. Got an excellent shooting-stick my dear wife gave me if I need an occasional rest. Wouldn't impose on Mrs. Ringwood, of course, bring sandwiches. They say there's a shortage of policemen, only fair to do my bit."

The mental picture called up by this offer was irresistible, and made Richard want to hug him on the spot; but he restrained himself to a courteous refusal and a promise to ring him up at Fleet in Hampshire if volunteer forces were needed later.

"We'll take care of her, I promise. By the way, has she had any callers here? Anyone inquire after her?"

"Oh yes, rather. That Taffy feller came along with his beard; funny fish, isn't he? But he brought some beautiful flowers. I believe that native wife of his rang up too, the nurse said it was a foreigner, couldn't hear the name. And then that young Shrubsole's been, too – three times, in fact, once yesterday and twice today, rough diamond, I should say, fidgety, wouldn't you? Bound to be tiring."

"He didn't see her?"

"Oh no, rather not. Gloomy too, said they were all going to lose their jobs. Wanted to ask Janet something about their archaeology, very insistent. But of course as the nurse said, that was quite out of the question. Janet was relieved really, I think, though of course she didn't want to hold up the work, she's such a little brick, you know. In fact we didn't tell her he'd come back again. No point in worrying her when she's getting on so well. They say she's a splendid patient, splendid. Remarkable powers of recuperation." He beamed and wiped his eyes. "Amazing, isn't it? When you think that three days ago … but character always counts, doesn't it? Under Providence, of course."

Richard tore himself away, urging the old man to go home – he looked very fragile – and promising to call upon him at need to supplement the forces of the Metropolitan Police. Then, after a word with the nurse, he entered the sickroom.

Janet still looked pale, sitting up in bed in her rough hospital jacket, but she was much more composed, and thanked him with real warmth for the offer of hospitality. He felt that today there was no need to beat about the bush. He told her that Sir Alban Worrall had been poisoned. At first she could hardly believe it, but her incredulity took the form of practical and intelligent questions. When Richard's answers had convinced her, she was distressed; but again, her distress took a practical form. How could she best help the police? No, she was not tired at all.

"And I don't think my brain's working more slowly than usual," she added with a sad little smile. "I've always been a bit of a plodder, you know. But as Sir Alban used to say, better late than never."

He would, thought Richard, and began by asking for certain soil specimens. Janet brightened. Yes, she had taken samples of every type of soil on all the digs, but they were down at her cottage at Cholsford.

"I could easily go and fetch them once they let me out of here."

"Nonsense. I've got to go there myself tomorrow, anyhow, to make sure your property's all right. Tell me where they are and I'll get them."

"Really? Well, there's one of those big birds'-egg cabinets in the sitting room, on the north wall. The soil specimens are all in the sixth drawer down, in matchboxes. They're labeled, so it ought to be quite simple. You'll let me have them back, won't you? It's useful to keep the record."

This seemed to be the only thing that worried her; strangers tramping over her house she accepted with almost unnatural complaisance.

"Now," he said, opening his notebook. "I want us to go over the whole story together, beginning with that last night on Mouse Island (or do you call it Pontikonisi?) that you mentioned in your letter to *The Times*. I'll read what you said. *Returning from a late stroll shortly before midnight, I saw his unmistakable figure standing in moonlight beside the newly opened trench, in earnest conversation with a young Greek workman. It was a key to his whole life, and perhaps to his death, for such unsparing activity may well have sown the seeds of that fatal illness which led to his untimely end. He is said to have left no close relatives behind him, but his friends will not forget.* Did he know you were about?"

"I don't expect so. I'd generally be asleep in my tent by about eleven, but I had a headache that night, so I went down to the shore for a bit of air. I don't think he saw me coming back, so of course I didn't disturb him."

"It seems a bit odd, his talking to a workman at that time of night."

"Oh, but that's so *like* him," she explained. "He was so keen. He'd been working in the hut, you see – he preferred to have it to himself when the others had knocked off work – and no doubt there was some point he wanted to check up immediately. He was very scrupulous about siting. He wouldn't have got the workman out of bed, of course – he'd probably just come back from a jaunt to the other side. They often came back pretty late."

"Did you hear what they were saying?"

"No, they were talking very quietly. I expect they thought I was asleep and didn't want to disturb me."

"Did you stand and watch them for some time?"

"No, of course I didn't. I – I wouldn't, you know, as they couldn't see me. No, I went straight into my tent."

"Which workman was it? Can you describe what you saw?"

"Oh yes. The moonlight was behind the Greek and he had a thing on his head, a sort of scarf they mostly wear, and the usual baggy Cretan breeches. So I could tell it was one of the workmen and I think one of the younger ones, because he was slim and his mustache didn't stick out past the side of his head as the older men's do. I couldn't see his face. But I saw Sir Alban clearly – the moon was full on him. He looked – rather wonderful, standing there so intent and serious and massive, with the steep rock going up behind him and that very clear dark blue sky. I never told him I'd been there, of course, but I'm glad I was. I'll never forget it."

"How were they standing? Both looking down into the trench?"

"No, he was facing it and the Greek had his back to it."

"About how wide was the trench? And how deep?"

"It was five feet wide exactly – we're particular about measurements on our digs. And we'd dug down seven feet in that section, I know, because I've noted the finds of the day before as occurring at from six feet three to six feet ten."

"Hm! As wide as a church door, and not so deep as – a grave. You seem to have been very rash, walking round at night among all these pitfalls."

She laughed at him tolerantly. "It wouldn't be the first time I'd fallen into a seven-foot trench, and it's quite all right. Not nearly such a bump as falling off a pony. Besides, we naturally knew exactly where all the trenches were."

Nettled by her grandmotherly tone, Richard became argumentative.

"Yes, I see there wouldn't be far to fall if one just slipped over the edge. But five foot's a nasty width. I mean, if you stumbled at one edge and fell horizontally across the trench, surely you could hit your head a nasty knock against the far side?"

She considered carefully, as always. "No. Because you'd put out your hands to save yourself, surely?"

Richard capitulated. "Yes, you're obviously right. I'd better stop trying to teach you your job and let you help me with mine instead. Well, to come to the next morning – when the boy fell over the cliff. Did you see the body? What were the injuries?"

"Yes, I – I saw it. His neck was broken. His head …" her voice was strained.

"Sorry, but you must try to tell me clearly."

"His head was hanging down over his chest at a beastly, unnatural angle. The back of it was smashed in. There was one kneecap broken, but no other bones. The skin and flesh had been cut about a good deal by sharp bits of rock. He was found half in and half out of the water, and there were – there'd been crabs."

"How horrible for you. I've applied to the police at Corfu for a report." He passed hastily on. "He was the son of your Greek foreman, I believe?"

"Yes, poor old Stavro. His only son, a boy called Spiro. He must have been climbing for gulls' eggs – he often did, he was very adventurous. It was Stavro who found the body. I wish one of us had, it must have made it even worse for him. Oh! Something's just occurred to me. Whoever the Greek was who was talking to Sir Alban the night before, it probably wasn't Spiro. He wouldn't have been up so early if he'd been late the night before. And also, we found his knife in the trench later on – he must have dropped it the day before. Well, if he'd been back there in the evening, he'd certainly have seen it and picked it up. They don't like to be without their knives, you know. Like us with watches."

"I see. Yes, I think you've got something there. Well, the boy was found about – six? And Sir Alban was told when?"

"About eight. I went over to the mainland to tell him as soon as I could, but of course there were things to see to first. He was looking ill even then, I thought. He and Ian and Iorweth were all having breakfast on the terrace. Zoe was having hers in bed, but she called to us from the balcony – I suppose she must have realized from our voices that there was something wrong. There were a lot of things to cope with. Indeed, I'm afraid it was the worry that brought on his first attack … Oh! But you say he didn't have an ulcer at all. I can still hardly believe it."

"I'm just passing on the doctor's report. He may be mistaken, though I think it's unlikely … The breakfast was prepared by the hotel staff, I take it? None of the members of the dig – workmen or archaeologists – had anything to do with it?"

"No … *Oh!*" She looked horrified. "You mean, someone tried to poison him that morning? Iorweth or Ian? No, no, that's impossible! I'm sure it was a proper illness. I looked in the medical dictionary and all the symptoms were exactly what it said for gastric ulcer. Yes, we always took a medical dictionary; it's useful sometimes when you're in the wilds. We had it on the yacht. Yes, it's still there; I'll get it for you when I'm out of here."

He assured her that it could be found by the police. Whose idea had it been, he asked, to consult the dictionary under the word "ulcer"? She could not be sure; not hers, she thought. They were all there, Worrall, Shrubsole, Zoe, and ap Ifor, and all making suggestions while she did the looking up. They had tried appendicitis and various other things first, but gastric ulcer was the only disease that exactly corresponded to Worrall's symptoms, and when she had treated him, on the voyage home, according to the instructions, the treatment had seemed to work. And Dr. Chevet had confirmed the diagnosis, she understood. No, she had not seen much of Sir Alban since their return to England. He had been staying quietly at his club, and the rest of them had all been busy sorting and cataloguing the finds.

"I went to see him twice," she said. "Once to arrange about some lectures, and once about his will. He wanted to leave his money in trust for Minoan archaeology, and he had some questions about the Greek law for me to see to; I generally tried to take that sort of thing off his hands a bit. And then, of course" – she faltered very slightly – "I saw him in the Minos the day he died."

"I know. Sorry to make you talk about it. Macdonald said he insulted you grossly in public; Macdonald was horrified. Was there any conceivable reason for such an outburst? Sorry, I know you hate to remember it."

He watched her, fearing that she would collapse as she had done yesterday. But although she looked wretched, she was perfectly steady.

"I'm afraid I behaved very stupidly yesterday. It's different now I've had time to think it over. He must have been in great pain. Perhaps he knew he was giving me his last instructions. And then I wasted time by arguing." Then she muttered, looking down like a schoolboy at fault, "Must have been getting on his nerves for years, I s'pose. Everybody's, for that matter. See that now. Wish they'd told me before. Always was a clumsy fool. Same with Ian."

"I gather you and Mr. Shrubsole weren't on very good terms?"

She flushed. "Sorry he should say that. I've got a very high respect for his work as a whole, though he hasn't of course got Sir Alban's field experience."

"Did you have an actual quarrel with Shrubsole?"

She looked uneasy. "We may have disagreed about a point of interpretation. That's bound to happen sometimes."

"About the Nausicaa Ring, for instance?"

"Really I don't think I can discuss another archaeologist's unpublished finds." Janet's blobby, boyish features took on a strangely formidable dignity. "Sir Alban's successor will be the person for that, and I should think it very incorrect to anticipate his decision. It's always been our tradition to publish as a team, not as individuals. I daresay Ian wasn't quite himself – he was very disappointed that the dig had to be cut short, you know – and I expect I was clumsy and tactless, as usual, and didn't give his point of view a fair hearing. Was there anything else you wanted to know?"

"Yes. Tell me what was on the table when you left Sir Alban in the Minos. Can you remember?"

She remembered easily. She was still sipping her first glass of sherry; Worrall had finished his second and ordered the bouillabaisse. (He would!) It had just been placed on the table when Shrubsole had passed and upset the dish of olives Janet had helped to pick them up (she would!), so she had not actually had an eye on him all the time; she obviously did not grasp the point of the question. Richard explained.

"The poison was probably given in capsule form either in the bouillabaisse or in the sweet. So it may have been put there by the waiter, or the proprietor, or Shrubsole ..." He watched her.

"Or Mr. Macdonald, or me." She put her hand across her eyes. "Sorry, I can't seem to take it in. It seems so fantastic – *poison!* Why *should* anyone? Couldn't it have been – suicide? If he was very ill, and not himself?"

"Hardly anyone would deliberately choose such a painful death. Or so public. And the timing's wrong, too. Look, Janet – I may call you Janet, mayn't I? – I feel quite sure *you* didn't do it. But even for you, I could find several motives that look credible enough on paper, as well as opportunity. Don't you see, the only way to get at the truth is to suspect everyone till we find good reason not to? I've half a mind to show you my notebook, just to demonstrate what a lot there is against everybody. But no, I'll wait till you're better."

She looked very washed-out. Indeed, her hair and freckles were the only bits of her that held any color; her face was white and her gray eyes as cold and dull as a winter sea.

"No, I'm all right," she protested. "I don't want to hold you up. Do show me, please."

He showed her the table of motive and opportunity that he had made that morning, for Shrubsole, the ap Ifors, and the two Greeks.

"Yours is over the page," he said, "with some other rather secret stuff, so I won't show it to you. It's all nonsense anyway."

She seemed not to hear him, she was reading with such concentration. It gave her a curiously intimidating look – her big forehead lowering, her jaw square and heavy – but when at last Richard held out his hand for the book and she looked up, her face was as puzzled and candid as a girl's.

"I don't understand," she said. "Who's Georgios?" (She pronounced the name right, but after all, one would expect that from anyone with a working knowledge of modern Greek.)

"The waiter at the Minos. He's having a love affair with Zoe ap Ifor. Didn't you know?"

"A – a love affair?" He had never seen anyone blush so thoroughly. Face, neck, even the parting in the carroty hair, were deeply suffused. "Are you sure? Yes, I can see you must be. Please don't tell me. I'd rather not. Oh! How could she? Poor Iorweth!"

"He may not know. I certainly haven't told him. Or he may know and not mind. He adopts a fairly pagan attitude, doesn't he? Liberating the Life Forces and so on?"

"I don't understand married life, of course," mumbled Janet, like an embarrassed schoolboy. "Probably never will. But surely, a promise is a promise. Everyone knows that. This is absolutely ghastly. Oh dear! And I feel it's partly my fault."

"*What?*"

"I expect she was lonely, without a woman friend. They say most girls are," said Janet as though speaking of a different species. "I did try to talk to her a bit, when she was hanging about the site. But I'm afraid I grudged the time. Couldn't think of anything to say, either. Oh dear! Sir Alban would have known what to do. He got on splendidly with her." It was almost a wail.

"Do!" Could she really be so blind? There was only one thing you *could* do with Zoe. And you couldn't even do that if you were a woman. "Why do anything? You and I aren't responsible. Our only interest in the affair is evidential. Their guilt made Zoe and Georgios feel insecure, and insecurity can make people turn dangerous. I notice you don't comment on their other lapse."

"Other lapse?" She stared at the notebook again. "Oh! *Feared exposure for antique faking*. Sorry. I don't understand that either."

"No? Zoe passed a packet of faked Minoan objects – mostly seals – to Georgios yesterday. It obviously wasn't the first time. I managed to intercept the parcel."

"You intercepted it?" She was formidable again in her angry intelligence. "But that means we shall never find out who it was intended for!"

"So you agree with me that it was probably intended for a member of the expedition?"

She caught her breath. "No! No! I never said so. Of course I don't."

"Odd," said Richard as though she had not spoken. "When I showed it to Shrubsole *he* was extremely frightened and he, too, insisted that he knew nothing about it."

"Ian frightened? But *he* …" She stopped for a moment, and then, once more the cautious and controlled scholar, said:

"How do you know the things are fakes?"

"I asked Macdonald. Here's what he said. Oh, by the way, I shall need a complete and thorough account of the so-called Nausicaa Ring. Will you do it, or shall I ask Macdonald?"

She flinched, but managed an answer.

"I think it would be extremely incorrect to put out a description at all at this stage. It's always been our tradition to work as a team, under a leader, and not to publish mere personal opinions. Sir Alban …"

"Yes, but he's dead. And I'm not asking you to publish. Still, I take it you'd rather I asked Macdonald."

"No! No! I'll do it, if you want me to. As soon as I'm well enough, that is." She had been offering to run errands for him by train only five minutes ago. "But I can't see that it's relevant."

"Listen, Janet. Let's stop pretending. You'll never make a good liar, anyhow, even when you're trying to be professionally correct. You know quite well that there's something fishy about the Nausicaa Ring."

"I've never said so."

"No, but I've seen what you wrote about it. And I know Shrubsole suspected Worrall of having planted it in the trench and of pretending to find it afterwards. And I know you quarreled with him …"

"Why? Did he say so?"

"It's obvious you were quarreling about the ring. My guess is that you first of all defended Worrall to Shrubsole, out of loyalty. But you were really worried. You quieted your conscience by writing a private description for yourself. Then, I think, you tackled Worrall himself on the matter."

She looked miserable but only said, "What's this got to do with – murder?"

"By itself, perhaps nothing. But look how it links up with the new fact – the fact that fakes are now circulating, and *after* Worrall's death. Don't you see that it means that *somebody else* was going to buy them? Not, as you suspected in your heart of hearts, Worrall?"

"I'm sure Sir Alban wouldn't have had anything to do with buying even genuine antiques," she said. "He attached such great importance to proper siting." Still, she sounded enormously relieved.

"Well," went on Richard brushing aside the interruption, "what's the alternative? Someone else was buying the fakes. Someone who wanted to discredit Worrall, who planted the Nausicaa Ring in the trench knowing that it would take Worrall in at the time. And knowing that later on, when it was proved to have been a fake, people would suspect Worrall himself of having planted it there and 'found' it. Well, who would that be? Who was the last person in the trench before Worrall walked along it and picked out the ring? Do you remember?"

"I – I think it was Ian."

"Yes, and Ian was the first person to question the authenticity of the find, wasn't he? And he hated Worrall, didn't he?"

"What are you saying?" She had hardly breath for the question.

"I'm suggesting that Shrubsole wanted Worrall out of the way. That he first tried to discredit him as an archaeologist by making him 'find' a fake. That for some reason the plot didn't work. Perhaps one of the workmen saw him plant it and told Worrall the truth – that may be the explanation of your moonlight scene. Or perhaps Worrall had his own suspicions. Anyhow, the plot failed. And if there was an attempt to poison Worrall next day, that failed too. Though the attempt to shut the workman's mouth may have been more successful. Spiro's death may fit in there. But meanwhile, the people who were selling him the fakes – Zoe and whoever is in it with her – start turning nasty. They say they've still got a lot of antiques left on their hands, and Shrubsole's jolly well got to buy them, or they'll inform against him. He can't – he hasn't got enough money. He's in a desperate situation. So ..."

"No." She spoke calmly and with absolute conviction.

"Janet, please! It's all very well to be loyal to your colleagues, but not if it means putting on moral blinkers and refusing to face facts. There's no virtue and no sense in such an attitude."

"I agree. I've been thinking a lot about loyalty while I've been lying here. And I came to the same conclusion. Loyalty hasn't got anything to do with blinkers. It's just the opposite. If you give your loyalty to somebody or something, you have *more* knowledge, not less. It isn't the particular phase of the person or thing that you have to be loyal to. It's the whole – the past and the future and the purpose and the context – everything seen in the round. ..."

"*Sub specie aeternitatis?*"

"Something like that. So you mustn't think I'm frightened of facts. Only, just as I ought to have been sure Sir Alban didn't do anything dishonest about the ring, so now I *am* sure Ian hasn't done what you accuse him of. You see, you've only met him over this business, but I really know him. I don't only know what he's *done*. I know what he *is* and what he stands for. And that's complete honesty, specially about scholarship. He'd no more touch a fake than he'd – he's often made himself unpopular by being so scrupulous. He'd never get himself out of a jam at the expense of anyone else. He's utterly responsible. I'm not being blind to facts, honestly I'm not. I just know the other sort of facts too."

"Most policemen wouldn't say they were facts at all, but I'm not inclined to ignore them any more than you are. Though I must say, Ian is lucky to have you to stand up for him."

She blushed again and murmured "Rot!"

"No, I mean it. He hasn't been an easy colleague, and I know his attitude to Worrall distressed you. I think you're being remarkably generous."

Janet looked down at her square, freckled hands and said nothing.

"Still, you must admit that there's a strong case against him as things stand at present."

"No stronger than against me. I had the same or better opportunities at Corfu and in the Minos. I could have done everything that you're accusing Ian of."

"Including the attempted murder of yourself, from behind?"

She crammed three fingers into her mouth, like a child caught out.

"I'd forgotten that. But honestly I don't think that's relevant. I'm sure it was just a stray lunatic attacked me. I know I've sometimes annoyed my colleagues. I wish Sir Alban had told me before. But surely, not as much as that?"

"Don't be silly. They all obviously think the world of you. But just imagine you're the murderer and take another look at this letter you sent to *The Times*. Don't you see how threatening it can look? You say the scene by the trench was '*perhaps the key to his death.*' And '*his friends will not forget.*' "

"M'm. S'pose it *could* be taken like that. But it's so silly. I mean, obviously, if I'd suspected anything like that, I'd have gone straight to the police. Wouldn't I?"

"Being you, yes. But some people would have preferred to blackmail the murderer. Your letter could be read in that sense."

"Anyone that knew me would surely realize I wouldn't do a thing like that. Don't you think so?" she added wistfully.

Poor thing! Sir Alban's burst of temper in the Minos had wrecked her confidence very thoroughly.

"Any normal person would, of course. But you can't expect an unconvicted murderer to think normally or see things straight. He's jumpy. He fancies threats everywhere. Now just think. Which of your colleagues was like that?"

The answer was unexpected.

"Iorweth. He's been an absolute Cassandra from the first, and when poor Spiro was killed and Sir Alban was taken ill, he kept saying that he'd expected it. I didn't know if it was just his funny way or whether that awful Zoe had been getting at him. I don't believe in second sight, do you? My father was always very much against it."

Both tone and words belonged to a different generation; Janet was for a moment exactly like her old uncle.

"I certainly prefer a natural explanation. Did Iorweth seem unhappy? Ill?"

"Oh, no. In a way, he almost enjoyed talking about the next victim. I don't mean he was unkind, or gloating. He was most sympathetic. But –"

"He liked a spot of drama. I know, I've heard him on the subject myself. How long had he been working with Worrall?"

"Officially, only this year. But he'd spent a lot of time with us in Crete the year before. Why?"

"Were there any finds last year that might not have been genuine? Did you have any reason to suspect his integrity as an archaeologist?"

"Well" – Janet spoke carefully but without emotion – "He's rather gullible, of course. Still, that isn't what you mean, is it? There was just one thing that happened – at least I think it happened – which was rather odd. I haven't said anything about it because I can't be sure. It was last year in Crete, at Zero. We'd had a very good week – the same party as this year – and there were a lot of finds in my department, each of which of course I'd labeled on the spot, as I always do. But I went down with malaria before I'd had time to list them. When I came back after ten days, I had the impression – and mind you, it was only an impression – that there were fewer gems and seals there in the boxes than I remembered. I did ask Sir Alban about it, but he said he'd been looking after everything and he was sure it was all right. He made a joke about my seeing double, I remember. And he was probably right, because I was running quite a high temperature those last few days."

"But now you're not so sure? In fact, you suspect ap Ifor of stealing some of them?"

"Oh, no! Goodness, no!"

"Well, what are you trying to say about him? He wasn't in the Minos when Worrall was poisoned, like Ian. He hadn't a special grudge against him, like Ian. And yet you seem to want me to arrest him, and not Ian. Why?"

Janet blushed again – and Richard half expected a lie, but she looked and spoke with staggering frankness.

"Oh, no! I don't want you to arrest either of them. I want you to arrest Zoe. You see, I know Ian's too honest a scholar to have done these dreadful things, and Iorweth is really a very kind, harmless little man. I know them both. But I never really got to know Zoe. And now you've actually proved that she's a bad woman. I heard rumors about her, you know, even in Crete. So there you are."

"My dear girl! You've read Plato and Aristotle, and yet you think that's an argument!"

"Well, I was never much good at philosophy. They either make you prove something you know already or disprove something that doesn't matter. Very unpractical. But character always counts, doesn't it?"

Richard almost shouted. "You say that in good faith? You, a classic and a historian, God help you? Yes, I see you do. All I can say is, you've got a very feminine mind."

At this moment two nurses came in, asserting that they were to wash Janet at once. Richard's good-bye was hasty. But outside the door, he was still recovering from his astonishment. Why had Janet looked so pleased at a remark that he had meant to sting?

Of course! Sir Alban had told her that she wasn't a proper woman at all.

Chapter 13

THE bedroom was dark except where a ray from the street lamp came through a chink in the curtains. The late traffic outside had ceased and the district was quiet. The large hump and the small hump in the double bed were quiet, too, at first sight; but from time to time each of them stirred cautiously, taking care not to disturb the other. Then the eiderdown quilt slipped off and Richard and Clare both uttered a sigh of exasperation and grabbed at it. Each realized that the other was awake and both together cried, "Did I wake you up, darling? I'm so sorry."

They laughed and, this time in deliberate unison, repeated the family formula for this frequent trick of simultaneous utterance:

"Dialogue, not chorus."

The rules of the game demanded now that Richard, as head of the family, should speak first.

"So you can't sleep either?" he said, gathering his wife into a more companionable position. "How heavenly. Well? What are *you* lying awake about?"

"Just planning about Janet. The only things I can remember out of those Home Nursing lectures are *Always warm the bedpan,* but we haven't got one, and *The patient should be lifted in a single firm movement*. Do you think I could lift Janet in a single firm movement? She looks pretty hefty."

"Don't be silly. She'll be perfectly capable of lifting herself."

"And we've only got two pillows in the spare room, both rather thin ones. I wonder if we ought to buy a bolster. I can put sofa-cushions, of course, but they're not so nice … What's keeping *you* awake, darling?"

Richard shifted restlessly. Even in Clare's arms he could not lie at ease tonight.

"It's this damn case. I've got nearly all the pieces of the jigsaw, but I'm not convinced that I'm joining them up right. They fit – they fit almost too neatly, but they don't make a convincing picture. It isn't human nature."

"What d'you mean? You're always telling me that no one's free from temptation – that you and I are just as much potential murderers as any thug in jug. You always get so cross when I talk about good people and bad people. Don't say you've changed your mind!"

"No, of course I haven't. This isn't a matter of morals, it's a matter of personal style, taste, values – call it what you like. Even the criminal has his personal code – there's someone or something he cares about, and some role where he sees himself as hero. If it was Janet I suspected, I wouldn't be so surprised. You see, Worrall was what *she* most cared about and perhaps that ideal was shattered even before his death. But Shrubsole cared for something more enduring – sound, unbogus archaeology. If he didn't he wouldn't have toiled like that for ten years with no money and no recognition and everybody against him. I just can't see why *he* should have turned faker. It's a betrayal of all he stands for."

"Couldn't he have told himself that he'd never have a chance to work in the right way – *his* way – without money or position? And that the end justified the means, and the work he'd do when he led his own expedition would make up for the bad things he'd done so as to get there?"

"It's possible, I suppose. Though he doesn't strike me as a casuistical type, somehow. Capable of violence, yes. But uncompromising. I do see Janet's point in a way; Zoe and her lot are much more the type. *They* haven't got any abstract loyalties that I can see."

"There, darling! The case is only two days old, and you're going to find out lots more tomorrow. Try to sleep. Relax. Wiggle your head down a bit, it's squashing my arm."

They lay a little longer in close but somehow separate discomfort, till Clare said:

"It's no good. We're nothing but knees and elbows and toenails. We'd better make ourselves some tea."

"Oh good! I've been dying to turn on the light and look at my notes."

"And I've been longing to go and have a look in the linen cupboard. Be an angel and fill the kettle while I collect the tray."

To drink tea together in bed in the small hours of a sleepless night is one of the pleasures of matrimony too seldom celebrated. It combines the present reality of mutual society, help, and comfort, with the half-forgotten glamour of feasts in the night nursery, when bumpers of foaming Eno's washed down the cheese biscuits spread thickly with Swiss milk. Soon Clare had quite forgotten her domestic problems and Richard's case began to look interesting and hopeful.

"You said just now that you'd got nearly all the pieces," said Clare. "What is there still to come? Reports from the analysts?"

"Partly. They've proved that the stuff on Shrubsole's shoes is the same mixture as what I got off the sink at the Minos – honey and soil. But I can't prove that it's actually soil from the site on Mouse Island till I've fetched Janet's specimen from her cottage at Cholsford. Also, I must find out where the fakes are coming from. The maker must be an unusually skilled chap with a lot of archaeological knowledge. I'd like to go through the private collections of Sir Alban, ap Ifor, and Janet, to see if any fakes have crept in there. Besides that I'm still waiting for the Greeks to answer my inquiries, and the archaeologists to make up their minds about the seals, and I've still not had time to go and search Worrall's yacht."

"It sounds a lot. All the same, you really feel that the most important evidence is in your hands already?"

"It's only a feeling – a sort of hunch that I've seen or heard the key to the whole thing, and somehow failed to recognize it."

"But surely you must really think it was Shrubsole by now? The circumstantial evidence is so strong, and the motive, and you said yourself he was queer."

"Yes, but the other three are queer too. It's true that Shrubsole is the most quarrelsome, and I think he's probably got a well-grown inferiority complex. But the others are just as batty in their way. Zoe's obviously nymphomaniac as well as being up to some funny business with the fakes. Iorweth is a self-deceiver and superstitious; he cuts his history to fit his fancies, and he's got an equally unreal view of his own wife. And even Janet, whom I like the best of the bunch, is stuck at the emotional age of fifteen and seems to be quite lost without a father substitute. Incidentally, I'm very much afraid she's cast me to fill the part next. She behaved most curiously today – kept on blushing and appealing for my approval."

"Father figure my foot! It's just your fatal charms. But I'll sort her. I'll deal with her. I know! Couldn't we have Macdonald to tea and palm her off on him?"

"No good. He's the sort that likes them pretty."

"Well, perhaps even that could be arranged. At least she could be made to look presentable, I believe. We must find her *some* light relief, after all. So far, our only social plan for her is to stick around and see if Shrubsole has another go at murdering her. That isn't very gay."

The flippant tone did not quite hide her apprehension.

"Darling! I'll put her off. She can easily go into lodgings under guard."

"Of course not. I want to have her. It's a much more interesting way of helping you with your work than just having the Bloodhound to dinner."

"I don't see how you or Janet can possibly run any risk if you do as I say."

"Of course not. I was just enjoying my spot of drama. Well, to be quite honest, the thing I find alarming is the idea that I'm going to meet a murderer face to face. Uncanny, somehow."

"But I've told you before, murderers are just people like us. We've all got it in us to do the same. But anyhow, we can't be absolutely sure that Shrubsole is a murderer. Janet was strongly against the idea."

"That might just be because she's too frightened to give him away. I know she doesn't a bit want to see him, because her old uncle told me so. He's a complete heart-winner, isn't he?"

"He says you're a regular little fairy."

They both yawned at the same moment.

"Chorus, not dialogue," said Clare, and turned out the light.

* * *

Having moved the telephone on to the breakfast table, Richard used it all through the meal with mounting exasperation only heightened by his wife's sympathy. She left him at it and began her housework. At last she heard him rush upstairs, making the ejaculation which Napoleon prophesied that the world would make at the news of his death: "*Ouf!*"

He sat down with a bang on the bed, which Clare was making, and burst into speech.

"Well! I got through to everyone in the end. It would have taken half the time in America; still, I suppose it would take all day in Yugoslavia. Want to hear my program?"

He got up and paced about the room, which Clare was trying to tidy.

"First I go and report and collect a car. Then I meet Macdonald outside the B.M. at ten and take him off for a quiet chat. He *can* come to tea today, by the way, so you can start palming off Janet at once. Then I call on Shrubsole's elocution teacher at ten-thirty. She's called Meriel Montagu, and boy! Can she elocute! She sounded a dream over the telephone. After that I'll visit Worrall's yacht, and then go straight on down to Cholsford to get the soil specimen and nose round Janet's cottage a bit. I'll get lunch on the road and be back in good time for tea."

He began putting on a pair of shoes which Clare had just set aside for cleaning.

"I rang up the hospital to ask what time we should fetch Janet, and they said we were to ring back after eleven, when the doctor's been to see her. Can you do that? And then get on to my chaps and they'll see about a car and an escort. I'll leave it all fixed up so that you don't have to do anything but just let them know the time. And I'll arrange for one of them to stop on here and keep an eye on things till I get back. Damn! I've broken a shoelace."

"Here's another pair of shoes. I'd put them *both* on if I were you."

"Have you got everything clear? Good! Well, good-bye, darling."
"Good-bye. *Ouf!*"

* * *

Macdonald was punctual to his appointment and Richard had a short conversation with him in the police car, where there was no risk of eavesdroppers. Macdonald handed him a slip of paper.

"Here's some sort of list – just a few people I've been able to hear of who are known to have done replicas or restorations of Minoan stuff. I found some of the names in Evans's writings (I must say he was generous about giving his assistants their due) and I got a few more by casual asking around, I hope without arousing any suspicions. Mind you, the list isn't complete, and I don't know where the men are now or even if they're still alive. They seem to date back about thirty years as far as I can see, and you'll notice they're mostly foreigners. I've put their nationalities."

Richard thanked him for his trouble, and next asked him whether Worrall or any other members of his party had been private collectors, and if so whether Macdonald had seen their collections. Would any of them have bought fakes?

Macdonald had seen Worrall's collection, which was at his house in Crete. Its whole value lay in the fact that it was above suspicion. Worrall would not even buy surface finds from peasants. His objects must be vouched for by an archaeologist who had checked the exact locale and stratification – he was almost overcautious. To tell the truth, he hadn't much natural flair, and he may have tried to balance this deficiency by his insistence on correct technical methods, in which, of course, Miss Coltman would have been of great assistance to him. Even so, he made howlers from time to time, and his reputation was in need of refurbishing. People were beginning to say that he ought to have found out something really important after spending all that money. He had dug up plenty of objects but they did not add to one's knowledge of history.

Ap Ifor also had a collection, of which Macdonald spoke with wry amusement. It consisted of supposedly talismanic Minoan jewelry and he liked to wear it – rings on his fingers and amulets round his neck – for he claimed that its mystic influences gave him important historical intuitions. Macdonald had never examined the whole lot, but certainly ap Ifor would wear a real Minoan ring one day and a fake the next. Unwittingly, for he had spent large sums on both.

Shrubsole had no collection, and Miss Coltman, he thought, was also too poor to buy antiques, unless Worrall had occasionally given her a few. All finds made on digs were of course the property of the Greek government, and though some might be exported with their permission, none belonged personally or by right to the archaeologist who found them. The treasure-hunt days were over.

Richard thanked Macdonald and returned him to store.

* * *

Meriel Montagu's voice, even over the telephone, had a voluptuous music that promised no common encounter; and the uninviting approach to her flat did not take the edge from Richard's eagerness to see her. He went down a dark passage by a shop and up a narrow stair, and found her front door with a large visiting card printed in Gothic lettering under the bell, which he rang. The door swung open and the siren voice called:

"Come in, please! The first door on the right."

The front door closed behind him – it was evidently worked by some mechanism – and he advanced, observing that someone had lately cooked a rich breakfast. He smelt coffee, bacon, oranges, and possibly kidneys in the air before he opened the first door on the right.

The room was almost filled by a large sofa. The sofa was quite filled by a large woman. She was not old and might even have been beautiful if there had been less of her. A rose-pink housecoat enhanced the effect. Theatrical photographs covered the walls; a telephone stood on the chair beside her; and she was reading *Picture Post*.

"Come in, please. Don't be nervous. People are always surprised by the door opening like that, but I really had to have it. There isn't room for two in my teeny little hall, is there?"

She swept the telephone off the chair on to the table, and covered it with a doll in a crinoline.

"Sit down. Well, how can I help you, dear? Is it social or public speaking? Tell me *all* your troubles."

He had closed his eyes for a moment to enjoy the voice – precise as a jewel, rich as Devonshire cream, soft as a featherbed – magical, if you didn't look.

"Sorry! I ought to have explained on the telephone. The thing is –"

"But my dear, you speak beautifully already. You only need a little breath-control. Put your hands here, over my diaphragm. Now, feel me breathe in. Keep your hands on me. Now I'm using my breath to talk, aren't I? But you can still feel the reserve, like a kind of air-cushion. The secret is, to stop before it's all gone, and take another breath." She did so. It was like refilling an observation balloon. "You want to keep plenty in hand. Now you try."

She unbuttoned his jacket and laid two warm cushiony hands on his chest, remarking that he had a wonderful diaphragm. He took a deep breath and talked fast while it lasted.

"I haven't come to learn elocution incidentally why is anybody with such a lovely voice as you wasting it on the desert air you ought to be speaking great poetry no I'm just a policeman come to ask some questions about Mr. Ian Shrubsole."

Her laugh was a lovely sound, too. She thanked him for his compliment and apologized for her mistake.

"I'm too impulsive, that's the trouble. You might say it's ruined my career."

Pressed to explain, she admitted that her impulsiveness had taken the form of never refusing good food. She had preferred eclairs to orchids, chocolates to chinchilla, so consistently that public appearances had now become impossible. She couldn't even get into the new lifts at the BBC. But she seemed quite resigned and just as ready to help in detection as in breath-control.

She described Ian Shrubsole as "one of those boys on the upgrade." She had many pupils in this category but none so promising, so quick in the uptake, so intelligent in applying the rules. He had had two lessons a week for just under three weeks. At first he had been shy and sullen, but had soon got over it and shown real interest. This week, however, there had been a setback. He had missed his Monday lesson and had been ten minutes late for his Wednesday one, and then he was all on edge and his breathing was haywire. *He* said it was a sick headache, but Miss Montagu, not knowing he was in trouble with the police, had put it down to Love. Her voice made the word sound infinitely credible and attractive – if only you didn't look.

* * *

In Worrall's yacht, empty but for a couple of Greek sailors in charge, what first struck one was the luxury of the owner's cabin compared with the monastic simplicity of the other quarters. Richard sat in Worrall's well-sprung chair and gazed round him. After all, this was the nearest thing to a home that the man had in England; his room at the club had been anybody's bedroom. But even this cabin, where he had spent so much time, told you little about him. Comfortable, yes. No expense spared. But it was like a business man's office; the best materials had been used, but the general effect lacked color and patina. Even the drinks in the cupboard were only whisky and gin. A lot of empties, too. A few archaeological books, *Who's Who*, half a dozen new novels that you would find in any good circulating library, and an aroma of cigars were the only clues to personality. The medical dictionary was there and opened of itself on the article about internal ulcers. Cigar ashes on the page suggested that Worrall himself had read and reread the passage.

"Poor chap! He must have been worried," thought Richard, and set off on the drive down to Berkshire.

* * *

Ian Shrubsole had started *his* journey earlier. Indeed, he had looked out the last stage – the walk from the station to the house – on an Ordnance Survey map on the previous day, and memorized the landmarks. There were some Neolithic earthworks nearby which would have interested him before. Before! The word tolled in his head, ringing out that golden age when he had only thought himself unhappy and insecure. Well, you live and learn. No (let's be accurate) you learn – you learn a lot in what people call a shortened course. No background, they'd said. What the heck! I wouldn't mind that now if I could just count on a bit of foreground, if I could just trust people and be sure of staying alive. Jumpy, they'd said. Both of them. My godfathers! If they only knew!

Jumpiness at least hadn't impaired his topographical training, which brought him accurately by field paths to the house. It had been a good idea to arrive in the dinner hour, when there was no one in the fields. The house was well-screened, too, down a lonely lane, hidden behind its hedges and apple-trees. Maybe he'd get away with it.

If you had to do this sort of thing, archaeology and ironmongery were the perfect training. He had brought tools. The seals on the door came away intact. It was a much easier job than detaching a brittle piece of bronzework from a rotted leather shield. As for the lock, his father had taught him all about locks years ago; and relocking the door, refixing the seals, and climbing back through a window were the actions of native intelligence. Or was that jumpiness too? So what? Who wouldn't be? He fastened the window behind him, still wearing the thin gloves which were yet another proof of his forethought.

Now he could get down to it. But he was clammy with sweat and shivering, and his stomach felt as if a sharp hand were squeezing at it spasmodically, and when he tried to turn away from the window, he found that he was unable. He simply didn't dare.

"They're just waiting for that. As soon as my back's turned –"

And yet there was nobody in sight, and the house was well screened. Ah, but that's no security. What hides me can hide them. They can creep up gradually behind all those bushes. They're no novices, you know that.

"Oh, what the heck!" he muttered, and fumbled in his pocket for the Blis-sprins – a sedative to which he was addicted. Not that they were strong enough to make much difference, but at least one had taken action of a sort. One had done something about it. His hands were shaking, but at last, after taking off one of his gloves, he managed to pull out the cellophane strip with its separately wrapped tablets. How quiet it was here! He tore three tablets off still in their wrapping, dug them out at last, and swallowed them. While they were still in his mouth, he felt better. He had taken action to deal with his nerves, therefore he felt better. By the time the taste had faded, his hands were steady. He replaced his glove. Only a few moments afterwards, he found that he could turn away from the window, look about the room, even appraise it.

"My godfathers! That looks like Sheraton, or something; must have cost a packet. Wouldn't have expected this style, would you, to look at her? Well, in the circs, it's no wonder if she wasn't keen to … Gosh! I suppose all those silhouettes are ancestors! That one's a bit like, come to think of it. Why! Every darned thing in the room's a genuine antique. Regular bijou mansion. Yes, but it'd take a heck of a lot of keeping up. She *might* have needed the dough. It was a reasonable hypothesis."

He suddenly found himself in action. He threw his little crumpled pellet of cellophane into the pile of wood ash on the hearth with such vigor that it half-embedded itself in the gray dust. He opened the desk. Propping the flap with his head, he began to rummage. Then he opened all the drawers, lifting a paper here and there. What he found seemed to please him.

"Good," he muttered. "But still not quite good enough. Literary evidence is only half the story. You've had that dinned into you often enough. Well, my lady, let's see what you've got in that natty little cabinet thing, shall we? Maybe we'll be in the clear after all. Ah! No lock there, either – a good sign."

The slow, expert scrutiny calmed him; once he even smiled. But the light was bad, for the trees outside filtered it green and dim, as though the room lay at the bottom of a river. He took out a drawer and carried it across to the window, and this time, so deep was his concentration, he did not even glance outside. Having finished work on the drawer, he took it back and carefully slid it home in its place. That was when he heard the car. He dropped on all fours, panting, as he used to do with the doodlebugs.

It must be them. The car must be coming here, there wasn't any other house in the lane. Somehow, they'd heard about the search. Perhaps even trailed him all the way from London. Or they might have had the idea independently. They might be trying to get in first, having failed to do so at the Minos. One thing was sure; finding him here, they would have no mercy.

What could he do? Sprint out of the back? But if they found the door unlocked, they'd know he'd been there, whereas if they found everything locked and sealed (thank goodness he'd done that!) they just conceivably might overlook him. Still, they'd come into the house. Bound to. There was only one chance for him. He must hide.

While these thoughts flashed through his head, and fear actually sharpened his wits, he had crawled across the room and out into the passage, shutting the door behind him. He began to explore the house for a refuge. There was no cellar, and the kitchen cupboards would not lock. The engine of the car stopped, just as he saw a short ladder leaned against the kitchen wall. A ladder. That might mean a loft upstairs; indeed (again his training was useful) the pitch of the roof would suggest one. Worth trying anyway. Hugging his ladder, he rushed upstairs, hearing the door of the car slam as he did so. They were getting out, then.

There was no loft-hole in the landing ceiling nor in either of the bedrooms, which he entered on all fours again so as not to be seen through the windows.

"I'm keeping my head, aren't I?" he thought. "No! My godfathers! I've been a darned fool. They could have seen the bedroom doors moving from outside even if they couldn't see me. And any movement is a giveaway. Oh heck! Still, I'll have to open that other door. There's nowhere to hide here."

Opening the bathroom door was a terrible effort, thinking of the watchful eyes in the garden. But he did it, and what he saw was an immense relief. There was a muslin curtain over the window, so movements here couldn't be seen from outside. And, oh wizard! There was a square loft-hole with a loose wooden trap, in the ceiling over the bath. The perfect place, if he could only make it. There were heavy footsteps crunching up the gravel path; several people, he thought, and they weren't even bothering to be quiet. Why should they? They knew they could crush him as easily as treading on a snail. They were old hands at this sort of thing.

He poked at the trapdoor with the end of the ladder. At first it wouldn't budge. Then it came loose with a clatter, and slipped sideways, jamming in the hole. But at last he got the ladder in position, climbed up, and dragged it after him into the loft. It was not easy to maneuver in that confined space, but his training had given him an almost automatic dexterity. Just before the front door opened, he had replaced the trap and crawled away into the most remote corner by the eaves.

How queer it was up there! Overhead, a little light and a good deal of draft seeped through the crevices between the stone tiles. The floor consisted of big joists with deep spaces between them. He thought it would be wise to lie in one of these spaces out of sight; but just as he had stretched out (and the footsteps were indoors now, clattering over the stone floor downstairs) he remembered how houses are built. You have joists over the ceiling. But the ceiling itself, the plaster, is only attached to thin lathes nailed to the underside of the joists. He was lying, therefore, on nothing but lath and plaster, a flimsy support, especially in an old house like this. He might fall through at any moment into the room below. So, although he felt the enemy very near, he changed his position, and lay along one of the joists instead, which was rough and splintery and dirtied by birds. It ran to the edge of the roof, where it ended in what looked like a hole partly blocked by a bundle of rags. Had he dared, he would have crawled along and moved the bundle aside, so as to have a peephole and see what was going on. Luckily, he did not dare; for the supposed bundle of rags was a big barn owl dozing beside its nest, which it had made there for years and would certainly have defended. Left to itself, it was a most unobtrusive companion.

* * *

Richard Ringwood, finding the village policeman at his meal, had insisted on going to Miss Coltman's cottage alone, and was glad to do so. He told his driver to stay in the car, and opened the gate in the high hedge. It was an unpretentious old cottage of gray stone, with apple trees in front, a vegetable plot behind, and a few flower-beds, the whole, like its owner, kept in rough but decent order. Unconsciously Richard fell into his old leisurely country ways, planting his feet firmly and slowly, stopping to watch a tree creeper and light a pipe, pulling up a few promising young plantains, as he would have done in his father's garden. He noticed that the man who kept the garden in order when Janet was away had planted up the vegetables excellently; but the flowers wouldn't come to much this year. He had probably hoped to use some of the vegetables himself. Pity. The flowers must have been very charming formerly.

He removed the seals from the front door and unlocked it with the key he had brought. Before him was a flagged passage with a kitchen on the left and a living room on the right. He strolled round, making sure that the fastenings were secure, and then went into the living room, still smoking his pipe. He stood idly for a moment, enjoying the feel of the place and made indolent by the rustic peace. It was not difficult here to "get the atmosphere".

This place, unlike Worrall's cabin, was rich in atmosphere, and neither impersonal nor luxurious. Every bit of furniture, from the big ugly Edwardian desk to the elegant little rosewood sewing table, had been used – and perhaps ill-used, there was little evidence of polishing – for years, and one could to some extent guess at the owners. Surely it was Janet's long-dead mother who had imported the sewing table, the Tonbridge box, and the Spode bedroom china. Equally, the desk, the big leather armchair, and the fishing-rods outside, must have been Major Coltman's. The threadbare Turkey carpet would have started life long before the family came into being. But which of the three Coltmans had chosen to cook on an oil stove? Who had collected the complete works of Rider Haggard? Who had typed the card, brown in a dank and peeling bathroom, PULL GENTLY BUT DO NOT HOLD DOWN? How much of all this was Janet's family and how much the real Janet? Hard to say. Silly, too. As if people were only real when they were rootless!

And despite its shabbiness and total lack of convenience, this house was a good place to have roots in. Richard, as he went through the desk, felt increasingly heartless and ill-bred; it all seemed so innocent and touching. Janet and her father had kept each other's letters – long affectionate letters about very dull affairs – and they filled three drawers. A fourth contained their extremely simple legal and financial papers: the cottage had been bought in 1927 and then sublet for a while; the income tax – and therefore presumably the income – was consistently low. Major Coltman's will was in this drawer; he left everything to his daughter and asked her to destroy her mother's letters.

The rest of the desk was devoted to archaeological notes, mostly abbreviated and technical, but here and there with a phrase one could understand: *fortunately the first test pit struck the town midden*. But on the whole it was a barren field. Unlike most people, Janet seemed never to stuff unanswered letters and bills into her desk and forget them, for it contained no recent personal papers whatever. Of course, she may have had a clear-up before coming to London. Or somebody else – perhaps her would-be murderer – might have come in, between her departure and the sealing of the house by the police. True, the desk hadn't been forced; but probably the keys had been lost long ago; the keyhole was full of dust. It was easy enough to burgle. He turned to the birds'-egg cabinet.

The specimen of soil was there, labeled "Pontikonisi, topsoil," with dozens of others as exactly catalogued. He also found a small collection of Minoan antiquities, all fully labeled and none, he thought, valuable or striking. Worrall had given her most of them, but two large and lovely sherds of painted pottery were labeled in her hand "gift of Ian Shrubsole". That reminded him to look for gelatine and hydrochloric acid. He found both in good supply, just as Shrubsole had foretold, the one in the kitchen and the other in a corner cupboard in the sitting room.

He sat down rather despondently to think. But it is almost too noisy to think in the country. There were pigeons in the chimney and what sounded like rats in the roof, not to mention some tits who were behaving in a very impertinent manner on the windowsill. She must feed them. Well, what had he hoped to find? Threatening letters, signs of breaking in, a cache of faked antiquities? He did not know: only, after a thorough search, he found his vague hopes to be disappointed, as an archaeologist's are when he uncovers some ancient dwelling quite empty of pottery or bones or any sign of its former occupants. But (damn those pigeons! Can't they say it a new way?) what does he do then? *Fortunately his test pit strikes the town midden.* People throw things away, and rubbish is not often, if ever, collected in rural districts. Richard went out into the garden, drawing deep breaths of the delicious soft air.

The rubbish was tidily disposed in a little dell in the far corner. An admirable pit for vegetable compost, a dustbin for tins and bottles, and a bonfire for whatever would burn. It had been lighted not long ago, for the few scraps of unburned paper at the edge had not yet turned brown or sodden. She must have had her bonfire at the last possible moment before coming to London; it hardly looked a week old. What had she been burning?

Letters and photographs, and a good many of them to judge from the ashes. She had done it thoroughly, too. There were none of those wads of unconsumed paper that you find in a carelessly tended bonfire. The few tiny torn-up scraps that survived had blown to the edge, probably when she raked through the center. He gathered them up. The largest piece was typewritten and read "… ee to it at once … ever" and bore Worrall's cramped but coarse signature. The other fragments were in Shrubsole's hand, but torn up so small that one could not guess what they were about. "Should con …" (convince? condemn?) "is aftern" (this afternoon?) "d like to" (I'd like to? he'd like to?). One could only say this, that the fragments looked more personal than archaeological.

Here was a bit of a photograph, no bigger than a thumbnail. The detective's visual memory, as highly trained as an archaeologist's, could place it. It was part of a snapshot from the packet ap Ifor had sent him, a group of the whole party, workmen and all, taken on the site, and this fragment was a bit of a workman's head. Wasn't it rather ruthless of Janet to destroy the photograph so soon after it had been given to her? But perhaps you would expect her to be ruthless in a way; as rigorous as a nun in the elimination of nonessentials. She had preferred a tent to a hotel at Corfu. And here, the contents of her dustbin suggested that she lived chiefly on tinned baked beans.

Pouching his uninformative scraps of paper, Richard walked slowly back towards the house along a cinder path edged with catmint that had been allowed to sprawl and spread. Something white lay half-hidden under a thick spray – a man's handkerchief. Oh well! No doubt Janet, practical and unfastidious as usual, was still using up her father's stock. He picked it up. Surely this was rather odd? First, it was folded just as it had come from the wash, unused, and still clean inside, though rather grubby on both outer surfaces. Secondly, it wasn't Janet's. It bore the name I. Shrubsole in marking ink. Now most of us are fairly dishonest about other people's handkerchiefs. We find them, send them to the wash, and put them away with every intention of returning them; but usually end by adopting them next time we have a cold. Still, one wouldn't expect the conscientious Janet to behave like this, especially when she had dozens of her father's handkerchiefs upstairs. Besides, in this mild weather, she would surely be using smaller ones. But if one assumed that the handkerchief had been dropped here by Shrubsole himself – say, some time last week – why was it unused? He would surely have had recourse to it on the long journey down. And anyhow, even if he *had* sneaked in some time, perhaps to remove incriminating letters, would he have dared to light a fire in the open? It was just possible. The house was secluded and if anyone saw the smoke they would assume that it was the jobbing gardener burning weeds. Possible, but unlikely daring. He had better search the house again for traces of Shrubsole.

He began by reexamining the door. The seals were unbroken, but – how had he missed it before? – he noticed now that the backs of them bore two distinct impressions of the grain of the wood, one superimposed over the other. Someone had prised off the seals with a thin heated knife, and afterwards (probably with the same instrument) had reheated them and pressed them back into position. It was a clever job, and if Richard hadn't been talking to archaeologists this week and becoming interested in their methods of observation and deduction, he might never have spotted it.

He went in, looking for fingerprints. There were none that interested him on the furniture, but he did notice the little ball of cellophane glittering among the ashes of the hearth. He picked it out and spread it with tweezers and penknife.

Blissprins. You'd have expected Janet, if she used it at all, not to buy a patent brand, and to take it either upstairs or in the kitchen, where the tap was. Better just make sure it *was* Janet. He used his fingerprint apparatus. A clear impression, and unusually moist. Yes, the prints were Shrubsole's. He'd been here, and recently. It was he who had removed the seals, and whatever he had done here, he had done in gloves. But he'd taken off his right-hand glove to unwrap the tablets. And – how had he missed it before? Here was a bit of damp leaf-mold under the window. Richard himself, on his first entry, had only been walking on the gravel path. Could the man be still here, and hiding? He rushed out and called his driver. Then he began to search downstairs.

No one in the cupboards. No cellar. No one in the sheds. The driver appeared, and Richard told him to search the garden and watch the house to make sure that nobody got away. He went upstairs into the two bedrooms, but there was nowhere for anyone to hide in those Spartan and bare cells. The bathroom, he thought, was equally discouraging, but he looked in to make sure, and immediately noticed the loft. He tried to think where he had seen a ladder, but did not remember one. Well, he would have to go and look, but he might as well have a preliminary try. A wooden board lay across the bath, rough and messy with old soap, doing duty for a bathrack. He seized it and poked its end against the trapdoor, which lifted easily.

"Shrubsole! You'd better come down!" he called, but there was dead silence. He could not reach to get in, so he left it and ran downstairs for a ladder.

He did not find one, of course, but he did notice the two marks, a foot apart and ten feet up, where it had leaned against the kitchen wall, and he guessed the rest. Well, he must improvise. He raced upstairs again, lifted a table from Janet's bedroom, and carried it into the bathroom. He could not place it directly under the trapdoor, because the bath was in the way, but he put it as near as possible and set the bathroom chair on top of it. Useless; the approach was too oblique to keep balance. He dismantled the erection and started again. This time he stood the table upside-down across the bath right under the loft-hole and stood the chair upon it, between its inverted legs. Now he could reach easily. He mounted and heaved at the trapdoor. It did not budge.

He banged again, this time at one corner, and it rose a few inches before knocking against something hard and coming to a standstill. The person in the loft had wedged it somehow, perhaps with the missing ladder, and if he had any sense he was sitting on it. Richard, his blood up, began to shake and push at the loose panel with all his might. From the sounds above, there was some sort of free fight going on in the loft overhead.

* * *

When Ian Shrubsole heard the bath-board hit against the panel, and heard his name called, he was terrified, but not too terrified to think quickly. He remained absolutely still until he heard the footsteps receding, and then scrambled quickly over the joists and dragged the ladder down, so that one end rested against the top of the trapdoor, and the other was wedged against the sloping roof. For extra safety, he added his own weight, sitting on the ladder. They wouldn't easily get in now. He heard them returning, still in silence; they must have had all their plans laid well in advance to work thus without consultation. It was a regular campaign; there were footsteps in the garden as well as the search party indoors. What would be the next move? The footsteps returned and heavy things were banged about; he heard a sharp ring of metal. Then he saw in a flash what the plan must be.

They'd rigged up some way of reaching the ceiling, by heavy furniture; but if they couldn't move the trapdoor, they would shoot through it. The metallic sound was somebody putting down his gun. (In fact it was the brass claw of the table-leg bumping on the bathtap. But he was not to know that.) Therefore, to remain in his present position was madness and suicide. He must just hope that the ladder held the door down, and get as far out of range as he could.

He crawled desperately, instinctively through the shadows towards the little beam of light that came through the partly stopped hole under the eaves. As he crawled, his brain still worked. Suppose he could enlarge the hole! It might even be big enough to get through once he had removed the obstruction. Anyway, he'd be able to see. It was awful being shut up in this dark place, with its creepings and rustlings, not knowing what they were doing in the real world outside. It would be awful to die here in the shadows without ever seeing the light again. He struggled, careless now of noise, over the last joist to the hole, and thrust his hand towards it. His hand encountered no resistance, for he had put it right behind the obstruction and down the hole.

The next moment was blind panic. A soundlessly, flapping nightmare was upon him, a lamp-eyed horror that beat and tore at his face. He tried to stand and run, but hit his head on the roof and fell half-stunned. He was utterly afraid because utterly bewildered. Here was something that his mind – his one weapon – could not place except in terms of screaming skulls or harpies or vampires. That he was involved with a real creature simply did not occur to him; he reacted as though to a ghost or an infernal machine. Like a child diving under the bedclothes, he flung his arms across his face and rolled down between the joists, moaning.

Richard meanwhile had worked the trapdoor into a diagonal position and now it and the ladder together fell through the hole into the bath with a deafening clatter. He mounted the ladder and put his head through the hole. He could see nothing, but he heard the moaning. He climbed up and stood peering into the half-darkness. As he stood, a big pale shadow drifted noiselessly past his head, staring at him with an eye at once blank and piercing, like that of a nihilist philosopher lecturing on ethics.

"Shrubsole!" he called. "Come on out."

Still no answer. Like Ian, Richard moved instinctively towards the light, and there he found him prone.

"I can see you. Don't you think we'd better go down where we can talk? Come on!"

Shrubsole at last lifted his head and stared wildly.

"Who's that? Who is it? Inspector Ringwood?" He sounded absurdly relieved.

"In person. Well? What's the matter? Are you hurt? Why! There's blood on your face! What on earth have you been up to? Trying conclusions with the owl?"

"The owl?" Shrubsole stared again and then laughed hysterically. "Did you say *owl?*"

"I saw a fine one just now. Did you disturb it? I've heard they'll fly at your face sometimes, if you come near the nest, but I never actually knew it happen before. Not surprising really; they're more hawk than anything else. Must be pretty startling, I should think."

"But – but do you mean there's nobody – nothing here but an owl?"

"Of course not. Why should there be?"

"I – I'm going to be sick," gasped Shrubsole.

"Come over the hole, then, and do it in the bath."

The owl licked the last of Shrubsole's blood off its claw and settled back to sleep.

Chapter 14

HUDDLED in Major Coltman's armchair, Shrubsole suffered interrogation. He admitted to breaking in, but not to lighting the bonfire; he owned the Blissprin wrappings in the hearth, but denied having dropped the handkerchief in the garden. He had not been anywhere near the rubbish heap. The scraps of paper were in his writing, yes, and the handkerchief was one of his own; but he couldn't identify the scraps as anything he remembered having written lately, and the handkerchief was certainly not the (now rather dirty) one he had put in his pocket this morning. He could not have dropped it there on a previous occasion, for he had never been to Cholsford before. He observed that the ink on the scraps of paper was old, and that the dirt on the outside surfaces of the handkerchief was most of it not garden mold – it looked more like house dust to him – but of course the police wouldn't want to bother with details like that, he supposed, with a halfhearted sneer.

Urged once more to account for his presence, he denied, strenuously and repeatedly, that he had removed anything from the house or introduced anything into it.

"I was just looking," he said, "but of course I don't expect you to believe that. Well, go ahead. Why don't you arrest me and get it over? I can't stick this cat and mouse business."

His teeth chattered with nerves and nausea, and Richard felt, more strongly than ever, the curious sympathy, almost tenderness, of the hunter for the hunted. He had sent his sergeant off to make some inquiries in the village, and he and Shrubsole were quite alone.

"You're cold. Have my coat," he said, and threw it round the angular shoulders. "You still haven't told me what you were looking for. Or why you left London after promising to stay put. Or why you were obviously so terrified of being found here."

"Well, you've found me. Isn't that good enough for you? Where's the handcuffs?"

"I've seen people begging to be arrested before; it's one of the normal psychological reactions of those under suspicion. They think they'll somehow make things all right by punishing themselves. But it doesn't work, Ian, I swear it doesn't. Nothing makes them feel better except telling the truth. 'Unpack your heart with words,' doesn't Hamlet say?"

"You're misapplying your quotation, aren't you?" retorted the other with a ghost of his old aggressiveness. "Hamlet thought only drabs went on like that."

"*Touché!*" Richard's laugh, quick and spontaneous, seemed to warm the air. "I deserved it too, after all that rhetoric. Still, you *had* better tell me about it, hadn't you?"

Shrubsole felt the intimacy as strongly as Richard, but it gave him no ease.

"You wouldn't believe me. I know you're against me. You've had a down on me right from the start, haven't you?"

Richard busied himself with his pipe. In their tortuous way, he felt, Shrubsole's words were a cry for help, and now, if ever, was the moment to establish contact. How? Tell him the truth, perhaps, and tell it as placidly and objectively as possible.

"Well, to be quite honest, your manner did annoy me at first. I mean to say, nobody likes to be treated as an enemy, a snob, and a fool from the word go, do they?" He struck a match. "But afterwards, of course, I realized that it was just your way. Apparently you treat everyone like that."

Under cover of a cloud of smoke, he watched these ideas sinking into Ian's mind. They were evidently new to him.

"Since then, of course, I've got to know more about you. I've come to respect your work – your courage and integrity as a scholar. Lots of people would have paid lip service to Worrall for the sake of his position, especially people like you who had had a struggle to get into the archaeological world at all. Well, you didn't, and I admire you for it. And then I met your mother and realized how decent you were to your family and how fond they were of you. Macdonald and Janet gave you a good press, too."

"Yes?" A whisper. There was a person looking out through the hot black eyes now, a tortured person but a real one, younger and more vulnerable than the man he had seen before.

"So you see I got over my personal prejudices quite quickly." He smiled. "I hope you don't mind my being so frank. I'm afraid the police angle isn't so easy to get over. Like to see my notes about you?"

Shrubsole shot out his hand and drew it back as quickly, at once suspicious and scandalized.

"But you shouldn't – I mean, it must be illegal – surely that isn't a serious proposal?"

"It is, actually. There's nothing here but facts about you – facts you know already. But I wonder if you realize what sort of an impression they make to an outsider."

He took the notebook with timid avidity and read its whole catalogue of damning items: the quarrels with Worrall and Janet, the time, place, and opportunity he had for killing them both, his chance of "salting" the trench, his possession of the necessary tools and materials for each crime, the stealthy visit to the Minos … Here he gasped and broke off.

"Was it you, that night in the Minos?"

"I was there, yes." Richard did not mention the third intruder.

"What the …"

"And if you say 'what the heck' or 'my godfathers' again, I shall scream. If you want to swear, for God's sake swear!"

"Sorry," Ian muttered. Richard had spoken the words half-jokingly, but he seemed crushed out of all proportion. He went on in his hangdog way:

"You've got good reason to suspect me; I see that now. I've been a darned fool, and I suppose I'd better tell you. I thought I could do the job better than you. That's why I went to the Minos that night; I thought you were being stupid, giving them notice like that so that they'd have a chance to clear up all the clues. I was pretty sure the knife was a Greek job, you see, and I thought you hadn't spotted its significance. Sorry if I hurt you, but I thought you were one of *them*. In fact, I didn't expect to get away alive. I didn't today, either, for the same reason. When I heard the car, I thought it was *them*."

"I see," said Richard, trying to look as if he did. "But in that case, why didn't you just stay at home and keep out of it? Why stick your neck out?"

"It was – I had to *know*, you see. I had to know where I stood. I'd had four different ideas of the setup at different times, beginning at Corfu. And I – you won't believe me, of course – but *I had to know!*" He almost screamed the words, but then muttered. "Think that's silly, eh?"

"No, I don't. Will you tell me these four different views that you say you formed at different times? As clearly as you can?"

"It's easy enough to be *clear*. That's just expressing thought processes, and I can do that perfectly well."

Looking at him, Richard realized that this wasn't boasting. It was self-deprecation. And it was the truth. Shrubsole was an unsatisfactory specimen in many ways, but he *could* think.

"I understand. *Knowing* needs evidence as well as a clear head. Well, perhaps we can supply some of that. Go on."

Shrubsole began, like a lecturer of the most boring kind dictating notes.

"One. At Corfu, when Worrall found the Nausicaa Ring, so-called, and Janet at first questioned his interpretation but afterwards accepted it, I thought Janet had at last seen through him – it wasn't by any means the first shady thing he'd done. I thought she'd told him so and that he'd made some kind of bargain with her. I thought he'd promised to show up the other fakes and the other people if Janet promised not to expose him personally. I thought the gang had somehow got wind of this bargain, and that Worrall, caught between two fires, had been frightened into shamming ill and abandoning the dig. My suspicion was increased when Janet destroyed her own description of the ring in front of me. She didn't know I'd taken a copy first. I went on trying to persuade her to go back to her original, honest opinion, but she hedged and …"

"I know – loyalty, team spirit, incorrect. So you quarreled."

"Yes. But after that lunch in the Minos on Monday, I thought I'd misjudged her."

"Why? Because she'd had that row with Worrall?"

"Yes. I thought she'd taken my advice after all and told him she wouldn't play his dirty game. As for his death, I thought it was natural, and good riddance, too, as neither Janet nor I could have gone on working for him, but we were quite likely to keep our jobs once he was dead. I didn't think he'd have had a chance to alter his will, you see. Frankly, I just couldn't believe our luck."

Richard's distaste showed only in a slight flexing of the nose.

"And this, er, euphoria of yours continued until?"

"Till I found Janet wouldn't speak to me and had gone out of her way to attack me in her letter to *The Times*. Then I thought – what the heck? She's one of them after all. She's planning to chuck me out, get control herself, and carry on with the game as before. My godfathers?"

"The idea distressed you. But then?"

"Yeah, it distressed me. The idea of having no job and no colleague I could trust distressed me. Funny, wasn't it?"

"I apologize. Obviously we aren't talking about your feelings at the moment. Later, you say, you changed your mind. You spoke of four phases of opinion."

"Yes. Four. After I heard she'd been stabbed. I couldn't think why on earth that should have happened, unless she was honest after all. Unless she *had* taken my advice. Unless she *was* going to finish the lot of them and they knew it. In that case, I was partly responsible. It was because she'd decided to take *my* advice after all that they tried to kill her. But I hadn't any proof, one way or the other. I had to get it, specially when you …"

"Didn't seem to be handling the case very cleverly. Well, what did you hope to find?"

"Where that knife came from, for one thing. You know I went to the Minos that night, after you'd phoned me up."

"And – here?"

"I wanted to see if Janet had anything – fakes, or evidence against *them*, or threatening letters. To prove her guilty, or make sure she was innocent. I had to *know*."

"Innocent of the crime of faking? What about murder? You realize that on the evidence she could easily have poisoned Worrall herself?"

"Oh, that, yes. On the evidence at the time, I suppose. But in that case, why was she the next victim? Doesn't that let her out?"

"Technically, no. She might have intended to confess it and involve an accomplice, who therefore turned against her. Or one of Worrall's people, as the waiter suggested, might have killed her to avenge him. That hadn't occurred to you?"

"Everything occurred to me. I've been thinking of nothing else, I tell you, and I just don't know what to believe. I've found nothing either for or against her here. I suppose the evidence *could* be read to make her have done the murder. I suppose she might be involved in the other thing too – the fakes – which to my mind is worse. I shall try to find out. But how, I don't know." He looked exhausted.

"Well, I suppose you realize how thin your story sounds. Suspecting all you did, you want me to believe that you took these mad risks just to clear her, although you thought that you had not only the police, but also *them* after you. I wouldn't have called you a Quixotic type. Why did you do it? It isn't even as if you'd been engaged to her, or anything."

Shrubsole's sallow face flushed a little. "Not likely, is it? I can't expect you to understand, I don't suppose. It was the uncertainty. I had to *know*. I had to make sense of it. Otherwise I didn't know where I stood. I'd always regarded her as a sound, honest scholar, you see; I'd based a lot of my own work on her expert opinions. You don't realize how one has to rely on colleagues, and what hell it is if you can't."

"I do understand that, of course. But it doesn't seem worth risking your life for, especially if you half think the said colleague is a murderess and you know damn well she was nearly a murderee. Your actions just don't make sense."

"It wasn't only that." Shrubsole sounded exasperated. "I had to *know*, you see. For my own sake – for my own safety, if you like, because until I knew just how things stood I couldn't be sure of anything. I didn't know who to trust. I might be the next victim, and it would be just as bad if they threw suspicion on me or if they tried to kill me. I thought they'd do the second, and when I was set on in the Minos, I was convinced of it. Of course I never realized it was you. But I knew you wouldn't believe me if I came and told you that. I'd have to have proof. So I came down here to find it – to find something that definitely showed that Janet was in it with the others, or else that she was being blackmailed by them. Well, I didn't find anything. I just piled up suspicion against myself. And I'm still in the dark. I suppose *you* don't think that's anything to complain of, do you? Because *your* intelligence isn't the only weapon you've got. It's like that owl – it was hell not being able to understand what it was. But you don't believe me, do you? You think I'm putting it on?" He looked ghastly, staring and twitching. "Well, when they finally get me, you'll see."

"And who exactly are *they?*"

"Why, Worrall's gang, of course. The people who ran the fake business. The blokes he paid to do his dirty work, murder the boy, maybe, and stab Janet. Zoe, I suppose, for one, I thought you'd know."

"Well, and who else? Iorweth? Mikhailopoulos? The waiter? Where's your proof?"

"I don't know. It must have been a pretty big network if it could operate in Crete and Corfu and London, but that isn't surprising. Worrall had a name for paying his men well, and he must have had other holds over them too. Most Greeks have been in trouble with the law some time or other."

"That doesn't explain why the system should continue to operate *after* Worrall's death."

"No, it doesn't, does it?" He sounded baffled and tired to death. "Unless they're working for Janet, or think that I or Janet could pin something on them now. What a hope! I've just hindered you and put myself in the queer. In the dark, too, which is worse. Darned fool!"

"Damned, not darned, for God's sake. Sorry, I shouldn't pick on you; I'm on edge too. Look, Ian, I want to believe you. I damn nearly do. But I'm not at all sure my chief will agree with me. I'm going to propose a bargain. Suppose I don't arrest you. Suppose I leave you free and give you police protection against the threats you think are hanging over you. That'll satisfy my chief, because you won't be able to run away. Will you do two things in return? Find out about the faking business from beginning to end – we'll put all our resources at your disposal – and more important still, find out just how Janet Coltman comes into the picture. I suggest that the best way of doing that will be to enlist her help in the first inquiry. She's keeping some vital bit of information back, I feel sure, even if she's innocent herself. I can't do anything with her; I just mention Worrall and she shuts up like a clam."

"But – but if I'm under suspicion for stabbing her? And breaking into her house? You wouldn't take the risk of leaving her alone with me, surely? Anyhow, the nurses won't let me in."

"There won't be any nurses. She's at my house by now, I hope, staying with my wife. I imagine I can protect her. Well, is it a bargain? Here's the car outside. We can drive you back."

"But – I've got a return ticket."

"Oh hell! We'll stop at the station and get them to take it back. Come on!"

He stood up shakily and clutched at the desk for support.

"Dizzy? Take my arm, I've got some brandy in the car."

"I'd say just the same, drunk or sober," said Shrubsole, every inch the underdog. "So you might as well save your money."

Richard gasped. Back to the old attitude so quickly! Then a second glance at the deadpan face, which he now knew better, convinced him that this was the unspeakable fellow's idea of a joke. Perhaps all his earlier remarks were too?

"Never mind," he said, trying to reply in kind, "my money comes out of your rates and taxes, don't forget."

In the car, gingerly holding the flask, Ian remarked:

"My mother took to you in a big way." Richard's heart expanded. "But of course, she always does, it's just like her." Richard's heart contracted. "Mind you, she's no fool either."

Richard's heart gave it up, and he got out of the car and bought Ian a sandwich.

* * *

"Thank God you've come!" said Clare, as the lavatory door shut safely behind Shrubsole. "*Such* a party upstairs! I'd hardly got Janet settled before that awful Iorweth ap Ifor arrived – the hospital had given him our address – and as he'd brought a huge basket of grapes I didn't like to send him away just like that. Janet seemed perfectly willing to see him, but he's embarrassing her madly now she's got him, she's quite tongue-tied. And Sergeant Frewin, who was quite cozy at first, is sitting on the coffin stool by the bed, buttons and black stockings and all, doing an official dumb watchdog act; and he's walking up and down stroking that horrible little beard of his and holding forth on the Life Forces, and shows no signs of leaving; and Macdonald's not come, though goodness knows where he can sit down if he does. Do go and cope, darling, I haven't even started to get tea."

"Right. You take over Ian. He's been sick, so be kind to him."

He ran upstairs and heard Iorweth's jackdaw voice in full spate behind the bedroom door.

"... shy of the subject, of course. But as a married man, and married perhaps in rather a specially significant way, I feel I have a kind of mission to break through this conventional, sterile crust of yours. You don't realize the splendor of Life-giving. You'll remind me that the Goddess also has her virgin aspect – Dictynna, Britomartis – ach! Of course I know that!" You could tell he had inside knowledge by the way he made the Greek names sound just like a living language, in fact just like Welsh. "But it isn't your virginity that's at the root of the trouble, Janet *bach*, it's your negative attitude. You don't appreciate your own significance in the threefold pattern. You refuse to see that the Virgin is always the potential Bride. *Nympha*. The Welsh word is *Mamau* which of course means Mothers as well as Nymphs and is by lallation akin to the Anatolian *Ma*. Surely you must see that it's a blasphemy for you, a woman, a Life-bringer, a Labyrinth of flesh, a potential Cave of Being and Milk-bearing Tree – and the potentiality is in some ways more significant than the act –"

Richard waded in to the rescue. Janet, lying against a frilled pillow and wearing Clare's pretty nightgown and dressing-jacket, looked rather appealing, but flushed and awkward as a schoolgirl. Sergeant Frewin on the coffin-stool was stiffly attempting to melt into the background, having long ago lost the thread of the monologue. Only Iorweth was at ease, and sprang towards him with a glad cry and a rattle of amuletic jewelry.

"Hallo," said Richard. "I'm afraid I've been sent to break up the party. Could I have word with you before you go, Iorweth? See you presently, Janet."

Hustled on to the landing, Iorweth continued to tell Richard how he was sure that Janet's safety depended upon her adopting a more reverent and positive attitude to the Mother Goddess. He was cut short.

"Quite. Where's your wife?"

"She likes to spend the afternoon alone. It's a question of the reintegration …"

"Yes, yes. Will she be resting tomorrow afternoon too? Could you come along here alone, then, for a conference? Good. And have you got your private Minoan collection here in London? All of it? Could you possibly bring it with you? I need someone to educate me in a hurry about all this, so that I can understand about the Nausicaa Ring."

He did not flinch. On the contrary, he seemed delighted to oblige.

"By the way," added Richard on the doorstep, "is the Minos shut on Sundays, do you know?"

"I don't know. But I could easily ring up and find out for you."

Was the man a consummate actor or a consummate fool?

* * *

He returned to the sickroom.

"Well, how are you, after all that? What do you think, Sergeant Frewin? Has he tired her out?"

"Really, Inspector," replied the policewoman, sitting as it were to attention, "I hardly knew where to look. I did wonder if you'd want me to make a charge for obscene language, but he went so fast, I …"

Janet laughed heartily. She seemed quite herself again.

"Oh! He always talks like that. He's quite harmless really, apart from his inaccuracy. He *will* keep mistaking querns for fertility symbols."

Richard gasped. You never knew where you were with this woman.

"All the same, I'd rather not see him again," she went on. "You see, I couldn't bring myself to tell him about – you know." Her shyness returned. "He hasn't been told, has he? First I thought he knew and wanted to ask me about it, so of course I felt I couldn't refuse to see him. And then I thought he didn't and I wondered if I ought to tell him, but you'd said not to. It puts me in a terribly false position, you know, not having it out with him. Don't you think it's a duty?"

So that was it! She was shy, not of Iorweth the disciple of fertility, or even of Iorweth the suspected crook, but of Iorweth the deceived husband. He dismissed the policewoman and sat down in her place.

"Human situations are like teeth," he said. "It's always a mistake to have them out if you can possibly avoid it. And there isn't the least necessity for you to see him if you don't want to. But I would rather like you to see Ian Shrubsole for a minute. Could I bring him up? He's down in the drawing room now."

Her jaw dropped in uncouth dismay.

"Don't leave me alone with him! Please!"

"Of course I won't. You're getting full police protection till further notice."

"I didn't mean that!" Her hand flew to her mouth. "I told you yesterday, I'm sure he's innocent. Why d'you think I need protection? Have you found out something else?"

She might protest her belief in his innocence till she was blue in the face, but she couldn't disguise her fear. More than ever, it was clear that she was keeping something back.

"Yes, Janet, I have found out a bit more, but I don't think I'm quite ready to make a charge yet. Meanwhile, I'd like you to hear Ian's version from his own mouth."

He called down, and presently Shrubsole came edging into the flowery little room like an earwig entering a sweet-pea, but more conscious of the incongruity.

"Hallo, Janet."

"Hallo, Ian."

"You look all right."

"Yes, I'm all right."

"I came to the hospital three times."

"Yes, I know."

An unyielding silence on both sides.

"I haven't told her about today, Ian," prompted Richard.

"Today?" Janet looked up for the first time. "Good gracious! What on earth have you done to your face?"

"That was your owl." Shrubsole gave a hysterical giggle. "I suppose Iorweth would say it was Athene the Guardian rallying round in person. I notice you don't refuse to see *him*. Well, I can't wonder. Specially after today. No good saying I'm sorry, I suppose. You won't believe me anyway."

"Perhaps if you made it clear what it is that I'm supposed not to believe," Janet began in the formal lecture-room voice that she usually reserved for the Nausicaa Ring, "and what you're supposed to be apologizing for ..." She broke off. "I say, are you all right? You do look awful."

"That's it! Go on! Why don't you tell me I'm nuts right out and get it over? You've implied it often enough, Pete knows! Specially when I've said something you can't answer."

"I've done nothing of the sort! *I'm* not the one that backs up bad arguments by personal abuse, as you know very well." She sat up, formidable in her cold and eloquent indignation. "It was *you* who said *I* was blinded by my emotions. It was *you* who accused *me* of being incapable of intellectual honesty. *I* didn't drag in the personal issue, it was *you*. Just because I happen to have a respect for better and riper scholars than myself! Just because I won't jump to conclusions! Even about my own special subject, which incidentally doesn't happen to be yours!"

Really, thought Richard, she looks like Pallas Athene on the warpath. This isn't acting. But why does she – both of them for that matter, for Shrubsole was also quivering and glaring – get so worked up about this old controversy of theirs? Surely they're not so madly one-track that they think it's more important than murder? Or – are they afraid to talk about that?

Shrubsole's answer, which came out as something between a cringe and a snarl, was almost equally off the point.

"Well, I've apologized, haven't I? I'm sorry I said that, and I'm sorry I broke into your cottage today, and I'm sorry I thought you were in the racket. I'm beginning to think now that you weren't being deliberately dishonest, you were just being stupid. I misjudged you. I can't say more than that, can I?"

To judge by the tense way Janet was breathing through her nose, she was not mollified, and no wonder. Richard attempted to bring the discussion back from the unreal atmosphere of *odium archaeologicum* to present facts.

"Yes, you jolly well can say more," he interposed. "And I'll say it for you. Look here, Janet, this tiff about the Nausicaa Ring has become pretty unimportant, hasn't it, in view of what's happened since? Unless it all connects up? Well, when you were stabbed, Ian here thought it *did* connect up. He thought there was a gang who were putting over fakes in a big way, and he thought you'd taken his advice and had it out with Sir Alban. So he concluded that somebody found out that you knew too much and tried to put you away. Before that, he'd thought you might be in the gang too."

"Me!" She was outraged.

"I don't think he actually suspected you of the murder."

"Of course not." She brushed the suggestion aside impatiently. "Well?"

"Well, he tried to make amends. He tried to find out who *was* in the gang, as he calls it, and what they were doing, and which of them had attacked you. He didn't tell me, as he thought I'd bungle it. I don't blame him. So he worked by himself and took a lot of risks in doing so – not only the sort he expected, but he unconsciously piled up some very nasty circumstantial evidence against himself. He broke into the Minos on Thursday night and only got away after being in a fight and leaving me plenty of proof that it was him. And I found him in your cottage today, hiding in the loft. *He* said he was looking for papers to prove you were either fighting the gang or being terrorized by them. *I* thought he was removing something that incriminated him, but now I'm not so sure. Tell me, did you burn any papers in his writing just before you came away? And photographs? Could it have been you who dropped one of Ian's handkerchiefs by the path on the way to the rubbish heap?"

"Oh, yes, I expect so. I did burn a lot of rubbish last week."

"But somebody else's perfectly good handkerchief isn't rubbish."

She again looked mulish and flustered. As her uncle had said, she was a very bad liar.

"Yes. I … I was having a thorough clear-out, you see, to make room for all the new stuff. I have to save space. Anyhow, I can assure you that I *was* destroying papers, last Friday, in fact, and there may very well have been a handkerchief among them." She still looked guilty. "It – it was only an old one, anyway."

"Well, in that case I believe you, Ian, when you say that you left things as you found them. And I hope you'll accept his explanation too, Janet, anyhow as a working hypothesis. Will you?"

"I suppose so," she muttered, looking wooden.

"You were more generous yesterday. When I suggested he was the likeliest suspect – and I showed her my notebook, too, Ian – you said you were absolutely convinced of his honesty. You said that nothing would make him stop putting the truth first, even if it was damaging to himself. You said he was tactless and nervy and aggressive, but absolutely straight. Don't you think so any more?"

She was silent, but Shrubsole spoke instead.

"Well, of course she doesn't. Since then I've sneaked into her house with a skeleton key. I can see it looks bad. Listen, Janet, I don't care a darn about the personal angle, I just want to get at the facts. You can think what you like. *He* says you've got other reasons as well as that ring for thinking there was some shady stuff going on. Well, so've I. And I want to *know*. Don't you?" He stretched out his hand in appeal.

"Don't touch me!" said Janet, recoiling.

"I needn't say," added Richard, "that if you could see your way to working together, it would make my whole case much easier. You both seem to think it doesn't matter having an unconvicted murderer at large."

"All right," said Janet, but still fought a delaying action. "But we can't start yet. The B.M.'s shut on Sunday. And half the objects we need to inspect are in Crete or Corfu still."

"Oh, what the …! We can start on what's here, can't we? Monday morning?"

"I don't know if I'll be well enough by then."

"Monday afternoon," said Richard, "unless we let you know to the contrary. I'll get you driven home now, Ian. And you'll get protection from now on."

"Huh!" He gave a sudden, barrow-boy's grin. "You mean you'll see I don't run away. Well, I can't, see? We English criminals can't afford it with hotels the price they are. *I* can't run up Mount Ida and get meself suckled by the goat Amalthea."

The combination of Cockney pathetic irony with classical myth was too much for Richard. He burst out laughing and even Janet could not help laughing too – the idea of Shrubsole as an infant Greek god was irresistible. As they got up to go, the atmosphere suddenly lost its tension. Just then the bell rang.

"That'll be Macdonald, I expect. Will you have him up now, Janet, or after tea?"

"After tea," called Clare from below. "She ought to rest a little first. Come on down, you two."

Shrubsole went out abruptly. On the landing he turned, with the old shifty hunted stare. "Macdonald, eh? What does he want? Did she ask to see him?"

"No." Richard tried to soothe him. "But she seemed very pleased at the idea. He's *simpatico*, don't you think? And she needs cheering up, poor girl. Why? Don't you trust even him? I thought he was a friend of yours. Why don't you come and have a word with him?"

Shrubsole was at his most prickly.

"Thanks all the same, I'll leave the social stuff to you. I don't feel like small-talk just now. I'm funny that way. *Nevropatico*, see? I can talk Italian too, I don't think. Well, enjoy yourselves. And don't forget to tell them about the owl, that's good for a laugh, I bet."

He ran downstairs, turned at the door, and said with extraordinary violence:

"Jabber, jabber, jabber! Think it'll get you anywhere?"

Chapter 15

By lunchtime on Sunday Janet looked much healthier and was obviously happy with the Ringwoods. Her reverential attitude to Richard no longer alarmed him, for she had conceived an equally wholehearted admiration for his wife. In ordinary social intercourse, Clare's hummingbird beauty and quick wit would have made Janet awkward and inarticulate; but one cannot be shy for long of a really sympathetic nurse. Besides, Clare had confided in her ("Four months and still not a suspicion of a baby, not a hiccup. D'you think I'm barren, or impotent, or something?"), and had kissed her good night as a matter of course. It was the nearest thing to a home that Janet had known since her father died, and she thrived on it, not indeed forgetting her troubles, but more conscious today of the kindness of her two comforters.

The case was not discussed in her presence. Though Richard now and then slipped away to telephone to the four men whom he had posted to watch for him; though he took two foreign calls which gave him lively satisfaction; though a policeman was sitting over the *News of the World* in the kitchen, Janet remained unaware. She simply reposed and expanded on the family bosom.

It seemed quite natural, though in fact it was prearranged, that Clare and Richard should be asking her after lunch about the ancient Cretan religion. They had been looking at pictures of the Minoan seal-rings.

"Was it just another form of the same old Near Eastern stuff – a whopping great Earth Ma and a poor little Air Pa? Was King Minos the Goddess's consort and did he have to perform a ritual mating and death and rebirth every year?"

"Poor man, I hope not," said Clare. "*So* exhausting for him!"

"I don't think so," Janet replied, "because he renewed his strength every *nine* years in the Dictaean Cave, whereas sacred copulation has to be *annual*, you see. Otherwise there'd be no point in it."

Clare stifled a giggle. "Then who's the poor little man you see standing by the Goddess in the pictures, looking so frightfully henpecked? A priest or something?"

"Well, that's a disputed question, but many people now think that he was an Eniautos-Daimon."

Clare looked puzzled and her husband explained.

"The Year-Spirit. Something to do with Spring, as Noel Coward puts it."

Janet now looked puzzled in turn.

"Coward? I'm afraid I haven't seen his work. Is he an American anthropologist?"

"No," said Clare. "It's just a song. I see; the god's little because he's really just a sort of annual stunt, whereas the Goddess is huge because she goes on forever. How rational. I *am* disappointed. When I saw those pictures, I imagined wild thrilling orgies. You know, song, sex, and slaughter. The Sacred King opening the furrow. Streams of human blood. Ululation. Sinuous pneumatic women with nothing on doing a can-can."

She stopped, her husband having kicked her under the table to restrain her ribaldry. But Janet did not seem shocked except perhaps by Clare's ignorance.

"Oh, no. You very seldom find the nude represented in Minoan art. You must have been misled by the early codpieces. The female dress *does* of course expose the breasts, but it was so general that I doubt if it had any erotic significance. In fact Nilsson speaks of the prudishness of Minoan art. The figures are always draped, at least with some form of loincloth. Even the ordinary fertility-symbols aren't usually represented, unless you want to read a phallic meaning into the form of the baetylic shrine."

Richard directed another quelling glance at his wife, but it was unnecessary. She sat pink and speechless.

"Explain to me about baetylic shrines, Janet," he said. "I've never quite made out what they were for."

"Well, I think Evans was right. They were originally single upright stones, representing the deity in a rude aniconic form."

"Not shaped like a human figure, you mean?"

"No. Quite aniconic, but treated as a seat of divinity. They'd oil it and circumambulate it and so on. Where you see more than one stone – and of course on the seals we notice both triliths and biliths – the supporting stones would be for protection or the accommodation of offerings. There's generally a sacred tree planted by the shrine."

"Biliths and triliths," murmured Clare. "What heaven!"

"But didn't they have statues and pictures of their gods too?" Richard asked.

"Certainly, inside the houses, but it isn't uncommon to find the iconic – in this case the anthropomorphic – coexisting with the aniconic form. In fact, it seems to be the rule in glyptics – that is, in gem engravings."

"I see. I suppose it's a sort of label, like putting lilies in a picture of the Madonna. So if I see a baetylic shrine and a large woman by it, I can bet she's the Goddess in person, can I?"

"Yes, or the god if it's a male figure. Just occasionally a human votary might be the right interpretation, but it's doubtful."

"And if I find human figures on a ring without any, er, rude aniconic stone or baetylic shrine – shut up, Clare! – I'll know they're just ordinary human beings getting on with everyday life?"

Janet hesitated, but only for a second.

"I suppose so, possibly. But as far as I know, such secular representations simply don't occur on the seals. They're invariably religious in character, and always include the sacred stone or tree. Generally both."

She had made the admission! Richard concealed his excitement and signaled to Clare to carry on the conversation.

"But, Janet, what did they *do?* Apart from oiling and circumambulating the rude aniconic stone, which sounds a bit pedestrian. Didn't they have *any* orgies? Not even prudish ones?"

Janet plunged into a cautious account of bullfights and open-air dances, which she made sound like a cross between a rodeo and a church fête. She did not stop till Clare took her up to rest. Iorweth ap Ifor was nearly due, and Richard wanted to spare her the crisis for which he was bracing himself.

* * *

He arrived in a taxi, wearing an overcoat in spite of the warm weather, and empty-handed.

"Haven't you brought your collection?" Richard asked in dismay.

"Oh yes, indeed I have, Inspector." He took off his coat gingerly, refusing help, and held on to it. "The fact is, my wife – she has wonderful gifts, as you know, but we have to remember that she's also a human vehicle – well, no doubt it *is* more risky to carry valuables about in her country. Could you be so kind as to lend me a box or tray?"

Richard brought one, and Iorweth began to empty his pockets, beginning with the overcoat. There were dozens of little boxes and parcels.

"She doesn't even like me to take things to the museum, unless I'm actually wearing them. So I thought it better not to bring a case."

"You didn't tell her?"

"Oh, indeed I told her I was coming here. She always likes to know where I am. But I thought it better not to mention I was bringing my collection." He undid the top of his trousers, hitched up his shirt (his green silk pants were a wonder to behold), and untied a tape that encircled his stomach. "This little amulet is obviously intended to be carried inside the navel, as you see it has an omphalos on it. But I found it caused soreness, so I just get it as near as I can without discomfort. Yes, I thought it better not to worry Zoe with what is after all merely a difference in culture. Not race, mark you, because the Welsh, as I think I told you …"

"Perfectly right, I'm sure. The main point is, you've brought the things. Let's come and sit down."

Iorweth would have made a wonderful salesman. He had the power – founded on successful self-deception – of making the worse appear the better article; and if that failed, he could make you feel a cad for questioning his veracity. Yet even to Richard's amateur eye it was apparent that many of his treasures were fakes, though a few – for instance, the rudest of the figurines, and some of them were very rude indeed – looked genuine. No one could possibly have made them look like that on purpose. Eight signet rings, five with gold seals and three set with big engraved stones, were outstanding in workmanship and astonishingly well-preserved. Somehow they seemed a bit too good to be true.

"Where did you get these?"

"Oh, surface finds reported by various peasants, though I'd forgotten I had so many of them," he replied. "I think I've kept a note of the localities somewhere. Zoe has a wonderful instinct – or is it something deeper? No! If one uses the word instinct with a full and reverent sense of its meaning, there *is* nothing deeper – Zoe often hears of these finds before anyone else. Sir Alban was very struck."

"Did she ever find anything for *him?*"

"Well, that's rather a delicate question. He did make a rule at one time not to accept anything that hadn't been noted *in situ*. Humoring poor Janet, no doubt; she's terribly hidebound in some ways, as he often agreed when I was alone with him. Still, I think that now" – he made a sanctimonious death-face like an undertaker – "I may tell you without harm that he did sometimes break his rule. Yes indeed. But he sold the things later to Americans, so I've heard. Conscience doth make cowards of us all. Yes, poor man! How deeply true!"

The telephone rang outside and Richard ran to answer it. A stolid, official voice.

"Sturt speaking. Your man's just gone off in a taxi. I think it was sent for him, the driver had a job persuading him to go. He's taken a suitcase and a brown-paper parcel. Wearing a navy suit and black hat. I didn't follow as instructions were to give you a ring at once."

"Good. Take down this address and join Samuelson there as quickly and unobtrusively as possible."

He had hardly settled again in the drawing room when the telephone rang again.

"Samuelson here," a new voice rapped out. "A man's just arrived in a taxi. Dark, slim, foreign-looking, blue lounge suit, black hat, cases and parcel. The porter says he often visits here, afternoons. Right?"

"That's him. I congratulate you. Look, I've sent you Sturt and I'll be along myself as quickly as possible. Can you cover the entrances?"

"There's three. Jukes is on the fire escape. Do what I can."

Richard rushed back.

"Got your latchkey, Iorweth? Look, we've got to go along to your place quickly. Never mind the things. I'm leaving someone here to keep an eye on them. Yes, a proper policeman. He's here now. Come on. I'll explain in the car. There's something fishy going on in your flat."

He pushed him protesting into his overcoat and out of the front door.

Iorweth clutched at Richard's arm as the car swung round a bend.

"Well, Inspector? Well?"

His jackdaw voice, his ruffled plumage, his bright nervous eye, made him more birdlike than ever; and Richard remembered, with irrelevant pity, that the jackdaw is inconsolable for the desertion of its mate, and will only take a new one if it has actually seen its former partner dead.

He spoke briefly of the evidence that Zoe was unfaithful, and was about to speak of his more serious suspicions. But Iorweth never let him finish. He burst into a hysterical flood of speech. Where most men would have taken the news in stunned silence, or expressed a single attitude, Iorweth expressed all in turn. He raged and lamented, denied and admitted. Now he reproached her tenderly, even with tears, and now vowed divorce, repudiation, and revenge. In one breath he spoke of forgiveness and a new start, and in the next of her punishment and his own suicide. It was like an anthology from six different melodramas, and yet the man did not seem to be acting; there were real tears in his eyes and an unmistakable break in his voice. And they were approaching Missenden Mansions. Richard saw Sturt at the main entrance and they exchanged imperceptible signs of recognition.

"For God's sake, Iorweth, control yourself! I need your help and you probably need mine. We've got to get in quietly. Which is the best way?"

"The parcels entrance." He was unexpectedly practical though the tears stood in his eyes. "Go past the building, first right, and right again under the arch."

The car drew up in a glass-roofed court like the loading yard of a big shop. Iorweth went first, and after a quick reconnaissance beckoned them indoors. But Richard left his driver on guard and followed alone. It was Iorweth who led the way to the service lift and worked the mechanism, though quivering with emotion and sibilantly muttering; and Iorweth who led the way through the maze of carpeted passages on the third floor, past the rows of identical green doors. Richard had hoped to see Samuelson, the best of his subordinates, but there was no sign of him; one could only hope all was well. At last they came to Flat 108. Iorweth handed Richard the key, and stood unexpectedly quiet and patient while he oiled the lock and soundlessly unlatched the door. It swung inwards for a foot and jammed against some obstacle within. He squeezed in, Iorweth following. The hall was full of luggage, and angry Greek voices were arguing in the bedroom. Iorweth laid his ear to the keyhole.

"What are they saying?" whispered Richard.

"I can't understand. Can you?"

"No. We'd better go in."

"No! Wait! Wait till ..."

Richard glanced at his face and was appalled at the tortured fury of it; yet he had never seen the man look so intelligent. He was a truer Welshman than he knew, capable of a rage subtle, underground, and secret, containing itself until it had found its mark.

The voices had died. "Now!" breathed Iorweth, and flung open the door.

Zoe released Georgios from her embrace, and drew herself up to face the intruders. Though fully dressed, even to smart high-heeled shoes, long gloves, and a tiny black hat with a diadem of osprey plumes, she still looked primitive and magical; her eyes implacable and enigmatic in her high-nosed face, her dancer's hips tensed as if to spring. And even as Richard watched her, she extended her right arm, bent at the elbow, in an attitude of … (what nonsense these archaeologists talked! It was just the Cretan attitude for emphatic speech.) Her arm, like the rest of her, was loaded with expensive modern jewelry.

"What you doing here, gumshoe?"

"Zoe! I … I …"

"I brought him," said Richard. "And he knows. You were just going to bolt, weren't you? But you couldn't find the other faked rings, and Georgios Aiakides wouldn't take you without. Why, Georgi? Were you going to plant *them* on old Mikhailopoulos too? Or did you still hope to sell them?"

The waiter was tongue-tied and pale green with fear, staring out of his long eyes like an animal in a trap.

"Look, Inspector!" hissed Iorweth, plucking at his arm. "She was taking all the jewels I gave her. My mother's jewels, too! It iss worth thousands of pounds, thousands!"

"So what?" Zoe's stillness was as violent and threatening as a volcano's. "Listen, gumshoe! Listen, mister! He give me jewels, sure, he give me money. But he *not* give me …"

Her gesture was even less prudish than a fertility-symbol, and Iorweth made a strangled sound of protest.

"Not good. Not strong. Not enough," she continued brutally. "Always you talk, talk, of mother, of baby, of spirit, just like old priest. So what? I take Georgios, he's good, he's yong, he give me love, don't you, honey? A-ah!" All three men stirred involuntarily at her amorous sigh, as seaweed stirs at the margin of a whirlpool. But now, without the least loss of intensity, she became businesslike.

"Listen! I don't want no trouble, Iorweth. I meet you. You let me alone, I give you the jewels of your mother. Yes?"

"No! No! All the jewels are insured in my name. The furs too!" He almost danced with emotion. She took one menacing pace forward, and he shrank.

"Listen! I have give you plenty love, no? Four month, maybe five month, I have no other man, only you. You think it is pleasure? You lousy little *spado*, how you say, unch! You think I give my love free? To you, unch!" She laughed.

"Take her in charge, Inspector! Take them both in charge! She called me a eunuch! It isn't true! It isn't true!"

Richard took a step forward. Zoe's arm moved. She was stripping off her heavy gold bracelet.

"Oll right! Oll right!" she shouted in her vibrant contralto. "You take the jewels, old *spado!*" With the athletic precision of a dancer, she hurled the bracelet and caught her husband squarely on the nose. "And tell this police fellow to scram. I don't take nothing, only Georgios."

"No!" the young man screamed, suddenly finding his tongue and leaping forward. Richard drew his gun and the group froze again, Georgios extending his right arm, bent at the elbow, in the attitude of ... of one about to do a deal.

"Listen, sir!" He pleaded with Iorweth. "I don't take her, no. She's beautiful, O.K. But without jewel, she don't buy me the hotel. Too bad. I must wait, buy hotel myself, then have beautiful girl. You think I'm crazy, sir? How can I keep girl without money?"

Zoe screamed at him in Greek, but he was concentrating on ap Ifor.

"And listen, sir. I tell you something nice, maybe you won't make me no trouble, you be so pleased." He smiled bewitchingly. "You think you are *cocu?* With horns, yes?" He gesticulated to make things quite clear. Iorweth pawed at Richard's arm in a frenzy.

"Take him away! Take him away!"

"But wait, sir. This is nice, what I tell you. I have sleep with Zoe, yes often, she's a fine girl. But I don't make you *cocu*. For this Zoe, she is ..." He paused dramatically and they all looked at him.

There was a shattering bang. Zoe had taken a small pistol from the bosom of her dress and shot Richard's gun out of his hand, which was momentarily paralyzed with the shock.

"Watch *him!*" shouted Richard, disentangling himself from Iorweth and springing towards Zoe. But Zoe, moving like a whiplash, was already out of the window. He climbed after, shouting down to Jukes who was supposed to be guarding the bottom of the fire escape. Zoe was halfway down the first of the three flights of steps already, going as fast and smoothly as a cat. Richard clattered after her. He saw Jukes at the bottom. Zoe, a high-heeled shoe in each hand, was streaking down right into his arms, but at the top of the last flight suddenly became aware of his presence. Without a second's hesitation she flung her shoes at his head, first one and then the other. Both hit him hard in the face. She turned and fired her gun at Richard, but he sprang aside just in time, and the bullet ricocheted, ringing on the steel of the stair. Richard came straight on, and Jukes had begun plodding up to his assistance.

But Zoe was no longer on the stairs. She had mounted the narrow handrail of the little square platform at the turn by the first floor and stood there, poised on an inch of slippery iron, every tense curve outlined against the sky, in an enchanted second of suspended movement. Richard almost expected her to fly. Not that she looked spiritual; far from it. She was flesh raised to such sovereignty of perfection that it seemed potent in its own right to transcend the ordinary laws of nature. As he gazed, she launched out, taking to the air with the sureness and grace of a swallow.

Of course she didn't fly. But she took off with such superb confidence that Richard began to think that, in spite of the height of the drop, she might land on her feet and run. He ought to have told Jukes to stay below. These thoughts flashed through his mind in the fraction of a second between her spring and her fall, before he leaned over to look down. She was falling now, feet together, arms spread, breasting the air like some divine bird, all that pride and mastery falling to be a mass of broken bones and blood. For he could see now that a big open sports car was drawn up immediately beneath her. She could not miss it.

She did not miss it. She dropped, as she had intended, plumb on to the cushion of the passenger's seat. The springs must have been wrecked; but Zoe was unscathed, and before Richard had pushed past Jukes, who was turning clumsily to run back again, she was in the driver's seat and had started the engine. The car was shooting out of the yard by the time he reached the ground. He ran out into the street after it, but it was already out of sight. He returned.

Jukes was standing at the bottom of the fire escape, a high-heeled shoe in each hand, looking stolidly dazed. Richard was almost too angry to speak to him.

"Well, Jukes?"

"Well, sir, it just goes to show. People oughtn't to leave their cars unlocked. Did you get the number, sir? 'Fraid I missed it."

"NBG 666," said Richard between his teeth. "Send out a general call at once. And give me those shoes. For God's sake! Want to keep them for a souvenir, or something?"

"No, sir, I ..." He saluted, and as Richard ran back up the fire escape, added under his breath, "As if I needed any blooming souvenir! God, what a woman! I'll catch her. I'll catch her. Only to see her again, just once."

* * *

Richard climbed in through the window to find the bedroom empty, a chair overturned, and the door open. The hall door was open too, and he could hear a voice in the passage. He went through.

He found a curious scene. Samuelson (his best man, a London Jew of the toughest, clever, decisive, and devoured by ambition) was sitting on the lid of a large laundry basket across a corner in which Iorweth stood penned and panting.

"Samuelson!"

"Inspector Ringwood!" he snapped. "Sorry I can't stand up."

"Well?"

"Report? Couldn't cover all the entrances, see, so I popped into this basket outside the flat – I made the porter tell me the number. Heard you coming with the second man, but I couldn't contact you. After a bit, there was a breakout. The first man was an easy cop."

"And the other?"

Samuelson jerked his head at Iorweth. "This is him. Laid into the first one like a wild cat."

"What? Did the other one get away?"

Samuelson showed his teeth. "Oh no! He's in this basket. For safety. Couldn't keep the other one off of him, and the two together were a bit more than I could handle by myself, see?"

"Mm." It was always hard to praise this man who was so patently and in a way so justly asking for it; but as an indirect compliment he added, "The woman got away."

"Tck!" said Iorweth. It seemed inadequate.

"She won't get far. She was in a stolen car, and it's bound to be stopped. She doesn't know her way about London, does she? Samuelson."

"Sir!"

"Never mind the Sir just now. Watch this man. I'm going to get the other one out. He sounds as if he'd fainted or something."

Samuelson got off the basket, but the lid was not raised.

"Georgi!" called Richard.

"Nè," replied a faint voice, and Georgios showed his big eyes over the rim. He saw Iorweth.

"Panagia!" he cried, and pulled the lid down. Even two policemen and the invocation of the Virgin were not, it seemed, sufficient protection. At last, encouraged by Richard, he came up again, and extended his right arm to Iorweth in a gesture limp but still Minoan.

"Please, please listen, sir. Is nice, what I try to tell you. You are *not* dishonor, no *cocu*. Zoe, she already have two hosband in Crete."

"She's married already?" Iorweth was incisive. "Who to?"

"Two men, sir. First to boy in her village. Then to *propriéteur* of the restaurant where she dance at Candia. My cousin in Crete, he write and tell me. Everyone know."

"In that case, Inspector" – Iorweth spoke with sudden formality – "I won't prosecute, provided that you can recover my property." He might, for all the emotion he showed, have been discussing his father's coal mine.

"Ah, good! I come out now." Georgios, his fears allayed, began to rise smiling from his vessel like an Eniautos-Daimon in Spring. But at a sign from his officer, Samuelson grappled him. There was a click, and the smooth brown hands were manacled. He screamed.

"There's the matter of the faked rings," said Richard. "And more, too. Take them both for questioning."

"No! You can't prove nothing on me, sir! Nothing!"

"Nothing? Louis Rosenau in Rotterdam? Andreas Bagadakis in Candia? Planting the seal in Mikhailopoulos's guitar on Thursday night?"

"Ah! Panagia!" Georgios turned pale. "But I only work for Zoe. Zoe's the boss, sir, I swear by God. She don't evven pay me much. She" – his voice broke – "she give me love. Oh my God! Just for love and little money, I got all this trouble."

He buried his face in his fettered hands and wept. Richard pitied him, but Iorweth took no notice whatever.

"If you want me to come too, Inspector, perhaps we could be making a start. There's no point in standing here."

Samuelson rasped, "Bracelets for him as well, Inspector?"

"Bracelets?" For a moment Iorweth looked bewildered, and then, as he understood, his face became the picture of affronted dignity. "It iss unnecessary. I am cooperating, of course."

"No bracelets," said Richard. "But I must warn you that you are under arrest. I'm not at all sure that you're so innocent about the fakes as you pretend."

* * *

Richard did not get home till after dinner that night to tell his story to Clare and Janet.

"Yes, we got Zoe in the end. But not before she'd managed to stash away all the jewels – God knows where, she won't say – and shoot up two policemen, and wreck the car. Maybe we'll crack her in the end, but … Lord, she's magnificent! She's awful! She makes Medea and Clytemnestra look like old rope."

The two women did not share his enthusiasm.

"She's a murderess, I suppose," said Janet heavily.

"You and Ian just get the facts about the faking," he replied, "and I think I can promise you the rest of the story tomorrow. Wait till then."

"And Iorweth? Is he in prison too?"

"Under house arrest. Why, Janet? What is it?"

"I was wondering if I'd be allowed to ring him up or something. It must be so awful for him."

"Do ring him up, of course, if you don't mind the line being tapped. But he's surprisingly calm – sort of cutting his losses. Odd, after all his histrionics at the time."

"I don't think so," Clare said. "He can't do anything now, so why get worked up? Celts are like women, essentially practical in their emotions."

"Still," Janet said, her voice troubled, "it's awful for him, isn't it? I mean, living with someone all that time, and then finding you'd been living in – I mean, not properly married after all. He must feel dreadful about it. Sort of" – she blushed – "impure."

Richard marvelled inwardly, but all he said was:

"Well, you come and cheer him up on the telephone. I'll put the call through at once, and then you must go to bed. I want you fresh for tomorrow."

Chapter 16

EARLY next morning a young constable, on his way back from night duty at Missenden Mansions, called with a letter from ap Ifor to Janet. He said that ap

Ifor had been unwilling to let him read it but very anxious for it to be delivered.

"It's kind of you to come out of your way," said Richard. "Miss Coltman can read it in my presence, and no doubt she'll be willing to show it to me."

He took it in with Janet's breakfast tray, and she willingly agreed with his proposal. A few minutes later, Clare found him on the stairs, reading the letter and spluttering.

"Good Lord! It's ridiculous. You never saw such stuff – devotion, and ethnology, and a panegyric on virginity, and a clear statement of income and prospects, and touching appeals for sympathy, all mixed up. Pages of it. *What* a moment to choose!"

"You can't mean …? He hasn't asked Janet to *marry* him? Oh, do let me see!"

"Better not. It's incredibly funny, but the little man seems to be in earnest. And Janet's frightfully upset – couldn't even bear for me to read it in front of her. She thinks it's an unkind joke."

"Poor Janet! Why?"

"I think Worrall's abuse is still rankling – ugly, unfeminine, etc. The letter'll have to be tested for code."

But Clare had already hurried to Janet's room.

"… but silly, of *course* he's serious. I admit it's a bit sudden, but these uxorious men are known to be quick on the rebound. Look at Coventry Patmore."

"If it was someone like you, I'd believe it. But – just look at me!"

She pointed to the reflections of Clare and herself in the glass. They certainly formed a contrast; emotion had made Janet more like a boiled gooseberry than usual. But Clare smiled and said:

"Very nice too, except for your hair, which does need doing better. Who on earth did you go to?"

"My charwoman kindly trimmed it for me. But Clare, do you honestly think he's serious? Oh dear!"

"Of course he is, and you might look a bit more pleased, I must say. It's always flattering when people want to marry you, even the absolute nonstarters."

"But it puts me in such an awful position. In the middle of all this! What ought I to say?" She pulled at her mouth with one finger with her old childish awkwardness.

"The classic form is that you are resolved never to give your hand save where you have already bestowed your heart, but you'll always regard him as a brother. I used to vary that a bit, myself. They prefer it."

"Then you don't think I need say yes? He says he's unhappy."

"I think you could do better than him. Don't you?"

"I hate that way of talking. You don't understand. I don't mind not having married, Clare. I can see it would have been nice in a way, but it wasn't *meant*, and I'm quite happy as I am. Only I can't bear the suggestion that I'm still sort of – angling. Honestly I've never given Iorweth or anyone else the least handle for that."

"I expect that's the attraction. Zoe seems to have been a mass of handles – curved ones too, damn her! Come on, my dear, drink up your coffee and don't look so worried. I say! I'm not being an idiot, am I? Does Iorweth attract you at all?"

"Good gracious, no!" Janet shuddered. "What a beastly idea, after Zoe too! Horrible!"

In the shock of this new problem she seemed to have almost forgotten the shadow of the greater one that hung over them all, and Clare thought that nothing would be gained by reminding her.

"Well, tell him you wouldn't want to be anyone's second wife. That lets him down gently. Better than telling him you couldn't bear him at any price. Why not write now and get it done?"

The letter, painfully produced, ran as follows:

> DEAR IORWETH,
>
> I expect I ought to be grateful for your proposal, especially as it is the first I have ever received. I know you are unhappy, otherwise I would not have rung up last night, and I am sorry. But I think it would be disgusting to marry someone with a previous wife even if she wasn't one really, in fact worse. Please do not take this personally.
>
> JANET COLTMAN.

"No, no!" said Clare when Janet asked if it would do. "It's not human enough. You ought to say something like – let's see – *Dear Iorweth, I am very touched by all the kind things you say so beautifully*. No. I didn't see his letter, of course. That's just a thing one has to say. *I do wish I could say yes*. No. I know you don't, but you must be civil. *But I have a horror of second marriages. I should wish to be the first woman in my husband's life, as he would be the first man in mine*."

"That's very well expressed." Janet was taking it all down.

Clare bit her lip. She had thought the parody rather too broad. "*Please think of me as, Always your friend, Janet*."

"Is that quite true? I mean, I can't be always his friend if he turns out to be guilty, can I?"

"Richard says yes. I was terrified of meeting Ian Shrubsole for the same reason yesterday, but Richard said criminals were just like the rest of us – just people. I must say, I found Ian very human and I got on all right with him. And you consented to work with him today, didn't you? Why not give everyone the benefit of the doubt?"

"Work's different. And Ian – Oh, Clare! I wish I could start at the museum now, and get it over. Can't I? I feel all right."

"No, the doctor said to have a trial run first to see how you are. And Richard's fixed everything for the afternoon, anyhow. Let's go for a walk and call on my hairdresser. He's a Greek, so he'll be right up your street."

* * *

The process which Clare afterwards described as "oiling and circumambulating Janet and making her less rudely aniconic" could never have been attempted if poor Janet had not been so dazed with the events of the day. But Richard had said, "Build her up. Give her back her confidence." Clare's plan was less frivolous than it seemed on the surface.

When they entered the pink, softly-lighted saloon, Clare drew Semonides aside and gave him a rapid false impression of Janet's fame and influence, even hinting at an impending interview in the highest quarters. She did not believe in doing things by halves. Then she turned to Janet and said aloud:

"This is Mr. Semonides, Janet. He's an artist."

"Really?" said Janet. "Do you paint pictures?"

"Ah! No, Madame. In Greece, pipple don't take art serious like they do in London and Paris. It's only pictures of Christ and the Virgin. But" – his bulk loomed over her – he was sleek and curled and highly fed as a sacred bull – "You wait, my dear! When you look *so* wonderful, *so* glamorous as I will make you, you'll tell all your friends, 'Semonides is a great artist.' You'll be beautiful, you see." He turned off the mechanical ecstasy and shouted, as if to a dog, "Doris! Get ready to shampoo my lady!"

A highly decorated blonde, who was walking up and down picking up hairpins from the floor with a magnet on a string, jumped to obey him. Semonides, enormous in his double-breasted, padded suit, began to circle Janet in her chair, making spasmodic dashes at her with scissors and comb. Then he seized her violently by the head and began to sing in a brassy falsetto, dropping cigarette-ash all over her, and Clare knew that he was having his inspiration. He was always at his most intolerable then.

When Janet returned to him, dripping from her shampoo, she began a timid conversation in Greek. Semonides, now working mechanically, answered her in a much more natural voice than before and they were soon talking with animation. Clare wondered what on earth they had found of common interest. It was an hour and a half before Janet was finished.

It would be an exaggeration to say that she looked "so wonderful, so glamorous, so beautiful." But one could now see that her head and brows were nobly modeled, and that her hair was the color of mellow copper. It was doubtful if Semonides had ever heard of Donatello, or would have considered his statue of the young John Baptist as "serious" art; but he had achieved a curiously similar effect. When the two girls got home, Clare said as much. Janet looked in the glass with more interest.

"Yes. Perhaps even more like Polyclitus. I wonder if Greek boys had to go through all that to get the effect. Oh dear!"

"What is it?"

"I do feel a fool. At a time like this, too."

"You look absolutely charming. And didn't the Spartans wash or something before the battle of Salamis?"

"Comb their hair before Thermopylae. Yes. But I do wish I'd got my ordinary clothes."

"They were all over blood. It's lucky I had that dress of Mummy's, it might have been made for you. I say, what on earth did you find to talk to Semonides about? He sounded almost human with you."

"We started by talking about his home town. After that, he was telling me about his Greek friends in London, and trying to get me to go to his brother's restaurant. I mentioned the Minos, and he began abusing Mikhailopoulos. He says he's much older than he looks. Apparently he's been coming to Semonides in secret to have his hair and whiskers dyed. They're quite white really. I thought it was rather nasty of Semonides to give him away, but he was puffing his brother's place, of course. Greeks do have very strong family feeling."

"Well, when *we* get to the point of having our hair and whiskers dyed, we'll go elsewhere. Oh! Excuse me, there's the telephone." She ran downstairs.

"Yes? Oh, Richard, darling! She's perfectly all right, we felt so safe with your chap plodding along behind. And she had a long conversation in Greek with Semonides, and he's done wonders with her hair. No, no incidents of any kind, unless you count a rather sweet little urchin who sold us some violets at the corner outside here. He insisted on pinning them on for us himself. What like? Black eyes and a nice smile. Yes, I suppose he could have been a Greek, though I didn't notice any accent, he spoke rather well, in fact. Oh! Very young, he even had a red toy engine. Your man came up in rather a threatening way, saying, 'What's all this?' and the child took to his heels. I was cross with him for making a fuss, because Janet was just feeling nice and cheerful and then she looked bothered again. As if a little *boy* …! What! I don't think so. I'll make sure. Hi! Janet, did the little boy say anything to you? No, she says not. He looked poor, yes. No, I didn't notice his shoes. Yes, we each put our own flowers in water. Why? Surely poisoned posies went out with the Borgias. We both adored this little boy. Right, darling, she'll be ready at two. I can hear her washing like anything now."

Janet was scrubbing soot off her hands. She had put them right up the bedroom chimney, where she had hidden the tiny piece of paper written over in Greek. Her heart was still pounding so loudly that she could hardly hear the tap running, and forgot to wash away the traces of soot from the basin.

* * *

The Keeper had put a better and more private room at the disposal of Inspector Ringwood than those usually assigned to junior visiting archaeologists; and he had promised Richard that the Research Laboratory would give instant help if required. When Richard and Janet arrived, they found Ian Shrubsole already there and working at a big table littered with objects, books, and tools. His escort sat in a corner, bored and hungry, and was glad to be dismissed.

Ian had risen to greet Janet, and there was a moment of perceptible tension between them; but once he had handed her his notes, and they settled to discuss their plan of work, the atmosphere eased. The expert on his own ground, as Richard had noticed before, has a dignity no less impressive for being unconscious; and both Janet and Ian were touched with a new, tranquil air of authority. Their voices, normally overloud, were hushed to library pitch, and they spoke in a kind of shorthand of ellipses and abbreviations. Richard felt like a raw undergraduate, ignorant and out of things. Also it occurred to him that if Shrubsole were really hostile to Janet he could threaten or bully her under his very nose, the significant words cloaked by the lowered voices and technical language, or hidden in the morass of archaeological notes. Yet he could not constantly interrupt by asking them to speak up and explain. Scholars must be allowed to concentrate. All he could do was to attend, watch Janet's face for signals of distress, and protect her from physical violence. Presently he asked if they had now worked out a program. It was Ian who replied, with such concise confidence that it was quite difficult to keep up with his points.

"We have five foci of suspicion. One. We both conjectured, independently, that some seals disappeared from the dig in Crete last year while Janet was ill. Some that didn't disappear are on loan here in the museum. We must look at them again and see if they are related in type to any of the seals at present under consideration, the ones in private hands. We might be able to spot the thief. Two. Iorweth and I both heard that Worrall had bought some rings and sold them later to Americans.(Janet says she can't believe it. You're investigating that by cable, I think? You expect an answer today? Good. Three. The gold rings in ap Ifor's collection. Janet does the stylistic analysis. I'll see to the metallurgy."

"Metallurgy? I don't understand."

"To see if the gold is ancient or modern. Modern gold is much purer than prehistoric Aegean gold, which contains up to twenty-five percent of natural alloys which have not been refined away, such as silver, tellurium, mercury, antimony, and bismuth."

"How do you find if there's any – er – bismuth and so on?"

"Spectroscopic analysis of minute quantities." Shrubsole tapped his fingers on the table as if he were impatient. "You observe the different colors of the rays emitted. It could be done with chemical reagents and solvents, of course, but it's slower and wastes more of the metal."

"I see. You'll send your specimens along to the research laboratory here, I suppose."

"No, I'll go along myself. I always do."

Richard was almost hypnotized into acquiescence by this new, impressive Shrubsole, but just in time he remembered to say:

"I don't know if we can allow that. The Keeper said we could use the scientific experts here."

"I'm a qualified archaeological chemist myself, and I can do the job quicker. You agree, Janet?"

"Yes. He's always done our lab work himself – the chemistry, that is. Not bones or soils. I'll file them myself, Ian, if you don't mind."

A trained chemist! thought Richard. Why haven't I been told this before? This means that he knows about poisons. But apparently not to be trusted with a file.

Aloud he said, "You really want him to do this, Janet? You wouldn't rather send it to the museum people?"

"Of course not. Ian can be much quicker, and besides, I can be sure he won't injure the objects. Can't we start?"

"I'll just finish outlining the program," said Ian, assuming and ignoring their assent. "Four. The parcel obtained from Zoe ap Ifor, and the ring found in the guitar at the Minos. Same plan as for Three. Five. Worrall's last find, the – er – Nausicaa Ring." The atmosphere was tense again, and he deliberately did not look at Janet. "The other points may throw light on that."

"What about the pottery?" Janet asked. "There was some found in the trench with the Nausicaa Ring, and there were some sherds in Zoe's parcel."

"I've already done that. Check it if you like. It's genuine." He turned to Richard. "But you'd expect that; it's an old faker's trick. He offers a group of objects for sale in a single lot, saying that they've all been found together. The group contains some expensive items and some cheap ones. The cheap ones – sherds and so on – will be obviously genuine, and thus help to convince the purchaser that the expensive item – in this case the ring – is genuine too, since it was 'found' with them. You agree, Janet?"

"Of course. You ought to add, perhaps, that the genuine things have to match the fake in period; otherwise they'd tell against it rather than in favor."

"That's obvious, surely. Though in this case we must reserve our judgment till you've reconsidered the metal objects. You agree?"

"Of course."

"I've got you your usual books. Want anything else?"

"Oh! Thank you, Ian. Envelopes, emery – how topping, you've thought of everything."

"Just a minute." Richard was uneasy, he could not say why. Was it merely the intimidation of the amateur before the expert that made his hackles rise like this? Or was it – danger? "I'll have to get an escort for you if you're going off to the lab, Ian. Is there a bell I can ring?"

There was no bell, and the passage outside was empty. Unwilling to leave the room even for a moment, uneasy as he felt, he shouted into the academic solitudes, an outrage which he had to repeat several times, standing in the open doorway, before an old man nursing something in his arms came out of a room farther down the passage and asked what was the matter. When Richard explained, the old man thrust his burden upon him (heavens! It was a mummy's leg, toenails and all. But it felt surprisingly dry and inorganic) and went off to fetch an attendant. Richard looked behind him. The black head and the copper one were close together, poring over the table, and the murmur of voices sounded peaceful enough.

Waiting, as always, made him more aware of his own state of mind. Why did he feel so uneasy about the case still? There was plenty of evidence against Zoe and Georgios – the parcel on the floor of the flat, the ring in the guitar (Georgios had confessed to putting it there, at Zoe's orders), and lastly, yesterday's desperate attempt at flight. But there was also evidence against Shrubsole; and lately a second, even more distressing suspicion had crept into his mind. Suddenly the matter-of-fact sensuality and self-seeking of Georgios and Zoe had come to appear too shallow, too childishly human to inspire the monstrous, deliberate decision of repeated murder. Lecherous and avaricious as they were, the objects they pursued were positive and in themselves desirable. Zoe wanted an acceptable lover and plenty of money; Georgios wanted his own hotel and a beautiful woman. But in face of "trouble," Zoe had been willing to part with her jewelry, and Georgios with his mistress. Surely this realistic self-regard, however sordid, was poles away from the inhuman, fanatical passion that could plot murder in cold blood? So –

But footsteps sounded in the passage, and presently a museum official stumped into view, rudely anthropomorphic in his brown uniform. Of the old man who had gone to fetch him there was no sign.

The attendant consented to take Richard's telephone message, but refused to relieve him of the mummy's leg. That was 'Andling Hobjects, against the rules, and not his work. So Richard was obliged to stand in the doorway waiting for the old man to come back. A shuffling step in the distance gave him hope.

Suddenly he heard behind him a sharp movement and a stifled cry. He spun round. Janet, flushed and breathing hard, had half-risen from her chair. Shrubsole was on his feet, facing Richard with that black stare of his that gave nothing away.

"What's happened? Are you hurt, Janet?"

"No. At least, I – I bumped my scar on the back of the chair and it did hurt for a minute. It's all right. Sorry I made such a row."

"What's that in your hand, Ian?"

"Emery stone," he snapped, showing it. "Are you all right, Janet?"

"Of course. I … *Look!* Look, Ian, in his hand!" They were both staring in horror at the mummy's leg, which Richard was swinging by the ankle. Surely they were used to such things? They both assailed him with angry instructions.

"Mind that!" "Give it to me!" "Haven't you any idea …?" "Put it down there!" "Mind that loose bit!" "Seems all right." "No thanks to him."

Richard was thoroughly browbeaten, and when he again asked Janet what had made her cry out, she stuck to her story. He was sure she was lying. Something was being kept from him, and now he did not even know whether he should mistrust one or both of them.

All his instincts had made him spring to Janet's defense; she was a girl, wounded, and his guest. But in fact it was she who had first diverted attention to the mummy's leg, and of the two she was the more composed at present. He reconsidered some of her past remarks. "Ian was the last person in the trench before Sir Alban found the ring." "Ian was angry when the dig broke up." "Ian! No, I don't want to see him! Don't leave me alone with him!" If it had been her policy to discredit him, she had pursued it subtly and almost impalpably till now. Perhaps this time she had overreached herself, and was trying to retreat. At any rate, they both seemed anxious to pass over the incident and get back to work, and Richard could do nothing but acquiesce, with silent resolutions to watch the pair of them like a lynx.

The table was full of seal impressions, seals, electrotypes of seals. The rings looked very much alike to him, for the design was harder to distinguish in intaglio, and he was amazed how quickly Janet and Ian could pick out the ones they wanted. The method seemed to be that of collation; you compared the object you were working on with similar objects or reproductions from the museum collection, and also with photographs or drawings of others in dozens of books. A slow process and muddling to watch. The afternoon wore on, broken only by the arrival of an escort for Shrubsole, and (later) by a visit from the old man in search of his, or rather some defunct Egyptian's, leg. Shrubsole was going off to the lab under guard from time to time, with gold filings in little envelopes. Richard was under the impression that he had been taking the samples of gold from the rings himself, with his emery stone, but he was surprised to see Janet hand him a couple more envelopes when he went off for the third time. Ian looked at her in a curious way, too.

"These aren't labeled, Janet."

"I labeled them inside the flap. You know I always do, then it doesn't rub out."

Shrubsole took them and went without another word. When they were alone, Richard asked which rings those last two specimens had been taken from.

"Just a minute," said Janet, her finger on an index, "Fetishes, fillets, ah! Flywhisks. Could you possibly save your questions till we've finished? I keep losing the thread."

Ten minutes later, she asked if she might wash. Richard went with her but of course waited outside. She took three minutes and came out – he supposed it was natural – looking a little embarrassed.

Soon afterwards, Shrubsole returned, and went straight back to his place by Janet at the table, but his police guard drew Richard aside and whispered:

"I hope it was all right, sir. He asked to go to the lavatory. Locked himself in for four minutes. Seemed a long time."

Shrubsole's ears were sharp, for he turned and said:

"Sorry I didn't ask him in too. I'm not used to these public-school habits, see."

Even the jeering note rang false. Richard asked him why he had taken so long.

"What the … Well, really! If you must know, and Janet will excuse my mentioning it, I suffer from constipation. You can ask my mother."

His embarrassment was real – he was even blushing – but one could not say whether modesty or guilt was the cause. Janet, on the other hand, seemed perfectly composed.

"It's all this sitting about. You'll be all right when you can get some decent exercise. Now, can't we stop talking and get on? There's still a lot to do."

Really, thought Richard, she has an extraordinarily fine head. A sort of Athene quality. When she's looking formidable like this, you can see it.

"All right," he said. "But I shall reopen the question. Meanwhile, Smith, you'd better close the lavatory, and bring me the key."

The low voices went on.

"Ian, what's the provenance of that square seal with a potbellied daemon holding up a hind? I can't place it."

"Necropolis of Phaestus, I think. Monumenti Antichi. Yes, here it is, isn't it?"

"Yes, thanks awfully. You see the point?"

"The decorative whorls are pointing upwards. Wait, what about that one from Hagia Triada? Upwards again, see? Why do ours point downwards?"

"It *might* be a glyptic *hapax legomenon*."

"Hm! It might be something worse."

So it went on, often inaudible and generally unintelligible. At last they presented him with a "rough report," which ran to six foolscap pages, with a summary attached. The summary read:

(1) *Crete, last year*. A Late-Minoan I site. Seals at present available for inspection are undoubtedly genuine, chiefly L.M. I, consisting (*a*) of religious

scenes of a well-known type and (*b*) of a few earlier animal-motifs. It is possible that some seals of the (*a*) type were stolen by a member of the dig, and if so, could have been reintroduced this year as new finds.

(2) *Rings sold to Americans by A.W.* Police inquiry pending.

(3) *I ap I's rings*. Forgeries of L.M. I, so skillful that we should not have condemned them on stylistic grounds alone. But spectroscopic analysis shows that the gold is not Minoan, but modern, though artificially alloyed with silver to produce the pale Minoan color.

(4) *Z ap I's parcel*. Pottery genuine, valueless; periods mixed, none of right period for the rings, which are L.M. I forgeries as in group 3 with one exception, the amethyst. This, though its setting is modern, might conceivably be a genuine piece. It is stylistically correct and there is no means to determine the age of the material, ancient and modern amethysts being indistinguishable.

(5) *Agate ring found in Minos*. The setting is of modern metal as above. The gem is of fine workmanship and stylistically convincing, but one detail, i.e. the pattern on the ritual garments worn by the daemons – has so far only been found oriented in a reverse direction.

(6) *Nausicaa Ring*. A seal of L.M. I period similar to Cretan finds. The gold is ancient and we believe the ring to be genuine. It is consistent with pottery found by I.R.S. in same stratum.

"*What?*" Richard almost shouted. "You say the Nausicaa Ring's genuine after all? It can't be! It can't be!" If it was, his almost completed case fell to the ground, and he had been sure it was solved. "Listen, Janet. That first night in hospital, when you were delirious, you kept saying *There was a baetylic shrine! There must have been a shrine!* In your written description you said the same. And, Ian, when you showed me the ring, you told me that Minoan artists never left a blank space like that blank under the tree. You said the design couldn't have been just worn away, or there'd be a cavity. You thought – yes, I know you didn't say, but I guessed all the same – that the shrine had been deliberately rubbed out and the cavity had been filled with plain gold. You thought – or led me to think – that Worrall had done it so as to turn the ring into a picture of the Nausicaa story. Didn't you? Was the gold on the blank part tested?"

"Yes," said Shrubsole. "I tested it myself."

"That right, Janet?"

"Yes, of course."

Neither appeared to be lying. Their faces looked clear and at peace. But Richard was not satisfied.

"It *must* be a fake. Even if it was genuine originally, it must have been tampered with. My God! I'll have another opinion. Give me the thing. Where is it?"

He turned to the littered table, picking up one after another the rings of pale gold.

"This it? No! Come and find it, you two."

They all looked for a long time, but in vain. The Nausicaa Ring had disappeared.

* * *

Richard had seldom been so angry. Angry with himself because he had trusted them; because he had been awed, by his intellectual snobbery, into not interrupting them when he did not understand. Angry most of all with Janet, whose integrity he had believed proof against corruption or fear. She had helped to trick him; had perhaps been in it all along. He stared at them and they stared back. How did they manage to put on that virtuous expression? Like martyrs. Well, it was too late now.

"You're both under arrest. Smith, keep the man here and search him thoroughly – really thoroughly. Then secure him and search both the lavatories. You'd better send for a plumber. I'll take the woman to be searched in custody."

"Wait a minute. What's the charge?" Shrubsole's voice was calm still. "Suppression of evidence? Is that a ground for imprisonment?"

"You can't prove it," added Janet. "Things do get lost, sometimes for months. Ask any archaeologist. Don't they, Ian?"

"The charge" – Richard spoke slowly – "will be murder in the one case and wilful abetting in the other."

"Then I confess," Shrubsole said. "Not to your charges, because I'm not a murderer and I wouldn't help one. But I did put that ring down the lavatory."

Janet intervened.

"Don't be an idiot! Why on earth should he? As a matter of fact, I *dropped* it down the lavatory by accident, as Ian knows very well, because I told him. I ought to have told you, but I didn't like to. Anyhow, we've done the work on it and it makes no difference at present whether it's there or not. Though I expect it can be recovered. Every word in our report is perfectly true, and Ian hasn't got the ring. Honestly."

"What would Janet want to destroy a genuine object for? It was me. I hated Worrall's guts, if you want to know, and I was darned if I'd leave him this to his credit, even posthumously."

"No, it was me. If I *must* say it, I … I wasn't convinced it was genuine, actually. But I didn't want to attack Sir Alban now he's dead. Need it be made public?"

"You're both very clever, aren't you? Cleverer than I thought, with your pseudo-quarrels and hesitations and your sham simplicity. Well, I'm applying ordinary police methods from now on. Undress the man completely, Smith. I'll take the woman."

Shrubsole sprang forward, and Janet put up her hand defensively crying

"No!" Richard and Smith held him. He stood as steady as a rock. There was nothing the matter with the man's nerves.

"Go on, then," he said. "We'll both be out by this evening."

So they were searched and taken into custody.

* * *

The ring was on neither of them, nor could it be found in either lavatory though a plumber plumbed profoundly. Richard made Smith take him along to the laboratory and show him the bench and sink where Shrubsole had been. Smith, the police escort, had watched him throughout. Sometimes he had held his samples in a flame and watched them through a "sort of microscope thing." Sometimes he'd "done things with bottles of stuff and test-tubes." He'd washed up himself and swilled down the sink. The lab boy corroborated. He had wanted to see too, but the copper had told him to keep off, and Shrubsole habitually preferred to get his own apparatus. No one else had been in the lab, except one of the staff of research chemists, who was still working up at the far end. Richard went to him and asked if he had noticed what Shrubsole was doing.

"Shrubsole! Never heard of him. No, of course not. I was busy."

What *had* Shrubsole been doing with "bottles of stuff"? He had said that he was using the spectroscopic analysis, which only involved a flame and a "microscope thing." No chemicals. Or had he been using them to destroy the ring? But – destroy gold? Surely gold is practically indestructible – that's why it has always been prized. Gold. … Suddenly a phrase from his undergraduate reading flashed into his head. John Locke was a stodgy philosopher, and comic relief was rare in his pages. All the more memorable, therefore, the absurdly rhythmical definition of gold, recurring chapter after chapter like a refrain:

"A body yellow, fusible, ductile, malleable, weighty and fixed, and soluble in *aqua regia*."

Richard turned excitedly to the research chemist.

"What's *aqua regia?* Does it really melt gold?"

"Dissolve, not melt. Yes. It's hydrochloric and nitric acid mixed in equal proportions. Why?"

"Could you see if someone had been melting, I mean dissolving gold in *aqua regia* at this sink? Would we find traces of gold in the U-pipe?"

"No, it wouldn't *be* gold any more. The acid might burn through the pipe if it wasn't swilled at once."

"It was, I'm afraid. Thoroughly swilled. Look, the thing is, I think someone's just destroyed a Minoan gold ring here by dissolving it in, er, *aqua regia*."

"That's bad. Why didn't you stop him?" He paused. "There won't be anything in the sink or pipes if he swilled it. I wonder if … I say, look at this!

There's a fresh acid been spilled here, on the bench. You can see the stain. I'll analyze that if you like."

He did so. It was indeed *aqua regia* – a mixture of nitric and hydrochloric acid. But of the presence of dissolved gold there was no trace, so the proof of destruction was incomplete. Shrubsole must have spilled his solvent before he used it.

Accidentally? Perhaps, though Richard had seldom seen a man with defter hands. If accidentally, he had condemned himself, for Richard believed that the destroyer of the ring was also the destroyer of life. But if he had spilled the acid on purpose, so that the police would *think* that the ring had been destroyed … It was difficult to conceive the motive for such an action, difficult to imagine what could possibly have forced Shrubsole to it. But perhaps an hour in a detention cell would have made him readier to talk. Richard went to him at once.

Chapter 17

HE was standing upright like a Cockney St. Sebastian, in the far corner of the cell; and sat down, at Richard's suggestion, as steadfastly as he had stood. He was like a man who is about to undergo a serious operation; separated, obedient, fatalistic, yet curiously dignified. Richard came straight to the point.

"You didn't put the Nausicaa Ring down the lavatory, did you? You destroyed it with acids in the lab?"

"How did you get on to that?" The old, street-Arab mockery flickered for an instant.

"Locke. Don't you remember? *A body yellow, fusible, ductile.* …"

"*Malleable, weighty and fixed* …" Shrubsole took up the chant. There was something compulsive about the rhythm.

"*And soluble in aqua regia*. You spilled some on the bench. You admit that?"

He laughed. "O.K. I admit it. What the heck! I resign. I ought to have realized you'd remember that tag. So what?"

The two men had exchanged roles. It was Richard who played the nervous man now. He spoke jerkily, looking at his own tightly clasped hands as though he could not bear to look at Shrubsole.

"Ian, for God's sake think what you're saying! If it was really you who destroyed the ring, and not Janet, then it must have been you who killed Worrall. You could have only had one reason for destroying it – that it was *your* fake, evidence against *you*, not Worrall. That *you* stole it in Crete last year while Janet was away ill; that *you* altered it and planted it in the trench this year for Worrall to find; that Janet could still somehow prove all this against you if the ring once got out of your hands and into hers. And if you *did* plant it, everything else follows, because that was the first step of your campaign to break Worrall, and when that failed, and Worrall, and perhaps the boy and Janet too, got to know about it, you had to take other steps. You had to set about eliminating them. Look, I want to be fair to you. We found traces of acid, but not of dissolved gold. I can't *prove* you destroyed the ring. And if you can show that you didn't, the case against Janet is as strong as it is against you. I – I can't *see* you doing it, Ian. Not since I've got to know you, watched you at work and in your home. I do see that you had every reason to hate Worrall, even to want to disgrace him publicly. He was bogus and insolent and heartless, I know that; I can see that you'd want to get back on him. But – the last step, Ian? Can't you at least tell me *some* extenuating circumstance? Did Worrall threaten your career? Did he even threaten to set his 'gang' on you to kill you? Were you desperately frightened of him? Are you still frightened of Janet? For Heaven's sake, tell me the truth! It's the only thing that can help you now."

Shrubsole touched Richard on the knee, and Richard flinched and looked up, to see the deadpan face softened and undefended as he had never seen it before; the whole man seemed to look out from it. He was anxious, yes, and still thinking hard; but he looked at Richard with a queer sympathy. He didn't look like a murderer.

"Don't worry," he said. "I didn't kill anyone. But – thanks for kind inquiries."

"Then why did you destroy the ring? Or – didn't you? Did you just make it look as if you had, because you were frightened and had to seem to obey orders? You silly ass! She can't get at you now. Nobody can. Why won't you tell me the truth?"

"Just a minute. I want to get this straight. If I say I destroyed the ring, you're going to charge me with murder, relying on the circumstantial evidence in your notebook and on your theories about my motives. It doesn't sound to me a watertight case. If I say I didn't destroy the ring, you'll charge Janet. Why?"

"The circumstantial evidence against her, up to the time she was stabbed, and that needn't necessarily be connected with Worrall's murder, is if anything more serious than it is against you. She was with Worrall more continuously, and she helped him to draft the will, which at once protected her from being found out a poisoner, and made sure that she'd profit by his death. As for motive – well, violent revulsion from a long, obsessive, hero worship is obviously a much more explosive and dangerous emotion than your own detached, settled dislike. Discipleship to Worrall was the mainspring of her life for years. One can imagine how violent the reaction would be."

"That's no case at all, and you know it. Listen. Janet *didn't* destroy the ring, and didn't want it destroyed either. Because when we got back to England, she gave it to me to look after. She said that if I accused her of being biased and trying to hide the truth, I'd better make sure that no one tampered with the thing before it was tested. She made me promise not to do any work on it without her, and I didn't. But she wouldn't have let me have it at all, don't you see, if she'd really been trying to suppress it. And she *didn't* want to lead the expedition. She said this afternoon that she wouldn't stand for election. Listen, *I* destroyed the ring, and I'll tell you why. I was still jealous of Worrall, even though he's dead. I couldn't bear the idea of him being right after all. That's the kind of bloke I am, if you want to know. But I don't think you can hang me for it."

"She gave you the ring to take care of, you say? When?"

"When we started work in the B.M. three weeks ago."

"But she didn't know you'd got a copy of her own description?"

"No. She'd torn up the original on the boat, in front of us all."

"And you swear the ring was genuine? Would you – an archaeologist – destroy a genuine thing?"

"I've told you already."

"Yes, and I don't believe you. Either the ring was bogus or you didn't destroy it. Won't you – can't you – tell me the truth? Don't you see that you're putting a rope round your own neck?"

Shrubsole paused, and then answered steadily:

"I don't think you'll charge me. And at present I've no more to say. Except –"

"Yes?"

"Nothing. You're a good bloke, that's all." And he would not say another word.

* * *

Feeling even more unhappy than before, Richard went to Janet. She had been lying on her bed, but sat up when he came in. She was pale and moved cautiously as though her wound was hurting her, but insisted that she was perfectly comfortable. How long did he think she'd have to stay? What about Shrubsole? Someone ought to go and put away the things they'd left on the table at the museum.

Twenty-four hours ago, her stoicism and her professional conscience would have touched him; now, whether they were clever acting or something more like insanity, they irritated him violently.

"Damn the table at the museum! The one important thing has gone from it already, as you know very well. Why do you persist in shamming stupid? You must realize by now that the person who took it is also Worrall's murderer!"

Janet gave one of her glances of formidable, hawk-eyed intelligence.

"No. Why? I don't see that at all."

Her assurance put him on his mettle.

"Surely you do. But if you want a summary, here goes. First, no one *would* have destroyed the ring if it had been genuine, because there'd be no reason to. Second, if it was faked, the only person who'd want to destroy it would be the person who'd tried to use it, and knew that this could still be proved against him if the ring didn't disappear. Third, the person who was using it (assuming that he's still alive and therefore wasn't Worrall) was using it to discredit Worrall. And when this trick didn't work, and was seen through, he'd involved himself so deeply that his only hope of getting off was to kill Worrall before Worrall took steps against him. (Perhaps Worrall wasn't the only victim, but I'm concentrating on him for the moment.) Now do you see? Now will you come clean and tell me all you know about the ring? I ought to warn you that you yourself, from the police point of view, are in just as bad a position as Ian Shrubsole."

"*What?*" She looked really alarmed for the first time.

"Yes. It's him or you, and your opportunities were equal if not better. You helped to draft that curious will. You spent much more time with Worrall. And I know – I absolutely *know* – that you haven't been frank with me. For the last time, will you answer me fully?"

"Yes." She whispered, looking down at her freckled hands. "Sorry. Yes, I will."

"First, was the ring genuine?"

"No. Yes. That is, it was a genuine Late Minoan I seal, but part of the design had been rubbed away and the hollow had been filled up with modern metal. There! It's out now, and in a way I feel better. Wish I'd said it before."

"So originally the ring was the ordinary type of 'religious scene' – nothing to do with Nausicaa and Odysseus?"

"No, nothing at all."

"And Shrubsole planted it in the trench for Worrall to find it and make a fool of himself, having stolen it on last year's dig and altered it? And when Worrall fell into the trap, you realized what Shrubsole had done and warned Worrall against him?"

"Good gracious, no!" Her jaw dropped, and she thrust two fingers into her mouth with a look of half-stupid dismay. "Never thought of such a thing. Oh, dear! This is all my fault. I – I didn't want to be disloyal to Sir Alban. See I was wrong now. Look, I know really, knew all the time in a way, that he – Sir Alban – did it himself, the ring business, I mean. No one else could have. I was worried the day he found it, but next day, when he was taken ill, I – I thought it would be best to carry on as if everything was all right. Really, I suppose I was sparing myself as much as him. I was – upset. I had admired his work very deeply once, you see, and I owed him so much. I shelved the whole thing and gave Ian the ring to look after, because I knew that whatever the explanation was, he could be trusted. I just concentrated on getting Sir Alban well. When we'd been back in London a fortnight, though, and he did really seem so much better, and asked me to lunch at the Minos, I thought I could raise the question again. I told him that I was sure the ring wasn't genuine. I let him see that I thought he'd put it in the trench himself. I hoped he'd have some explanation. But – *he offered me money to hold my tongue!*"

"And you refused it? That was when he turned on you and abused you and you left the restaurant?"

"Of course. It was – awful. But then, oh! Then he died, and I was sorry. I did owe him so much, and there was nothing else like this he'd done, as far as I knew, and I thought that perhaps his mind had been deranged by his illness, that he hadn't been himself. I *couldn't* turn against him. You do see? Not that it's an excuse, really. But I thought that I'd get the ring back from Ian before he'd tested it – he'd promised not to, till I was there – and then I'd, er, lose it. Hush the whole wretched business up. And I did, today, as I hoped. I gave Ian a false sample of gold to test, from another ring, and I put the real ring down the lavatory. *Put*, not dropped."

In spite of the unmistakable anguish in her voice, Richard was still not sure how far to believe her. There had been moments during her recital when she had avoided meeting his eye, and this had proved a danger signal in other conversations.

"I see. Well now, to go back to when Sir Alban was first taken ill at Corfu. What were the symptoms?"

"I told you before. Bad pains, tummy ones, and he was sick."

"Did you actually see him vomiting?"

"Oh, no! He went to the lavatory."

"Well, did you *hear* him vomiting? Was there any mess afterwards?"

"I did hear him, yes. I think we all did, because Ian was rather disgusted – thought he could have been quieter. But I don't know about mess, naturally. The crew saw to things like that."

"I see. Now when you all got together and consulted the medical dictionary. Who suggested looking up gastric ulcer?"

"I don't remember for certain. I've got an idea it was Sir Alban himself, but I couldn't swear to that."

"That would fit in. What did he have to eat on his way home?"

"I tried to keep to the book. Tinned milk, eggs, fish – things like that."

"What about drinks? I may say that I found a good many empty gin and whisky bottles in the cabin."

The hawk behind Janet's blobby face stooped and pounced on this important new fact.

"What? Why on earth didn't you tell me? That's extremely strange. He always had his empties taken away at once, as there was so little room in the cabin. And I know there weren't any there when we started, because I gave the place a thorough tidying when I settled him in. But I don't see how he can have been drinking gin and whisky on the voyage home. It would have been bound to make him very ill, because I know it said in the book that spirits were dangerous. He'd certainly have had another attack; and he didn't."

"If he'd really had an ulcer, he would have. Not if he was shamming."

"Shamming!" She was all mind now, no room left for emotion. "But – don't you see? That explains everything – the will, the way he wouldn't have an X-ray ..."

"Go on!" Richard watched her narrowly.

"I never understood why he should have wanted that clause put in about being buried whole and unmutilated. It was so unlike him, somehow – unconventional and a bit morbid – more the sort of thing Iorweth would think of than Sir Alban. I was puzzled, but I thought that perhaps his nerves had got upset by his illness. But now I see. Something I said must have given him the idea. I'd been telling him how a friend of my father's had an ulcer and they'd operated at once and he'd got over it in no time. It was the same day, later on, that he started drafting the will. I protested a bit, and said that if the X-ray showed that an operation was necessary, he'd simply have to have one. I told him about how they'd give him a barium meal and an X-ray. He asked a lot of questions, I remember, and then dismissed me suddenly, as if he wasn't very pleased with what I'd said. Well, of course; if he was shamming, he obviously wanted to avoid being found out. The will took a line against operations."

"Yes? Go on." If this was a performance, it was masterly.

"I'm only thinking aloud, it may be wrong. But if he *was* shamming, we have to ask ourselves why. My guess is that something went wrong with his plans the day before. He didn't expect us to question his find. Or Zoe ap Ifor knew that he'd 'salted' the dig, and was blackmailing him. Something like that. Something that made him want to run away."

"Yes, that occurred to me, of course. And why, in that case, was he murdered?"

"I can only guess. But suppose Zoe went on blackmailing him, and suppose he in turn found out about her fakes and about – about her and the waiter, couldn't she have decided to kill him for her own security?"

"She could indeed. But she wasn't in fact there when he was poisoned."

"You're sure? Well then, couldn't the waiter have done it, acting on her instructions?"

"I doubt if he'd have been willing. The first time I ever saw them together, I had the impression that he was trying to break away from her. In fact, I'd say that she was the pursuer all along."

"Oh! How beastly! What about the owner of the Minos? Could he have done it?"

"Again I don't see why he should have taken the risk. He'd no motive; he didn't know Worrall, he wasn't poor, and he had a certain reputation to keep up."

"Well, I think it must have been the waiter. Because it all fits in with my being stabbed afterwards, don't you see?"

"Listen, Janet. Everything you say applies just as much to Shrubsole. If Worrall had offered *him* money too, and he'd refused; if he'd then threatened him with unemployment or even violence; if Shrubsole had killed him before he could carry out his threats; if you'd then seemed to offer a new threat because of the unconsciously apt phrasing of your letter to *The Times*; above all, if he'd planted the ring himself as a trap for Worrall and he knew that sooner or later something about it would make you realize – say, if you did the test yourself or sent it to the Research Lab …"

"No! Because *I* was the only person who handled the ring. *I* tried to pass it off as genuine. *I* threw it down the lavatory. And I know that last year when I was ill, it was Sir Alban, not Ian, who had charge of the seals. No one else could have stolen one. Please, you *must* believe me. I ought to have told you before, but you must see now that it's true. Sir Alban was the dishonest one, and I was too, because I backed him up. Ian's right outside the whole thing. I'm very much to blame, for mistaking cowardice for loyalty and getting rid of the ring, and I'm sorry. That's all."

"So you stick to it that *you* destroyed the ring. Even if the admission should involve you in a charge of murder?"

She looked at him steadily. "Yes, I did destroy it. I think you know I didn't murder Sir Alban. But – well, I deserve to be punished for what I have done. And I don't believe an English jury would give me a worse punishment than I deserve, now I've owned up."

Almost exactly what Ian Shrubsole had said. They were too clever, these two; they realized every weakness in the arguments against them and they had called his bluff. Yet they both seemed to be alarmed, and he was sure that neither had told him the whole truth even now. Well, he must try to find it out for himself.

First, he rang up his wife. She was in and promised to do what he asked her at once. Then he returned to the museum, taking with him not only Smith (who had watched Shrubsole on his journeys to the lab) but also that inestimable woman Frewin, whose special talents were to be even more useful today than they had previously proved to be in the Minos.

* * *

They gathered round the table still littered with the afternoon's work. Sergeant Frewin was shown the drawing of the ring and told to go ahead; but instead of searching the room she sat and asked them obvious questions like "When did you see it last?" and "Who came in and out?" and "Who touched that?" And of course she heard about the mummy's leg and was immediately interested. But of course no one knew where it was now; and the old man had gone home; and they did not even know his name. But Richard became shamelessly and fiercely persistent and gave no one any peace till at last the thing had been found and examined. There, sure enough, tucked between the folds of musty, brittle linen and the light, dried flesh, they found the Nausicaa Ring. It looked different now. The space under the tree was no longer flat, for the gold that had filled up the hollow was gone, and where it had been there were faint marks like the remains of a picture. And Richard thought he began to see light.

"Miss Frewin, you're a genius. You've saved an innocent person and set me the worst puzzle of my life, and I probably can't do it. But – *hommages*." And he kissed her hand.

She loved it, but she and Smith were both stiff as they all drove back to Scotland Yard. Richard himself was so deep in thought that he had forgotten they were there. When he arrived and heard that his wife was waiting in his room, he took the stairs four at a time and almost snatched from her the sooty little scrap of paper she offered him.

"I found it in Janet's chimney. There was soot on the washbasin. Otherwise I'd never have thought of looking there. It's Greek to me, but that doesn't matter so long as it is to you too, because then *you'll* understand it."

"It's Greek all right, and very good Greek too. It looks like a quotation from the anthology. Funny, I'm sure I've seen that hand before!"

"*Hand?* What, doesn't everyone write Greek letters the same?"

"No, people who write it a lot have their own characteristic handwriting in Greek too. *Got it!*" He looked up in triumph. "Clare, that little boy, the one who sold you the violets. You say he had a red engine. Could he have been Ian Shrubsole's brother? Here's a photograph. Was he at all like?"

"Yes. Goodness, yes! Eyes and forehead exactly like. Why didn't I see it? So the note was from Ian. But why the secrecy? What does it say?"

"It says – but this is nonsense, it must be some sort of code. On the surface, it looks like one of the epigrams from the fifth book of the Anthology, and yet I know that pretty well and I don't remember this one. It's rather good, too."

"What's it about? Book *Five?* Richard, isn't that …?"

He told her. And then she told him what she had supposed him to know already. He found the idea new, preposterous, and absolutely convincing.

"Well, now you see, it's all right. Aren't you glad? You don't suspect them of the murder now, do you?"

"I'm glad in a way; I've been feeling more and more sure that both those theories were wrong. In fact, I've been working on an alternative all the time, but some of the evidence for that has taken time to collect. Clare, I do know who did it now. That is, I can convince myself. But I doubt if it will convince anyone else."

When he had expounded his case, she said, "I'm afraid I'm convinced, and I wish I wasn't. You'll hate it. But look, it isn't really *proved*, is it? Your two bits of guesswork remain guesswork unless you can somehow force confirmation of them. So – can't you drop the case? Oh! I'm sorry, darling, I see I shouldn't have said that. Of course you have to keep the rules. But I still don't see how you can strengthen those two weak points."

"I do. Not very nice though. You'd better go home."

"Why? What are you going to do? Will you be in danger?"

"Not the sort of danger you mean. Oh! Clare, I'll have to get them together and play on their nerves. Someone will crack, someone will slip, someone will turn traitor, if I plan it well. Mass torture – there's a tradition that it sometimes works better than the screw *in camera*. Given a clever and ruthless torturer ..." She could not bear the bitterness in his voice.

"Darling, don't. Look, it isn't any good my talking. I shall go and pray for you. Good-bye."

She hurried off, and he took up the telephone and began to issue a stream of complex but pellucid instructions.

Chapter 18

A SINGLE customer in the Minos was being served by a new waiter when the police party trooped in at seven and commandeered the back room. Mikhailopoulos took the invasion with (for him) surprising meekness, only begging them to finish as soon as possible and "not make him no trouble." Today he was Odysseus disguised as the conventional *restaurateur*, deferential in a sober pinstripe, his zest and swagger subdued into attentive watchfulness; Odysseus the beggar in his own hall. Richard told him that his presence would be required, and he shrugged and took a humble seat when all the others were comfortably settled.

The prisoners filed in under guard; Georgios and Zoe wearing even their handcuffs hieratically, like the Minotaur's latest victims; ap Ifor unfettered, red-eyed, morose, and smelling of whisky; Janet and Ian mulish, nervous, and closely guarded. Macdonald had come by request, and looked grim and unhappy. The dimly illuminated room, with its snaky frescoes, reminded him of those sinister little underground chapels at Cnossos, which scholars less cautious than himself had called chambers of sacrifice.

The tables were put together in one long block, round which they sat, Richard at the head of the improvised board, and the guards standing behind.

"Samuelson! Just make sure that ap Ifor and the proprietor are unarmed, please."

Ap Ifor carried no weapons, but a pistol was found in the breast pocket of Mikhailopoulos, and a knife tucked into his sock suspender. Ian suddenly spoke up.

"No doubt you know that country-bred Cretans habitually carry arms? It doesn't mean a thing. We had a quarrel break out on the site once, and every one of the workmen produced weapons from under their clothes – at least two each. It's just the national habit. You agree, Janet?"

"Of course."

"You agree too often." Richard's voice was harsh. "Please don't interrupt me." He addressed the assembly at large. "Before we proceed to our reconstruction. I have two pieces of fresh evidence that have recently come in.

"First, Worrall, as you know, was said to have sold some Minoan gold seal-rings to American collectors last year, secretly. This turns out to be true. We traced the owners, had the gold analyzed, and found that the rings are fakes of exactly the same kind as those found in the ap Ifors' possession.

"Secondly, we have discovered the source of these fakes. They were made in Rotterdam by a shady little jeweller called Louis Rosenau, who has now confessed. He's related to one of the craftsmen formerly employed by Sir Arthur Evans for restorations and replicas. Rosenau never actually worked for Evans, but he watched his cousin and learned the technique; and during the last two years, at the instigation of Zoe ap Ifor, he began to make and sell his own fakes. He'd known her parents, and he tried to beg from her when she paid a visit to Rotterdam with a sultana merchant who was her protector at the time. Zoe refused Rosenau her charity but saw how she could make him useful to her. The fakes were received and disposed of by a schoolmaster in Candia called Bagadakis. He collected sherds of the right periods, arranged the seals with them in matching lots, and bribed various peasants to say they'd found them on likely sites. Zoe paid the peasants something through him, but he worked free. Zoe, as she would put it, gave him love. I suspect that she blackmailed him, too."

"Oll right!" Zoe looked murderous. "I make him plenty trouble now, sure! This Bagadakis, he –" She tried to raise her arm in the accustomed gesture, but the handcuffs prevented her.

"Shut up!" Richard's voice imposed itself with the roughness of a trumpet. "Rosenau got twenty percent. Zoe got the rest. She forced Georgios to act as her accomplice in London, partly because his family in Crete were among the peasants involved, and partly for love, in her sense of the word. That is, in return for being used and then eaten alive by a human widow spider."

There she sat, gathered and malevolent, her swelling breasts and thighs almost bladderlike above and below the narrow waist, her eyes two black points of venom. Iorweth looked once and groaned.

"Don't pretend you didn't enjoy it, Iorweth. It gave you the same kind of kick as fertility religions and matriarchy. You like having a woman to grovel to. But let's get back to the case. We will now take events in order, beginning from the time last year when Worrall first realized his reputation was slipping, and Janet first began to see through him. In spite of his money and his knighthood and his team of experts, Worrall hadn't really arrived. He knew that the inner circle, the real archaeologists, despised him. He wanted to have a resounding success next year, something spectacular; Homer come true. The Corfu site was promising, from what people said.

"Well, there you have the setting, down to the moment when the Nausicaa Ring was found. Clearly the ring and the murders were connected. Clearly Worrall's death had something to do with archaeological prestige. He found an object which, if genuine, gave him enormous kudos, and if faked, ruined his reputation irretrievably; and the moment he found it, trouble broke out. So the troublemakers must have been people to whom archaeological prestige was supremely important. Therefore I rule out Zoe and Iorweth ap Ifor, in spite of his prophecies of disaster and her faking activities. Because it's become quite clear to me in the course of my investigations that neither of them depends on whether Worrall's reputation stands or falls. Murder for the sake of archaeological prestige wouldn't be worth their while. That left me with the prisoners Coltman and Shrubsole as my main suspects."

Both the latter, hearing their bare surnames so menacingly spoken, stiffened with alarm, and Richard took it as a good omen for the success of his "war of nerves." He continued in the same cold, analytical vein, ostensibly addressing his chief, who had come in unannounced and ponderously installed himself in the background – an incident which did not add to Richard's self-confidence.

"Both prisoners displayed almost pathologically strong feelings about Sir Alban Worrall. Shrubsole's kink was obvious – one that we are constantly coming across in crimes of violence. He wasn't a personal success, he felt; and he blamed his unpopularity on other people's class prejudices. Oh! No doubt when he quarreled with his colleagues in Athens or Crete or London, he told himself that he was crusading against bad scholarship and nepotism and the power of the purse. But what he really resented was that people like Worrall, rich, bogus, and self-confident, were the top dogs while he was an underdog. And that Coltman and ap Ifor always took Worrall's word against his.

"That's an obvious kink, as I say, and for a time it blinded me to the fact that Coltman's attitude was equally pathological, though less simple. Her trouble was that she'd centered her whole emotional life on Worrall and the success of his expedition. Not on Worrall the man – it would have been comparatively healthy and realistic, if she'd been in love with him – but on her idea of Worrall the archaeologist, a sort of phantom hero that she'd made up for herself to satisfy her loneliness after her father died. Something she could live for, work for, devote herself to utterly. So long as the idol remained standing, so long as Worrall the archaeologist lived up to her idea of him, I think that she was perfectly happy and fulfilled. But if she found that she couldn't be his disciple any more without flagrant dishonesty, she'd have nothing left to live for. If the idol were to fall, it would bring the sky down with it."

Janet Coltman gave a long shuddering sigh, but he went on:

"Well now, at first my theory was that Shrubsole had prepared and planted the ring in the trench, in order that Worrall might find it, hail it, make a fool of himself, and lose all his archaeological prestige. I further believed that Worrall had somehow spotted Shrubsole's plot and was threatening to expose him; and that Shrubsole, sooner than lose his last foothold in the archaeological world, had killed Worrall before he had time to put his threats into action. And that he also attempted the murder of Coltman when he thought, after reading her letter to *The Times*, that she too knew what he was guilty of. It wasn't until this afternoon that I changed my mind. The destroying of the ring put everything in a new light.

"It showed, you see, that Worrall *hadn't* been killed by someone who wanted to discredit him. On the contrary, he must have been killed by someone who wanted to preserve his reputation, and the good name of the expedition, at all costs, even at the cost of Worrall's own life. Worrall the man had died so that Worrall the archaeologist might live. How did I know this? Because the destroying of the ring could have no other motive but this same fanaticism. No one must ever be able to retest the ring and prove it a fake. Like Worrall, it must disappear before anyone had a chance to prove it bogus. So Shrubsole was let out."

Richard felt that he was on very thin ice now. He could only hope that the logical flaws in his discourse might be covered up by the confidence and violent denunciatory tone of their presentation.

"Coltman had suspected for some time that her idol had feet of clay. When he produced the ring, she really knew it. But she couldn't bring herself to face it at once. Perhaps she questioned the workmen. Certainly she listened to her colleagues. And we know that she spent a sick, sleepless night, with her head throbbing. In the morning there came an unexpected excuse for procrastination – the boy's sudden death, Worrall's equally sudden illness – and I expect it was a relief to her to plunge into a whirl of organizing and sick-nursing, and put off the showdown. But it was only put off. On the way home, she couldn't help looking at Worrall with new eyes; and it wasn't very long before she saw, intelligent as she is, that his illness was only feigned. He was a sham right through, then, and a coward as well! Scared to stay on the dig he'd salted, scared to be X-rayed, scared to be questioned about the fakes he'd got from Zoe last year. Coltman suddenly realized how despicable the man was. And he was in her power.

"That, I think, was when the temptation came. Why not play on his fear of having an X-ray by planting on him the idea of making this new will, so that he could tell the surgeon, 'I don't believe in operations. Why, I've even put a clause about it in my will.' If the will also secured the future of the expedition, and provided against a post mortem, so much the better. Why not strangle the whole controversy about the ring at birth, before the outside world had heard about it? Why not, finally, make the sham gastric ulcer the cover for a real death by poison? No one would ever know. And once Worrall the man was out of the way, Worrall the archaeologist could flourish posthumously in the Expedition endowed by him, which would increase its prestige, and, under more reliable leadership, do better work than ever. One can see that there's a sort of insane poetic justice about the idea."

Janet Coltman sat as though stunned. He paused a moment and then began formally: "Janet Coltman, I arrest …"

"No!" Ian Shrubsole was on his feet. "It was me, not Janet. I mean, *I* destroyed the ring, she didn't. It's true that she didn't want it published, but that was just loyalty. I must say, I don't see anything psychopathic about that. I agreed with her, actually; there was no point in having a public scandal. But *I* took it along to the lab, and it was *my* idea to destroy it, not hers. Only – Janet, I haven't had a chance to tell you this – I didn't destroy it after all. I hid it. Because when I'd removed the layer of modern gold he'd put on, I found traces of the original baetylic shrine that he'd attempted to erase. And it was interesting, because it looked a different type from anything that had been found before. *He* wouldn't have known that, of course, but there were striking affinities with the palace cult. Nilsson's theory might have to be modified. You do agree, don't you, that I couldn't conscientiously have destroyed a thing like that? And as for you" – he turned to Richard – "if finding the ring in my possession is all you need to let Janet go free – and I don't see that you've a shred of a case against her apart from that – well, you'll find it where I hid it this afternoon …"

"In the mummy's leg. We did. Now confess the rest, Shrubsole, because you've dished yourself at last!" He turned on Shrubsole a ferocity as violent as it was assumed.

"Why don't you admit it? The whole thing's so obvious. *You* stole the ring last year while Miss Coltman was away. *You* altered it and planted it for Worrall to find. *You* called attention to its unauthenticity. But your scheme went wrong, didn't it? Young Spiro had seen you slipping it into the side of the trench, and he told you so early the next morning when you went back to do some more work of the same kind. You killed young Spiro, didn't you, there by the trench, and then you took his body and threw it over the cliff?

"That boy didn't, I think, break his neck falling down a cliff. For one thing, the fracture was of a very peculiar kind. When we come across that kind of fracture, it's practically always the result of a sudden backward fall in which the victim hits the nape of his neck against a projection – an old-fashioned high fender, for instance, or the edge of a high curbstone. The trunk is still falling when the neck receives a sudden violent blow which forces the head forward with a jerk. The spine is fractured at the neck, and the head dangles right down over the chest at an unnatural angle. And that's how Spiro died, because I've had detailed accounts of his injuries from Miss Coltman and the Corfu police. That cliff hasn't got rocks of a shape to make such a fracture likely. Secondly, the Corfu people now think that the battering on the rocks occurred *after* death. Considering the nature of his injury and the fact that his knife was found in the trench, it is certain that it was in the trench that he met his death.

"It was five feet across – just the right width for the far edge to catch the back of his neck as he toppled over backwards from your blow. He died in a matter of seconds, whether you'd intended it or not. He was out of the way. But what you didn't realize was that he'd told Worrall at midnight, and Janet had witnessed the interview. Hence what followed ..."

"Stop! Oh, stop!" Janet had never looked so unhappy or so forceful. "That isn't true. Ian didn't kill Spiro. But I've just realized who did. It was Sir Alban, and I saw him do it. But I didn't – honestly I didn't realize till this moment that it was – that."

"Yes?" Richard's trick had worked. "Go on, Janet. Try to be clear."

Janet spoke brokenly but with an obvious effort to present her facts accurately and in order.

"I saw Sir Alban hit or push Spiro, and he fell into the trench. I didn't realize that such a fall could have killed him, so I didn't say anything. I – I didn't think it mattered to you, and so I sort of – pushed the memory of that blow to the back of my mind. It – it wasn't a thing I wanted to remember. It spoiled my picture of Sir Alban. Oh! You're right! I *have* been dishonest, with myself and with you. I'm so ashamed now.

"They were by the trench, as I said, that night. Spiro was standing at the edge with his back to it, and the moonlight behind him so that his face was in shadow, and Sir Alban facing him in full view. Spiro was talking excitedly and gesticulating a good deal, and coming up closer and closer. He must have been accusing him of planting the ring, I think; because if he'd been trying to blackmail him, surely Sir Alban would have paid? He offered *me* money later on. I don't know. But I think Sir Alban must have mistaken his intentions. He must have thought Spiro was going to attack him. Perhaps he'd got out his knife and was fingering it – it's a thing Cretans will do in an argument. Anyhow, whether in annoyance or alarm, Sir Alban lashed out at Spiro, because I actually saw him.

"I mustn't give a false impression. What I saw was this. I saw Spiro coming up close to Sir Alban with his hand raised, and I saw Sir Alban give him a kind of push or blow in the chest and he fell backwards. There was no sound and I knew the trench wasn't deep. Spiro had gone and Sir Alban was standing there alone. And I went into my tent. The argument, whatever it was, was settled; and I didn't want to talk to Sir Alban. I pushed it to the back of my mind. You can guess why. I suppose that Spiro was dead by the time I got into my tent.

And I suppose that Sir Alban must have carried the body along the trench to the end, where there were steps and he'd be unseen from the part where the workmen and I were, and that he threw it over the cliff. I can't believe that he meant to kill him – just to knock him down. The next day he was frightened, and pretended to be ill just so as to get away."

"Thank you, Janet," said Richard, suddenly human again. "Sorry I had to abuse you two idiots to make you talk. Anyhow, you're cleared now, so neither of you need have any qualms about announcing the engagement."

The four other people round the table started and stared. Ian and Janet sat speechless, wooden, and apparently parboiled. As Clare had remarked, nothing but love could possibly make two sensible persons look so goopy.

The Bloodhound intervened unexpectedly. "What's this? Engaged, you say? In that case, don't believe a word they say. They'll be shielding each other."

"That's just why I didn't trust them *till* I discovered their engagement. They *were* shielding one another, and I couldn't see why, unless one of them was acting so under duress – and their behavior was certainly most suspicious. But now I can prove that they were engaged at the time. I've got, er, documentary evidence. A little boy brought Miss Coltman this note today, hidden in a bunch of flowers he sold her. I suspected that he wasn't just a casual contact, but he hadn't given a verbal message, so I got my wife to search for a note. She found it; and thought on reflection that the child looked like Shrubsole. He was actually his youngest brother. And the note's in Shrubsole's hand, too." He passed over the sooty little piece of paper with Ian's Greek verses on it.

"What's all this? I can't see to read it. Here, you read it out. And translate it – literally."

With an apologetic glance at Shrubsole, Richard began:

"*For the sake of a ring I incurred your heart-wounding anger. Let me now destroy that one, and take from my hands, O most desirable* (girl or woman – the adjective's feminine) *another* (ring, understood) *the symbol of*, er, *future mutually encircling love madness*. I'm afraid my translation doesn't do justice to the original, which is really very pointed and elegant."

"Damned affected nonsense!" said the Bloodhound, glaring over his dewlap. "What's it mean, if anything?"

"Oh! It just means that Shrubsole's apologizing for the fuss he made over Miss Coltman's attempts to hush up the 'Nausicaa Ring' scandal, and says that he's willing to destroy it if she will accept an engagement ring from him in return. Very simple and businesslike, really, though I think he invented one of the words in the last line, to make it scan right."

Shrubsole made as if to speak, but the Bloodhound got in first.

"And does this explain *all* their suspicious behavior?"

"Yes. The little disturbance this afternoon when my back was turned was just, er, *mutually encircling love madness* – he kissed her. And the handkerchief in Miss Coltman's garden – well, my wife and Sergeant Frewin both suggested independently that Janet had perhaps kept a little hoard of things that reminded her of Shrubsole – letters and snapshots and this handkerchief – and that she burned them all when they quarreled. The handkerchief accidentally got left out, because she dropped it on the way to the bonfire. Is that right, Janet?"

Janet nodded and muttered something about having been very silly.

"And why the secrecy about your engagement? Was it simply shyness, or ...?"

"Darn it!" burst out Ian in his old explosive manner (now softened by a new sheepish grin), "I couldn't let her be publicly associated with a suspected murderer."

Richard could not hide his affectionate amusement. "It's an odd thing, but I think that you and Mr. Coltman are going to find you have a lot in common. Well! You can both go at once if you like. There's no longer any reason to detain you. I'm staying to make my arrest."

Ian glanced at Janet and said, "We're staying too. You agree – darling?"

And Janet, with the blush of a schoolgirl and the vocabulary of a professional woman, replied, "Certainly, I agree. The matter concerns us all, doesn't it?"

"Very well, stay, but I'm afraid you'll be distressed." Richard had become businesslike and impersonal now, but the lines in his face had deepened. "The point at which the police took up this case was after the attempted murder of Miss Coltman. Inquiries soon made it apparent that she was the third of a series of victims, of whom the second, Worrall, had died in London three days before. Worrall's body was examined, and it was discovered that he had not had a gastric ulcer at all; he had been poisoned. I decided to start from there.

"It was physically possible for the poison to have been given by the following persons – Miss Coltman, Macdonald, Shrubsole, Georgios Aiakides, or Mikhailopoulos. But in the case of the first three having administered the poison, its action must somehow have been delayed – say, by its being given in a gelatine capsule – for if Worrall had swallowed it in liquid form when they were by his table, the agony would have been immediate; it wouldn't have been delayed until the end of the meal. Now, although Worrall did wolf his food, it's difficult to believe that even he could have been got to swallow a large capsule without knowing it. And another thing. When the agony actually began, a diversion occurred so that it wasn't noticed at once. The rabbits. Surely that diversion wasn't a chance thing, but part of the murderer's plan?

"Mikhailopoulos told me that the rabbits got out of their hutch because the door was rotten. I looked at those hutches. They were all well made of excellent wood, and his story didn't convince me. I'd seen Mikhailopoulos myself, on the previous night, putting on a new door and chopping up the old one for firewood. It was hard to chop. Why burn it? Because the wood wasn't really rotten at all, and he was afraid I might find this out. What is more, we found a sack wrapped round the fig tree which had fresh rabbit dung in it, and I realized then that someone must have put those rabbits in the sack and let them loose deliberately, just when Worrall's poison began to take effect, in order to create a diversion.

"He gave the hydrochloric acid in the *ouzo*, of course. Worrall swallowed it in a single gulp, as he always did, so that there was not much burning of the mouth and throat. Even so, he protested at the taste. '*Just you wait, sir*,' says Mikhailopoulos. '*You feel the quality in a moment.*' And he went off to let loose his rabbits. The diversion was a great success. No one saw that Worrall was ill until he was past the power of coherent speech.

"You didn't know that hydrochloric acid took so long to kill, though, did you, Mikhailopoulos? They'd told you it was deadly and so you'd concluded that it was also instantaneous. You had to ring up the doctor quite soon, because people were watching you; there was a delay before he came, but still, he did come, and Worrall was still alive. A nasty moment for you. But by an amazing stroke of luck, as you must have thought, you got a second chance. You were able to travel alone with him in the ambulance. There, it was easy to hold a pillow over his face until he died. He arrived a corpse, and the doctors said, as doctors so often do, that the patient had died of shock. You went home, hardly able to believe that it had been as easy as all that.

"Two days later, someone showed you Miss Coltman's letter in *The Times*, and you knew it wasn't going to be easy after all. She said she knew *the seeds of his death*. And *his friends would not forget*. On top of that, she turned up in person and asked you for the address of your nearest relative. To a Cretan, this all added up to one thing – she'd taken up the feud and would avenge her master – you were under threat. So you followed her and stabbed her with the knife you'd made to use on Worrall. No one but a Cretan would be so knife-conscious as to make a special knife for one murder lest his own should give him away. Well? Must I go on?"

Mikhailopoulos stood up and met Richard's eye without the least sign of alarm.

"I give you my word, sir, as man of honor, I have not done this thing you say."

Even now, Richard found it hard not to believe him. The word *honor*, on his lips, seemed still to be something valid and indubitable. Macdonald must have felt the same, for he interrupted:

"Why on earth should Costa Mikhailopoulos want to murder Worrall? I happen to know that they hardly knew each other."

"*Costa* Mikhailopoulos hardly knew Worrall. But *Stavro* Mikhailopoulos, Costa's brother, knew him very well indeed. Stavro was the foreman on the dig, and Worrall killed his son, Spiro."

The whole room stirred and leaned forward. Richard went on:

"It was a blood feud after the old Cretan pattern. From the very beginning I had a sense that something mysterious and primitive was at the bottom of the crime. None of the usual motives made sense. Nobody gained by Worrall's death. At first, I tried to make myself believe that Iorweth's talk of sacrifice was seriously meant. I asked myself whether he might be mad enough or besotted enough to have been duped by Zoe into a 'ritual murder,' to suit her ends. But it didn't seem to make sense, and other casual talk I'd heard did. Georgios and Mikhailopoulos both suggested, quite naturally, and as the first thing you'd think of, that it must have been Worrall's *relations* who stabbed Janet to avenge him. Ian said that Cretans didn't usually murder, *except for blood feuds*. Mikhailopoulos made a great point of telling me that Worrall was merely a customer, not a guest; that he'd never offered him a drink on the house. If he'd regarded Worrall as a guest, you see, his code would have made it dishonorable to kill him, because guests in Greece are sacred. And all through his evidence there sounded this note of honor, honor, honor – a Homeric system of ethics quite different from our own."

"Yes," Ian said. "I agree that most of what you say is in accordance with Cretan ideas, but you've missed the big point. While Stavro, Spiro's father, is alive, it's *his* feud, and Costa can't take it on for him. The avenger wouldn't be Costa, it would be Stavro. And Stavro's in Greece."

"Stavro isn't in Greece, and he *was* the avenger – Stavro there in front of you, who has been running the Minos while his brother had a holiday in Paris, ever since you got back. Costa was quite a different type – you could see that just by looking at the house or talking to Stavro. Costa had lived in London for years, and would certainly have heard of Scotland Yard (even Georgios had, and he's been over here less than a year). This man hadn't. Costa had a stock of silk pajamas and an up-to-date Western European bathroom. This man didn't wash, and he slept in his shirt with a knife under his pillow. Costa kept accounts and had a checkbook. The accounts and checks stop three weeks ago. Costa cherished his fig tree because it reminded him of home. Stavro had so little understanding of the sorrows of prolonged nostalgia that he spoke quite casually of cutting that fig tree down, because it gave easy access to burglars."

"Even so," said Janet, "you can't be right. Stavro's much older than his brother, and he's got white hair. Oh! But ..." She gasped, remembering.

"Yes, Clare's Greek hairdresser told you this morning that he dyed his hair. I'd guessed already, as a matter of fact. I saw the anxious way he examined it in the glass, and I'd noticed the hair on his arms and hands, which wasn't black, as you'd expect, but grizzled and grayish. Well, Stavro? Are you still afraid to tell the truth?"

The guards started towards him, but Richard checked them with a gesture. Even now, he hoped against hope that this splendid enemy, whom he had come to like so much, might escape defeat. After the first dozen words, his hope failed.

"Stavro Mikhailopoulos is afraid of nothing – nothing. It is true. He killed Worrall. He tried to kill Miss Coltman. But first, this Worrall have killed his son, his only son. You think he get justice in Corfu? No! Stavro can't buy justice. He make justice, like a man of honor.

"If this Worrall have stay in Greece, Stavro would do like his fathers. Kill him clean, with the knife or the gun, and after, go to the mountains. But Worrall's a coward. He run to hide in London. Here, no mountains, many police. Stavro don't like to give the death of poison, it is not the way he like to kill, but here, is no other way. Listen, Worrall has kill his son. And he is customer, *not* guest. Listen, sirs, listen, God, not guest. Not. I swear it."

He raised his hand in solemn asseveration and let it fall again.

"It is sin to kill, yes, I know. But Stavro is clean of the blood. The blood of his son is on Worrall, and his sin, that is on Worrall also. But the lady, Miss Coltman, is clean of blood, and you see, the *Panagìa* has save her, not let her die. But She don't save Worrall. Because it is justice. She let him die, and God will not be angry."

He made the sign of the cross in that broad, sweeping way that one so seldom sees in the West.

"Stavro Mikhailopoulos," Richard said, hating his task, "I arrest you for the wilful murder of Alban Worrall on …"

"Stavro's not here, sir. He can't hear you …"

Two men hurried upstairs on Richard's orders. Soon they returned.

"Dead, sir. Stabbed himself with a knife right through the heart, like someone in a play. This note was beside him."

Richard went up close to Costa Mikhailopoulos and examined him. He saw now that the hairs on his arms were black, and that there were the first threads of gray in his hair. His bulk owed more to flesh and less to muscle. He was a grand-looking man, but missed the heroic grandeur of his outlawed brother.

"You let him do this, Costa? Take his own life?"

Costa answered steadily. "What else can he do? In England you choke a man with a rope, like a dog, not shoot him like a man of honor die. Stavro's not afraid to die, he risk to die many time; but to die like a dog, no! God will forgive him, and I will pay for his peace.

"You want to hear what Stavro say to me? Last night, when I come back from my holiday, he don't tell me nothing. He don't want to make me no trouble. This evening, we are sitting upstairs, and we see out of window, back, front, police, police, everywhere. Then he tell me, quick. 'My God, Stavro!' I say. 'Why the hell you don't tell me before? Why you don't let me help? Now we have trouble.' 'Not you, Costa,' he say. 'Go down, quick, and make the police talk. Don't worry. I won't make you no trouble.' He give me one kiss, and I go. *Ai, ai! Stavro!*"

Tears ran down his face and lodged in the curling hair of his whiskers.

"I'm sorry, Costa," said Ian suddenly. "We all are, darned sorry. Anything we can do – funeral, lawyers ..."

Costa did not reply. Shaking the tears from his face as a bull shakes off flies, he took his dead brother's *kithara* from the shelf by the door and played. The instrument no longer sang with the full voice that it had sounded before it was broken, but Richard recognized the tune as the same that Stavro had been playing four nights ago by the fig tree. Ian, Janet, and Macdonald recognized it too, and looked at each other with sudden understanding.

"You know the words?" Macdonald said. "It's an old Cretan song.

Weep not for the eagle
Flying against the storm.
Weep for the bird
That has lost his wings."

"Lot of rigmarole!" The Bloodhound's heavy, official voice came from the back of the room, harmonious as a saw on glass. "Don't waste time. Bring him along for questioning. The law's the law here."

THE END

If you enjoyed *The Cretan Counterfeit* ask your bookseller for the first Inspector Ringwood mystery, *The Missing Link* (0-915230-72-0, $14.95) also published by The Rue Morgue Press.

The Rue Morgue Press specializes in reprinting traditional mysteries from the 1930s and 1940s. To receive our catalogs or to suggest titles telephone toll free 800-699-6214 or go to our webpage: www.ruemorguepress.com. As of November 2004, The Rue Morgue Press has more than 50 books in print.

Some of our Anglo-Irish titles include:

Joanna Cannan. This English writer's books are among our most popular titles. Modern reviewers have compared them favorably with the best books of the Golden Age of detective fiction. "Worthy of being discussed in the same breath with an Agatha Christie or a Josephine Tey."—Sally Fellows, *Mystery News.* Set in the late 1930s in a village that was a fictionalized version of Oxfordshire, both titles feature young Scotland Yard inspector Guy Northeast. *They Rang Up the Police* (0-915230-27-5, $14.00) and *Death at The Dog* (0-915230-23-2, $14.00).

Glyn Carr. The 15 books featuring Shakespearean actor Abercrombie "Filthy" Lewker are set on peaks scattered around the globe, although the author returned again and again to his favorite climbs in Wales, where his first mystery, published in 1951, *Death on Milestone Buttress* (0-915230-29-1, $14.00), is set.

Joan Coggin. Meet Lady Lupin Lorrimer Hastings, the young, lovely, scatterbrained and kindhearted daughter of an earl, now the newlywed wife of the vicar of St. Marks Parish in Glanville, Sussex. You might not understand her logic but she always gets her man. *Who Killed the Curate?* (0-915230-44-5, $14.00), *The Mystery at Orchard House* (0-915230-54-2, $14.95), *Penelope Passes or Why Did She Die?* (0-915230-61-5, $14.95), and *Dancing with Death* (0-915230-62-3, $14.95).

Sheila Pim. *Ellery Queen's Mystery Magazine* said of these wonderful Irish village mysteries that Pim "depicts with style and humor everyday life." *Booklist* said they were in "the best tradition of Agatha Christie." Beekeeper Edward Gildea uses his knowledge of bees and plants to good use in *A Hive of Suspects* (0-915230-38-0, $14.00). *Creeping Venom* (0-915230-42-9, $14.00) blends politics, gardening and religion into a deadly mixture. *A Brush with Death* (0-915230-49-6, $14.00) grafts a clever art scam onto the stem of a gardening mystery.

Sarsfield, Maureen. These two mysteries featuring Inspector Lane Parry of Scotland Yard are among our most popular books. Both are set in Sussex. *Murder at Shots Hall* (0-915230-55-8, $14.95) features Flikka Ashley, a thirtyish sculptor with a past she would prefer remain hidden. It was originally published as *Green December Fills the Graveyard* in 1945. Parry is back in Sussex, trapped by a blizzard at a country hotel where a war hero has been pushed out of a window to his death, in *Murder at Beechlands* (0-915230-56-9, $14.95). First published in 1948.

Some of our other recent titles include:

Stuart Palmer. *The Puzzle of the Blue Banderilla* (0-915230-70-4, $14.95). Schoolteacher Hildegarde Withers (Anthony Boucher's favorite female sleuth of the Golden Age) heads down to Mexico City when Inspector Oscar Piper finds himself in over his head. First published in 1937. Picked in *The Reader's Guide to the American Novel of Detection* (1993) as one of the 100 best American detective novels of all time.

Lucy Cores. Her books both feature one of the more independent female sleuths of the 1940s. Toni Ney is the exercise director at a very posh Manhattan beauty spa when the "French Lana Turner" is murdered in *Painted for the Kill (*0-915230-66-6, $14.95) "Miles better than most of today's product."—Jon L. Breen, *The Weekly Standard.* She's a newly minted ballet reviewer when murder cuts short the return of a Russian dancer to the stage in *Corpse de Balle*t (0-915230-67-4, $14.95). "This brilliant novel...presents a vivid portrait of the backstage workings of a dance company...eye-catching cover illustration...must read mystery."—*I Love a Mystery.*

John Mersereau. *Murder Loves Company* (0-915239-69-0, $14.95. Young Berkeley professor James Yeats Biddle finds love and murder while looking into a murder at the 1939 San Francisco World's Fair. First published in 1940. "A classic of its genre...characters are well-rounded and alive...Some of us were lucky to have lived in those times. Those who were born too late can relive some of that happiness as they read this light-hearted adventure tale."—*Nob Hill Gazette.* "The cover is stunning, and this book is highly recommended."—*Deadly Pleasures.*

Frances Crane. *The Turquoise Shop* (0-915230-71-2, $14.95). Mona Brandon's artist husband disappeared several months ago. Had he just grown tired of his domineering, artsy wife or was it his body lying out there in the desert, rendered unrecognizable by turkey vultures? And was it just a coincidence that a handsome private detective from San Francisco just happened to pick that time to show up in Santa Maria to pursue an art career? Young Jean Holly, owner of The Turquoise Shop, hasn't much use for Mona, who uses her wealth to dominate this small New Mexico community. Mona isn't very popular with much of the local Mexican population, especially after she sent one of their own—a beautiful teenager—to prison. When murder strikes a second time, this time at Mona's enormous adobe mansion at the edge of town, suspicion falls not only on her but on several of the artists and writers she had encouraged to move to Santa Maria. Mona is loosely based on Mabel Dodge Luhan, a wealthy Easterner who came to Taos in 1918 and turned the town into a mecca for the arts, luring D.H. Lawrence, Georgia O'Keeffe, Robinson Jeffers, Ansel Adams, and many others there.